Praise fc
Jean-Marie Blas de Roblès

"Those of you who stay with Blas de Roblès's
ultimately quite satisfying novel will find yourselves
with a new European literary star to steer by."
—Alan Cheuse, NPR

"Psychodrama meets history meets mystery—vintage
Umberto Eco territory, as practiced by French philosophy
professor turned novelist Blas de Roblès."
—*Kirkus*

"This encyclopedic and mystifying novel, full of picaresque
adventures, delights and fascinates. . . . A marvelous,
dizzying galaxy, spiraling to the end of the novel."
—*Le Figaro littéraire*

"This dazzling book is itself such a mountain, overflowing with
visions that dramatically enlarge the reader's imaginative horizons."
—*Booklist* (starred review)

"Blas de Roblès simultaneously channels Umberto
Eco, Indiana Jones, and Jorge Amado."
—*Publishers Weekly*

"*Where Tigers Are at Home* is a great enough work that I
would gladly travel through its treacherous pages again."
—*Rain Taxi Review of Books*

ISLAND OF POINT NEMO

JEAN-MARIE BLAS DE ROBLÈS

Translated from the French by Hannah Chute

OPEN LETTER

LITERARY TRANSLATIONS FROM THE UNIVERSITY OF ROCHESTER

Library of Congress Cataloging-in-Publication Data: Available.
ISBN-13: 978-1-940953-62-5 / ISBN-10: 1-940953-62-6

*Cet ouvrage, publié dans le cadre d'un programme d'aide à la publication,
bénéficie du soutien de la Mission Culturelle et Universitaire Française
aux Etats Unis, service de l'ambassade de France aux Etats Unis*

*This work, published as part of a program of aid for publication, received
support from the Mission Culturelle et Universitaire Française aux Etats
Unis, a department of the French Embassy in the United States*

·

*This project is supported in part by an award from
the National Endowment for the Arts*

ART WORKS.
arts.gov

Printed on acid-free paper in the United States of America.

Text set in Caslon, a family of serif typefaces based on
the designs of William Caslon (1692–1766).

Design by N. J. Furl

Open Letter is the University of Rochester's nonprofit, literary translation press:
Dewey Hall 1-219, Box 278968, Rochester, NY 14627

www.openletterbooks.org

For Elaine

"We all died at the age of twenty,
without realizing it."
—*André Hardellet*

ISLAND OF POINT NEMO

I

The Mystery of the Three Feet

The Tigris, now invisible, to the right, the bare heights of the Gordyene Mountains to the left; between the two, the plain looked like a desert swarming with golden beetles. They were at Gaugamela, less than three years after the hundred and twelfth Olympiad. Darius had lined up some two hundred thousand foot soldiers and thirty thousand cavalry: auxiliary Indians, Bactrian troops led by their respective satraps, Scythians from Asia, an alliance of mounted archers from the Persians, Arians, Parthians, Phrataphernes, Medes, Armenians, Greek mercenaries, not to mention those from Hyrcania, Susa, and Babylon; Mazaios commanded the soldiers from Syria, Oromobates those from the shores of the Red Sea. They also boasted fifteen elephants and two hundred scythed chariots for which the King of Kings had cleared the stones from the soon-to-be battlefield.

Alexander slept.

Under his orders, the Macedonian army—forty thousand foot soldiers and only seven thousand horses—was deployed in an oblique front. The phalanx in the center was protected on its flanks by Nicanor's hypaspists and Perdiccas's and Meleager's battalions, by Parmenion's Thessalonian cavalry on its left wing, and by Philotas's on its right. The sun, already high, made their helmets and cuirasses gleam, and their shields dazzled.

Still Alexander slept. His companions had the greatest difficulty waking him, but when he rose, he mounted Bucephalus and rejoined the right wing, at the head of the Macedonian cavalry.

Darius, at the center of his elite infantry—ten thousand Immortals, so called because whenever one died in the course of combat he was immediately replaced—gave the order to attack. He set the bulk of his cavalry on Alexander's left flank and sent his chariots to thrust through the central phalanx. The king of Macedonia did not seem concerned. He led his cavalrymen toward the right, as if he wanted to skirt the front on that side, provoking, as in a mirror, the same shift in the opposing cavalry, but with the effect of severing it from the rest of the troops and stretching out the front. While Parmenion was subjected to the Persian assault, the phalanxes were preparing themselves for impact. When the chariots were no more than fifty meters away, this human hedge, bristly with lances, opened to form several aisles. At the same time, the trumpets sounded, and all the foot soldiers began to strike their iron shields with their swords. This incredible clamor spooked the teams of horses; some halted abruptly, causing the chariots to tumble, while others instinctively rushed down the lanes formed by the soldiers. Closing back in on them, the phalanx swallowed and digested them with jabs of its sarissas. It must be admitted, however, as Diodorus said, that some chariots, having avoided this defense, did terrible damage in the places where they landed. The cutting edges of the scythes and other metal fittings attached to their wheels were so sharp they brought death in a number of different ways—taking off some soldiers' arms along with the shields they carried, cutting off others' heads so suddenly that when they landed on the ground their mouths were still mid-roar. Several unfortunates were cleaved in two and died before they felt the blow.

Once Alexander calculated that he had drawn the Persian cavalry far enough, and as it was preparing to attack, he abruptly turned his horses half around, revealing the corps of slingers that his advance

4

had concealed. Leaving these skilled warriors to pelt the Bactrian cavalry with their stones, he rushed into the breach and galloped off toward the center of the opposing army, right at the Immortals protecting Darius. An excellent opening! A line of red ink between the paragraphs of the battle! In the sandy dust raised by the combat, thousands of men are gutted in the terrible melee; swords and Macedonian javelins send blood spurting into the air, splatter the yellow robes embroidered with lavender, split hooded heads, rend wicker shields; axes and curved swords descend on the hoplites, smash crested helmets, slice, kill, mutilate unrelentingly. Caught up in a parallel fury, the men butcher one another, their disemboweled mounts gnashing their teeth. The dying continue to advance; they choke on pink foam, stumble, entangled in their own entrails. A single cry of pain seems to emanate from the mounds of the dead and wounded, whose bodies cushion their assailants' steps. The Immortals are as resurrected as they can be, they are not renewing themselves fast enough to scatter the Macedonian wave. And suddenly, behold, they are disbanding, the Persian center is broken, Darius is fleeing. It is at this moment, as Alexander sees his opponent's motley chariot disappearing in the dust, that a messenger reaches him: on the left flank, Parmenion and his Thessalonian cavalry are faltering before the Persians; without reinforcements they will not last long.

It was at this moment that Miss Sherrington chose to shake her master's shoulder: "Monsieur, please, Monsieur Canterel . . ."

Martial Canterel was stretched out on a bed that had been imported at great cost from an opium den in Hong Kong. The battlefield was spread out across the floor, occupying almost the entirety of the parquet surface; twenty-five thousand lead soldiers, which he had spent several days positioning in order to reproduce this pivotal moment: should Alexander go after Darius, or rescue Parmenion?

"Miss Sherrington?" he said, raising glassy eyes to hers. "I'm listening."

"You have a caller," she said, holding out a card to him. "And, if I may, you should stop smoking that filth. It's not good for your health."

"It's medicinal, Miss Sherrington. You can address any commentary to Dr. Ménard."

Canterel took a look at the card and sat up immediately.

"By the Holy Candle of Arras, Holmes! Holmes is here, and you didn't tell me! Why haven't you sent him up?"

Miss Sherrington raised her eyes to the heavens, as if she were dealing with an imbecile.

"I've been trying to wake you for ten minutes . . ." And, indicating the opium kit that was lying on the bed: "I've brought your medication, or do you need even more?"

"Out of here, please, and spare me the sarcasm."

Martial Canterel was forty-five. Imagine a thin face, hair slicked back and sticking up in all directions—the hair of a man who sends for his barber each morning and gives him as a model a portrait of Louis II of Bavaria at the age of eighteen—big green eyes with lashes so thick that one would have thought him naturally made-up, a nice nose, and—between a French mustache and a tuft of hairs forming a fan under his lower lip—a fleshy little mouth with a disconcerting pout. His mustache was no less bizarre: very thick beneath the nose, it rippled out horizontally, stretching to an uncommon length before rising up, and then fading into tawny whiskers. Canterel maintained it obsessively. Add to this a braided frock coat over a waistcoat of quilted silk, a white-collared shirt with a double bow tie the color of a Périgord truffle, cashmere trousers, and gray beaver boots, and you will understand that the figure whom we are examining cultivated the appearance of a dandy.

Canterel inspected his attire in the mirror. He was adjusting his collar when Holmes entered, followed by a black man whom he did not know.

"Hello, my friend!" Holmes said, stepping forward with his arms outstretched. "Just what are you playing at, Martial, having me wait at your door like some common delivery man?"

"Stop, not another step!" said Canterel, flatly.

"What's the matter?" asked Holmes, worried, tottering on one foot.

"Look in front of you, old chap, you were about to trample Cleitus the Black's squadron!"

"By Jove!" he said, seeing the armies of lead soldiers that covered the floor. "Have you gone mad, my dear friend? What is the meaning of this?"

He put on his spectacles and carefully squatted down for a closer look.

"Very nice, a splendid collection! I've never seen a set so complete . . . Alexander and his companies! The Immortals, Darius on his massive golden chariot!"

"Mine's only gold-plated . . ."

"Regardless, Canterel, it's absolutely extraordinary!"

Holmes stood up in order to take in the whole scene, waved his hand vaguely as he deliberated, and grimaced. "At first glance, this looks like the Battle of Issus, but there is something that doesn't quite make sense in the left wing . . . I'd say the Granicus or . . . No! Of course, it's Gaugamela, right as Darius is turning to run from the attack of the Macedonian center!"

"Splendid," said the other man, "it's quite easy to visualize the nasty position that Parmenion's troops have found themselves in, and how Alexander could still lose the battle . . ."

"And whom do I have the honor . . . ?" asked Canterel, allured by the shrewdness of this remark.

"Allow me to introduce Grimod, my butler," said Holmes.

"Delighted," said Canterel, eagerly shaking his hand. "Grimod?"

"Grimod de la Reynière," continued Holmes, noticeably embarrassed. "It's a long story, I'll tell it to you one of these days. But I am here regarding a more important matter. Would it be possible to discuss it while not standing on one foot?"

"Forgive me," said Canterel. "I will find us a more suitable place. Miss Sherrington," he called, guiding them toward an adjoining room, "tea for me, and a Longmorn 72 for our guests, please." He turned to Grimod. "I know Shylock's tastes, but you may also have tea, if you prefer . . ."

"Not to worry, the Longmorn will be perfectly fine," said Grimod with the smile of a connoisseur.

They took a seat in a parlor that overlooked the Atlantic through three bay windows, through which they could see nothing but the dividing line between the blue of the sky and the blue of the ocean, as if the chateau were at the back of a frigate.

"So," said Canterel, "what brings you to Biarritz?"

Before letting Holmes respond, it would be well for us to dispel any misunderstandings about the man. Although he bore the name of the illustrious detective, John Shylock Holmes had inherited nothing from that line besides a questionable sense of humor and a strong confidence in his own expertise. Former curator of the Bodleian Library at Oxford, he worked at Christie's in Art Restitution Services; his talents and contacts sometimes enabled him to assist Lloyd's in negotiating certain delicate cases. Gifted with a prodigious memory, he was a man of sixty, and neither his excessive portliness nor his devotion to aged malts prevented him from traveling the world in search of rare objects. A habit that explained, without excusing, his propensity for wearing suits that he ought to have thrown out long ago. A receding hairline; a crown of curls that were too jet-black, in all honesty, to be anything but dyed; grizzled side-whiskers that descended to his chin; round, thin-rimmed glasses with smoked lenses that pinched the end of his nose; and a hint of rosacea on his cheekbones: all these features combined to give him an ever so slightly grotesque appearance.

As to the man who has been presented to us under the name of Grimod, it will suffice, for the moment, to say that he stood two heads above either of them. A tall, strapping man the color of burnished metal, whose muscles strained against the seams of his clothing without detracting from their elegance: an eggshell suit and silk shirt made by the hands of Cavanagh, the Irish tailor at 26, Champs-Élysées. It took Canterel only a glance to identify their maker. Two things were discordant, however: the deep scar that ran across half his forehead to his hairline, and the fact that he had not seen fit to take off his right glove.

"Have you read this weekend's *New Herald*?" asked Holmes, pulling a notebook from his jacket pocket.

"You know very well that I never read the papers . . ."

"Anyone can change, even you. But let's move along. That means you did not come across this astonishing bit of news. I'll read it to you: 'Last Monday, a hiker on a beach on the Isle of Skye, in Scotland, was surprised to discover a human foot cut off at mid-calf; mummified by the salt, this appendage was still shod in a sneaker. Two days later, thirty kilometers to the east, at the source of the loch at Glen Shiel, the sea washed up a second, quite similar foot. And, yesterday, to the south of Kyle of Lochalsh—that is, at the tip of an equilateral triangle formed by the two previous points—Mrs. Glenfidich's dog brought his mistress a third foot, hewn off in a similar manner and also wearing the same kind of shoe. These gruesome discoveries are rare in a county where there are neither sharks nor crocodiles; moreover, the police have not had report of a single disappearance in two years.'" Holmes paused for a moment and lifted one finger, drawing Canterel's attention to the end of the story: "'The plot thickens: regarding what the locals are already calling the "mystery of the three feet," it should be noted that these are three right feet of different sizes, but shod in the same type of shoe.'"

9

"What is the make?" Canterel demanded.

"Ananke . . ."

"I hope you haven't come all this way just to tell me that?"

He placed a ladyfinger in a cookie-dunking device that Miss Sherrington had brought in and left near his cup, and used it to soak the cookie in his tea for several seconds.

"Ananke, you say?" he resumed, bringing the moistened cookie to his lips.

"Yes," said Holmes. "'Destiny,' the Greeks' unalterable 'necessity' . . ."

"Except that this make does not exist," continued Grimod, sniffing his glass of scotch.

"However," added Holmes, "it is the name of the jewel that was stolen this week from the heart of that same triangle, Eilean Donan Castle . . ."

"To the point, Shylock, get to the point!" exclaimed Canterel.

"The Ananke," Holmes continued without losing his composure, "is the largest diamond ever excavated from an earthly mine: eight hundred carats once cut, appraised at over fifteen million florins! This marvel belonged to Lady MacRae, widow of Lord Duncan MacRae of Kintail, in other words a certain Madame Chauchat who should not be completely erased from your memory, if I'm not mistaken."

"Chauchat, Clawdia Chauchat?" Canterel murmured.

"The same," said Holmes, pulling a cigar from his waistcoat pocket. "It is she—and the insurance company that offers my services at an exorbitant price—who has recruited me to retrieve this magnificent stone."

Canterel's face had darkened suddenly.

"Obviously, this changes everything," he said, massaging his temples with two fingers. "Miss Sherrington, I beg you, I am going to need some more of my medicine . . ."

II

Breathtaking View of a Worker's Backside

At this point in the story, the voice stops, immediately replaced by the kind of background music that increases cows' milk production. Monsieur Wang looks at his watch and shakes his head at the punctuality of the performance. Five o'clock on the dot, good work. Not a bad idea to bring this guy on, he reflects, adjusting his cufflinks. Once more, the proverbial wisdom has proven true: without going into the tiger's den, how can one hope to lay a hand on its cubs?

Wang-li Wong, "Monsieur Wang" as he makes everyone call him to keep all the natives from mangling his name, is the Chinese manager of B@bil Books, an assembly plant for e-readers in La Roque-Gageac, in Périgord Noir. An adolescent's peach-fuzz mustache, in spite of his forty years, his hair slicked back in short, gelled waves, a three-piece suit with a tie and a white-buttoned collar. The Asian aspects of his features are faint. He looks more like a Japanese modernist from the sixties than a Chinese man. Perhaps this is the result of the outdated shape of his horn-rimmed glasses.

He is sitting at his desk, in a modern, industrial space improved by several Asian antiques, including a gilt nautilus shell adorned with mer-people, its feet shaped like eagle talons.

On the adjoining terrace, a small, deluxe pigeon loft holds several nests made of precious woods. Monsieur Wang is a pigeon-fancier;

he owns six pairs of carrier pigeons, including one star—Free Legs Diamond—for which he paid a hundred thousand euros, putting him ahead of most of the competition.

A proponent of "lean management," Wang-li Wong works to streamline activity within his company. In pursuit of this goal—and at the urging of Arnaud Méneste, the former owner of the factory that his plant is replacing—he is trying out the practice of having a "storyteller" read aloud during the workday. He followed along with the whole of the first reading, astonished to find himself taken in by the nonsense. The name of the author, a writer of serial novels from the previous century, already escapes him; in any case, the workers appeared to be enthralled, but did not raise their eyes from their work. The initial figures are clear: far from slowing production, the reading sped it up. Even bathroom breaks decreased.

This thought brings the manager's gaze back to his iPad. Stroking several icons with his finger, he brings wide shots from the surveillance cameras up on the screen, then zooms in on the assembly lines to wait for closing time. The stations are set up in long parallel rows separated by clean, gleaming aisles. Yellow lines on the ground indicate the paths reserved for forklifts, reminding the employees not to let their stools or trays cross this strict boundary. A hundred workers sit per row, heads lowered under the harsh brightness of the fluorescents; almond-green gowns, latex gloves, caps, and breathing masks: a long line of surgeons bent over the golden innards that are their destiny. Monsieur Wang is only interested in the women. He doesn't know all of their names, but he uses nicknames to distinguish among them: the white-haired slut, the weasel, the fatty with the mustache, smirk, gloomy, loon, nympho, Charlotte . . . The beautiful, the sweet Charlotte Dufrène. He lingers on the oval of her face, examines her big green eyes under thick eyebrows. Milky-white skin, lips the color of a swollen vulva, messy hair escaping from her bouffant cap. Every fifteen minutes, she glances lovingly at the man seated to her right.

Fabrice Petitbout. This lapdog, with his pale mop of hair, needs no nickname. The eyes of a husky, the goatee of a sickly ginger. He has a tongue piercing, a black titanium barbell that makes him lisp on the rare occasions when he speaks. Those two have managed to get places next to each other on the line; they must have messed around a bit, but they've never fucked—Monsieur Wang would bet his life on it.

Bell. Production halts. Not all of the workers react the same way. Some spring up immediately, others—the majority—remain seated for a few seconds, their eyes closed, their chins lowered, as if meditating; a few stretch their muscles, their elbows bent back behind their heads.

Monsieur Wang touches his iPad, and it displays the women's restrooms. He installed these cameras himself. Sophisticated equipment. Locker rooms, showers, toilets, nothing escapes him: there is even a sensor that opens a video feed on his screen every time someone turns the lock on a stall. The same equipment exists in the men's room, but he has only looked at it once, when Jaffar stuck it to the white-haired slut during a break.

Here come the women, chattering away as they enter the locker room. Wang has turned off the sound, but he knows he will be able to hear everything on the recordings. He has amassed dozens of hours of this over the last six months on a hard drive in a safe in his office; more than enough for his simple, professional pleasures. They start undressing in front of the narrow lockers that line the walls. Not at all like a striptease, since there is no trace of seduction here. This is the weary disrobing of young girls who have woken too late. The manager, for his part, sees nothing but panties rolling down thighs, an abundance of breasts, buttocks, pelvises, moist variations of liberated flesh under the fluorescent lighting. All of it excites him, even the lumps of fat that deform their hips and the magnifying effect of the flab on their rumps and knees. And finally—Charlotte. He expands the window to see her better. No one wriggles out of a slip the way she does, a trout freeing itself from a net. Her bosom bulges out, protruding and convex; seeing her squirm without losing her shape, he is sure that she would feel firm under his hands. Charlotte enters a shower stall between two white-tiled walls. She scrubs her hair, head thrown back, washes it, massages it. Flecks of suds fall on her breasts, hang from the fuzz on her crotch. To rinse, she turns around and bends down, presenting a breathtaking view of a worker's backside. She turns again, washes between her legs, knees bent.

Wang-li Wong has pulled out his penis; having jerked at himself for a few seconds, he discharges onto the screen of his tablet.

Standing motionless by the door to his office, in his blind spot, the Director of Human Resources has not missed a single moment of the scene. A strange smile spreads across her face; it would be impossible to say whether it is one of complicity or scorn. Louise Le Galle silently retreats and disappears.

III

Talkative Soles

"Pigeon shit," said Holmes, attempting to scrape some dried droppings from his shoulder.

"Seagull, actually," corrected Canterel, while Miss Sherrington placed his container of opium in front of him.

"A pipe made of stingray and shark vertebrae," rhapsodized Holmes, his eyes shining. "And, if I'm not mistaken, a Yixing terracotta bowl? You don't deny yourself anything, my dear fellow!"

Canterel remained focused on the wad of *chandoo* speared on a long needle that he was heating over a lamp.

"Where is she?"

"Well, where do you think she is? In Scotland, of course, at Eilean Donan Castle. She's waiting for us there."

"And the feet?"

"The coroner is a good friend of hers, we will be at our leisure to examine them."

"Which means that you have not yet seen them?"

"Correct. I didn't want to skew your first impression . . ."

"And, if I may," said Grimod, "there is a train to Paris in two hours."

"We can do better than that," replied Canterel, exhaling the smoke that he had been holding in his lungs for several seconds. "Do you know how to drive?"

"Yes," said Grimod.

"Very good. You will be able to relieve Miss Sherrington at the wheel."

He turned to the housekeeper, raising an inquisitive eyebrow.

"It's all ready," she said. "The luggage is in the car. We can leave whenever you wish."

"I'm very lucky to have you with me, Miss Sherrington. You are an extraordinary woman."

"Thank you, Monsieur. I shall remind you of that on occasion."

What Martial Canterel called his "car" looked nothing like an automobile. It was a Cottin & Desgouttes coach, its motor modified by the brilliant Devonshire mechanic Harold Bates. When he bought it, Canterel had had its interior refurbished in a way that gave it the comfort of a small apartment in the style of Haussmann. Inside was a lounge hung with silk damask, a breccia fireplace with a brass fireback, Venetian mirrors, five medallion chairs of solid cherrywood—one of which turned toward the wheel to function as the driver's seat—wide bay windows with embroidered tulle curtains, a functioning kitchen, perfectly soundproof toilets, a bathroom with portholes, a tiled Roman tub, a red copper water heater, and a mirrored scale; additionally, two bedrooms with foldaway double beds—which served as stylish work desks during the day—and a private space that allowed the driver to make use of the same commodities. From the outside, the vehicle had the appearance of a hearse fit for a circus giant, all the while giving an impression of luxury and power. Luxury, thanks to the Coromandel screens—signed by Liang P'ei Lan and dated 1693—that adorned the body of the car; as for power, this came from the stainless-steel pipes that escaped from the hood to join a pressure gauge toward the back of the coach, before connecting to a kind of flat tank that doubled as the vehicle's roof.

"My word!" exclaimed Holmes. "Where do you hide these things, Martial? What does this palace on wheels run on?"

Canterel threw him a look that expressed his complete disinterest in the question.

"Methane," replied Miss Sherrington, whispering in Holmes's ear. "There is a nozzle in the rear that can extract this gas from any manure; calf, cow, pig, chicken, anything. The methane is stored up there, then redistributed and converted by a special carburetor. We can go for two hundred kilometers, and refilling only takes half an hour . . ."

"If I may," said Holmes, concerned, "how *do* we fill up?"

"We are in France, Monsieur, we are surrounded by shit."

They took a day to reach Calais, slept in the car, and embarked the next day on a ferry bound for Dover. Canterel did not say three words the whole voyage. He smoked more than usual, switching between periods of lethargy and long moments of scrutinizing the transparency of a strange photograph engraved in glass that seemed to fascinate him.

Eilean Donan Castle did not appear until the end of the afternoon. Heavy purple clouds rested on the Cuillin Range and the solitary mountains of the Five Sisters of Kintail; through a patch of blue sky, light was still gilding the surface of Loch Duich, the crenellated walls, the massive keep standing on its islet eaten over with green mosses and heaths. In the shadows of evening, the castle was striking. Starting the car across the thin stone bridge that straddled the loch, Miss Sherrington shuddered in displeasure; she closed her right hand into a fist, thumb and pinkie out, to ward off evil.

A wizened servant was waiting for them at the bottom of the stairs leading up to the main doorway. He invited them in, then went ahead of them, showing them the way to a huge chamber, the ceiling of which revealed sturdy oak beams. Settling down in front of a monumental fireplace where a recently kindled fire was crackling, they curiously examined the colored coats of arms, the tall stained-glass windows whose pointed recesses formed many smaller rooms, the gallery containing portraits of kilted ancestors, the sabers over carved stone lintels—all of it bathed in the amber light of an enormous chandelier and the candles that were artfully placed around the room.

A door slammed; Lady MacRae appeared, the nonchalance of her gait contrasting with the violence of the sound that had preceded it. She was wearing an ensemble of dark-red silk, the bodice trimmed with Spanish lace, obscuring but not concealing the advantages of a bosom that Martial had once been at his leisure to contemplate. Black roses had been stitched to the top of the waist of her pleated silk skirt, which sat low on her hips. Her bronze-colored hair was pulled up in a chignon. At forty-four years old, she was more beautiful than ever; her half-closed Kyrgyzstani eyes seemed dazzled by a low sun, her voice beguiled through a mixture of childlike softness and sudden, throaty derailments.

"You are welcome, Messieurs," she said, giving each of them her hand to kiss. "I hope that you have had a pleasant journey."

She took a seat on a couch beside Grimod.

"We came as quickly as we could," said Holmes. "Our friend's automobile is very comfortable."

Lady MacRae addressed Canterel. "And so, you have come," she said with emotion.

While a Malaysian valet, dressed all in white, serves them refreshments, and outside the fog is finishing erasing Eilean Donan Castle from the charcoal drawing of the Highlands, let us endeavor to become better acquainted with the lady of the house. When she appeared in Canterel's life, thirteen years earlier, Lady Clawdia MacRae still bore the name of her French husband, a civil servant whose absence never ceased to cause gossip. People said he was posted in Dagestan, somewhere in the Caucasus. Supposedly well-informed persons asserted that his wife was, for her part, of Russian blood, with a maiden name ending with "-anov" or "-ukov," which her sharp cheekbones and slightly slitted eyes seemed to substantiate. The only undeniable facts were that Clawdia Chauchat was recovering from some kind of chlorosis at the Sanatorium Berghof, near Davos, and that no one had ever seen a wedding ring on her finger. Certain ladies believed that she had engaged in various encounters with men who passed through the facility, but did not, for all that, consider her a loose woman; at worst, they accused her of neglecting her manicure from time to time—a fact that sheds light on her incredible ability to charm.

Martial Canterel, too, had found her "delicious." They had met in Biarritz, during her stay in the Pyrenees, one of the trips that she had frequently gone on to get away from the stifling atmosphere of Berghof. The story of their passionate love deserves to be told, but it lasted only three weeks and interests us only because of its disastrous results: after having returned to Davos with another man—Mynheer Peeperkorn, a Dutch millionaire spoiled by the Tropics—Madame Chauchat realized that she was pregnant with Canterel's child. Whatever the reasons for her decision, she chose not to tell him anything and gave birth to a daughter she named Verity. Seven years later, long after the death of Peeperkorn, and at the exact moment that her mother was becoming a lady by marrying Lord MacRae, Verity had gone to sleep on a church pew and never woken up. In a moment of great distress, Clawdia had written to Canterel to inform him both that he was the father of a little girl as gracious as she was bright, and that, by the gravest of misfortunes, this girl had just turned into a Sleeping Beauty. Having thus learned of his child, Martial made unsuccessful pleas to see her, then his responses became less frequent, and then he stopped sending letters altogether. It had now been four years since he had heard anything about his daughter, or about the woman who was, to him, ever the bewitching and mysterious Madame Chauchat.

"How is Verity?" asked Canterel, avoiding her gaze.

Clawdia rubbed her neck.

"No noticeable changes," she replied, icily. "But I don't believe that subject interests you very much."

"That's not the case, as you can see."

"She's still sleeping. I had her moved to Glasgow, where I go see her as often as my occupations allow. At least once a fortnight, no matter what. She has grown up, she's a young woman now. But it is painful to see her."

Canterel looked at her, making that strange little grimace that is the prelude to a question, then changed his mind.

"The doctors know no more today than yesterday," Clawdia continued. "It's some kind of lethargic slumber, her brain has not gone through any changes, she may continue to sleep for the rest of her life or wake up this very moment, no one can say."

Holmes waited for silence to settle in again, then cleared his throat. "I would not want to hurry you, Lady MacRae, but you know very well that, in this kind of situation, every minute counts. When will we have the chance to examine the sinister items you told me about?"

"Right away, if you wish. The coroner brought them by the castle this afternoon. My late husband was very generous with the county, which accounts for this little bending of the rules. Come with me, they are in the kitchen."

They followed her there. The valet opened the heavy door of a tall icebox and pulled out a wooden box, which he placed on the serving table. Having donned a pair of white gloves, Holmes lifted the lid, uncovering the three shoes they had come to examine.

"Sizes 42, 39, and 37, the investigation found. Rubber soles, white leather uppers, brand Ananke on a machine-sewn insert . . ."

He cautiously brought them out one by one and set them on the table. Each one still contained fragments of bone and waxy flesh from the feet that had been severed at the ankle.

"It is strange that they were severed in the same place," remarked Clawdia, with a look of revulsion.

"No, it is quite normal, in fact," responded Grimod. "When a body decomposes in the sea, it is common for the head, hands, and feet to detach. The extremities always give out at the thinnest point, but normally it all stays on the sea floor; in our case, the rubber soles allowed them to float up."

"As for the shoes' shape," suggested Holmes, "it must have preserved the contents for longer."

"It certainly helped," said Grimod, prodding the flesh, "but when bodies—and feet in particular—are left in seawater, they can change into adipocere, or 'grave wax.' The lack of oxygen combined with the influence of the cold and the damp causes a process similar to saponification; thus, the flesh becomes waterproof and takes on the waxy look that we see here. However, this makes any calculation of time of death very problematic. I highly doubt that the tests will give us anything."

"May I see the soles?" asked Martial.

Holmes tilted the shoes, and Canterel bent down to inspect them, hands behind his back for fear of touching them.

"And here's the odd thing," he said. "The pattern of the nonslip grooves is different on each, even though they are the same model."

"You're right," noted Grimod. "I'm going back up to our rooms to look for something to take their imprints."

"Don't trouble yourself," said Clawdia. "What do you need?"

"Ink and paper. A sponge, as well."

A look from Lady MacRae sent the valet off in search of the required equipment.

"Well," said Holmes, "I believe that's everything on this side of things. For now, we have three right feet, that is to say three bodies, and one . . . 'necessity.' It's not much, I must say."

"Where was the diamond?" asked Canterel.

"In my safe. A Delagarde Amiens with a lock and combination. It was not forced open, and I don't understand how it's possible."

"The key?"

She looked him right in the eye, tugging on a small gold chain that slid the key between the curves of her breasts. "I always have it with me."

"How did you come to have such a jewel in your home?"

"Unusual circumstances. I always leave the Ananke in the Royal Bank of Scotland, but the Duchess of Kent was supposed to visit me, and I had promised to show her the gem. No one knew about it."

Holmes shook his head. "Besides the employees at the bank, the deliverer, and the security officers who accompanied him . . . Let's say between fifteen and fifty persons. That's a lot of people, milady."

The valet returned, and Grimod quickly began taking the shoes' imprints. Having swabbed the soles with an ink-soaked sponge, he applied them to three pieces of rice paper. The macabre remains went back into the icebox, and everyone returned to their seats by the fireplace to go over what they had learned, though they did not refrain from partaking in some of the best malt in Lady MacRae's cellar.

"It's extremely confusing," said Grimod, passing the imprints to Holmes. "This does not resemble anything I recognize."

"Indeed," replied Holmes. "The circles in these tread patterns appear to have been placed completely at random. You'd swear they were leopard spots . . . Perhaps there were three machines, one for each shoe size, with their own unique patterns?"

"Unlikely . . . I would lean more toward a custom-made fabrication, but that doesn't make sense."

"These three shoes, however, seem to have the same pattern of wear on them," said Canterel.

Miss Sherrington took a look at the impressions, ranked them from largest to smallest, then held them out to Clawdia for her to pass on.

"Not very talkative, your Russian dolls," she said, giving them to Canterel.

"More than you would believe," exclaimed Canterel, looking at all three together through the transparent paper. He adjusted them a little and smiled briefly in satisfaction. "Look, each of the imprints works as a fragment of the same stamp, we must assemble them in order for them to acquire meaning. Layered on top of each other like this, the markings on the treads come together to form a word: 'Mar-ty-rio.' That's what I read, anyway."

Holmes leapt out of his chair. "Terrific, my friend! I knew I was right in bringing you! Let me see that. 'Martyrio' . . . It's right there. Incredible!"

"Except that we have gotten nowhere."

"Martyrio, you say?" asked Grimod, looking thoughtful. "I've seen that word somewhere before. Wait . . . It was in the *New Herald*, in the same issue as the discovery of the three right feet."

"Kim, please," said Lady MacRae.

The Malaysian valet took a few steps and returned with a touch-screen framed in varnished wood. Grimod scanned it silently with his finger.

"There it is!" he said, separating the page out. "'Chung Ling Soo finally returns to London. After his triumphant tour of the United States, the celebrated Chinese magician Chung Ling Soo will be presenting his show at the Wood Green Empire, February 5-7. He will, for the first time in years, perform his "Condemned to Death by the Boxers," the extremely dangerous act that made a name for him at the Martyrio Circus before he went off to do his own show.'"

"Well," muttered Miss Sherrington, "I get the feeling I should repack the bags . . ."

IV

A Lovely Odor of Roasted Turnips

Carmen is the unfortunate wife of Dieumercie Bonacieux. The latter does not smoke or drink, he showers her with attention, he works hard, he is handy around the house. He is not ugly, despite having big teeth and a slightly stupid smile. Even his receding hairline is not without a certain charm. But his *thingy* doesn't work. "Your husband is affected by 'sexual blindness,'" the doctor said, "what is called genital ataraxia," he even specified, fearing that they had not understood. And it's true that, though she had tried a thousand ways to tantalize him, Dieumercie could not get it up. To make matters worse, he turned out to be one of the twenty-five percent of patients on whom even the strongest dose of Viagra has no effect. As for yarsagumba, the Tibetan fungus with a reputation for being an aphrodisiac, that did him no more good than any old omelet made with mushrooms. Or even truffles, at that price.

Given that this impotence threatens their relationship, Dieumercie is ready to try anything to fix it. Yesterday evening, his wife convinced him of the benefits of a foolproof technique, a method she heard about from a friend who is a nurse. The results should be visible by the time he returns from the factory.

At the moment we meet her, Carmen is sprawled out on the sofa bed, limbs outstretched, skirt hiked up to her belly button. Her eyes closed, she is masturbating with a duck neck. She has cooked the rest; there is a lovely odor of roasted turnips wafting through the room.

His mind on the assembly of the circuit boards that are passing between his hands, Dieumercie has a vague feeling of unease. In spite of his efforts to think about other things, images of his wife fussing at his penis play through his mind on a loop. Again he sees her insert the thin, plastic hose into the bag of serum, then hang it from the hook in the bathroom. She pulled on latex gloves, snapping them against her wrists. You'd think she had been doing this forever. A professional. Finally, she got down on her knees in front of him, disinfected him with ether, and stuck a long hypodermic needle into the skin of his balls. Having secured the catheter with surgical tape, she connected the needle to the other end of the hose. Scrotal infusion, my dear . . . A poisonous-sounding term that had not seemed to give Carmen pause, but that had made his back prickle with sweat. She made him sit on the edge of the tub, and he waited there while the liquid flowed in. Good Lord, a liter! When he began to panic, seeing his scrotum swell to the size of a handball, she reassured him from afar, her eyes never straying from whatever crappy game show she was watching on TV: it was normal, the serum was going to filter gradually into his cock, and the next evening his engine would be all revved up. He heard her blowing her nose, then she added, laughing: And I'm all stuffed up!

She was right, but also wrong. What he now has between his legs looks just like a large beer can, but a soft one. Dieumercie is worried. Besides the fact that at this very moment he is having trouble walking normally to leave his post, he knows already that this plan is going to fall to pieces.

V

The Chinese Cut Short

When the carriage dropped them off at 7 Cheapside, High Road, in front of the marquee at the Wood Green Empire, they were fifty minutes late. They hurried through the doors; under the colored poster announcing the show, in big red letters: "Chung Ling Soo, the marvelous Chinese magician, inimitable and rare jewel, remnant of the Yellow Empire."

Holmes showed their tickets to an usher. They followed her up the grand staircase, ran down the deserted corridors, then cautiously took their seats in the central box that Lady MacRae had reserved for them.

Chung Ling Soo was on stage, which was sumptuously decorated with painted canvases meant to represent the interior of the Summer Palace by means of lanterns and views of pagodas. He was wearing a robe of embroidered silk that touched the ground; his hair, which he had shaved from his most of his head, fell in a long braid that he had draped over his right shoulder. The audience burst into applause. The magician had just pulled a live goose out of the gutted drum that hung from his waist, a fowl that joined—next to an aquarium full of red fish—an improbable number of rabbits, bouquets, and multi-colored umbrellas. Chung Ling Soo bowed, his hands together, not moving a single muscle of his face, and then the curtain fell.

"Topping show," murmured Holmes. "We should have gotten here on time!" And, reading the program over his glasses: "There is only one number left before the end."

The lights had come back on for a short intermission. As was typical of Edwardian architecture, the interior of the Wood Green Empire gave the impression of both luxury and rococo exuberance. The hall was a jewelry box hung with red velvet, in which the stucco, gilding, crystal chandeliers, and Ionic columns decorating the arches over the loges seemed to exist only to illustrate the line from Shakespeare that was embossed on the cornice: *All the world's a stage.* Welcomed into the show, the spectators felt lifted into the same halo of glory as the actors, as if they, too, were transfigured by the limelight. The audience could see, on the trompe-l'oeil canvas at the front of the stage, an imaginary proscenium flanked by twisted columns and stairs leading up to a tableau curtain at the back, whose heavy cloth was gathered up at the sides of the stage.

Knowing that the change of scenes would last only ten minutes or so, the spectators had not gotten up, but were stirring in their seats, loosening stiff muscles, carrying on about the virtuosity of the acts, or trying to explain the tricks. The audience was certainly not fit for an opera, but neither were they the patrons of vulgar music halls. They were dressed up, and in the orchestra, amid the tailored frock coats, certain young women would easily have outshone those who were watching through their binoculars from the twilight of the galleries.

"I am going to start being bored very soon," said Canterel, massaging his temples. "Are you sure we need to attend this . . . thing?"

"Absolutely certain," replied Holmes. "It's the only way. He's been informed about us, we are going to meet him backstage after the show."

"But really, shouldn't it be possible to track down this Martyrio Circus by some other means?"

"I checked," said Grimod, "and as strange as it seems, this circus is no more real than the Ananke brand of shoes. And it was Chung Ling Soo himself who insisted that the journalist mention that particular detail."

"If you say so," grumbled Canterel, fanning himself with his program.

In the orchestra pit, the musicians were finishing up their tuning. The lights and the conversations died away gradually. A few prudent coughs accompanied the first bars of a dramatic overture in which the dissonance of the flutes mimicked a Chinese chorus. The spotlights came up, and at the crash of a gong, the curtain rose.

The set had changed completely, the action now taking place in the heart of Peking, beneath the walls of the Forbidden City. Preceded by standard-bearers, a band of Chinese drummers streamed onto the stage and arranged themselves in the background. Finally there appeared a squadron of Boxers in almond-green turbans and black tunics, all armed with rifles and led by a rebel officer from the imperial army. Decked out in a winged helmet topped with a plume, the man was wearing a thick belt of red silk from which his saber hung. The participants lined up on the left while a series of gong and cymbal crashes accented the appearance, stage right, of an ornate palanquin. Chung Ling Soo emerged from it slowly, wearing a buttercup-yellow Mandarin cap and a robe of yellow silk embroidered with dragons. He planted himself in front of his enemies, challenging them with his noble comportment. On the officer's order, four of the soldiers stepped forward to form the firing squad.

An assistant, also dressed in the Chinese fashion, stepped toward the spectators.

"The Great Chung Ling Soo speak no language but his ancestors', he send to you by my mouth his lamentable apologies. During Boxer Rebellion, His Excellency choose to stay true to Emperor Guangxu's youth. Imprisoned by rebels, he was sentenced to horror of fiery squad. Exceptionally, he agree tonight to show you how he escape death, thanks to front teeth's magic power."

He went on in the same pidgin to convince two people from the audience to come up on stage and examine the ammunition, the powder, and the rifles, then asked them to identify the bullets by putting on each of them a mark of their choosing. With this done, the assistant loaded the weapons under their watchful eye and invited them to go back to their seats.

"Officer," he pleaded, turning to the Boxer leader, "mercy for Chung Ling Soo!"

A drum roll accentuated the officer's scorn and the slowness with which he lifted his saber to give the order to fire. In this moment of extreme tension, the assistant crossed the stage and came to a halt for a moment by Chung Ling Soo. He saluted in farewell, then handed him a china plate. Smiling, the magician covered his torso with it, like an ersatz shield.

"Aim!" the officer bellowed.

The soldiers pointed their guns; the saber came down.

"Fire!"

The blast made the audience jump; even Canterel, who was finishing up some intricate origami with his program, could not prevent his lower lip from trembling a little. Through the thick whorl of smoke, Chung Ling Soo could be seen staggering under the impact. With the consummate skill of a mime, he opened his eyes wide, made one of those faces that, for his public, took the place of speech, and bringing the plate up to his mouth, he spat out one bullet, then two, then three, gave a look of amazement, searched around for the fourth with his tongue, and abruptly regurgitated it in a gush of astonishingly real blood. He fell to his knees, gasping.

"Fuck, something went wrong! Lower the curtain! Lower the curtain, damn you!"

Having set the plate on the floor, in an admirable gesture of pro-fessionalism, he collapsed.

This had been the first time in fifteen years that he had spoken on stage; it was also the last.

VI

Casa Beaubrun

His fingers caress what look like the colorful bindings of the Collection Hetzel. There are millions of them, like books stored on their sides along the walls of the cave in which he is buried alive. *Monte Cristo, Romeo and Juliet, The King of the World, Sancho Panza, Antony and Cleopatra, Don Diègue, The Crown of Diamonds, Excalibur, The Breath of the Jaguar,* products that he had imported, for their more or less affirmed place in literature, others that he had produced from scratch, *Athos, Les Esseintes, Vintage Peeperkorn, Abelard and Heloise, Extraordinary Raskolnikov, Baskerville . . .*

After putting so much passion and care into manufacturing French cigars that would not yield in any way to the best of those produced in the Caribbean, Arnaud is unable to digest the injustice of his failure. A diffuse resentment has his stomach in permanent knots, it's enough to make him scream sometimes, doubled over in the depths of his lair.

Now that Périgord has turned into an amusement park for tourists seeking out prehistory, it is almost impossible to imagine that France was, not so long ago, a Mecca for tobacco growing. Even so, it is still common, walking around this place, to spot at random large wooden sheds with vented sides that make them look a bit like belfries. These are the old, abandoned tobacco barns. One comes across them there, in the middle of the fields where farmers still grow a little corn and rapeseed, those remaining few who have not transformed into rough innkeepers, their farms turned into lodgings.

His grandfather had escaped this decline. His father, too, in a sense. When SEITA had refused to pay a fair price for his bundles of tobacco, Louis Méneste moved on to rapeseed so he could reach retirement and finish paying for his son's engineering studies. The day his son was named top of his class at Epitech, Louis had called to congratulate him, then hanged himself. His wife followed him to the grave shortly after.

Having done well in school, Arnaud Méneste had accepted a generous offer from an American information security firm and emigrated to Florida, never suspecting that he would return twenty-two years later to take up the craft of his forebears.

Arnaud settled in on his ancestral lands, counting on the network of troglodytic dwellings that ran through the cliff bordering Dordogne. He had spent his childhood exploring these labyrinths, and was familiar with their every bend and curve and knew how intelligently the people who had sought refuge there in the Middle Ages had arranged them. There was always a fresh breeze blowing in the dog days of summer, as in the shaded hearts of Saharan medinas. In winter it was the reverse: the stone oozed stored-up heat, and a few embers in the hearth were enough to maintain a comfortable temperature; no one in human memory had ever caught the slightest whiff of mildew.

As he had foreseen, these grottos turned out to be perfect for drying tobacco leaves. Hung from the ceiling on hooks, the plants browned without rotting, all the while keeping the suppleness required for the shaping process. The perfect humidity. Even the Dominican workers he brought over at a steep price to make up his staff were astonished.

He set up the factory at the top of the cliff, just a hundred meters from the caves; it was a huge, rectangular stone building in the style of the region's farmhouses, now marred by its new owners' additions.

My god, what a shame . . . He has to stop thinking about all that, he tells himself, going into another room. This is an alcove with rounded corners and high ceilings, at the center of which stands a very simple canopy bed made of exotic wood. One of the few desires that Dulcie allowed herself to voice in all the time he has known her. She is lying perfectly still in a white cotton nightgown that belonged to her grandmother. Dulcie Présage . . . When she had first introduced herself, at the Dominican tobacco company he was visiting, Arnaud had been captivated by her name as much as by her beauty. An island girl with big lips and a limpid smile. Eyes the color of jatoba wood, though she has not opened them in six months. The feeding tube in her left nostril looks like one of the nose pins that Rajasthani women wear, it traces a smooth curve over her cheek up to her ear. She is sweating a little. Her pores glimmer slightly on her ashen skin, distant stars in the night sky. He runs a sponge over her, feeling like he is brushing off a chalkboard.

Dulcie is Haitian, but she worked as a *torcedora* for Don Esteban in Santiago de los Caballeros. A great opportunity. Her maternal great-uncle, Yvrose Beaubrun, a schoolteacher in Port-au-Prince, had gone into exile in the Dominican Republic in the twenties. There, he had freelanced for the daily *El Caribe* before being recruited to be a reader at La Aurora tobacco factory, where he officiated for fifty-nine years. The hurricane that hit the island in 1975 *only* killed eighty people, but among those unfortunates was Marie-Frumence, Dulcie's mother, a hundred-gourde hooker in the suburbs of Jacmel. The kid was only five at the time; some kind souls took it upon themselves to bring her to Santiago, to the last known member of her family. Yvrose took her in unquestioningly. He brought her to the factory during the day and taught her in the evenings. By watching the workers, then imitating them, Dulcie learned to select the leaves, trim them, distinguish the parts of the plant that should make up the filler, the binder, and the wrapper. Recipes for assemblage and fermentation; a knack for cutting and rolling; the necessary balance between the *ligero* (the leaves from the top of the plant, the cigar's power), the *seco* (the middle leaves, the aroma), and the *volado* (the bottom part, the burning); techniques for germinating seeds and transplanting them into the field, then cultivating them indoors; no part of the long process that leads to an excellent cigar escaped her.

By listening to Yvrose day after day, she acquired an almost unhealthy taste for novels. Seated at the foot of the reading platform where he ensconced himself—the *atalaya*, the "watchtower," the "sentinel"—she took in *Les Misérables* as one might receive a sacred text. Then *Monte Cristo* in the same way, *Robinson Crusoe*, *Don Quixote*, *Anna Karenina*, *Moby-Dick*, *Twenty Thousand Leagues Under the Sea*. Popular fiction alternated with works of great literature, edifying biographies with history books. Lope de Vega, Dante, Shakespeare, the lives of Thomas Edison, Benjamin Franklin, Bernard Palissy, the six volumes of Álvaro Flórez Estrada's *Elements of Political Economy*, Michelet's *History of the French Revolution*, Montesquieu's *The Spirit of the Laws* and *Persian Letters* . . . The other women cried as they worked, made comments while on break, then forgot what they had felt so fiercely during the reading. This was a natural phenomenon, and, if we can be honest for a moment, one that concerns us all: what remains in our memories but a blurred, dusty summary of those books that once turned our worlds upside down? Dulcie, however, remembered everything.

"The blood of a jeli runs in your veins," Yvrose Beaubrun told her one day admiringly, when she was reciting the actions of Edmond Dantès with the graceful ease of a griot.

Upon her great-uncle's death, she became the top roller at Don Esteban. When Arnaud met her, and they recognized each other as two halves of the same fruit, finally reunited, the young woman had an intellectual background and a political awareness that far outstripped his. It was she who passed on to him her love of books and initiated him into the complex delights of the cigar, and she who helped him come to understand his own father's attachment to tobacco growing. Ten years after their marriage and their move to Florida, it was for her that he sold his business and returned to Périgord. He replowed and resowed the fields of his childhood, tripled the size of the barn to make it a model workshop; at Dulcie's urging, he hired two experienced Dominican rollers to teach the women he recruited locally. At the end of the year, Casa Beaubrun began to produce the first French cigars: a *Jean Valjean* with a brown cap, which burned in several modules; a simple corona *Rastignac*; and a *Salammbô* with mild Creole notes. Several reviews from specialists hailed the company's birth without concealing their misgivings about its future. Put to the test by the top experts, Casa Beaubrun's cigars were found comparable to Havana's best, worthy of representing luxury "à la française."

Smokers, however, balked at the idea of a product that was missing one of the subconscious factors that gave them pleasure: exoticism. Although Dulcie and the forty women she supervised were producing three thousand cigars a day, Arnaud never managed to sell more than a fifth of them. At this stage, it was necessary to find investors so they could promote their brand and continue to operate. Paying for distribution rights in airport duty free shops was the keystone to their marketing strategy, but the cost was prohibitive. Adding to their expenditures, they leased more farmland to increase their yield, with the objective of minimizing the amount of tobacco they would have to import. This endeavor was starting to pay off when the price of tobacco jumped yet again, more than ever before, thwarting their efforts; that same autumn, a storm devastated Périgord and reduced them to nothing: sales dropped, banks pulled their support. At the beginning of the third year, Arnaud called his workers together and announced the factory's liquidation. A Chinese buyer was proposing to turn the facilities into a "hub for information technology production."

He swore to retain all the employees, provided they took a pay cut and expedited the factory's conversion into an e-reader assembly plant.

Once alone with Dulcie, Arnaud Méneste was resolved to tell her the whole truth: the Chinese group was buying Casa Beaubrun at a price that would not allow him to pay his debts; as he alone was liable for the company, even his lands were to be swallowed up by his bankruptcy.

"We've lost everything," he had told her, taking her in his arms.

She gave a strange moan and went limp; in the moment he thought that she was voicing her pain in some bizarre manner, that this was how they cried over in the Caribbean. A stroke, the medic announced, we have to take her to the hospital.

She has not come out of her coma since that terrible moment.

It only took two weeks for him to get her out of the hospital in Sarlat and bring her home with him.

In his caves, besides the cigars he managed to save, he has hundreds of journals, from his father and his grandfather, who could never separate themselves from the written word. Books, too: Great-Uncle Yvrose's Spanish library, and all that Dulcie bought later. Day after day, he draws strength from them to invent the next part of the story that he will read the following day to the employees of B@bil Books.

He is just a voice, a tenuous bridge between two shores.

VII

An Additional Horror

When they arrived backstage, behind the curtain where Chung Ling Soo was lying, a short man whose arms were too long for his body was shouting himself hoarse trying to keep people away. Holmes recognized him immediately.

"Scummington! How the devil did you manage to get here so quickly?"

"I was in the hall. This sorry fellow is not who he was pretending to be, I was keeping an eye on him, on assignment. But you, Holmes, what reason do you have to be here?"

"The pleasure of enjoying a nice evening out. My friend Canterel is absolutely mad about illusionists."

"French, I presume . . ." He gave a nervous start, stiffened, and nodded his head, as if seized by a cramp in his neck. "Inspector Sipe Scummington, Scotland Yard."

This strange manner of introducing himself did not appear to elicit any response; Canterel merely gave a brief smile of confirmation.

"And you know Grimod, my butler?"

"I do," said Scummington, without even glancing at him.

"Then you know that he has some medical experience . . ."

"I do. But at present it is unnecessary. The bullet went through his heart; he's dead."

"Will you permit me to confirm this?" asked Grimod.

"Very well." He stepped aside to let them pass. "Take care not to get your nice clothes dirty, he bled like a pig."

Chung Ling Soo had been laid out on his back. On her knees beside him was a young woman dressed as a geisha, sobbing and holding his hand. Grimod checked for a pulse in his carotid, the site of the impact, and rose. There was nothing to be done.

"My condolences, madam," said Holmes. "He was a great artist."

He felt a hand on his shoulder: Canterel, holding a finger to his lips, was signaling him to look at the body. With the tip of his cane, Canterel discreetly lifted the magician's robe just enough to reveal a protruding shoe.

"Holy hell!" murmured Holmes.

On Chung Ling Soo's left foot was a blood-spattered white sneaker; the Ananke-brand symbol they discovered on it added an additional horror. Where his other foot should have been was only a peg leg with a rubber tip.

"Ah, yes, who would have guessed it?" said the inspector, forcing his way into their huddle. "The great Chung Ling Soo had only one leg. His disability did not hinder him, quite the opposite, since he made use of it in some of his illusions, according to what his assistant told me. One less leg leaves space under that robe to hide all sorts of things, not to speak of the number where his assistant saws his leg off!"

Canterel frowned, annoyed by the indecency of saying such things only two steps from a woman who was sobbing over the corpse of her husband. He was about to let out one of those barbs that had alienated him from the world when Holmes, sensing the danger, hurriedly cut him off: "What happened?"

"I don't know yet, but it was certainly an accident. A dozen conjurors have kicked the bucket doing this kind of thing. Houdini himself said it in his time, it's too sophisticated, the slightest technical error and you're toast . . ."

The arrival of the police and the paramedics brought an end to the discussion. Chung Ling Soo was loaded onto a stretcher and taken to the hospital along with his wife. One sergeant caught sight of Grimod, who was examining the rifles used by the firing squad.

"You there, the negro, who told you you could touch that?"

"Leave him alone," Holmes intervened, "he's with us."

"What do you mean, he's with you? Who are you, for starters?"

"Sergeant Bedford?" said Scummington.

"Oh, excuse me, Inspector," he said, snapping to attention. "That . . . person was tampering with the weapons, and I thought I should . . ."

"That will do, Sergeant, I have the situation in hand."

"What a tragic story!" said Holmes, offering the inspector a cigar. "What do you know about his true identity?"

"The fellow was no more Chinese than you or I. His real name was William Ellsworth Robinson, an American of Scottish origins. His wife, too: 'Suee Seen, the living doll of Shanghai,' but in reality Olive Path, a chorus girl from Ohio."

"And?"

"So far, they seem irreproachable, though you'll agree that this practice of playing at being Chinese all day, even behind the scenes, is at least a little peculiar."

"*That* is Great Art," said Canterel, examining the lead balls that were still sitting on the plate, "making your whole life a part of your pursuit of excellence. I would imagine that these are indeed the projectiles marked by the audience members?"

"It seems that way to me," the inspector replied. And, addressing Chung Ling Soo's assistant, "This is the time for you to explain yourself. How did the bullets wind up in his mouth?"

"He put them there himself," the man said, now speaking in perfect English. "When I load the rifles, I swap out the bullets marked by the spectators and hold onto them until the moment that I pass them to Chung Ling Soo, along with the plate. When the soldiers pull the trigger, they set off blanks. The guns are rigged. Everything else is just staging."

"So how did it misfire?"

"I took apart the rifle in question: the partition between the blank and the real powder had worn through. When the first exploded, it set fire to the second, so the gun really went off."

"You must check the guns, though, don't you?"

"Of course, but even though we were making big money, he begrudged any expenses. It was always too soon to replace the parts . . ."

"A stinginess that cost him his life," the inspector concluded smugly.

Canterel hastily whispered a few words into Holmes's ear.

"Well!" replied the latter. "All that's left for us to do is take a look around the poor man's dressing room!"

"That's not necessary, to my mind the case is closed."

"Oh, of course I agree, but . . ." Holmes winked at the inspector. "It's not every day that an opportunity arises to learn a few of a magician's secrets. That's what my friend Canterel just whispered to me. Aren't you curious to know how he pulled all those little animals out of his drum?"

"Not in the least. It's rigged, that's all. Anyone can do it, once they know how it works . . . But go on, if it interests you. As for me, I have to accompany these idiots to Scotland Yard to take their statements."

They hastened to salute the inspector, then plunged into the depths of the theater.

"What a worm," said Canterel, referring to Scummington.

"Worse than you suppose," replied Holmes. "He's a former Pinkerton. A scab and a pervert, I've been told; he drinks other people's piss . . ."

A stagehand directed them toward Chung Ling Soo's dressing room. As soon as they found it—the placard on the door and the warning against unauthorized entry left no doubts—they closed themselves in.

"This was no accident," Grimod informed them gravely. "The partition between the round and the secret ramrod was deliberately damaged."

"You're sure?" asked Holmes.

"One hundred percent. Normal wear and tear doesn't leave filings . . . And I asked his assistant, so I also know that Chung Ling Soo never told anyone, even his wife, where he got those shoes. He received one once every six months, size 42, which he only wore for performances."

As he was listening to his companions, Canterel began to snoop around the room. Wood Green Empire was known for the opulence of its interior design, but also for the comfort and spaciousness of its artists' rooms. Besides a huge dressing room, complete with vanity and folding screen, the space included a salon where the magician had stored some of his materials. Having lingered over the contents of a trunk, Canterel was getting ready to examine a support overloaded with Chinese attire when he suddenly felt another presence in the room. His jump undoubtedly saved his life; at the same moment that a gunshot brushed his waistcoat, a man shot out from under the silk clothes and bolted for the door, shoving Holmes and Grimod as he passed. Thrown off balance, Grimod grabbed at the unknown man's jacket and held on so tightly that the latter wriggled out of it to escape more quickly.

"Stand down, he's armed!" said Holmes, holding Grimod back. "It's not worth getting yourself killed. And you, old chap, no harm done?"

White as a sheet, Canterel was inspecting the gunshot residue left on his garments by the blast. "That rogue ruined a thousand-ducat waistcoat! If I ever catch him . . ."

"Still, he left us a few tidbits," said Grimod, combing through the pockets of the jacket. "And, if I'm not mistaken, I've found a document that may very well be of service to us . . ."

He produced a stamped, addressed envelope. Printed in red, a Chinese dragon framed a handwritten address: *Mr. Hugh Palmer, 97 Morrison Street, Peking, China.*

Holmes quickly unsealed the flap. The envelope did not contain a letter, but rather a long ribbon folded in a zigzag, like those they had seen come out of Chung Ling Soo's mouth less than an hour earlier. A series of signs, in the same handwriting and ink as those on the envelope, were inscribed vertically:

TDOWIKOυ HINANηίτ ETAYGδμα DSRM00άί IREO2ύχ AEOS/δο MFNC1έ OLTO50 NEHWAε DCEPV ATIEά NIRKV

"Looks like a job for you, Canterel!" said Holmes, holding the strip out to him. "Our ruffian is going to be in deep trouble: it looks as if he has lost what he came to fetch . . ."

"Let's get out of here. I look like a beggar, I have to change before I can think."

They hailed a cab and returned to The Langham, London. As soon as they arrived, Canterel arranged to meet them at the hotel bar, then rushed to his room.

"Ah, there you are!" said Miss Sherrington when she saw him. "Where did you run off to? The slums of Southwark?"

"Think again. It was only a variety show; it is impossible to attend boulevard theatre without coming back a little splattered."

It seemed to him that the gunshot had contaminated his whole outfit. He removed all his clothes, giving the order to dispose of them.

"Do I make myself clear?"

"Yes, Monsieur. As usual. I will go directly and throw these in the municipal incinerator. Just as well, I can't imagine what sort of unfortunate would wear your cast-offs on his back! He'd be sent straight to Bedlam . . ."

"For this evening, I will stay in my cream silk ensemble, white shirt, and dove gray socks."

"And for your shoes? High altitudes, mountain pastures, damp undergrowth?"

"Alice! Enough of your impertinences, please! My Guyanese python shoes will do nicely."

Still in his underclothes, walking around the room, he examined the ribbon for the first time. Letters from the Latin and Greek alphabets, numbers, a backslash . . . The puzzle promised to be gripping.

Miss Sherrington reappeared, her arms full of clothes.

"And now he's throwing streamers!" she said, snorting.

Canterel started to get dressed, though not before he updated the tally that kept track of how many times he had worn each garment. After three marks for shirts and ties—fifteen for suits, hats, and overcoats—he got rid of them.

When he joined them in the hotel bar an hour later, Holmes and Grimod were already seated in heavy brown leather armchairs. Sitting two tables away, three elderly gentlemen talked loudly, deep in an impassioned conversation that was quite obviously, thanks to certain recurring words, on the subject of Talleyrand and the Congress of Erfurt.

"So," asked Holmes, "have you had time to take a look?"

"Yes, but I haven't gotten far, I'm afraid."

He handed Holmes the ribbon and got out a paper onto which the message had been scrupulously copied.

"It's very odd, it does not resemble anything that I have had the chance to study. If it is merely a matter of a simple encryption through the transposal of letters, the presence of the Greek characters will complicate any frequency analysis, but I should be able to figure it out in a few hours. If we are dealing with a code involving the substitution

43

of words starting from a unique key, it will be much more difficult . . . And, in any case, I will need my notes, which I left in Scotland."

"We're losing precious time," said Holmes, disappointed. "Waiter! Another scotch, please. What are you drinking?"

"Tea with milk."

"How would one go about doing a frequency analysis?" asked Grimod, who was scrutinizing the message doubtfully.

"In any given language, the frequency of the letters remains the same in the event of a simple transposition. In French, for example, the letter 'e' is the most common, then 'a,' 's,' 'i,' etc. If the encryptor made each letter correspond to another letter in the alphabet, all one has to do is replace the most frequent letter in the message with 'e,' and so on."

At the neighboring table, the tone had gone up another notch. In the midst of their heated debate, the three diners had forgotten their manners. Half up onto the table, one of them seemed ready to come to blows. "And what if Talleyrand wasn't a traitor, eh? Try thinking about that for two seconds!"

Canterel turned toward them, ready to give them a piece of his mind, but froze and picked up the ribbon. "If Talleyrand . . ." he repeated. "How did I not think of it sooner!"

"If you could enlighten us . . ."

"A scytale, Holmes! The method the Spartans used to send secret messages. The generals who needed to send correspondence to each other would keep perfectly identical sticks. When one of them wanted to send a letter, he would encircle his stick with a thin strip of paper, then write his message on it. Then he would unroll the strip, rendering the text unreadable, and send it along to the other general. To decipher it, the second general had only to roll it around his own stick. Simple, but effective!"

"And in our case?" asked Grimod.

"This system amounts to a kind of encryption through transposal. If it is indeed the method used here, I will eventually crack it. But there is still something that rings a little strange. Scytales produce groups of the same number of letters, but here we have decreasing numbers . . ."

"We'll have to go back to the theater," said Holmes, "and try to dig up that damned stick."

Canterel suddenly sat up straight. "Call the car, quickly!"

"Where are we going? Wood Green Empire?"

"No, the morgue."

VIII

Dead Stars above the Bed

"Hello, Charlotte, how are you?"

"Alright, and you?"

"I'm a little . . ."

"What's wrong?"

"Oh, everything's fine, but I'm always tired. You know, with my old bones and all, it's normal . . . And you?"

"I'm fine, fine."

Marthe is in her usual place, on the landing, in front of her open door, just across from Charlotte Dufrène's studio apartment. She looks like she has just escaped an assassination attempt; wide, bloodshot eyes, her hair stiffened into three plumes by the strength of the blast. She is a fright to see.

"And, well, sometimes I talk real loud, because Chonchon is deaf and can't hear. But he's going to get into trouble. He was at the clinic, but he didn't want to wait for his appointment. He's out of medication. What's going to happen to him?"

"I have no idea. And you, what about your doctor, and your benefits?"

"Who, me?"

"You have to move."

"Oh, there's no rush, the city does all that . . ."

She slumps a little. Dirt stains have merged with the garish pattern of her dress, which she has been wearing for several weeks. She enunciates every syllable when she speaks, with a tic that makes her close her eyes tightly each time, as if the slightest word could trigger a catastrophe.

"Gotta look for a piece of a man's glasses."

"What?"

"Wait, come here . . . Look, look a little."

She brings Charlotte into her hallway and shows her a shard of glass.

"Do you think that's a lens from a pair of men's glasses?"

"It's possible. Yes, it does look like it. Whose glasses, though?"

"Well, it's just, I found them on the floor, in my apartment. I'm worried they're Chonchon's . . ."

"Does he wear glasses?"

"Yes . . ."

"And would he have stepped on them?"

"I dunno. I found this after he came home. But tell me, is it a tinted lens?"

"It's dirty, sure. Hard to say. Maybe it's just from a broken jar?"

"Oh, so you think it's from a broken jar?"

"Possibly."

"Not from a pair of glasses?"

"I don't know. I'm not an eye doctor."

"But still, you don't think it is? It's such a little shard."

"Yes, you have to find the rest of it."

"I didn't think to look. But d'you think he'll be able to . . . ?"

"Of course he'll make it home."

"You're sure he'll make it home? 'Cause with just one lens . . ."

"If he's still got one lens, it's fine. Anyway, it's not like he's totally blind."

"You think he'll still be able to read his name?"

"On the buzzer? He's been pushing the same button for thirty years, he doesn't need to read it, he knows where it is."

"Even if his lens is broken, you think he'll still be able to see?"

"Yes."

"Ah, you think he'll still be able to see? Even if it's small?"

"Yes."

"Good. You think I shouldn't worry about it?"

"No."

"Mustn't cry, then?"

"Oh, no, crying doesn't help anything. Not right now, at least!"

"You say he'll still be able to see his name to get back here?"

"Yes, to ring the bell."

"I'm gonna cry . . ."

"There's no need to cry, Marthe. Well, good night, I have to get some rest."

Charlotte goes into her apartment and quickly shuts the three-bolt lock that protects her from the horrors of old age. She undresses, pulls her flannel shirt over her head, slides under her comforter, eagerly starting to visualize Fabrice's handsome face. They started to have a conversation over break today, she tries to remember the exact scene, but nothing appears, either in her head or on the ceiling. Her eyes settle on the phosphorescent stars glued above the bed by a previous tenant. Tiny ones, big ones, arranged any which way; the spittle of a consumptive Martian. Their luminosity gave out ages ago. They are dead stars, Charlotte has never seen them shine.

She concentrates on the idea of a lovely house in the country; she would be there with Fabrice, surrounded by children. On the front of the house would be a climbing vine and bougainvilleas. Words, just words that do not manage to bring a single image into her head. For a moment, she thinks she hears shouting, like kids at play, but it's Chonchon coming home, piss drunk, and Marthe scolding him. And just like every other evening, the wallpaper falls away, panel by panel, as if stripped off by an invisible hand, the walls pucker, become porous, melt away. Marthe's face appears to her, immeasurably magnified, dotted with bristles on her chin, her forehead wrinkled with oily arches. The bedroom is nothing more than an aquarium, Charlotte a breathing axolotl.

IX

The Diamond and Its Reflection

Presented with aplomb by Shylock Holmes, Scummington's card gave them easy access to Eagle Place, the London morgue. One of the attendants led them to the cell where the late Chung Ling Soo was temporarily resting on a black marble slab. As soon as the attendant left them, Holmes rebelled.

"But really, Canterel, we're not children . . . When are you going to explain to me what we're doing here?"

"The wooden leg," said Canterel, pursing his lips. "Take off the wooden leg, will you?"

Grimod understood immediately and did so, his eyes gleaming.

Once he had the object in his hands, Canterel examined it and quickly found what he was looking for.

"I knew it!" he said, showing them a horizontal groove cut into the wood in the top third of the leg.

He aligned the beginning of the strip with this groove and asked Grimod to hold it in place while he rolled it around the leg. Gradually, as it wound around, the message appeared. His glasses perched on the tip of his nose, Holmes spelled it out aloud: "'The diamond and its reflection are on their way. Moscow-Peking 02/15.' As for the rest, I apologize for my pronunciation, but Ananki d oúdé theoí machontaí."

"Ἀνάνκη δ οὐδέ θεοί μάχουταί," Grimod corrected, smiling. "'Not even the gods fight against necessity,' Simonides's famous words . . .'"

"But which in our case sounds like a warning!" said Canterel.

"You are extraordinary. I would pay dearly to know the series of deductions that brought you to this leg . . .'"

"Even if I had the answer to your question, I don't think you'd be able to afford my price, my dear. No offense, of course."

"That's not what I meant," continued Grimod, "though perhaps a more in-depth conversation on that topic would surprise you. Let's move on . . . I am more a being of logic than passion, I have studied Joseph Bell's theories, arguments drawn upon by the grandsire of our own Sir Holmes, whom I try to assist as much as I can in his work, but your method of coming to this conclusion astounds me, as it flies in the face of all deductive logic!"

"Perhaps," said Canterel, unwinding the strip very slowly, "perhaps it is simply a matter of a different sort of logic, just as true to reason, or what you understand by that word. If I weren't concerned about the contradiction in terms, I would speak of an irrational logic, a mental process that I have noticed can be found in the margins, in random encounters, and in a kind of pure poetry, the magic of its operation. Thinking about it a little, I would say that I am likely not such a bad poet."

"Please, Monsieur, or I won't be able to sleep tonight: how did you go from the ribbon to the scytale, and from there to the wooden leg?"

"You imagine I know how I did it?" asked Canterel, adjusting his tiepin. "You are wrong. I try to be . . . How shall I put it? To be truly present in my surroundings, and suddenly everything begins to signal to me in some strange way. I cannot write poems that an editor would agree to publish without making me pay the expenses out of pocket, but something happens within me that is along the lines of poetry. I must be some kind of sensor, you know. Reality often works the same way in which Raymond Roussel wrote some of his books—it feels like a bad pun. Coils, pythons, a stray scytale . . . Then the intuition that a conical stick was needed to produce that shift in the letters. It's no more than that: I lock on to the things that hide from the order that lies beneath the seeming frivolity of language."

"In the meantime," Holmes noted, concerned, "the main thing I see is that we are not the only ones on the chase . . ."

Half an hour later, they arrived back at the hotel bar.

Holmes banged his glass down on the table.

"Moscow-Peking," he said, fervent. "Do we agree that it can only mean a train?"

Grimod nodded, while Canterel merely raised his eyebrows.

"If all this is not just the product of our imagination, the diamond should then be traveling on the Transsiberian on February 15th to get to its recipient."

"Which implies," continued Grimod, "that the message was intended to take the same route a few days in advance . . . Waiter!" he said, with an authority that left Canterel puzzled. "The schedule for the Moscow-Peking, please . . ."

"Of course, Monsieur, allow me to go consult the Bradshaw's at reception . . ."

He returned less than ten minutes later—this was one of the horribly expensive little services offered by large hotels—with a piece of paper on which were written the upcoming departures of the incredible train that had linked Europe and Asia since 1891.

"The next leaves in three days," said the server, "which will not leave you time to make a reservation, unless you already have your visas in order. Still, you'll have to get to Moscow. The next departs in two weeks, on February 15th, which would be more reasonable. If you wish, we can arrange your voyage for you."

Holmes was delighted, but he shot a questioning glance toward Grimod.

"I'll thank you to take care of it," said the latter. "There will be four of us. I will find you again in a little while to go over the details."

When the waiter was gone, Holmes noticed that Canterel looked preoccupied.

"What's wrong, my friend? Do you think we're not making the right decision?"

"Of course not," replied Canterel. "It's a good lead, but today is the . . ."

"The fifth of February," said Grimod.

"That's what I thought. I'm concerned that there won't be enough to fill my trunks. I have some shopping to do, you see . . . My whole wardrobe is still in Biarritz."

The next day, Holmes drove Canterel to Savile Row, the street with the best tailors in London. The Frenchman left behind a small fortune at Gieves & Hawkes in exchange for several suits, and almost as much at Hardy Amies for shirts and accessories. Still more checks cut the fittings down to three days, a period during which Holmes used his connections to obtain the necessary visas for their trek. As for Grimod, he was sent to Eilean Castle to tell Lady MacRae of their departure. He was to gather their things and bring them back to London along with the car.

Canterel never stopped thinking about the message that was sending them off to the end of the earth; one of the words kept bothering him. He opened up to Holmes. "The diamond and its reflection . . . Why word it like that? Doesn't that have to mean that there was something else in the safe?"

"I would lean more toward a simple figure of speech," said Holmes. "That fits the exuberance of his persona, Chung Ling Soo was not one for discretion, if I am to believe what we saw of his show."

"Certainly not, but still. I hardly see the use of such a phrasing in this instance . . ."

"Come now, Martial, don't go looking for things that aren't there, our situation is complicated enough as it is, let's not add any more riddles. In any case, now that your wardrobe is replenished, I suggest you stop by and visit my friend James Purdey, a gunsmith. It would be well not to disregard the dangers that await us."

Making it clear that he believed he had all he needed in his luggage, Canterel acquiesced. They went to 57 South Audley Street, where they were received in the "Long Room" reserved for "serious" clients. The meaning behind this word: those rich enough to spend the exorbitant sums of money that transform a simple aesthete, astonished by the beauty of a weapon, into one of those exceptional men capable of buying it. With Holmes seeming uneasy, in Grimod's absence, at the prospect of making pecuniary decisions, Canterel came to acquire a Whitworth double-barreled rifle, which had narrowed chokes and jasper trim that read *Best Bouquet & Scrolls*, allowing the bearer to honorably face any wildcat in the real or figurative jungles he had to roam. He finished his shopping with a Mauser C96 and its holster, and insisted on presenting his friend with a 9mm Luger Parabellum that he was salivating over.

Once Grimod returned from Scotland, the car was delivered to The Langham, London's garage; Miss Sherrington looked after getting all the purchases from the last several days packed up and transporting them to Victoria Station.

Perhaps you will have formed a rather poor picture of Canterel, of a contemptible father wholly occupied in frittering away his fortune without sparing a thought for the child he had never seen? That would be a mistake, as he expressed his desire to go to Glasgow before their departure, just long enough to embrace his daughter; it was Grimod who dissuaded him: the Nord-Express from Paris to St. Petersburg was going the next day, on Saturday the 9th of February at 2:15 P.M. It would not arrive at its destination until Monday at 3:00 P.M.; they would then have to catch a connection on the 12th to get to the Russian capital the evening of the 14th and hope to make the Transsiberian on the 15th.

They had not counted on the unknown quantities that accompany all journeys of this scale. After a brief night, shortened by important reflections on the chase they were undertaking—but even more by Holmes's tendency to top up his glass of scotch before sharing the slightest opinion—all four of them clambered into a cab around noon. Ever since the reopening of the coalmines and the return to coke in all fields of industry, a thick fog had been pressing down on the metropolitan centers of Europe. The once-renowned "London fog" had easily regained its past acclaim, so much so that at that hour of the day it reduced the streets to dismal canyons populated by vague shapes. From the orangey dome that covered the city fell a snow of carbonaceous particulates that oppressed the throat and irritated the eyes.

Their cab was turning onto Grosvenor Place, a few hundred meters from the station, when a huge explosion forced the coachman to rein in his team. Part of the façade of a department store had collapsed in the blast, flinging massive stones into the street and showering down a hail of glass shards. A terrified young woman came out of the haze, carrying a baby covered with blood, then came a carriage drawn by a panic-stricken horse that had taken the bit between its teeth, followed by a man who was walking slowly, his head split open. Canterel was about to open the door to go help the wounded who were streaming toward them, when a second explosion, then a third lit up the sky in different places, though it was impossible to pinpoint them exactly.

"Bombings," said Holmes. "We have to get out of here quickly!"

At that moment, swarms of young people emerged from the fog, running. Ragged little kids, for the most part, who were fleeing with their arms full of the fruits of their looting: hams, cashmeres, gleaming copper pots, ratafia, porcelain dolls, clocks, dried cod, cellos, armfuls of umbrellas, sewing machines, chandeliers, mattresses, glass globes, cobblers' anvils, andirons, preserves, boiled leather mannequins, brass candlesticks, wheelbarrows brimming with marshmallows and gilt buttons, even a cast iron stove carried like a cumbersome corpse by four teens whose faces were black with anguish and smoke. Radiant Hermès scarves began to billow out above them, looking like the last shreds of a snuffed-out dream.

After this vision came the tramping sound of a stampede, then the arrival of several mounted policemen. Holmes quickly gave the coachman an order, and they managed to sneak in behind the mounted guard that was launching into pursuit of the looters.

Twenty minutes later, they narrowly managed to leap onto the Golden Arrow that was threatening to leave for Paris without them.

X

A Bit of Fog on the Lenses of His Glasses

Perhaps her daily dose of hormones, or her age, though more likely her overindulgence in candied fruit and her lack of physical activity have made her into a woman who is rather more than chubby; not obese but plump, with the advantage of having curves where they are needed, but also cascading flab in places that are repellent. A Venus by Rubens, not yet a Botero. Louise Le Galle knows this without wanting to admit it. She imagines herself more as a priestess at the Crazy Horse Saloon, with a name that crackles and allures: Nouka Bazooka, Choo Choo Nightrain, Bertha von Paraboum . . .

Since she became a woman, men have shown zero interest. She signed up for specialized dating sites: "Click through to screw!" A girlfriend had vouched for this practice, though she advised her to cheat on her photo. Twelve meet-ups at restaurants, twelve checks before dessert; eight of them asked to split the bill, two ran off so quickly that the bill was left to her, and the remaining two picked up the check but never called again. She amended her criteria, raised the age and weight of her desired man, but nothing worked. Fat guys wanted skinny women; in fact, the more old and misshapen they were, the less they would compromise on the beauty of the women they were meeting. She got to the point where she just wanted to sleep with a man, no longer cared about falling in love or building a relationship with him.

Poking around in the darkest reaches of the Internet, Louise was surprised to discover advertising slogans that plunged her into the depths of embarrassment: "Ugly girls still need cock: these chicks will fuck the first guy to send them a text. See their photos."

A site for virgins, she said to herself, perverts and ugly mugs, but still she had clicked, bitten by curiosity at the idea of comparing herself. What exactly did they consider an ugly girl? The results left her dumbfounded: these were young girls, so young, some of them barely sixteen, but still not a single one whose charms did not make her jealous! If these women were considered unattractive, where did she fall on the scale? Outside the curve, certainly. She was so upset to find herself left out of even the rejects—in spite of her job in human resources and her efforts to conform to canonical kinds of sex appeal—that she stopped looking for anything online. Others would have tried similar channels, ballroom dancing, aerial yoga, truck stops, but Louise found refuge in the rituals that, to her, reflected femininity: delicate lingerie, beauty creams—each more expensive than the last—and guilty alternation between dieting and gluttony. She was bursting with fat and bitterness.

So, when Monsieur Wang showed interest, she was even less choosy than before, and his status beguiled her.

The first time, it was the end of a long day of work, and they found themselves alone at the office. She was bringing him the cup of green tea and the crackers that he usually had at that hour. He checked that the biscuits did not contain any trace of peanuts, since he had a severe allergy, then settled himself deeper into his chair.

"I am exhausted, Madame Le Galle," he said, with an air of despondency. "The stress . . . I can't seem to relax, would you let me touch your breasts?"

Louise was still in her trial period at the factory. After a moment of surprise, she unfastened her blouse, then her bra, without taking either off. Wang slid his fingers under the structure in order to free her breasts, bent over the larger one, put his mouth on it, kneading the other with his hand. She did not feel compelled by some underlying blackmail, or even nervous. The full truth was that, in spite of its shocking nature, this request flattered her. Yes, flattered. This is what she was thinking as she clutched the back of Monsieur Wang's head.

He never goes any further. It isn't that she refuses to, quite the contrary, but he is content to simply continue this sporadic exercise with her. She is not even sure if he ejaculates anywhere besides on his iPad while watching porn. One thing is certain: Wang cannot stop himself from farting while he sucks on her breasts; it even seems like it increases his enjoyment, because he does it with his eyes closed, gravely, as if all his pleasure is released by the sonorous wind that he contrives to prolong, to replicate in detonations that grow shorter and shorter until they become silent.

And yet all this suits Louise. It's not as if she imagines that these are the actions of a man and his lover, but what does it matter. She admires him, his strength of will, his way of advancing in life, encased in principles and moral rectitude. Who cares if he farts, as long as he bites her nipples? She doesn't feel much, to tell the truth. It's the implants' fault; the surgeon had warned her, it takes several months for erogenous sensitivity to return; in some cases, very rarely, it is lost for good. In any case, he doesn't see the scars, or, if he has noticed them, he doesn't say a word, and she is grateful that she gets to feel desirable under his lips.

There, he's finished with his little routine. He says thank you, bowing stiffly and allowing her to go home. No smile, no kind word. Just a bit of fog on the lenses of his glasses.

XI

By the Virgin's Holy Robe

Contrary to what their departure from London might have indicated, the next part of their voyage unfolded smoothly. Unrest shook the French capital around the still-smoking ruins of the Department of Finance, but despite this the Nord-Express left Paris on time and took them non-stop to St. Petersburg, and they managed to catch the Transsiberian on February 15th as planned. We return to them on this day, two hours after the train rattled out of the Yaroslavsky Vokzal, the station in Moscow from which most trains departed for Siberia and the Far East.

The convoy was made up of seventeen cars and two wagons. On the outside, the coaches were made of teak darkened with bands of gold. All of the first-class compartments were decorated with mahogany and rosewood paneling and copper sconces. The beds, which could be converted into crimson velvet benches, were oriented in the direction of travel. Furnished with great care, the lavatories included small showers lined with Izmir tiles. In the marvelously tasteful central wagon was a restaurant whose walls, hung with red damask, rose to a ceiling painted with singeries. The adjoining car housed a smokers' lounge illuminated by ten beveled glass windows; a grand piano stood among club chairs and low tables of varnished satinwood.

It was here that Martial Canterel, Holmes, and Grimod had chosen to sit and wait for lunchtime.

"Let's go over it again," said Holmes, enveloped in smoke from his cigar. "There is no doubt that the diamond is traveling with us on this train. The person charged with delivering it to Peking cannot know that we have deciphered the message, or even that we are looking for him. This leaves us with two possibilities: either we sit quietly for him to deliver it to the recipient, risking that it might melt away once again, or we try to intercept it during the journey, which would be preferable."

"With the catch," responded Canterel, "that we are not the only ones on the chase."

"Yes," said Grimod, "but the others don't have the address that you managed to decipher. Even if they've followed us this far, we're one step ahead of them. It's up to us to make the most of it, and to remain vigilant."

He fell silent, having noticed another passenger approaching them with the obvious intention of making their acquaintance.

"Hello, Messieurs. Allow me to introduce myself: Dr. Charles-Joseph Mardrus, en route to the Orient."

He was a frail man whose long white hair—still quite thick for the seventy years of age that he later claimed, not without some pride—fell almost to his shoulders. A dapper old Liszt in need of conversation. Ten minutes later, they knew almost everything about his background and the reasons behind his journey on the Transsiberian. Born a Muslim into an illustrious Armenian family in Alexandria, he had converted to Coptic Christianity at a young age before dedicating his life first to Byzantine paleography, and later to medicine.

"But not just that," he clarified, "because no one can hope to heal the body without first taking care of the soul."

He had spent twenty years working on a *Compendium Philosophycum Essentialis*, a kind of abstract on clear vision and potions concocted to preserve it, as he himself explained it, promising to read them some excerpts once the monotony of the steppes had begun to infect the mood of the passengers, as he did not for a second doubt it would, even those who believed themselves to be well fortified against ill humors. He was on his way to Irkutsk, to the Znamensky monastery, where he was summoned by an appraisal of the greatest importance, since they had just found the Holy Robe of Mary, a relic that would relegate the Shroud of Turin to the rank of a common dishcloth. "Perhaps I exaggerate a little, of course . . ." He smiled at them all, displaying a set of teeth so white that they looked like an advertisement for a prosthetisist. The fact was that people were speaking about this linen as if it were a mandylion more precious than the Image of Edessa, and it was already drawing thousands of pilgrims eager to behold the direct testimony of their idol's real existence. "Devotees of St. Thomas, more than Christ, if you want my opinion . . . A mandylion? Sorry, that's a specialist's term, jargon . . . The Greek word for 'handkerchief.' That's what we call an imprint of Jesus's face on cloth. Having learned that Jesus was preaching not far from the kingdom of Edessa, King Abgar supposedly had his painter do a portrait. When the artist proved incapable of copying his features, Jesus applied a cloth to his face, and the image imprinted itself onto it. That is known as acheiropoiesa, or otherwise an 'icon made without hands.' For example, the Shroud of Turin or the Veil of Veronica, relics that we now know to have been created several centuries after the death of Christ. The Virgin's Holy Robe is doubtless also a medieval forgery, but looking at it, surprisingly, one hopes that it is not. I have a copy that was sent to me, would you all like to take a look? It's one fiftieth the size of the original . . ."

Without waiting for them to respond, he unrolled before them a sheet of Japanese paper upon which a woman's naked body was drawn in blood. Her breasts, her rounded belly, her shaved pubis, and even her vulval vestibule were there, revealed as if by a thin, transparent, damp cloth.

"Magnificent," said Holmes, spreading the drawing out on a chairback in order to examine it better. "This looks like nothing else I know of. You'd swear it was the stamp of a real body!"

"Indeed," said Dr. Mardrus, "and, in addition to its anatomical details, it is also in keeping with an inversion of forms. I imagine you likely know that women's left breasts are always larger than their neighbors to the right. In a painting, the left breast is therefore quite logically presented on the right."

"While here," said Grimod, "the larger of the two is on the left, as if the drawing resulted from the application of the paper to a real body."

"Precisely."

"And, if I may," said Canterel, making a show of looking out the window at the countryside, "the dark line that runs from the navel to the pubis suggests that this woman was pregnant."

"Bravo, dear sir, and of course that is what makes this relic so valuable: more than just an image of the Virgin, we are dealing with one of Christ *in utero!*"

Another passenger who was passing near them, accompanied by her ten-year-old son in a sailor suit, could not help but notice the drawing.

"How awful!" she exclaimed, trying in vain to turn her child's gaze away. "How can you flaunt such smut? And in first class! It's a scandal, I'm going to complain to the conductor!"

"I'll go with you," said Grimod, taking her by the elbow. "I do not understand how anyone can display such filth. If it were merely some actress, that would be one thing, but to dare to exhibit the Virgin Mary's nightgown! It's quite unacceptable!"

For an instant, the woman seemed bolstered in her indignation;

it appeared she was about to follow Grimod, but then she raised her eyes to his face and winced in astonishment.

"Oh my god! Who do you think you are? Don't touch me or I'll scream! You don't know who you're talking to!" She fled, trailing her brat by the hand.

"Well played," said Holmes.

Grimod cracked a smile.

"It's amazing, the way women go mad for me . . ."

"Shall we go to lunch?" Canterel proposed. "Would you like to join us, Dr. Mardrus?"

"Absolutely!"

He folded his sheet of paper carefully and followed them into the dining car. The head waiter led them to an elegant round table. On a white linen tablecloth, large porcelain plates bore the symbol of the Sleeping-Car Company, a design that was also engraved into the silverware and embroidered into the napkins folded in a double Tafelspitz. Hexagonal crystal glasses added a noteworthy touch of refinement, or at least showed how much the decorator had wanted to evoke that sensation.

While they were being served Ukrainian borscht cooked with Chablis wine, Mardrus continued to expound upon the Holy Robe, including several details regarding certain Syriac texts that may have mentioned it.

"Do you know that not a single piece of the Virgin's clothing has come down to us? There is the story of Galbois and Candide, two Arians who converted to Catholicism, who took the Mother of God's Dress, which had been bequeathed to one of her two Jewish serving women, from Galilee. The relic was kept in Constantinople, in the Basilica of Saint Mary Major, at the same time as the Maphorion, or Mantle, of that same person. A concentration that made the sanctuary the holiest place in the Eastern Empire! A 'regular miracle' occurred there each Friday at vespers: the silk veil slowly rose up and floated in the air until that same hour on Saturday, at which time it would float back down in front of everyone, softly and promptly, onto an ancient icon. A procession would then take it from that church to the sanctuary of St. Mary Chalkoprateia, where the Cincture of the Theotokos was kept. Yes, yes, dear friends! Her girdle . . ."

"Am I to understand," said Canterel, raising his right eyebrow, "that your archaeologists have put together the Virgin Mary's entire wardrobe, down to the implements that protected her chastity?"

"That would be saying a great deal," whispered Dr. Mardrus, "especially since the church in question and all its contents were destroyed by a fire in 1070 and, after its reconstruction, once again in 1434 . . ."

"Good, we can rest easy, then," said Holmes, opening his eyes wide at the covered dish their server was bringing over.

"Roasted fowl with Piedmontese seared quail," he announced, lifting the sparkling domed cover. "Would you like a little mustard?"

Confused by this unseemly proposition, then disappointed, Canterel glared at the waiter. This slight error of taste made the whole edifice crumble. Mustard . . . One might as well suggest a glass of vinegar to accompany the tasting of the Château Lafite that they were about to be served!

The wine had been poured and he was just enjoying its bouquet when the French doors separating the restaurant from the lounge crashed open, making everyone jump. Annoyed, Canterel could not help but turn around to identify the vulgar individual who was capable of so arrogantly displaying a lack of education.

Clawdia Chauchat was advancing between the tables, smiling and imperial. She was wearing a brownish-pink suit of wool serge, with a belted jacket, a skirt that narrowed at the ankles, and a hat with a wide, raised brim decorated with a double knot of umber silk in front, oversized and jauntily tilted to the side like a propeller.

She came straight toward them, carried by a wave of tense looks containing a mixture of naïve admiration from the men and annoyed suspicion from their wives. Holmes was the first to react, rising to greet her.

"Lady MacRae, what a surprise!"

"I would say, rather, what a landing . . ." scoffed Canterel, clapping slowly and silently. "Such finesse, well done, bravo!"

"May I ask what you are doing here?" Holmes asked gravely.

"You didn't really think I'd let you head off to the ends of the earth without me, did you?"

"This is a mistake. I told you how dangerous this expedition could prove . . ."

"Don't listen to him, dear madam," said Mardrus, genially. "Look around you: we are in a five-star restaurant on wheels, the only danger you could meet here is boredom . . . or indigestion," he said, leaning back to let the server slip a Lobster en Bellevue onto his plate.

"Dr. Charles-Joseph Mardrus," said Holmes, with a pointed look at Clawdia. "He is traveling with us to Irkutsk."

Grimod waved to the head waiter to set a place at their table for Lady MacRae.

"How did you do it," he asked, "I mean, get here at the same time as us?"

"A train from Glasgow to London, a boat to Ostend, and a mail-coach to Moscow. We arrived two days before you."

"We?" asked Canterel.

"My daughter and I, of course. She is the compartment next to mine. Kim keeps constant vigil over her."

"This is madness," said Holmes, bringing a huge mouthful of Siberian sorbet to his lips. "I don't understand how you could have done such a thing!"

"But what could be the problem with her traveling with her child?" said Dr. Mardrus. "On the contrary, it can only aid in her education, pique her curiosity, contribute to the development of her character.

Really, I don't see what is making you so anxious, you're doing her a great service!"

Clawdia took a sip of wine and looked at Mardrus with that kind of studied coldness, the feigned insensitivity that misfortune forges.

"It so happens that my child, Verity, is the victim of a mysterious illness that has kept her asleep for the last eight years, two months, and fourteen days. I very much doubt whether she will be able to enjoy the voyage other than in her dreams, or even whether she is aware of any of it."

Dr. Mardrus looked at her fixedly, tucked his hair behind his ears, and responded in a tone that chilled them, despite or perhaps because of its mildness.

"Once the pleasure centers have been damaged," he said, "it is impossible to know anything but segmented joys. But rest assured they are joys nonetheless, Madame, real, deep joys."

XII

A Butcher's Joke

"You're sure it won't be too bad?"

"Positive. It will probably feel a little warm, but no more than Tiger Balm or strong mint. Remember?"

"Not very effective, as I recall . . ."

"And it gave me canker sores."

Carmen has gotten wind of a new recipe for awakening her beloved's passion. This time, she is taking the method from a documentary she saw on TV. A film about beekeeping and the countless benefits of honey.

"An old folk remedy. Apparently people used it to treat arthritis. I don't see why it wouldn't work for you."

"If there was a joint in there, we'd know about it, don't you think?"

"Who said anything about a joint? The point is to make it swell, using venom. It expands and constricts the blood vessels and then . . ."

"Oh, oh, oh!" says Dieumercie, striking a pose from an operetta.

But Monsieur Bonacieux is not reassured, even less so when he catches sight of the jar that his wife is taking out of the cupboard. There are live bees imprisoned in it. A good number of them.

"Let's see," says Carmen, sticking the Post-it note where she has written out the procedure to his forehead. "First step, the tourniquet . . . Will you get your little bird out for me, please?"

"I'm not so sure about this. . ."

"Come on, *doudou*, it's for a good cause."

She helps him undo his fly and pull out his penis. He touches her breasts, trying to visualize salacious images. If he can get hard, here, right now, this whole business with the bees can be forgotten. He tries imagining his wife sucking off a dog, a huge dog, a Great Dane, but to no avail, as usual. In the meantime, Madame Bonacieux has looped her hair tie around his cock. She slides it up toward the base and finds the best position for the pink plastic bear cub on the band.

"This looks stupid . . ."

"On the contrary," says Carmen, patting his testicles, "you're very cute. This is already driving me wild."

As if to prove it to him, she pulls her thong down from her under her dress and shakes it off the tips of her toes. She has washed her hair, shaved, put on makeup. The fresh scents of soap and lavender emanate from her body as she cozies up to him to read the next part.

"Step two: we put them to sleep."

She takes the jar in both hands and shakes it vigorously, like a cocktail shaker. It works: inside, the dazed bees are still. Carmen unscrews the lid and takes two bees by their wings. With one bee between the thumb and index finger of each hand, she kneels down in front of her husband.

"Here we go," she says, focusing, as if she is getting ready to hook up electrodes to someone in cardiac arrest. "You ready?"

"Do it, dear," he replies bravely.

"Okay. Clear!"

Madame Bonacieux places the two bees on her husband's foreskin and squeezes them to get them to sting. Anxious, uncomfortably tickled by their touch, Dieumercie cannot stop himself from recoiling instinctively; when the insects react, they thrust their stingers into his glans. The effect is immediate, intense burning, disproportionate swelling. Monsieur Bonacieux begins to howl as he jumps up and down. His penis looks like a butcher's joke, a microphone made of bratwurst, ending in a big ball of calf liver. Each time he looks down upon this horror, he starts howling even louder. Frightened by this result, Carmen moves around him as best she can to observe his transformation. She still wants to believe.

"It has to work, *doudou*. Calm down, the pain will pass . . ."

Dieumercie is so disoriented that he is waving his arms wildly, trying to fight off a cloud. Suddenly, Carmen's thighs start to itch; she thinks, for a second, that Dieumercie's burning is contagious, she sticks her hand under her dress to scratch, then starts to writhe just like her husband. Now they are both yelling. Wakened from their torpor, the other bees have flown out of the jar and seem determined to avenge their companions' deaths.

XIII

I Survived the Terror of Russian Sex

After lunch, Canterel easily secured permission to visit his daughter. Clawdia accompanied him to the girl's apartment and left him alone with her for a quarter of an hour.

The girl was laid out on a sofa bed, her head resting on a fat pillow, her arms beside her body beneath the sheets. Two belts, one across her chest, the other across the middle of her thighs, kept her secured. Canterel took her hand and said her name several times, as if to wake her gently, watching her face, on the lookout for the least sign of a reaction. She must have looked more like Clawdia than him; he recognized the thick set of her eyebrows, her almond eyes, even the four beauty marks that formed a southern cross on her left cheek. But her gauntness, her skin tinged the color of germinated grain, the too pronounced tilt of her neck, the lace bonnet, knotted under her chin, from which transparent blonde locks peeked out, the claw-like stiffness of her fingers . . . it all indicated a slow death. He imagined the movements and rubdowns necessary to stave off bedsores, the nourishing enemas, the manipulations of basic hygiene that all resulted from this, and reflected in turn that it was foolish to have brought this poor child to a place where it would be so difficult to care for her.

He planted a kiss on her forehead and left the compartment, feeling helpless, as if her immobility were contagious.

Madame Chauchat was waiting for him in the passageway.

"How's the happy father?" she asked, looking out at a bleak landscape of wastelands and abandoned factories. "Not so easy, is it?"

"You shouldn't have," he said, after a period of reflection that went on slightly too long.

"Shouldn't have what? Left you alone, while I was married and pregnant with your child? Spared you the droning of a little girl who was intelligent, but hypersensitive, temperamental, and prone to morbid sulking? My late husband worshipped her, he passed his whimsies on to her . . . Spared you the tragedy of her illness, her indefinite distance?"

Canterel looked at her, and for the first time since they had come back into each other's lives, managed to fix on that thrilling green light in her eyes.

"You shouldn't have," he insisted, reaching out his hands in such a way that she could have grabbed them and brought them to her. "You know very well you shouldn't have . . ."

He turned around and left.

Holmes and Grimod had become railway sponges. From the moment they had left Martial to his paternal obligations, the two of them had been wandering through the train with an easy-going porosity that attracted all kinds of encounters. There is hardly any place that speaks to the smallness of the world so well as the corridors of a train, and our two comrades rubbed up against a number of individuals whose existence they had until then merely imagined, like the savages who were said to populate remote islands.

Our readers must follow us into these cars and let themselves be dragged—in sympathy, or friendship, we hope—through the series of chats that brought these men to dinner.

Between Vladimir and Nizhny Novgorod, Holmes spent some time in the company of a Haitian priest who claimed to be raising funds for his martyred bit of island from the tartar chief of Ulan Bator. It seemed to Holmes that Brother Célestin, as he had introduced himself with commendable sobriety, was drinking too many fine vintages for a man driven by such a noble cause, and that whatever money he might bring back from Mongolia would hardly cover his travel expenses.

For his part, Grimod had to endure the pompous chitchat of a merchant from Manchester who was transporting sixteen cases of anal probes meant for the dignitaries of the "yellow chamber," which was his personal nickname for the Chinese People's Congress. Just from a man's excrement, he swore, it was possible to learn whether he had ever gone beyond the borders of England: it takes 45 cm³ of an Englishman's urine to kill a one-kilo rabbit, but only 30 cm³ of a Frenchman's, and even less if he's from the Bas-Rhin. During their conversation, he decided to call out to two German officers who were laughing loudly, drunk on vodka.

"You there, if you were lucky enough to be English, imagine how much happier you'd be!"

"England was founded by barbarians," replied one of the Germans, sounding hostile, "and among those barbarians were your ancestors: the Angles!"

Grimod left him in the unhappy situation he had gotten himself into.

In the next car, he made the acquaintance of Achille Fournier, the humble designer of the national bicolored hat of the Sixth Republic. This young man was walking around with a large, shabby leather satchel overflowing with all the patents that he was going broke trying to maintain to protect his inventions. He was proud of them, and brandished them like weapons from the first moments of their meeting. Grimod was given the rights to a patent "to change the face of the world a little using long range siphons," to "an aquarium that automatically supplies live flies," and to "pigs suspended from the ceiling or raised in some other way, in order to nourish and then slaughter swine without letting those unclean animals ever touch the floor," a system that was meant to respect Talmudic taboos and that would secure his fortune among Jewish communities.

"Had I the necessary funds," he confided, "I would make a bicycle that runs on grain alcohol, which would prevent the friction caused by pedaling, which is very overstimulating, especially for the fair sex, who have sensitive membranes and delicate pelvises. I would ventilate the Chamber of Deputies using disc wheels, I would replace all bridges with tunnels, I would drain Lake Geneva to provide arable land for Turkish immigrants in Switzerland! But, oh well, I'm from Marseille, I'm only thirty, so I'm wrong."

In his defense, he was born in Vitrolles, and he augmented his Southern exuberance with the nervous irritability shared by all young provincial poets.

After Brother Célestin, Holmes was kept quite busy with Prince Sergei Svechin, the official waltzer to the Empress of Luxembourg and grand champagne-uncorker before the Lord. The gentleman was nearly two meters tall, a height ungraciously close to his royal partner's. Helped along by some Dom Pérignon, Holmes managed to get from him a blurred impression and three axioms that plunged him into the depths of long-term bewilderment. These were that the empress was nothing more than a pleasure machine, a jubilant battery that released copious fluids; that the woman had to be acknowledged as a hedonist concerned solely with the pleasures of the mouth—"the Brillat-Savarin of irrumation," Prince Svechin had said, rolling his Rs; and that her mouth, like that of all her peers, had something of the baseness that turns litmus paper blue.

As the prince believed in magnetism and boasted that he possessed the "gift," Holmes even had to suffer through the prince laying hands on his neck, an experience that, several years later, he claimed as the moment he had lost his last tuft of hair.

In Car 5, Grimod was approached by a sickly-looking Russian who charitably began to comfort him about his race by sharing with him a mathematical proof of the non-existence of Hell. Having established that mankind had appeared in the year 200,000 B.C., approximately, he calculated the number of humans who had lived on Earth up to our time.

"By applying to these givens the rule of compound interest," he explained, "I have reached the figure of 75 billion deceased. If we grant, with some indulgence, that all white Christians have been saved, maybe 5% of this number, there are 71 billion 250 million of the damned currently burning in Hell. Knowing that the average volume of a human, counting everyone from newborns to adults, is about a twentieth of a cubic meter, the weight of the damned would constitute a volume seven times greater than the Earth itself! It doesn't take a genius to figure out that this means Hell is a mathematical impossibility. As for the resurrection of the body, for the same reasons, allow me to laugh for a moment . . ."

Which he did, with his lips pursed, exhaling in short bursts of air that made his nose run.

"Admit it," he continued, having blown his nose, "admit it's enough to make you chuckle! Let's be serious: the soul is made of a colorless, etheric gas, that's as far as I'm willing to go. As for the Bible, it contains the most perfect treatise on gasometry there is, but nothing more, we agree, don't we?"

Grimod readily agreed, while the Russian shook his hand with the enthusiasm of someone who had just saved a man's life. Grimod took his leave, happy to see Shylock approaching. Together again, they were going into the bar car when they nearly walked into a person who froze at the sight of them, seeming to hesitate, then slipped past them into the corridor without even acknowledging them. Holmes only had time to take in his bowler hat and the black beard that was eating his face; Grimod noted his short stature and his detachable collar, glossy with use; but both of them noticed his tacky glasses with blue lenses. This incongruity, they noted admiringly, had prevented them from studying other, more significant details. As they sat down, they vowed to find out more about this gentleman.

The waitress who came to take their order left them speechless, a twenty-two-year-old Ukrainian whose name, Yva, was embroidered in red italics at the top of her apron. Her maid outfit, though spartan, could hide neither the military at-attention of her bosom nor the profile of her rear. One of those young women so instinctively seductive, thought Holmes, that every man who saw her walk by had no choice but to fix himself to her heels the way one dog sticks to another's asshole. The end of what looked like a tendril of bindweed was poking up from her blouse, rising up her neck to just below her ear.

"Did you see?" said Holmes when she had left.

"The tattoo?"

"Yes. It's rather unusual . . . I would be willing to give my whole body to see the rest of it!"

"It's not all that impressive," came Canterel's voice from behind them.

A towel over his shoulders, his hair wet, he was sweating in a mauve silk robe.

"Martial! Where were you?"

"In the fitness room. I needed to unwind a bit."

The waitress passed by, tray in hand.

"Ah! Yva, Yva!" said Canterel in a low voice.

She turned her head and gave him a quick wink.

Holmes was staring, open-mouthed.

"Don't tell me you . . ."

"Yes, my dear. But as you see, I survived the terror of Russian sex!"

"How the devil did you manage that?"

"Let us say that I gave my whole body. And added a little from my pocket, to be honest. Two hundred rubles; I have no idea how many ducats that is."

"The tattoo?" asked Grimod, smiling.

"A giant octopus whose tentacles are curled suggestively around her body. The work of a Japanese artist. Very frightening, I must confess, especially around its beak . . ."

Holmes forced himself to swallow.

"And what did you do with her?"

"What one normally does with an octopus: I harpooned her. And now, you'll excuse me, but I must change for dinner."

At this moment, a man sitting near them stood up.

"If I may, you did well: the octopus is a sucking monster, a favorite of the Demon! Allow me to introduce myself: Hégésippe Petiot, Belgian by birth, municipal official by profession, missionary by calling, prophet and Russian Orthodox by divine revelation."

"Good lord!" Canterel exclaimed, taking a step back. "Good evening to you all, I'm going to take a shower."

It did not take long for Holmes and Grimod, trapped by Yva returning with their scotches, to envy him for escaping so quickly. This fellow was dreadful! He was explaining how, while walking down Rue de Rome in Paris one November day, he had seen in the distance a terrible black cloud that had appeared to be announcing great wonders.

"And thus an unknown force," he said, "instructed me in a terrible voice: Look, Petiot, look! Turn your face toward the celestial machine!"

Petrified in the rain that had begun to fall, he had seen the cloud open up with a great crash; out of it came a dry, pale figure, flanked by a blazing squid and a hedgehog on which were speared a multitude of appetizing olives stuffed with pimentos.

"The apparition spoke to me: 'Tremble, Petiot, and quake! I died over six months ago, and am now resurrected!'"

Unaccustomed to seeing the dead resurrected in the clouds, our man indeed shuddered from his head to his toes and found the courage to ask his name: "Don't question me, you wretch!" the phantom had responded. "You already know me. I am . . . Bournissac! The accountant-god brought unjustly to court, but now aided by Saint Joan of France, patron of bad poets, who will return all this to order."

This Bournissac had been caught in the act of embezzling six months earlier and had committed suicide to spare his family the disgrace of a trial.

"Then," continued Petiot, "Bournissac and Joan of Arc informed me that, in my capacity as a prophet inspired by them, and as a moral Mamluk, I would one day be allowed to advise and guide the future Archimandrake of all the Russias."

The theophany was then reabsorbed and compressed into a white rhinoceros that had touched down lightly on the Rue de Rome before running off down the pavement. Hégésippe Petiot had thus developed a calling as an apostle that displeased his dear wife, but which overshadowed everything regardless.

"As for my wife's unthinkable opposition, Bournissac and Joan of Arc ordered me not to bother with it; they tell me constantly: 'Resist the bourgeois woman, Petiot, resist the bourgeois woman!' Which I did, by leaving her at her mother's house so I could devote myself fully to the spreading of the new faith."

Holmes and Grimod were glad to see him put on his hat and bow in farewell.

"If you run into a white rhino one day," he whispered, moving away, "let it come to you without fear: praise God and tell yourself that it is Bournissac resurrected!"

XIV

The Bitter Poison of Evil Passions

Arnaud lights a Montecristo and watches as the coils of smoke rise in a spiral, then stagnate halfway to the ceiling. He is dreaming the long nightmare of his sleeping wife; pen in hand, he makes up stories, aware of only one and dizzy with its absence.

Yvrose Beaubrun, Dulcie had told him, would read for two hours in the morning and two hours in the afternoon. The morning was dedicated to a kind of press review of the local papers. A selection of miscellaneous news items, for the most part, but also regional and international politics, never forgetting the "poem of the day," which always went over well. After the lunch break, he devoted himself to novels. The factory women—there were also men, but the women were in the majority—compensated him for his services by producing on his behalf as many cigars as he would have if he had worked beside them for the duration of the reading; often a few more, to thank him for the emotions that he was so good at conveying to them. The choice of the title was theirs: Yvrose arrived with a pile of books and read a dozen pages from one of the authors whose work remained in the running after ferocious negotiations; if any of the workers expressed boredom, the book was immediately abandoned. He would quickly begin another. When the magic set in, the whole workshop was captivated by the story, and from then on no one was allowed to interrupt the reading until the end of the book.

Reading aloud is at least as old as the rule of Saint Benoît, who enforced *lectio divina* among the monks of Monte Cassino, but its first appearance in a tobacco factory was in the nineteenth century, in Havana. The idea, it seems, came from a Spaniard, Jacinto de Salas y Quiroga, who visited Cuba in the 1830s; this humanist had seen it as a way of educating the slaves who were sorting beans on a coffee plantation. The project was not carried out, instead bearing fruit when it was found, thirty years later, in the prisons of the capital. Through certain incarcerated *torcedores*, who were released feeling that they had benefited from the readings, the practice was introduced in 1865 at the factory El Figaro, supported by a weekly paper devoted to artisans, *La Aurora*, whose creators were advertising their reformist spirit. "Today," a columnist had written that week, "in the very heart of the factories, during the most important working hours, the laborers are keeping their imaginations busy, inquiring into the scientific and philosophical truths best suited to their era. They are talking and discussing; they are reading the works of excellent modern writers and consulting one another on the points that surpass their understanding; and finally, they are doing what they can to learn and to move forward on the path of civilization."

At the end of the same article, however, this great momentum faltered, showing the all too familiar limits of philanthropy. The reading was educational, certainly, and enriching to those to whom it was addressed, but only if certain things were read: the workers at El Figaro had to take care, since they were paying the reader with their own labor, that they were read works worthy of being studied, with teachings that "do not plant the bitter poison of evil passions in their hearts." Worthy of being studied . . . All of the bosses' fears were contained in that phrase, and all of their blindness. How did they not understand that there was more rebellion in Edmond Dantès than in

Marx's entire body of work? Once the workers escaped into literature, no one would be able to pull them out of it, not because they were being read Bakunin or Proudhon, but because they could see in the books, as in a mirror, the reflection of their own misery.

This first initiative snowballed with a speed no one had foreseen. At the end of 1866, the five hundred tobacco plants of Havana—more than fifteen thousand workers, seventy-five percent of whom were illiterate—held reading platforms. This became all the plants on the island, then in Santo Domingo, Puerto Rico, and Tampa. In 1868, after the voluntary expatriation of the Cuban owners, fleeing the chaos of the first war of independence against Spain, there were readers from the factories of Key West up to New York, but also in Mexico, A Coruña, San Sebastián, and Seville!

"In Seville!" said Dulcie, her eyes glowing with pride. "Do you see?"

She never tired of telling him about the peaceful action of the cigar makers who had preceded her. These women had not been content with "good" authors, they had profited from all books without distinguishing between Dumas and Bakunin by anything other than the pleasure these authors gave them. And the light. It was through their attentive listening that the spirit of revolution had been infused, that a hope had begun to be born. The readings had been banned an incalculable number of times, but each time they had fought to rekindle the fire. In 1870, three hundred of these women, exiles in Tampa, had written to the author of *Les Misérables* to appeal to his sense of justice; Hugo had responded: "Women of Cuba, I hear your cries. Despairing, you have contacted me. Fugitives, martyrs, widows, orphans, you turn to an outcast; those who no longer have a home call to their aid one who no longer has a homeland. Certainly, we are oppressed; you have lost your voice, and I have lost mine; your voices moan, mine cautions. This is all we have left. Who are we? We are weakness. No, we are strength. Because you are moral strength, and

I am conscience. [. . .] All I have within me is that force, but it is enough. And you do well in contacting me. I will speak for Cuba as I spoke for Crete. No nation has the right to hold another under its thumb, no more Cuba under Spain's than Gibraltar under England's. One people does not own another people any more than one man owns another man. [. . .] Spain is a noble, admirable nation, and I love it; but I cannot love it more than France. And, if France still had Haiti, the same way I say to Spain: Give up Cuba!, I would say to France: Give up Haiti! [. . .] Women of Cuba, who have so eloquently shared with me your troubles and suffering, do not doubt, your persevering homeland will be paid back for its pain, so much blood will not have been spilled in vain, and one day magnificent Cuba will rise up, free and sovereign among its august sisters, the republics of America."

It was as if Jean Valjean himself had replied to them.

Arnaud lifted his eyes to his collection of cigars. How could he not see them, rolled with tobacco leaves, as if archived within the banded cylinders, as the thousands of pages recited over all the years in the dampness of the workshops. A library of papyrus that, in its admirable disorder, made neighbors of Byron, Mark Twain, Dante, Walter Scott, Conan Doyle, Jules Verne, José Martí, Nicolás Guillén, Dickens, Boccaccio, Pérez Galdós, José Hernández's *Martín Fierro*, Charlotte Brontë, *Lady Chatterley's Lover*, Blasco Ibáñez, Edgar Allan Poe, Maxim Gorky, Tolstoy, Nietzsche's *The Antichrist*, Marcus Aurelius's *Meditations*, *Uncle Tom's Cabin*, Darwin, Émile Zola, Engels, Gustave Flaubert, Pierre Loti, Dostoevsky, Marx, Errico Malatesta, John Stuart Mill, George Sand, Turgenev, Maupassant, Camille Flammarion, Lugones, the twenty volumes of the *Young Person's Treasury or Encyclopedia of Knowledge*, the twenty-one volumes of the *Collection of Best Spanish Writers*, Calderón's *Life Is a Dream*, Armando Palacio Valdés, Kropotkin, Chateaubriand, Schiller, Quevedo, Proudhon, Juana Inés de la Cruz . . . This mashing together of "good" and "bad" books was only a tiny portion of what Dulcie had in her head, of that great wave of stories and myths that had broken over Caribbean manufacturing.

All historians acknowledge this reading craze as one of the engines of the independence of 1898, and then the revolution.

As unlikely as it seemed, the readings in the factories continued under Castro without any major changes, aside from the allotment of a fixed salary and a civil service status for the readers. The introduction of the microphone, then of radio programs, replaced the platforms with control booths, and the readers had to learn to add in salsa music, sports results, and reports on Castro's glory; but no one ever questioned their choice of books. While the practice of reading aloud died out everywhere else, because of industrial mechanization or, since the 1930s in Mexico and the United States, the advent of strict censorship, it continues in Cuba and Santo Domingo to this day. Ever since, they have read the big hits of the nineteenth century, but also Juan Rulfo's *El llano en llamas*, Patrick Süskind's *Perfume*, Kyle Onstott's *Mandingo*, García Márquez, Agatha Christie, Pablo Neruda, Stephen King, Alejo Carpentier, Ernesto Guevara, Hemingway, Salinger, Faulkner, Proust, Kipling, Schopenhauer, D'Annunzio, H.G. Wells, and even Pierre Grimal's *Greek Mythology*!

Dulcie's knowledge on this subject was inexhaustible. One day, in December 1903, in Ybor City in Tampa, the reader at the José Lovera factory finished the novel that had been holding the cigar makers spellbound for a month. Before taking his break, he offered his audience a list of ten works; among the suggested titles was Paul de Kock's *The Cuckold*. Many of the workers immediately objected to this reading, considering it immoral. The other half of the cigar makers protested the opposite, and without anyone having read the book in question, the whole workshop flamed up over the suitability of the reading. At the head of the two parties, which clashed verbally until closing time, Jesús Fernández and Enrique Velázquez were the most aggravated. The night did not help at all, and they met with the same frustration the next day at the Lorenzana, the bar where they were wont to eat a quick bite before work. Insults came flooding out, humiliating and disproportionate, then threats, likewise so excessive that they forgot to use their fists and went straight for their weapons. A .38-caliber for Fernández, a .44 for Velázquez. They fired simultaneously, point blank. Both hit in the chest, they staggered away from each other, still firing. A second bullet struck Fernández in the stomach, a third ripped Velázquez open at the groin, the others missed their targets as the two men collapsed. They died at the same time, not pausing in their insults for a second.

That truth is stranger than fiction is a well-known fact, but that fiction can alter reality just as directly is what the people at the José Lovera factory learned the next day from the mouth of their reader, when the story of the shoot-out joined the ranks of the news stories in the *Tampa Morning Tribune*.

Out of respect for the deceased, *The Cuckold* was pulled from the list; the cigar makers agreed upon *The Human Beast* for their next reading, and life went on.

XV

The Noh Straddler

Let us leave Holmes and Grimod to gather their thoughts and discuss the curious passengers on this ship of fools, and follow Canterel after he left his companions behind and passed through two cars to get back to his room.

As he entered the last hallway, he saw the little man with the blue glasses, who was trying to open the door to his compartment.

"Hey, you there!" called Martial. "Might I ask what you're doing?"

"You can see very well," the man responded with a very strong Belgian accent, "I'm trying to get into my cabin, but the key isn't working . . ."

"What is your cabin number?"

"Car 6, Cabin 15."

"This is Car 7 . . ."

The man apologized profusely, doffed his hat, and hurriedly decamped. This person certainly appeared nothing short of fishy, but in his defense, thought Canterel, the numbers of the cars were so poorly indicated that anyone would have trouble finding his way around.

Once in his room, Canterel undressed to take a shower. Although it was much less spacious than the one installed in his automobile, the bathroom he was using was roomy enough for proper ablutions with hot water, a luxury that seemed to him quite natural in a steam engine where soot always managed to grease up your skin. His sessions with the chest expanders and in the bicycle room had left him dazed; his shower perked him up without quieting his mind. As soon as he had donned evening wear, he opened the two panels of his travel pharmacy, a walnut-wood box containing numerous phials with glass stoppers; from the drawer at the bottom, he pulled what he called his "wine list," a notebook where he meticulously recorded the medications he took and the effects he felt from them:

> *Sunday, February 10th. 17 hrs: 6 Phanodorms; 6 more around 1 hr 30 in the morning. Slept 4 hrs.*
>
> *Monday the 11th. Rutonal at 4 hrs 30; 3 at 6 hrs. 18 total for 3 hrs of sleep.*
>
> *Tuesday the 12th. 4 Soneryl at 17 hrs; 4 at 18 hrs 30; asleep at 22 hrs, then 13 during the night. Slept 12 hr 15, outward euphoria.*
>
> *Wednesday the 13th. 1 bottle Neurinase, little effect.*
>
> *Thursday the 14th. 20 Somnothyril; 1 bottle Neurinase, no lunch, euphoria all day.*
>
> *Friday the 15th. Rutonal at 9 hr = 34. 3 hrs sleep, wonderful euphoria.*
>
> *Saturday the 16th. 2 bottles Veronidin. Anxiety, little sleep. Muddled euphoria.*

Reading this last page, he decided on fifteen Rutonal tablets, waiting to see what happened. Opium, alas, gave off too strong a smell in the car; other travelers had complained.

Seated at the corner of the bench, Canterel took out his chronograph and once again verified that the time did not correspond to the brightness outside. This whole train was catching up to time; or outrunning it, which amounted to the same thing in terms of the floating sensation that the phenomenon produced. Rather pleasant, he admitted, stowing the timepiece in his pocket, not to be brought back to the present until their arrival.

He had made his first big trip as a child, accompanied by his mother. An intellectual, recently widowed and so eccentric that she seemed English, Marguerite had decided one day that she could no longer do without taking a trip to the Indies. She had hired a yacht and crew, convinced a dozen friends to come with her, and set off for Cannes, with her head chef, her chambermaid, and the ebony casket in which she kept her dresses. After several weeks of pleasant cruising, this little world saw the port of Bombay on the horizon. The ship was only a few cable lengths away when his mother asked someone to pass her a pair of binoculars. She scanned the coast for a moment, twisted her mouth as if she had just heard a sour note at a concert, and turned to the captain.

"So this is the Indies!" she said, handing him the binoculars. "No use disembarking, Monsieur, give the order to turn around, please; we're going back."

The guests had expostulated against this folly, then grown angry; the yacht had tacked about and set a course for France. For the whole return voyage, his mother had stayed cloistered in her cabin, accepting the presence of only her son and, every evening from ten to midnight, her paid companion, who would read *Twenty Thousand Leagues Under the Sea* to her.

Blood will tell, thought Canterel, setting his forearms down on the armrest that he had just hooked to the nickel bar of the luggage rack, a device shaped like a swing that allowed him to rest while maintaining decent posture. His face turned to the window, he watched the taiga pass by for a moment, then closed his eyes. The landscape, too, was a mental thing.

Three cars away, Lady MacRae missed nothing that passed the window she looked out of. Already dressed for the evening meal, she had taken a seat in the library lounge and was letting herself be rocked by the choppy motion of the train.

In the long curve that the train was following at that moment, the powerful locomotive could be seen moving toward the east, fleeing the night, as if frightened by the thick black smoke it spewed. Monotone hatching against the gray sky, firs and birches alternated with the hypnotic effect of a stroboscope.

Behind her, several travelers, mostly women, were making use of the amenities available to the passengers. Perfectly integrated into the luxurious setting of this paneled boudoir, several reading spinets produced a continuous humming sound, in harmony with the rhythm of the wheels on the rails. Seeing a place free up, Clawdia sat down at one of these machines; she settled into a still-warm chair in front of the glass triptych set in an old gold frame. Her feet worked the two pedals in a continuous motion, engaging the wheel and then the dynamo, which soon produced enough electricity to light the screen. Gloomily, she tapped out on the ivory keyboard an "adventure" code that soon produced a list of possible options. From among the suggested titles, she chose *Moby-Dick*, by Herman Melville, and activated the boxwood pull-tabs to confirm her choice. The device got right to the point: on the middle screen she could see the text of the last chapter, in which readers finally witness the hunt for the accursed whale, while one of the two panels that framed it displayed quavering but coordinated excerpts from the John Huston film with Gregory Peck, and the other showed the wrongs done to these poor creatures by the fishing industry. Caught up in the images, more than the text, Clawdia let herself be swept away by the scene, in which the whalers pursued the wounded monster.

"Heave, heave, me hearties!" yelled Stubb, with his bonny Irish face that looked like it had been carved with an ax, as the chalky mass of the sperm whale made its way through the gray swell.

When Queequeg jabbed in his harpoon, then Daggoo, then Tash-tego, she thought she could feel the blades plunge into her as they went into the beast's flank, the feeling was so strong that she had to hold back a whimper; caught up in trying to contain herself, she nonetheless heard a scream rise up in the library.

It was the wagon's babushka, her eyes full of horror, who was pointing at Clawdia, gesturing at something behind her back. Claw-dia turned around and could not stifle her own cry: hung by its feet outside the car, a woman's naked body was swinging outside the window, her face and dangling arms smearing the glass with wide, bloody streaks.

Informed of the incident, two conductors climbed onto the roof to untie the poor woman and bring her body back inside the train. Holmes and Grimod, drawn by the noise that all this commotion was making, appeared at just the right moment to lend a hand; it was not hard for them to help move the body to a service compartment, far from the eyes of the passengers. As they laid the dead woman out on a bench, they were sorry to recognize Yva, the pretty waitress, whose charms Holmes stopped contemplating from that moment forward. The young woman's ears had been cut off, her breasts and stomach slashed with a razor along the contours of her tattoo; her throat was slit open. A harrowing detail Yva's pubic hair had been torn out with such violence that it had left bruises, as if she had been skinned by an inept butcher.

At this last finding, Holmes and Grimod exchanged a quick look; in a less tragic situation, one would have glimpsed in this exchange, in spite of everything, the depth of their terror.

"Thank you, Messieurs," said one of the conductors, pulling a cover over the body. "We'll take it from here."

The two men joined Lady MacRae and, refusing to respond to the other passengers' questions, hurried to Canterel's cabin. After waking him from his slumber, Holmes began to tell him of the drama that had just taken place. When he reached the most intimate of the abuses suffered by the young woman, Canterel cursed.

"Great Scott!" he said, knitting his brows. "The Noh Straddler!"

"Yes," Grimod confirmed. "It's his mark."

"Who are you talking about?" asked Clawdia.

"The most sinister of assassins," said Holmes in a low voice. "No one has ever seen his face, but there is not a heinous crime, not a bankruptcy, not a famous con that does not involve his name being spoken at one point or another."

"Or rather his nickname," said Canterel, "since no one knows his true identity. On the rare occasions that anyone has glimpsed him, he has been seen straddling his victim, standing still over of her in an affected pose, like an actor in Noh theater, then grabbing at her crotch to yank out her pubic hair. He decorates the places he visits with these awful trophies. In the only cache that he didn't have time to remove before disappearing, the police also found masks fashioned from human faces . . ."

"And, God forgive me," continued Holmes, "a copy of *The Tarot as Guide to the World* bound in the skin of human breasts!"

"What a monster!" said Clawdia, shivering.

"Yes," Holmes said pensively. "At least now we know who our adversary is."

"Martial," Grimod interrupted, "could someone have noticed that you talked privately with Yva, maybe even imagining that she could have given you some kind of information?"

Canterel gathered his thoughts, then remembered the man in the blue glasses: he was the only person who had seen him come out of the bathroom where the young waitress was finishing getting dressed.

"Then we must begin with him. Here's what I propose . . ."

XVI

A Dying Rat

Fabrice is a tall young man, thin, his shoulders a little round, with greasy hair under his sailor hat. This is a black woolen cloth cap that he wears a little back on his head and that makes him look a bit like a tramp. He found it at a flea market. The hat of a boatswain from the Compagnie Générale Transatlantique, with the letters CGT embroidered in silver thread on the crown. He only takes it off inside the factory.

Same with his orange flip-flops. The rest he couldn't care less about. In any case, his overcoat covers everything else when he leaves his house. He's a *nolife*, spending all his time in virtual universes. He has given all of his free time to them. Blizzard games—Warcraft and others—hold no secrets for him. He is still passionately devoted to them, but for several months now he has been venturing into more sensitive territory: hacking. Not because he is attracted by the danger or is in it for the rush, but in rebellion and out of a sense of commitment. Returning to his first love, viruses, he programs bugs to train himself, and tests them, dreaming all the while of working out an algorithm that would prevent the digitization of a given text. He knows strange things, like the name of the French village that is farthest from a McDonald's. Occasionally, to relax, he goes on YouTube and watches a Congolese rocket fall: Troposphère V, he never gets tired of it. This Saturday, at the moment when we take an interest in his character, he is still in front of his screen after a whole night of battle. Along with thousands of nameless zombies, he relayed a new cyber-attack against Scroogle. A DDoS (Distributed Denial of Service) expertly orchestrated by Anonymous, which managed to block the site for nine hours. Sweet victory, but it was just a warning. The bastards who run that site said for years that they were digitizing the planet's libraries so they could put their contents online for free. And then overnight, they had introduced a fee to access millions of books. It was disgraceful. Disgraceful and despotic. Fabrice is a member of the Resistance; the operations he leads are legitimate acts of sabotage.

That is what he would ultimately say if he were ever tortured enough that he consented to give his opinion. But, in reality, he thinks so little that when he does use his brain, he feels like his nose is bleeding. The room he lives in looks just like the inside of his head, a sprawling mess of unconnected items, a scrap yard of computers piled with outdated motherboards, broken-down hard drives, edge connectors, power sources, memory sticks, ribbon cables. The link existed, once, but it was destroyed. All that's left of it is obsolete and disparate evidence, arranged in ascending size with obsessive attention to symmetry.

Girls don't interest him, nor do boys. However, if that same torturer were to ask him his girlfriend's name, he would have responded without hesitating: Charlotte, though they have never said anything on this subject. It is a tacit understanding, so obvious that it is never called into question.

Fabrice puts his computer in standby mode and opens the window. His room smells like skunk. He goes out, gets on his bike, rides down the main street, and pedals toward the cemetery. He is going to say hello to Eugène and Hortense Vitrac, his adoptive parents. He only goes to their graves when he is airing out his room.

That same morning, Charlotte had woken up early to go to the market. She also went by the drugstore to buy paint and the necessary tools. Her old neighbor Marthe is waiting in front of her door when she gets home.

"Hello there, dear."

"Hello, Marthe."

"Tell me, could you do me a little favor? A big favor? Can you buzz our intercom to check if it's working?"

She said this in one breath, without inflection, anxious to get her line out right.

"You know very well it's working. It always works . . ."

"You could just go check?"

"I'll press it very soon, when I go back down."

"You can't right now?"

"No."

"How soon're you leaving?"

"I have no idea, Marthe."

"You don't want to just go look, dear?"

"Not right now, no."

Marthe has finally changed her clothes. The dress she's wearing is just as dirty, but this one is patterned in a nautical map dotted with depth markers. She looks to the side, turns to the wall, her back hunched, searching for her words.

"Say, would you buzz our intercom to check if it's working?"

Charlotte sighs, sets her shopping on the landing, and climbs back down the six flights. She buzzes; Marthe answers right away.

"Hello, Charlotte? Is it working, dear?"

"Yes, it's working."

"Oh, thank you, dear, thank you . . ."

Charlotte climbs back up. She has not even finished shutting the bolts when someone knocks on her door. She opens it, furious.

"Yes, Marthe?"

"No point closing your door, I might need you again . . ."

"I don't know if I'm staying home today."

"Someone has to take me to the post office . . ."

"Why can't Chonchon take you? He spends all his time walking around town. He can easily do it."

Marthe rolls her big eyes, bloodshot and bulging. A plume of hair on the top of her head, and baboon tufts falling down the sides.

"He's lost his mind!"

"He's lost his mind . . . But he knows how to get home, right?"

"My dear, what did you say? I didn't hear you very well."

"He knows how to get home!" says Charlotte, slamming the door in her face.

Before she even unpacks her stuff, she goes and gets her earplugs out of her bedside table and starts to warm them up. Not fast enough: through two closed doors she hears her neighbor's intercom buzz.

"Oh my god! Are you coming up? Come up!"

She hears Marthe trip over the ripped-up carpet.

"I'm sick and tired of this carpet . . . Fucking carpet! Because that, that really, that pisses me off!"

Charlotte doesn't even take off her sweatshirt, she grabs her roller skates, opens the door, races down the stairs. She can't take it anymore, that old woman is going to drive her mad.

At the bottom, she bumps into Chonchon, blind drunk, who is trying to open his mailbox. He's a big, strong guy in corduroy pants, with a hat that matches his parka. He's trying to act normal, but his body is swaying back and forth. His glazed eyes are glued to the light of the digital clock.

"You're going out?" he asks, slurring his words.

"Yes. Your wife is calling you."

"Oh, boo her! She's completely . . ." He circles his finger next to his ear. "Completely batty. Sorry, excuse me, Mademoiselle . . ."

Marthe is upset. Her voice comes squawking out of the intercom and down the staircase.

"Hey! Chonchon, you down there?"

"Why don't you close the door? Whore!"

He puts his hands to his head, breathes through his mouth, then begins to mount the stairs, as if each step is an insurmountable cliff.

"Are you drunk?" yells Marthe.

"Oh, what do they know, anyway? They're wasted, they all are. And I do what I can . . ."

"Come up! Come on, Chonchon, come uuuup! Come on, Chonchon!"

Charlotte watches him go, one hand on the wrought iron railing, the other feeling along the wall. At this rate, it will take him an hour to get to the sixth floor.

Next to her, the intercom speaker starts up again, crackling.

"Charlotte, Charlotte! Chonchon is sick . . . Think he's coming up? D'you think he's coming up? Hello? Hello?"

But Charlotte has already left. Ill-at-ease on her skates, she walks more than she rolls, brushing against the walls. From a distance, with her hood up, she looks like a dying rat.

XVII

Leibniz is a Moron

Confident that the suspect in the blue glasses was occupied elsewhere, Holmes and Canterel stationed themselves at the two entrances to Car 6, while Grimod went into his cabin. He had had no trouble picking the lock and was getting to work searching the room.

Not ten minutes had gone by when Holmes started to sing a drinking song at the top of his voice. Feigning intoxication, he clung to the man whose things Grimod was so reprehensibly going through. Canterel quickly came over to lend a hand.

"Please excuse him," he said, blocking the passage as best he could, "I think my friend has had a little too much scotch."

"This is an outrage, let me through!"

"I've been a wild rover for many a year . . ."

"Look, Holmes, let this man go, you can see very well that he doesn't want your company."

"And I spent all my money on whiskey and beer . . ."

"I'm going to complain, you know! This is most improper!"

"And now I'm returning—re-turn-ing!—with gold in great store!"

"Damn you, let me go, I say!"

"Be reasonable, old chap . . ."

"And I never will play the wild rover no more!"

With great effort, however, the mysterious man managed to get through to his compartment. Still boxed in by our two accomplices, he was about to put his key in the lock when the door suddenly opened; seized by his collar, the man was pulled inside, while Holmes and Canterel rushed in behind him, apprehensive about this turn of events. Not content with smothering him half to death, Grimod had the barrel of a gun pressed into the man's jaw.

"Who are you?" said Grimod, his teeth clenched. "Why is all this in your luggage?"

He swung round, forcing his prisoner to look at the bench. Beside a little suitcase, whose false bottom had not been put back, were three revolvers, ammunition, two Model 24 grenades, and an assortment of beards and hairpieces worthy of Fregoli.

Canterel was the first to react. Seizing the man's beard with both hands, he ripped it off ruthlessly, then shrank back, stunned.

"Scummington!"

"In the flesh," said the inspector, losing his Belgian accent and regaining his assertiveness. To Holmes: "Could you ask your . . . your gorilla to lower his weapon?"

"But what is the meaning of this?" asked Holmes as Grimod, with tangible reluctance, released the inspector. "What an idea, disguising yourself like this! We took you for that poor woman's murderer . . ."

"You thought I was the Noh Straddler? If this is some kind of joke, it's in very poor taste, I assure you! He's the swine I've been trying to corner for months now. You can't imagine the amount of patience and investigation it took me to manage to be on this blasted train at the same time as him. Not to mention this disguise that's eating at my skin!"

As he was talking, he finished taking off a variety of pieces of latex, a nasal bridge, cheekbones, eyebrows, and false lashes, all of which was contrived to make his face unrecognizable; he looked like a leper sloughing off his own necrotic flesh, an effect accentuated by his whitish hives.

"You're allergic to that make-up," said Grimod, flatly. "You should stop wearing it."

"And risk seeing him escape me yet again? He knows my face, the bastard. He knows everything, foresees everything . . . There is something inhuman, supernatural about him. He's a demon!"

"A poor demon," replied Canterel, "if he has not succeeded in gaining what he seeks."

"You are mistaken, dear sir. It's only a matter of time. He will recover the diamond, believe me, even if he has to crush every last one of you. Lady MacRae should have called the police, not amateurs like you. I rate your chances pretty low if we can't even lay a hand on him!"

Holmes appeared taken aback by this outburst.

"What do you know, exactly?"

"I know more about it than you know yourself, Holmes. Do you really take me for a fool? I have informers, networks, I learned about the theft before you did! Your fine team is not without talent, I admit, but all I had to do was follow you, and even, at times, go ahead of you."

As the train had suddenly begun to slow, Grimod glanced at the window.

"I think we're arriving in Perm," he said, checking his watch. "If that rat is going to jump ship, he'll do it now. I'll go watch the platform."

"I'll go with you," said Holmes.

"Do what you will," Scummington jeered, "it's a waste of time, he won't flee. You're the ones who would be wise to get off here."

Canterel stared at him, then said to Holmes, "I'll be with Clawdia. We can meet in her compartment to take stock of the situation."

The train stopped, and Holmes and Grimod climbed down onto the platform to watch the other passengers' movements. In spite of the vendors who were crowded up to the windows selling food and trinkets, they could see that no one was getting off at this station. However, several Chinese men and a squad of Russian police were getting on. Half an hour later, they witnessed as the stretcher-bearers arrived, then as the remains, wrapped in oilcloth, were taken away. When the train departed, one policeman and two soldiers stayed on board to investigate Yva's murder.

Once they were reunited in Lady MacRae's cabin, Grimod took the floor.

"Well, let's continue. Perhaps the murder of this young woman is merely a coincidence, but honestly I find that hard to believe. If the Noh Straddler is our adversary, as Scummington's presence suggests, I urge you all to maintain the utmost vigilance. You've seen for yourselves that he will not hesitate to kill to follow the slightest trail."

"That poor woman had nothing to do with all this," said Clawdia, sadly.

Holmes shook his head. "It was enough that someone noticed the familiar way Martial spoke to her . . . No doubt this was only a grim warning."

"I'd wager, though, that he doesn't hold all the cards," replied Grimod. "Nor does the inspector, despite his claims."

"In any event," said Holmes, "we must proceed as if they do."

Canterel turned toward Lady MacRae and held out a lady's revolver with an ivory butt.

"It's loaded," he said. "It's a six-shooter, the safety is here; to take it off, you have to press it in and push it forward. Keep it with you, you never know. Miss Sherrington keeps the same one in her petticoats."

At dinner, the conversations were all, as one might expect, about the horrible murder of the waitress. The most absurd rumors had spread, until the conductors from the Sleeping-Car Company, by repeating their narrative over and over, had succeeded in endorsing a kind of minimal, official version of the tragedy. The murder had been particularly heinous, of course, but it concerned only the train employees; a story of jealousy or some kind of retaliation linked to the Russian mafia, nothing for the passengers to be alarmed about, in any case. Nevertheless, there remained an unpunished murderer on board, and, because no one could imagine that a woman could have committed such a barbarous act—it was not physically possible—all the men on staff were now considered potential culprits.

At Canterel's table, the atmosphere was just as oppressive, but for different reasons. Clawdia was picking at her food, eager to return to her daughter, who had been left in the care of Kim and Miss Sherrington. Luckily, Dr. Mardrus, who seemed to be maintaining his customary good humor, was doing his best to loosen everyone up.

"The best of all possible worlds, would you look at that! Our dear Leibniz was very nice, a mathematician of the first order, to be sure, but he was a moron. Imagine this: his god, a god in a powdered wig, alone in his tumbledown provincial castle, gets it into his head that he should create a viable world. Night falls, the wind whistles through the rattling windows, suppressing the flames in the impressive fireplace in the library, and there he trembles under his cloak, carefully spreading out the infinite playing cards of conceivable worlds. He looks at them one by one, weighs the pros and the cons, dreams for an instant of a land of thirty-six thousand pleasures, Atlantis, the Garden of the Hesperides; considers the Islands of the Blessed, Eldorado, Icaria, Thélème, Tamoé; examines Giphantie, Antillia, and the land of the Houynhnms; but there's nothing to be done: this god is infallible and can't help but see the shortcomings that would soon lead all these utopias to catastrophe. At the end of this long assessment, there remains only one viable world, the one that our bewigged god chooses to bring into existence: an optimal balance of goods and evils, the best of all possible worlds. A reality where one can increase the well-being of an individual without automatically diminishing the total happiness. But if you think a slightly worse universe than this one would be unable to survive, that it would self-destruct, as it must have done numerous times over the course of History, we arrive at the woeful conclusion that our world is at the same time the best and the worst that can be envisaged. So it's all nonsense."

"Schopenhauer?" asked Grimod.

"Not bad," Dr. Mardrus confirmed.

"Perhaps Vilfredo Pareto, as well?" said Canterel, his eyes vague.

"Just a pinch. Bravo, gentlemen, you know everything!"

Lady MacRae showed admirable patience, waiting until this brief pause before saying that she felt unwell and begging that they excuse her as she returned to her room.

For the next three days, a strange apathy seemed to come over everyone. Ekaterinburg, Tyumen, Omsk, Novosibirsk, towns and forests rolled by without provoking the slightest remark, apart from the perennial questions linked to the changing time zones. Since no one knew the answers, the passengers of this moving Babel drifted haphazardly through suspended time. Inside the cabins, the cold now left frost on the stainless steel of the windows.

After one day of investigation, the Russian policeman and his henchmen had gotten off in Ekaterinburg, case closed. The Mongolian cook who used to boast of dating Yva was nowhere to be found. This made it appear that he had managed to get off the train after his crime, a conclusion that left the passengers quite reassured.

Among themselves, Canterel and his friends remained armed. Aware that this was doubtless some kind of setup, they continued to be on their guard. Stubbornly sticking with his makeup, Scummington snooped relentlessly about the train, speaking to them only cautiously, and then only to advise them to "leave it to the experts."

Upon their departure from Omsk, a rumor went round the cars of yet another conflagration in Siberia, but the story was extinguished in Novosibirsk in face of the hypertrophied jaw of Colonel Yusupov, who embarked at that stop. Questioned about this new war from the moment of his appearance, the handsome man had burst into such laughter and held his sides in such a way as to banish any fears on this subject. A music and literature buff, and a smooth talker, the man shone in the salons, drinking a great deal of vodka and breaking each glass between his teeth, to the great excitement of the ladies. His dolman was decorated with frog fastenings of gold thread, his earring had a red diamond from Golconda. Or so he claimed, at least.

It was the afternoon of the fourth day after leaving Krasnoyarsk that terrible events conspired to prove him wrong.

XVIII

Dead Sheep Cove

Yesterday, Monsieur Wang took a trip to Biarritz to enroll Free Legs Diamond in the French regional championship. The actual start itself will take only a moment, at exactly 9 A.M., but what he has seen of the organization does not reassure him. Too much time spent on vagueness, waiting, niceties. These people are certainly enthusiasts—he will grant them that, at least—but they understand nothing about the beauty of a proper, professional gesture. They have not stopped dawdling, quibbling about this or that, rhapsodizing, as if they want to delay the moment when the action would begin. Five thousand birds to enroll, and they still did it by hand, with the aid of white-haired volunteers who typed in the registration numbers with just two fingers. Ten-digit registration numbers! To say nothing of the "electronic transponder" that they were required to use to time the birds' return flights—Unikons designed for the out-moded Minitel technology, but approved by the federation . . . In the age of the Internet and social networks!

The French understood nothing about what the world was becoming. Back when the Mediterranean was still the center of the universe, the combination of the region's Latin temperament and a certain Nordic discipline had done wonders to enforce its economic dominance. The day that center shifted east, this same Latinity served them again. Yes, he thinks, look how they are beginning to relocate Chinese factories to their own country, it's for the sake of their legendary haughtiness. Gold and jade on the outside, putrid wool on the inside . . .

Still, Monsieur Wang is worried for his pigeon. The inside of the basket held clean air and good quality grain, but the feeling of leaving his darling in a pigeonhole in the middle of nowhere, while he rolls away in his limousine, still shocks him. He knows that the organizers are aware of the value of his athlete, that they will fawn over him, but every time it's the same, he is left in suspense, foolish and helpless until the bird's return. A single day without his friend feels like three autumns.

Free Legs Diamond is an offshoot of the Steven van Breeman line in Hilversum. Wang had given him this name in reference to Jack Diamond, a gangster whose nickname was "Legs" because of how quickly he could run after committing a crime. "Free" was a reference to the feeling of emancipation, of regained liberty that he exuded when he shot up, a steel-blue projectile, as the baskets were unsealed and opened. A pureblood Janssen with the profile of a fighter jet, red eyes, proud crop. You had to hold him in your hands, to feel his muscles to understand. And on top of this, a champion's temperament. The looks on the other contestants' faces when they saw him! You could see in their eyes that the outcome was already decided.

Once he is finished with France—in two years, maybe three—Wang plans to return to work in China. Not just anywhere, in Hangzhou, near Shanghai. He has just bought a big apartment on the Champs-Élysées in Tianducheng, the twenty-square-kilometer "celestial city" that the Guangsha Holding Group brought into reality. There is already an Eiffel Tower, an Arc de Triomphe, a whole grid of paved avenues and French gardens. Beautiful new buildings lined up like the teeth of a comb. It is Paris, but Paris a thousand times better, Paris freed of its suburbs and its Parisians. He knows Zhang Xufei, the project's deputy director general. A classmate from university who has risen much more quickly in his field. Before the applications started flooding in, Zhang Xufei did him a great service by supporting his bid for a five-bedroom penthouse with a view of the Latona Basin at Versailles on one side, and of the Montmartre vineyards on the other. The broad, sunny terrace would allow him to finally set up a pigeon loft worthy of the name.

Three steps take him to the balcony, where he checks on Free Legs Diamond's box. There is a contact on the hatch; when the bird returns, it triggers a loud signal. The system functions well. The same can be said for the black Bakelite device—the sinister Unikon—where he must insert the pigeon's electric collar to authenticate the time of arrival.

Nine o'clock. And there, his darling has just taken flight. Five hundred kilometers to go; if all goes well, he will be home before nightfall. Wang pictures him launched, rowing through the air at top speed, drawn like a compass needle in the exact direction of the pigeon loft. A straight line that the wind bends and shifts, the stroke of a sword across the sky.

He grimaces, clenches his jaw to fend off this image, closes his eyes, knowing from experience that his mind will once again replay the brief horror film left to him by his parents. The person who is bitten by a snake fears rope for the rest of his life . . . Wang makes the best of it, the recurrence of these images is now only a slight mar on pure alabaster.

It was in the county of Jingbian, in the region of the dead sheep cove. There, his mother was growing two *mu* of sorghum by herself, in the absence of her husband, who had been deported the year before to another people's commune. Mao Zedong had finally died, taking with him his Cultural Revolution and his four million victims, but the way of things was slow to return to normal.

Wang does not know how much of this memory he has made up. Is a thirteen-month-old child capable of retaining such details, or do they have to be reconstructed? Anyway, he sees himself on his mother's back, in a blue canvas *mei-tai* that smells strongly of urine, garlic, and sweat. It's hot; his nose glued to the nape of the young woman's neck, tickled by the damp locks escaping from under her hat, he follows the gleam of the sickle's steel as it cuts the tops off the ears of sorghum one by one. There is gold, and brown, and the plaintive expiration caused by the repetitive motion occurring a few centimeters from his cheek. This steady rocking has almost put him to sleep when he feels the weight of a presence behind him and two arms creep under his mother's armpits. She turns around, and in this sudden movement, Wang sees a man's haggard face, his mouth twisted, a deaf-mute struggling not to say what he wants to express at any cost; then, in its place against the blue of the sky, a kind of arching red geyser whose droplets fall in a warm drizzle on Wang's eyelids.

Coming home unexpectedly, Wang's father had wanted to surprise his wife by grabbing her breasts from behind, as he used to two or three times a day before he left, but she had turned around so swiftly, sickle in hand, that she had decapitated him.

He had sunk to the ground like a rag. Later, Wang revisited this slow fall, disturbingly, when he saw a documentary on a praying mantises; it was the fall of the male, his body beheaded and then sucked of its juices by the female.

You and I, clever reader, would say that this explains many things, but Wang would disagree. *He* thinks the accident perfectly sums up the distribution of his parents' genes within him—he has his father's sensuality, and his mother's quick reactions.

XIX

The Sowers of Dread

The train plunged into a white desert as it crossed the Yenisei River. The steppe had given way to a rolling plain covered in a thick layer of snow, darkened in places with fir groves. Coming out of a long curve taken at reduced speed, the convoy was accelerating again when a series of reports rang out under the locomotive's wheels. It was the fulminate that railway repairmen lay down on the rails as a last resort to warn of a serious problem on the tracks. Only the driver could hear them: he understood the danger and braced himself on the brake pedal, activating the air brakes in all the cars. As the engine began to slow, with a dreadful screeching of metal on metal, the conductor felt the wheels give an unnatural jolt and prayed the train would stop before it derailed.

The first wagons made it past the obstacle somehow, but even as the convoy seemed about to come to a halt, Car 5 left the rails, dragging with it all the cars behind.

Inside, a number of passengers, thrown off balance by the sudden deceleration, were thrown to the ground or violently launched against the walls. Then the train gave another jolt, rattling over the ties, rocking wildly; the luggage waltzed in the crash. Clinging to whatever they could, the travelers wailed, believing that their final hour had come.

After one last judder, the train finally came to a stop. Thanks to the conductor's reflexes, none of the wagons had flipped, but three quarters of them now stood on the track ballast. In the middle of the general stupor, Grimod was one of the first to react. He checked that none of his friends had been hurt in the crash, then took it upon himself to help some of the other passengers up. Miraculously, there were no complaints more serious than some bruises and minor injuries caused by broken crockery or falling objects. As soon as they were somewhat recovered, everyone hurried to get out of the cars, despite the snow and the biting cold. Still in a state of shock, they wandered in small, shivering groups, exclaiming as they inspected the axles and already pestering the conductors. A machinist climbed onto the track to determine the cause of the accident: one of the rails had been completely unbolted for several meters, which pointed to sabotage. The wagons toward the front—which were broken up but still attached to those that remained on the rails—formed an unnatural angle, like a broken tibia; the jets of steam expelling from all of its valves made the locomotive look like it was foaming with rage.

No one noticed the carrier pigeon escaping out a window.

When the first gunshots rang out, people thought it was just another mechanical problem, but when two men collapsed, then a woman, her chest spattered with blood, everyone frantically sought refuge in the cars. To the north, armed groups had positioned themselves on the hillsides; fifty riders were wheeling around the edge of the fir trees, preparing to deploy the troops still hiding in the undergrowth.

Colonel Yusupov, observing these movements through a window, stepped to the side to avoid a bullet that shattered the glass.

"The Sowers of Dread!" he said, as if to himself, his pale face conveying the terror of an animal caught in a trap.

The employees of the Transsiberian, who had also recognized their attackers, fell to their knees in shock; the younger women were crying, the older ones admonishing them to control themselves.

The reader will be grateful, we hope, if we provide some more detailed information regarding the "Sowers of Dread."

Reviled by all, this name, which burns the lips that pronounce it, does not evoke just one enemy, but rather two adversaries united by the fear that they inspire. In the theriomorphic world of nomadic horsemen, there were two sides: on one, the horde of Cossack Epistemologists, and on the other, the Creationists, the hussars of the true faith. Two opposing ideologies that rallied under their banner a number of sects and splinter groups that were more or less allied.

The Epistemologists, mockingly called the "Canoe Cossacks" for their deftness in navigating the meanderings of rhetoric, asserted the definitive, incontestable nonexistence of any divinity. They drew so much happiness from the individual freedom that this gave them that they had taken it upon themselves to impose it on everyone as a supreme gift. These Cossacks were better known by the name of Zepistos, or even Zippos, so systematic was their practice of setting fire to the places they passed.

The Creationists believed the opposite: only a god could have brought our universe into being. Committed to martyr themselves in order to spread their message, they called themselves the "Creods," for "Creatures of God," and handed out "my brother"s and "my sister"s all over the place. They were feared for their propensity to blow themselves up next to you at the slightest provocation.

The Anarchist-Epistemologists marched with the Latter-Day Voltaireans, and also the Antitheists of Democratic Kampuchea, Babeuf's Henchmen, the Marxist Revival of the Urals, the Outraged Northerners, the Mad Southerners, the Independent State of the Gay Science, the Apostate Commandos, and the Fourierists of Passionate Attraction. They obeyed no one, not even the Atamans they would occasionally elect at the end of a long night of binge drinking.

Under the orders of the Commander of All Beliefs, the Creatures of God brought in a group of widely disparate cliques, including the

Enlightened of the Sacred Heart, the Iglesia Maradoniana of the Hand of God, the Algoran Templars (devoted for centuries upon centuries to a book in which the access algorithms to the Celestial City are inscribed, or so they claim), the Legions of Mary, the Black Hebrews, Omar's Taliban, the Gondwana Unification Front, the Worshippers of Kali, and the Sinai Shakers.

Hundreds of thousands of men and women professing that we are the result of a divine program, and just as many arguing that, on the contrary, we must get by on our own. Clinging to their convictions like limpets to a rock, they haunted the steppe, sowing fear. The Siberian equivalent of the mad, unforeseen outbursts that had begun to wreak havoc on the rest of the world.

Under the orders of Holmes, who—in spite of the scotches he had gulped down as an aperitif—had regained his old instincts from his days as an officer in the Army in India, our friends gathered in the library lounge, which had the advantage of being adjacent to Verity's compartment. At his injunction they had all put on their warmest clothes. Madame Chauchat, a mink coat with a matching hat; Grimod, a wolfskin greatcoat; Holmes, his hooded cloak from the Third Lancers Regiment; and Canterel, who took some time to reappear, a simple polar-bear fur coat whose collar ate up half of his face. Dr. Mardrus joined them, dressed for his part in a yak leather jacket lined with fur; it looked as if it had been through a lot, but seemed suited to the Siberian cold that was seeping into the cars. They had all collected their weapons. Besides the rifle and pistols purchased in London, Canterel had retrieved a rather stunning arsenal from his trunks.

The shots were only sporadic, as if their assailants, sure of their victory, were conserving their ammunition. The windowpanes were exploding one by one, though each time this happened one of the determined men who had gathered in that area would break the remaining glass with the butt of his rifle, then discharge his weapon blindly in the direction from which the blast seemed to have come. Scummington was nowhere to be seen.

Strangely, Lady MacRae proved to be more annoyed than frightened by this attack. She tried in vain to get the reading spinnets to work; the shock of the derailment, it appeared, had damaged the devices. Seeming bored, she informed Canterel that she was going to be with her daughter.

Several minutes after she left, a wave of panic caused all of the travelers to surge toward the front of the train.

"We have to get to the front cars, the train's going to leave!" people were shouting, panicking like the Parisians during the deadly strikes that had disrupted the railway there a month earlier.

Holmes looked at Grimod, Grimod looked at Canterel, and Canterel shook his head, his eyes indicating Verity's compartment: it was out of the question for them to transport his daughter under such conditions.

As one, Holmes and his butler agreed, but Grimod, crouching to get out of the way of the bullets that were blowing up the wall panels and decimating unwary passengers, slipped away.

"I'm still going to go take a look," he said, before crowding in among the clump of passengers that was savagely making its way forward.

In total pandemonium, men and women were trampling one another as they tried to gain ground, unmindful of even the most basic manners. A swarm of beasts transformed by a single instinct: to survive. Facing this obstruction, Grimod got off the train as soon as he could, on the opposite side from the attack, and began to run. The confusion was such that none of the passengers had for an instant considered leaving the deceptive sanctuary of the wagons. When he got to the junction of Cars 4 and 5, he saw a conductor finish breaking the coupling from the train body, then step back as the front of the train pulled away. Even as the latest arrivals screamed for them to wait, a wretched-looking man clambered over their bodies, took a bounding leap across the growing gap, and in a desperate attempt managed to grab hold of the back of the moving car. Scummington had finally reappeared!

"Hold on," he yelled, seeing Grimod. "I'll bring back help!"

His expression made him look both uneasy and sorry to be separated from Grimod this way, but in his eyes there was only the shameful relief of a man who has just selfishly saved his own skin.

Scornfully, Grimod watched his face shrink and disappear as the train rolled away. Then he quickly returned to his companions.

Squatting, his eye glued to his telescopic lens, Holmes was watching the movement of the troops in the hills. Long teams of horses were finishing towing what looked like two enormous torsion catapults out from the firs. The number of horsemen had grown considerably; three ranks of archers and crossbowmen, half buried in their snowy trenches, had gotten into shooting position.

"But who are they?" Canterel asked Prince Svechin, who was reloading his weapon.

"Beggars," he replied contemptuously, "madmen."

"Cossacks or hussars?"

"They're all the same breed. Can you make out their uniform?"

"Bright red pants," Holmes described, from behind his spyglass, "blue kaftans, multicolored belts, no sheaths on their swords, slightly curved blades . . ."

"Cossacks," the prince said with confidence. He got a flask out of his pocket and swallowed a mouthful before offering it around: "*Za vashye zdorovye!* Have a drink, we'll need it!"

"*Santé!*" said Grimod, taking the flask and bringing it to his lips.

"*Na zdorovye!*" said Holmes, preferring his own bottle of single malt.

"To ours," repeated Canterel, before swallowing a pipette of Rutonal.

"You shouldn't do that," Dr. Mardrus commented, adjusting his target. "Intoxication acts like a converging lens in a camera obscura; it diminishes all the proportions and thus produces an image that is less accurate than the original."

"Aye, aye," Holmes said in Gaelic. "But, at this moment, that's exactly what I need: to make what I see a little smaller . . ."

At that moment, an elephant knocked into Car 5. The muffled blow of its impact rocked the car's frame and shocked those inside. The beast, dying on the track ballast, drew tears with its long trumpet call.

Prince Svechin rolled over to the edge of the window and risked taking a look outside. To the west, a swath of the dusk was ablaze with an orange glow.

"Krasnoyarsk is burning," said the prince, gritting his teeth. "They must have taken control of the zoo."

All kinds of exotic animals were now flying toward them, most of them sinking into the drifts with a thud. Kangaroos, hyenas, pandas, pitiful giraffes twisting their disjointed necks, shivering all over.

Among the trapped travelers were several of the amiable clowns our friends had previously met, notably Brother Célestin, the trader from Manchester, Hégésippe Petiot, and the inventor Achille Fournier.

"Against a bull," the inventor whispered, as if it were a secret that he had chosen to reveal only under the given circumstances, "against a buffalo, an elephant, the best method to use is a bullfighter's: dodge to the side, very quick, until you can climb onto a tree or a rock. Against a wildcat, try to put a knife in its throat or grab its tongue: the beast doesn't care which!"

At that moment, a black panther burst into the wagon, but it was so dazed that it presented no danger. Canterel simply finished it off with a merciful shot from his Mauser.

As other pachyderms came crashing into the side of the train, Holmes, judging that the situation had become dangerous, gave the order to take refuge under the wagons. Canterel rushed to Claw-dia's compartment, and with the aid of Kim and Miss Sherrington got Verity outside, then slid her in among the axles with the others. Enveloped in a heap of covers, the girl looked like an Aztec mummy in the process of being buried.

When the first white rhino sank into a snowbank a few meters away, its four shackles in the air, its eyes rolling in shock, Hégésippe Petiot could no longer contain himself. Abandoning all reason, he extricated himself from his entrenchment and advanced across the snow with open arms.

"Bournissac!" he yelled, radiating happiness. "I'm here, Bournissac, come to me!"

Like a bus falling from the sky, the second rhinoceros flattened him, purely and simply, without leaving the slightest trace of his unique zealotry on this earth.

XX

A Flaming Rabbit is a Horrible Thing

"It's all in your head," says JJ, "you're overthinking it."

Monsieur Bonacieux shrugs and smiles sadly. He has heard this so many times, even from his wife, that the argument is no longer even remotely relevant. JJ, full name Jean-Johnny Hercule, is from Mauritius, and they work next to each other on the assembly line. Square face, military haircut, swarthy skin, he is an island colossus—his father was Maori—who seems to have grown in order to live up to his surname: 6'2", a hundred and twenty kilos of corded muscle. His voice matches his personality: that of a rugby player practicing the haka on a field in New Zealand. Astoundingly, in spite of his paw-like hands, he displays the dexterity of a surgeon. The only man Dieumercie considers a friend, even if they only interact at the factory.

"I must have a deformity, some genetic thing . . ."

"Cut the *kakakata*," says JJ, "don't beat around the bush with me. Have you ever had a hard-on?"

"Yes. Well, not a very good one, but yes."

"Then you can get one again, brother. What about your wife . . ."

"What are you saying?"

"Maybe she doesn't turn you on enough? Maybe she doesn't love you anymore? Or maybe *you* don't love *her* anymore?"

Dieumercie pictures Carmen's pretty face. He sees it floating over the printed circuit boards, with her wry little smile, her beautiful black hair divided into two asymmetrical masses. If she had stopped loving him, she wouldn't have concocted all those exercises to try to waken his desire. And if he loved her less, he would have stopped going along with them ages ago!

"It's not that, JJ, I don't believe it could be. I should go see a specialist . . ."

"This thing isn't for doctors, *kamarad*. I don't know where, but you picked up some *mové zer*. Someone's grabbed your tail, and they're holding on tight!"

"And how do I treat that?"

"Back home, you go see a *traiteur*; he fixes you up in two steps, three gestures. *Dokter san soulyé* . . . My father was one of the best on the island at getting rid of the evil eye."

Jean-Johnny checks that no one is watching them and slips something into his neighbor's pocket.

"A block of camphor," he says quietly. "You burn it in your house, and the malice returns to the sender. *System grandimounn*, guaranteed!"

That same evening, Monsieur Bonacieux talks to his wife about it. He's been hexed, they don't have to keep looking for the cause of his impotence anymore. Jean-Johnny has given him a sure fix, and his little trouser snake is telling him that this time it's going to work.

"JJ?" Carmen asked, astonished. "The big black guy?"

"Yeah. You know him?"

"Not really, I've seen him at the bakery. He seems nice."

"He's a good guy, my love! I told him about it, and he knew right away what the problem was. His father was a witch doctor, he inherited the gift."

Dieumercie gets the camphor out of his pocket and explains the process.

"You know what," says Carmen, "we'll kill two birds with one stone: we'll fumigate and flambé! I've prepared exciting new things for us . . ."

Seeing the bottle of rubbing alcohol that his wife is proudly showing him, Monsieur Bonacieux recoils.

"That's where I draw the line! Can't play with that stuff, it's too dangerous."

"No worse than the camphor, if you think about it. Louisette did a demo for me, you'll see."

"I won't see anything. And anyway, who's Louisette?"

"Louisette Bonbon, the woman who sells chickens."

"And what does someone who sells chickens know about rubbing alcohol? This is going too far!"

Carmen doesn't respond. She pulls up her skirt, pours a little alcohol onto her hand, and smears it onto her legs like moisturizer. A dab with a paper towel to absorb the excess, then she strikes a match. When she brings it near her feet, the flame feeds and changes at the contact. A blue glow seizes onto her toes, haloes them for an instant, dies away, and spreads, an ephemeral blaze. The short, harmless conflagration of a crêpe cooked with Grand Marnier. Her skin feels like clean glass, it's smooth, the stubble on her legs has not suffered.

"Mmmh!" says Madame Bonacieux, rapturous. "You can't imagine how good this feels. Take off your clothes, my love, this is going to do incredible things to you!"

Why not, thinks Dieumercie. At this point, how could it not get him going? And anyway he has JJ's camphor. He expects great things from the camphor.

Carmen does everything conscientiously. Once he is stretched out on the linoleum floor of the kitchen, between the sink and the stove, she pours half a liter of alcohol into an enamel bowl, prepares the paper towels, and kisses her husband passionately on the mouth.

"The camphor . . ." whispers Monsieur Bonacieux, holding his breath.

A wink, to let him know she hasn't forgotten, then she lights a charcoal incense tablet in a dish. Placed on the embers, the camphor block immediately begins to smoke.

"Out, evil eye!" she says, starting to rub Dieumercie down with the alcohol.

"Out!" he repeats, concentrating.

She carefully swabs his body with a paper towel, looks her husband right in the eye, with an adoration that she hopes is catching, and strikes a match by his toes. Blue wavelets begin to run up his ankles, work their way up his calves, climb along his thighs, linger around his penis. Carmen sees him shudder, convulse. She thinks it's going to work, until suddenly his pubic hair bursts into flame. A brush fire that sizzles and burns out as fast as it lit up. No harm done, besides the smell of burnt hair that overpowers the scents of camphor and alcohol, but Dieumercie felt the heat, heard his wife's gasp of surprise, and sat up sharply, worried for his penis, his upper body licked with wisps of flame, the same phenomenon was occurring on his chest hair, harmlessly, but more broadly, so extensive that it disturbed the slumber of Pile-poil, Carmen's white rabbit; it jumped, feeling the irresistible urge to change its viewing angle by leaping away, and in its bewilderment it miscalculated its trajectory and landed on the edge of the bowl, tipping it over and getting doused with alcohol, so of course it shot across the linoleum, skidded into the burning charcoal, and WHOOF, was engulfed in flames. It started to hop higher and farther than ever before, almost silently, with just that strange clicking sound that dwarf rabbits make, a flaming ball of fluff that swept saucepans from its path, grazing the walls, zigzagging, a vision of bared gums and napalm. A putrid horror. There's no other way to say it—a flaming rabbit is a horrible thing.

XXI

The Savage Division

The death of Hégésippe Petiot was followed by a sweeping volley of arrows, which pattered against the metal wagons.

"It won't be long before they attack," said Holmes. "Get ready!"

The cloud of arrows that had darkened the sky had not yet cleared when fifty Cossack horsemen began to rush toward the train. They charged at full speed through the snow, swords bared, roaring loudly enough for a whole army.

This first offensive was bravely fought off.

When he judged that they were the right distance away, Holmes gave the order to fire; all the armed travelers shot at the same time, and a good number of their assailants fell, unhorsed by the salvo. Even so, the losses were not significant enough to stem the assault. Several riders wrestled their spooked mounts back under control, then began to gallop forward behind those who had continued to brave the bullets. The second salvo cut down others, but there were still about thirty thundering down the hill to fall upon the cars. Ignoring the grapeshot, they got so close that the passengers could make out their fearless faces, distorted with the fury of combat; their curled mustaches, plastered down by the wind, the billowing steam of their breath.

Canterel closed his eyes, hindered by this too-clear vision. The others trembled, ramped up their shooting. They yelled and unloaded their weapons into the proud death that was advancing toward them. In its immediate violence, the scene recalled *The Iliad*.

His rifle over his shoulder, Martial Canterel rolled out from under the protection of the axles, stood up, sniffed mechanically, as if trying to test the thickness of the cold, then tossed two of the hand grenades taken from Scummington's cabin. The motion—precise, coordinated—was less that of a combatant than a juggler passing his batons, but it produced two impressive explosions in the very midst of the riders. Two thick plumes of dark yellow smoke stagnated there, slow to dissipate. Canterel was turning around when a Zepisto, his sword waving, came out of the haze behind him only a dozen steps away.

"Behind you!" shouted Holmes, caught off guard.

Canterel did not turn. Without losing his composure, he shouldered his weapon, aiming at Holmes.

"You're crazy!" Holmes shouted, trying to wriggle back into shelter. "Good lord, what's gotten into you!"

Astonished by his opponent's attitude, the Cossack hesitated for just a moment—long enough for Martial, calm as ever, to extend a kind of rearview mirror on the side of his weapon, adjust his target, and fire in stride. Struck right in the heart, the man collapsed.

"A rear-firing rifle . . ." said Holmes. "Where did you get that, old chap? It's splendid!"

"Saint-Étienne," Canterel replied. "It's the French version of the Krummlauf. I also have the model for firing around corners."

"I hope you have more than one," said Grimod, offering him the spyglass. "It looks like we may need them."

In the valley, out of range of the besieged passengers, some of the Cossack forces were making motions as if to take the train from the rear.

"They're not as stupid a I thought," grumbled Holmes.

Of all the travelers seeking refuge under the train, only Achille Fournier had been hurt in the attack. A bolt from a crossbow had struck him deep in the shoulder. No one noticed until he asked Prince Svechin to help him apply pressure to his subclavian artery. As the prince exclaimed that he knew nothing about and would have trouble even locating this artery, Achille assured him that it would be fine, if only someone would help him remove his shirt. Once his torso was bare, in fact, it became apparent that he was tattooed with the paths of his arterial vessels. Black circles marked compression points, dotted lines the places suitable for amputating limbs. Achille Fournier explained to Grimod, who was called to the rescue to finish bandaging him, that this was his greatest, and certainly his most useful, invention; by using this preventative tattooing on all soldiers, as he hoped one day would be the case—especially if Prince Svechin would agree to bring it to the attention of the Archimandrake—the deaths of many of those wounded on the battlefield would be prevented.

The quart of *eau de vie* that Grimod had made him swallow before extracting the bolt from his wound prompted the man to reveal other things. When he tried to demonstrate to the prince the importance of teaching infantry to march backward during retreats, since if a counterattack came they would be able to deal with the enemy more quickly, they concluded that he was either drunk or delirious with fever.

Holmes spread the word among the defenders to position themselves to protect both sides of the train, then returned to observing the enemies. Their numbers were still swelling; their horses were pawing at the ground, the attack was imminent. With their ammo almost exhausted, there was no chance this time that he and his comrades would be able to hold them off.

Canterel put a hand on his shoulder, as if he could read his thoughts.

"So they don't have any guns?"

"You don't need a gun to crush a bug, my friend. And, to tell the truth, we're hardly more than that."

"But they're not even using rifles . . ."

"Old school," said Prince Svechin. "You'll see that there are situations where rifles no longer do any good. That being said, perhaps they only want prisoners?"

Canterel turned toward Clawdia. He met her insistent gaze, and after hesitating briefly nodded his head: neither she nor her daughter would be taken alive.

In the dim light of evening, the bodies of men and beasts, stiffened by the cold, sketched grim shapes; torches lit up in the distance, fleeting wisps that shifted in the air like the souls of the dead. Fat flakes of snow began to flutter down over everything.

The second charge came without warning. An indistinct mass of Cossack riders took off down the hillside, signaling to the troops who had skirted around the back of the train. In a few seconds, a howling throng fell upon them from all sides. But while the besieged passengers fought as best they could against the violence of the assault, two squads used the element of surprise to attack the ends of the train from blind spots that were almost impossible to defend against. In spite of the fusillade that mowed some of the attackers down, a few managed to grab onto the handrails on the car doors and get into the wagons. They immediately began to set fires with their torches. When they leapt from the train several minutes later, all of the wagons were burning, spewing white smoke from their windows, where roaring flames flared up and blew out the glass.

A sizzling target in the Siberian night, the train appeared to be drawing legions of insects set on consuming it.

A shift in the wind carried the smoke back toward the hills, slowing and then stopping the charge from the north, catching their throats with the acridness of the burning varnish and lacquer. Visibility fell to less than two meters, as if they had been fired on by twenty batteries of coordinated cannons.

Our friends took this opportunity to concentrate their fire on the plain, but the number of Zepistos and their indifference to death were so unstoppable that there was nothing left for them to do but succumb. The Cossacks took the train little by little, terrible skirmishes raged under the axles, people fighting with their bare hands, and in melees where sabers gleamed and pistols cracked.

Canterel was ready. His last three bullets loaded into his Mauser, he was waiting till the last moment before keeping his promise. Grimod had used all his ammo and was bundled up in his greatcoat, his face whitened by traces of powder, ready to leap out and strangle the first person to approach them. Prince Svechin still had ammunition and was only firing at sure hits, spitting each time and grumbling: "Damn Cossacks!" Lady MacRae was rocking her daughter in her arms and crooning in her ear.

Holmes had only one cartridge left; mindful that it was his last, he aimed at the closest Zepisto and fired. To his great surprise, all the attackers fell at once, as if under heavy fire. He was still inspecting his weapon, trying to understand what miracle had brought about this result, when he heard the sound of a machine gun, then an engine running.

An armored train was approaching on the track parallel to the one they were on, but also coming from the direction of Krasnoyarsk; flanking the engine, six vans clad in black metal—three of them equipped with rotating gun turrets—were hammering away with all their might. With artillery fire, explosions, and continuous salvos shooting out from the train's armored shell, this incredible dragon sowed terror among the Cossacks and sent them running.

The monster came to a halt behind the burning wagons, keeping its distance from the flames. Immediately, soldiers climbed out to help the survivors out from under the wagons and get them on board the new train as quickly as possible. As soon as this transfer was complete, the convoy started back up. It left behind a wintry landscape strewn with bloodstained carcasses.

Gathered together in a single car, the survivors from the Transsiberian experienced one of those moments of unseemly elation that comes after the worst catastrophes. Some were crying or laughing, for no other reason than that they had made it out alive. Even the wounded seemed healed by their keen awareness of having been miraculously saved. Aside from the rather tipsy Holmes, who pretended to dance a quick jig, our protagonists were able to maintain their air of restrained dignity. Three quarters of the travelers had perished under the Cossacks' swords and were strewn on the ground behind them, left for the crows. Women and children, mostly. It would have been most indecent to celebrate. Among the fellow sufferers gathered in the coach, Dr. Mardrus was the only other one who showed the strength of mind that befitted a gentleman. The handshake Canterel gave him was like the dubbing of a knight.

The inside of the wagon was overcrowded with yatagans, rifles, crates of ammunition; an arsenal on wheels, ill adapted to housing refugees. The wood stove, however, gave off a comforting warmth, and the few soldiers who stayed with them—in spite of their fierce look, with their cartridge belts across their chests and strings of grenades on their waists—proved to be very considerate. These men had slanted black eyes above high cheekbones, weathered skin, and white, even teeth.

"Kalmucks," Prince Svechin whispered into Canterel's ear. "I'm not sure whether this change is for the better . . ."

He had not even finished uttering his doubts when the sentries guarding the door stepped respectfully aside, clearing the way for the officer in command of the train. In the red uniform of a Mongol dignitary, with the Cross of St. George pinned to his chest, sword at his side, holster hanging from the string of Tibetan prayer beads that doubled as his belt, General Ulrich looked around at the passengers, then marched deliberately up to Prince Svechin.

"Your Grace," he said, clicking his heels in front of the prince, "it is an honor and a pleasure to see you again after so long."

"Likewise, Excellency. Allow me to thank you, on all our behalf. You have saved us from certain death."

"I am happy that my actions pleased you."

His sunken cheeks, his disheveled blond mustache, and the wrinkles creasing his forehead gave the impression of a man grown old before his time—an image that clashed with the youthful tone of his voice and the fierceness of his bright eyes.

He took the prince by the arm, pulling him aside to converse. While they talked, the general could be seen turning toward the travelers and setting his gaze on some of them, as if to put faces to the descriptions Svechin was giving him.

When they stepped forward again, the prince had a worried look. He headed over to Lady MacRae and formally introduced her to this strange figure.

"Baron Ulrich von Hopelat, General of the Asiatic Cavalry Division . . ."

The baron bowed stiffly.

"My heart breaks for your daughter," he said. "I will make sure that a more comfortable place is found for you. We will be in Irkutsk tomorrow, God willing. You will be able to get on a different train and continue your voyage. Until then, you are my guests. My surgeon will see to your wounded."

He bowed again, gave an order in Mongolian to his sergeant, and left. Shortly thereafter, some soldiers came and dropped off a large number of precious rugs and cushions taken from their quarters. Then they brought the passengers bowls of borscht, water, and vodka.

When they were settled, Prince Svechin hastened to satisfy the curiosity of the little group gathered around him. He had known

Baron Ulrich at the Pavlovsk Military College in St. Petersburg, from which they had both graduated as officers in the same year.

"There was no denying that he had a fertile imagination," said the prince, "but that was his main virtue, and his actions already showed his lack of judgment."

Heroic and ambitious, however, he had carved out for himself a brilliant career on the battlefield. Wounded five times, decorated five times for his bravery, he had been promoted to the rank of general in the Archimandrake's army at the age of twenty-nine. The following year, when the implosion of Europe brought trouble to even the deepest regions of Holy Russia, he crossed his Rubicon. Leading a cavalry of two thousand men, he entered Mongolia and captured Urga, where he was welcomed as a liberator.

"That was when I lost track of him," Svechin added. Raised to the rank of High Bator by the Kalmucks, married to a princess of the blood, a distant descendent of Temüjin, he took the name Ulrich Khan and got it into his head to reconquer first Siberia, then the whole West, to create the universal Lamaist empire to which he aspired!

"Ulrich Khan, the initials embroidered on his epaulettes?" ventured Lady MacRae.

"Yes, the Cyrillic Y sounding like 'U,' and the X for the 'kh' sound."

Unfortunately for him, while he was waging war in Transbaikal, the Zepistos retook Urga, permanently robbing him of his home base.

Now, at the age of thirty-five, Ulrich was no more than a warlord condemned to roam across the steppe aboard his twelve armored trains, a kind of Flying Dutchman with neither roots nor homeland, but driven as ever by the fever of his visions, and inventing for himself a destiny that grew more romantic with each passing day.

"Quite the drama," said Canterel, condescendingly.

126

"Indeed," replied the prince, "though one would wish that its author were a little less cynical. The man is surrounded by real beasts. Whether he sanctions them or not, the exactions perpetrated by his troops have earned him the nickname the Red Baron, or the Mad Baron. As for his Asiatic Cavalry, it is known throughout Russia, and beyond, by the name of the Savage Division, which may allow you to imagine the subtlety of their operations."

Because of their fatigue, and perhaps also the glasses of vodka that they had downed, they soon sank into a drowsiness that dulled their reaction to these grave tidings.

Lulled by the low rumbling of the axles over the rails, curled up around one another like satraps, they did not see the mounted Buryats who escorted the train, lighting the way with their lanterns and making sure that no ambush could disturb the deepness of their sleep.

XXII

The Writing Disease

Among all the readers who officiated in the tobacco factories, the most appreciated were those who "set the tone," performing the texts like real actors on the stage. Some were so enthusiastic that they changed their voices for the different characters; others refused to, from lack of skill or on principle, but all were committed to moving their listeners, to carrying them as far as possible in their empathy for the novels' protagonists. With the advent of the microphone, the most skilled took it upon themselves to enrich their readings with all kinds of dramatic sound effects, with great claps of thunder and crackling fires. It was not uncommon to see a whole workshop in tears, continuing to work mechanically while the reader, throat tight with sobs, tried to regain control of his voice.

Most of them would not hesitate to alter the story in order to produce this effect. Especially in epilogues, so many authors had their creations die in torment, or gave them happy endings that lacked the necessary exaltation and effusion. So, at a minimum, the readers added embraces, a passionate kiss against the setting sun, a promise of eternity; and in tragic cases, Julien Sorel got off, acquitted by his judges, Madame Bovary breathed her last breath in peace, or even escaped the poisoning *in extremis* thanks to her husband's care.

Through reading, they ultimately contracted the writing disease. The most extreme case had been that of María Caridad González Martínez, a reader whom Dulcie admired endlessly. Improvising from outlines she would prepare the night before, or sometimes just from some simple notes, this woman had orally composed twenty-two novels before the eyes of her public: *Darkness and Destiny, Hearts of Stone, The Dream Factory,* countless tales whose weaving she revised as she went along, satisfying or frustrating the expectations of those listening at her leisure. Whether or not these books belonged to the realm of "good literature" was not the issue: they had succeeded in captivating her audience a thousand times better than the works of celebrated authors, because the words, the expressions, the turns of phrase she used were hers, they came to adapt themselves perfectly to her lips, rolled in her mouth like tamed delights; she knew how to modulate them, where to stop, to breathe, to push to make people laugh or cry. Because this was her music, because she knew how to make the nuances ring.

Arnaud does not need to look at his watch to know that he needs to tend to his wife. He sets his pair of scissors on the pile of old journals from which he cuts sections night after night, he articulates the joints of her fingers and carefully pulls back the sheet covering her. The radiance of Dulcie's naked form, despite the synthetic diaper; a black pin-up girl wearing a notched satin girdle, the plastic image of a Duke Magazine "playmate" from the sixties. Arnaud crosses her legs, places her arms under her breasts, accentuating her pose of Venus emerging from the waters; one hand at her shoulder, his other slides under her raised knee; then, pressing against her hip, he tips her body sideways. Not trusting the diaper's wetness indicator, he slides a finger under the elastic of the diaper, makes sure he doesn't need to change it. Bent over her, he then checks the condition of her skin, anxious at the thought of finding the least lesion that might signal the onset of a bedsore, touches her fingers and palms to oxygenate the areas that are at risk: heels, lower back, hips and pelvis. With this done, he covers her up, murmurs a word of love in her ear, tenderly kisses her temple.

He repeats these gestures every two hours, including at night, breaking up his own sleep into short periods spread throughout the day. In his solitary vigils, he is ready at any given moment to adjust the boat's course for the better.

Dulcie's nudity shocks him every time—by the tranquil rapture that spreads from it, but also because he is well aware that she would rather be dead than have to suffer these immodest examinations, even from him. He remembers her fit of anger while reading the novel by Pierre Louÿs, *The Woman and the Puppet*, when she came across his suggestive and contemptuous description of the Sevillian cigar makers. A harem of forty thousand eight hundred women, sweltering in the summer heat, were "charitably" given permission to work half naked! It was obvious that this fellow had never been inside a factory . . . He would have seen that all the workers there dressed decently, even in the worst heat, that not one of them would have deviated from that regulation at the risk of immediately being taken for a slut. As if it was hotter in Seville than in Santo Domingo or Cuba! No, but listen, listen to this: "Even the most dressed had nothing but shirts around their bodies (those were the prudes); almost all had bare torsos as they worked, in simple cloth petticoats with loosened belts, sometimes hiked halfway up their thighs. The spectacle was mixed. These were women of all ages, from children to old women, obese, fat, thin, and emaciated. Some were pregnant. Others were breast-feeding. Still others were not yet of marriageable age. There were all kinds of women in this naked throng, except virgins, probably. Some of them were even pretty." Can you believe that? The dirty asshole! "All kinds, except virgins," how could anyone be allowed to spout nonsense like that! She wept with rage, wounded as if it were an attack on her personally, and through her, an offense against all her fellow workers, against the entire body of cigar makers. Did you know there was a prison in the Seville factory? Cells where they imprisoned women suspected of having stolen tobacco, while they went and searched the women's homes, in the slums, to try to recover the stolen cigars. No police, no case, no judgment. If, by some unhappy chance, they found something that you had pinched or that a petty tyrant had planted there because of your pretty little face, you could be imprisoned for four or five years! There, right inside the workshop, with no recourse, with no hope, a whore at your keepers' disposal! Do you think they wanted to show their tits? Do you think that, do you?

It was fine for Mérimée, whom she half-heartedly exonerated, but here, nothing to be done, it was too hard to swallow. Pierre Louÿs? A liar and a nymphomaniac, a swine!

Arnaud returns to his work, finishing compiling the news items destined for the next morning's paper. He would like to have the talent of a Félix Fénéon so he could achieve the concision of *Novels in Three Lines*, or the skill of the falsely playful elegance of Sei Shōnagon's *The Pillow Book*. He imagines the workers' faces when, instead of the headlines from *La Tribune*, he reads the old news items that, smiling, he ushers to their destiny.

Last Telegrams of the Night

Things that present nothing out of the ordinary at first glance but take on exaggerated importance when attributed to a Chinese philosopher.

Mystery of the missing body. "When a tree falls in a forest and no one is around to hear it," the alleged murderer says smugly, "who can say whether it really made a sound?"

Things that vex true meat lovers.

A thirty-year-old British man puts ham in the shoes outside a mosque and decorates its gates with pork chops.

Things that awaken reasonable doubt in those who hear them.

"Kick in the door, we're both dead!" yelled the one-legged man, slumped over his wife's body.

Things that smell like sea air.

In Arcachon, on Avenue des Goélands, the septuagenarian kleptomaniac broke into cars using an oyster knife.

Things that are deliciously romantic.

He was working in the meat department, she in the fish department. Who could have possibly shot the butcher from Orne in the back?

Things that one is convinced could have inspired Max Ernst.
Before dying, the headless woman went to the hairdresser's.

Things that make one's eyes sting.
The Iranian justice condemns a man to be blinded with acid. The man had seen fit to do the same to the woman who refused to become his wife.

Things that seem to legitimize the use of brute force.
Brutally woken by blows from a nightstick, Michel-Ange Martin was struck so violently that he regained consciousness.

Things that do not bode well for marriage.
Fatal accident: leaving the road, a honeymoon bus weds itself to a pole.

Things that one realizes with alarm conform to an earlier dream.
Broadway, fire at Barnum's American Museum: a disabled war veteran swept away by a white whale.

XXIII

The Scorpions Loathe the Living

The first light of dawn filtered through the slit windows, streaking the sleeping bodies with pale, wavering zebra stripes. At the end of the coach, three soldiers—caps askew, tunics open—were stretching. Awake before the others, Canterel, Holmes, and Grimod spoke in low voices.

"It pains me to admit," Holmes was saying, "but we've been fooled. I'm willing to wager a case of the best Islay that the Straddler managed to get on one of the wagons that escaped. Even if he doesn't capture the diamond's bearer during the voyage, he will surely arrive in Peking before us."

"And so?" Grimod replied. "Until proven otherwise, we are the only ones who know the address of his destination."

"That's true," conceded Holmes, preoccupied. "And Scummington's on the case; he might very well succeed in foiling the Straddler's plans . . ."

"I doubt it, that man is an incompetent coward."

"You're exaggerating a little, don't you think? To have managed to follow the same trail as us, he must not be so very inept. What do you think, Martial?"

Canterel felt sweat running down his forehead in large droplets. His skin gray, mustache in disarray, he felt very nearly faint.

"Forgive me," he managed to articulate, "but I'm not in any condition . . ."

"What's wrong, old chap? Can I help?"

Canterel shook his head with a forced smile. Seeing his hands tremble, Grimod grasped the situation; he rummaged through the inner pockets of his coat and held out a cardboard tube that looked like a cartridge of buckshot.

"Ten grains, no more," he said, gravely.

"Thank you," said Canterel, his eyes shining. "I am in your debt . . ."

"What is it?" asked Holmes.

"*Savory & Moore* Chlorodyne," replied Grimod.

"Purified ether," Canterel added, already swallowing the remedy, "morphine hydrochloride and tincture of Indian hemp. I'll be better shortly."

As the train's motion slowed, a long whistle sounded, waking the rest of the travelers with a start. At the same moment an officer appeared, who hurried to set them at ease. The convoy was going to have to stop for two or three hours to fill up on water and coal. Baron Ulrich invited them to disembark and use the baths and restore themselves. The inn was under his troops' control, there was nothing to fear.

The train came to a stop in an open field, near a water tower perched on a high brick pedestal. Protected from freezing by a double-heated wall, the reservoir looked like a little log cabin with a snow-covered roof, with a metal chimney from which a continuous draft of white smoke spewed. A man was already working the crane arm to pivot it over the train. Right next to it, a motley assembly of blackened boards and framework formed the structure of the coal loader. Behind these service buildings, at the edge of a forest of snow-burdened firs, a large izba seemed to have been set down slightly lopsidedly by the hand of a clumsy model maker.

Despite the whole place's decrepit appearance—the pistachio green of the façade and the blue of the windows was flaking off, letting the grain of the wood show through—the inn cut a fine figure with its two symmetrical front buildings and the rounded skylight at its center.

They entered the common room. Most of the travelers sat down; faces drawn, clothes dirty and rumpled, they had the sad appearance of lost migrants. Some of them sought out news, interrogating the innkeeper about the possibility of rejoining the Sleeping-Car Company, demanding, ranting, bemoaning the loss of their personal effects, their money, the trunks that were still in the baggage car at the front of the train that had abandoned them. They were told that the telegraph line had been cut off for two days, and that they would have to wait until they got to Irkutsk before they would receive any answer to their questions.

A servant showed them where the baths were located, at the back of the inn. Describing these steam rooms, a wit once said, "They are to the Russians what the pipe is to the Germans"—that is, such a fundamental need that their happiness and their health seem to depend on it. Clawdia immediately wanted to try out their benefits on her daughter. As it was made clear to Kim that he was not allowed to enter the women's area, Miss Sherrington volunteered to help move her inside. They passed through a chamber fitted as a locker room before entering the banya itself.

Out of decency, this area was divided by a wooden partition into two separate rooms filled with the same sweltering heat of a Turkish bath. But, as the Russians see no drawbacks to letting the sexes mix in the baths, the partition was only as tall as a man and included a slatted connecting door. Set to heat on a large tiled stove, washing stones glistened in the dim light. An old serving woman sprayed them with water, setting off a new billow of steam. A bench of polished wood ran all around the room; white towels and pillows filled with aromatic plants were set out on it. Another servant, all smiles, showed them how to lash their bodies with the birch branches hanging in bunches from battens on the walls.

After having groomed Verity, with the assistance of Miss Sherrington—who had refused to disrobe completely and was suffocating in a linen shirt and knickerbockers with blue ribbons—Clawdia undid her bath towel and got into the hot water of a deep tub made of spruce staves. Closing her eyes, she let the heat pervade her, playing at making her chest sway lightly, content to feel herself floating, weightless. Mechanically, she checked the condition of the scars under her breasts, focusing on following their lines, in half-circles along the creases and, from the middle of these seams, coming up vertically to her nipples. The few men who had managed to come across this scarring—she tried to hide it from view through all sorts of subterfuges—had interpreted them as the result of some surgeon's unfortunate movement; she had never corrected these men, instead striking them from her mind forever. Canterel had been the only one who had softened at this soldering of pallid flesh, who had caressed it with the tips of his fingers, like a blind man feeling the hull of an armored schooner. It was to him alone that she had consented to recount the circumstances of her accident.

It was one Christmas Eve, at her parents' large country house in Montpellier-le-Vieux. She was seventeen and had just reread a message from a boy of her age who was arranging to meet with her at two o'clock in the morning, under the Door of Mycenae, the limestone arch where they had kissed for the first time, in the chaos of jagged rocks in that part of the Causse Noir. A storm was threatening. She had come down from her room to listen to the unbroken sound of her father's snoring, then gone back up to get ready. She would have had no need for finery, but she had wanted to inaugurate the tantalizing brassiere that she had found under the Christmas tree several hours earlier. A priceless wonder from Sabbia Rosa, a gift from her mother, who was trying to instill in her a taste for beautiful things. And it was true that this bustier, with its discreet metal frame, almost invisible under the raw silk from Lyon, had looked more like a luxurious treasure than a girl's undergarment.

She was just arriving at the arch when an endless roll of thunder began, echoing over the stumps of rocks that formed a landscape from some macabre folk tale around her. In the light of the rising moon, a dark nebula expanded, the striped core of the lightning. She stopped, frightened, as fat drops of rain broke on her forehead. It was at that moment that the sky seemed to open in two, and she fell in a heap on the moor: guided by the frame of her brassiere, a fork of lightning had struck her.

The scars were the indelible electrical mark of the metal ribs on her chest, the double lily of a meaningless brand.

Clawdia now relived this same feeling of helplessness when a hand suddenly clamped over her mouth, wrenching her neck back. The blade of a yatagan glinted for a moment before her eyes. She tried to call out, wriggled in her bath with all her might to escape this grasp, when a cry was heard, like the anguished wail of a dreamer cornered by his nightmare. Occupied by looking through the planks of the partition, Miss Sherrington turned around at this sound, her face reddened by a fever caused only in part by the steam. Without a moment of hesitation, she plunged her hand under her armpit and, in an astonishing movement whose stiffness was as remarkable as its speed, fired two successive shots at the attacker with her pocket pistol. He collapsed, mortally wounded.

At the sound of the reports, Grimod, stark naked, smashed through the door rather than opening it, and entered the room, quickly followed by Canterel and Prince Svechin, also unclothed. Clawdia was unscathed, luckily, but she was still shaking from the shock. Catching

Miss Sherrington's sidelong glance, Grimod covered himself with a sheet, imitated by his friends. The assailant was evidently a bather who had taken advantage of the fog of the steam room to sneak in among the women. He was lying on his stomach, his towel around his waist. Bending over him, Grimod checked for a pulse, then turned him over to examine him more closely. He was a man of Caucasian stock with a weather-beaten face, a tan that clashed with the sickly pallor of the rest of his body. In the course of this handling, his loincloth gaped open, revealing a frightful thing that looked like the swollen, brownish lips of a monkey's vulva.

"It's a woman!" exclaimed Grimod, stunned.

"A Skoptsy," said Prince Svechin, in a tone of negation. "Damn them! It's a eunuch, Creod scum!"

"He had the Greater Zeal, it seems," said Canterel; it was unclear how much he was joking.

"Indeed," replied the prince, a little astonished by the Frenchman's knowledge of this subject. "It is a total removal, what they call the Greater Seal. For the Lesser, they remove only the testicles."

"Good heavens!" exclaimed Clawdia, who was gradually coming to herself. "How is it possible?"

"It is Matthew's fault, dear madam. I quote the verse from memory: Matthew 19:12, 'For there are eunuchs who were born that from their mother's womb: and there are eunuchs who were made eunuchs by men: and there are also eunuchs who have made themselves eunuchs for the sake of the kingdom of heaven. He who is able to accept this, let him accept it.' Interpreted literally by a religious fanatic at the end of the eighteenth century, this simple phrase led to the creation of a sect whose believers castrate one another in order to reach Paradise more quickly. These 'White Doves,' as they call themselves once initiated, also mutilate women, in particular young girls, whom they immerse in a basin of hot water before slicing off their breasts; they chop the breasts into little pieces and then eat them in a ritual, like prophylactic communion bread. That's what was likely in store for you . . ."

"But that's insane," said Clawdia, her arms crossed over her chest. "To be nearly killed over such nonsense!"

"They are pests, scorpions who sting themselves to save their bodies from any capacity to feel lust. And, like all scorpions," the prince added, "they loathe the living."

They learned, furthermore, that the Skoptsy made up a force of one hundred thirty thousand adherents, spread through all of Siberia; they worked tirelessly to reach one hundred forty-four thousand, the limit, given in Acts, that would herald the coming of a Savior devoid of any sexual characteristics, a neuter Messiah who would secure for the world a kind of permanent vaccination against original sin. Canterel had picked up the yatagan and was examining it.

"You had a narrow escape," he said, running his finger along the edge of the blade. "It's razor-sharp."

"If it weren't for Miss Sherrington, I would be dead by now."

Everyone congratulated the housekeeper and asked her to recount the circumstances of her intervention. Without dwelling on where her attentions had been at the moment of the attack, she started by describing how much the heat of the room had been bothering her, and how she had thought she was going to faint if her discomfort got any worse, when she had heard Lady MacRae moan in that funny way.

"The kind of sound a dead chicken makes," she specified, "if you poke its carcass."

"How you're rewriting the story!" Clawdia interrupted, amused. "This person was smothering me, I doubt whether any audible sound could have escaped my throat. Even that of a dead chicken . . ."

Taken aback by this reasoning, Miss Sherrington fell silent, trying to recall the scene. She had been near the partition, not far from Lady

MacRae. The servants had left. Who then? It was at that moment that she turned toward the bench where Verity was sleeping.

Laid out, as always, the girl was breathing calmly. No change to her immobility, save that she had opened her eyes and, despite her lack of expression, was following their gestures with her gaze.

XXIV

A Horrible Disease Had Disfigured Her

Charlotte gets down from her stool, paintbrush in hand. She has stripped the diamond wallpaper, the phosphorescent stars, all the dead skin cells, all the ghosts; the walls have been washed, varnished, sanded. The second coat of Renaulac is finished, her room shines. It does indeed look like a fridge now. Better than paint, the advertisement said, "an enamel that gives the least object the luxurious appearance of a refrigerator." Everything is white, solid, impenetrable. She has even insulated the front door with foam seals to make it soundproof. And it seems to be working, not a sound since five o'clock this morning!

Charlotte looks at her watch and quickly gets changed. She has to hurry if she doesn't want to be late to the factory. She grabs her bag, opens the door, and cries out: Marthe is there, right at the door, hideous and miserable.

"What are you doing outside my door?"

"Sorry. There's someone coming up who stops at all the doors . . ."

"Well, fine. Listen, I don't have time. What's wrong?"

Marthe takes her by the sleeve, drags her into their den.

"Come, come in, my dear. I'm desperate, look, come . . . Chonchon took the wrong medicine. It happens a lot . . . Here, this one, what's it do?"

She shows Charlotte two containers of medication left on the table covered in transparent plastic that has gone fuzzy with grime. Through it, only the headlines of the newspapers protecting the Formica can be read.

"It's the same, the same as the other container."

"No, it's not."

"Yes, the labels say exactly the same thing."

"I'm desperate, give me a moment. This one's for me, and then that one . . . That one, what's that do, my dear?"

"How should I know, Marthe? I'm not a doctor! In any case, they're all the same . . ."

"Chonchon, he did it wrong. If he took one of those ones, it's gonna be so bad!"

"No, it isn't. Ask the doctor, he'll tell you."

"You don't think it's bad?"

"It's not bad."

"It's not gonna kill him, is it?"

"No, it won't kill him. He's tough, you know?"

The wretchedness of this place catches in her throat; she would like not to see, but her eyes register everything: the heaps of dirty laundry, battered suitcases, empty beer cans, the floor littered with garbage and broken glass, the cardboard packaging, the shoes. The big mattress lying on the ground, the office chair that's missing its back, the chest of drawers made of faux oak that is peeling off in strips from the eroded particleboard; it is a filthy alleyway on the night before garbage collection day. In a recess, behind the sparse ranks of a beaded curtain, a grease-caked gas stove sits next to a cracked sink. There is a kind of prayer mat fixed to the wall, showing Montmartre, the Arc de Triomphe, and the Eiffel Tower, and then some taped-up papers that have turned green from the moisture, receipts, reminders, a *Match* cover with large letters spelling out "Disaster: Runaway Train." A thermometer, a dome clock that only has an hour hand, and a badly stuffed hamster are sitting on the dresser. A framed black-and-white photo shows a young Swedish mother sitting near a cherub who is playing with some puppies.

"Charlotte?"

"Yes?"

"The post office, they withdraw money for people and all that?"

"Yes, of course."

"They do, huh?"

"Yes."

"I have to go to EDF today to pay my electric bill, but I can't go until tomorrow. D'you think they'll cut me off?"

"Oh, no . . ."

"I'm sorry. Chonchon was mad when he left. He told me: 'Get out, get the fuck out of here!' But when is he gonna come back?" She rolled her lips into the pout of a skeptical monkey. "I have no idea . . ."

"Of course he'll come back, he lives here."

"You think so? And you think I can go to EDF tomorrow morning?"

"Yes."

"They won't cut me off? I'm asking you, 'cause I'm desperate, you see . . ."

"Yes, I do see."

"It shows, huh? That I'm desperate?"

"Oh, it shows. Well, have a good day, I'm in a hurry."

"But you're coming back tonight?"

"Yes, I'm coming back, yes."

Marthe grabs the hem of her sweater.

"What's the number for emergencies?"

"It's this, the 1 and the 8."

"That doesn't bother you, does it? Wait, my dear. Oh, there it is, the 1 and the 8. Someone's very upset, because they're owed two months of rent. The deadline was the thirtieth."

"I have to go, Marthe!"

"But, tell me, they're not gonna throw us out like this?"

"Listen, I have no idea. You'll have to ask . . ."

Marthe takes her by the hand and pulls her over to the phone.

"Just a minute, come here, my pet. I'm desperate. Here, yes. Careful, the phone barely works. I'm desperate, Charlotte . . ."

Charlotte starts to cry as she checks the handset connection.

"Are you crying, dear?"

"Yeah . . . Come on, see if it works."

"No, nothing, nothing . . . The busy signal. I'll try another number?"

"If you want. Listen, I don't have time. What's the other number?"

Chonchon appears in the doorway.

"Your husband is here, he'll help you. I have to run."

Fabrice's mother, Lucette, had only waited one short year after her husband's death before she had replaced him. Fabrice had been six then, a bother. They sent him off to be raised in the country, by a couple of old friends, telling him that they were his grandparents. Eugène and Hortense Vitrac lived in Périgord, Lucette in Pigalle; she only made the journey once in two years before she evaporated.

The whole time, Fabrice had written to her every week, despite the disproportionate efforts that endeavor costs a child of that age. Especially since he would write a rough draft and then recopy it. His mother replied strangely, as if she were writing to an adult, in brief prattlings that made his heart tighten. In her letters she was always cheerful, telling a funny anecdote, describing the menu at a restaurant in detail, but never discussing the prospect of coming to get him. Though Hortense had kindly explained that this was certainly because she wanted to hide her pain at not being able to, she had hardly managed to console him.

And then, one day, Lucette stopped writing. The Vitracs stopped receiving their quarterly payment, the postman brought back their mail and Fabrice's with the notice "Wrong Address." Having gone to Paris to look for her, Eugène returned empty-handed. Fabrice's mother had disappeared; deliberately, it seemed, since she had contrived to cover her tracks. Fond of the child, Eugène and Hortense continued to take care of him without question.

For a long time, Fabrice came up with a thousand stories to excuse his mother. Gangsters had kidnapped her, she was in prison for a crime she had not committed, a horrible disease had disfigured her, she had died falling from a train and foxes had devoured her . . . But, when he was sixteen, Granny Hortense read him the short note that had accompanied the last installment of their payment: without giving any excuse or motive, Lucette begged them to take care of her child; she was abandoning him.

At the time, Fabrice had burned his mother's letters and forbidden anyone to speak of her in front of him. Now, approaching thirty, he would reread the drafts of the ones he had sent to her long ago. You might think it sounds like an exaggeration, but this is exactly what he would do, with tears in his eyes, at the tomb of Granny and Papa Vitrac, each time he pulled an all-nighter drumming away at his computer, trying to save the future of the world.

XXV

The Caspian Sea Monster

The train left an hour later, without any more mishaps among the passengers. A great deal was made of Verity's awakening, of course. Lady MacRae and Canterel displayed an unalloyed joy, but, having checked the girl's reflexes, Dr. Mardrus did his best to lower their expectations. Her recovery would be long, they would have to endure new trials, even more difficult than those they had gone through up to this point. The fact that Verity was following objects with her eyes showed that she had regained consciousness; but her face remained expressionless, her motor skills still lacking. There was nothing to indicate that her brain had not suffered some lesion that made her state irreversible.

"But she cried out," said Miss Sherrington, "she managed to warn me of the danger her mother was in!"

"We don't know that for sure," Mardrus corrected. "Even granting that it was she, it could have been a mere coincidence, an automatic response to the extreme heat of the baths. That was, in fact, your first impression: when one pushes sharply on the breast of a plucked and dressed chicken, said some philosopher whose name I no longer remember, the expelled air has the rather astonishing cry of an anguished bird; but do you believe that the woman who gives the same cry of surprise is any more conscious?" And, addressing Lady

MacRae gently: "Please don't misunderstand me. I'm not saying that your daughter is condemned, I'm merely saying that it is impossible to predict anything, and that you can't delude yourself, unless you want to suffer needlessly later."

If she continued to progress, as the doctor hoped she would despite everything, the poor child would remember nothing. At best, she would manage to recover the consciousness and memory of the little girl she had been at the moment of the shock that had plunged her into this catalepsy. But ten years had passed: "whatever happens, the lovely young lady we see before us has the mental age of a seven-year-old."

Not only would Verity have to relearn how to live, but she would also have to make up the lost time, which was no small task. They needed to prepare themselves.

In the meantime, they arrived in Irkutsk. Or, rather, they passed through it, as to their great surprise the train only slowed enough to allow a young Mongol in a fur hat to climb aboard, before accelerating to full speed and cutting through the city like a meteor. Half an hour later, Baron Ulrich came in to inform them in person of the bad news his agent had shared.

The Creationists had taken over Irkutsk; with the Virgin's Holy Robe as their standard, they were sacking and pillaging the city in the greatest of anarchy. His own troops were still holding the mouth of the Angara, and Ulan-Ude, on the other side of Lake Baikal, the railway junction where trains branched off to the south. The oriental line was still running, but the one across Mongolia had just been cut off at Naushki. Their own train, which had abandoned them during the Zepistos' attack, had only narrowly gotten through.

"Under these circumstances," said Baron Ulrich, "we must give up on getting you to China. The only thing I can do is leave you in Ulan-Ude, where you will be at your leisure to board a train to Vladivostok and take a boat from there to the destination that suits you. The good souls who have gone ahead of you dropped your bags off in Slyudyanka. We will stop there in a little over an hour to retrieve them."

This announcement was greeted with a profound silence, at first, then with various remarks of relief among the passengers; any situation being better than the prospect of remaining stuck right in the middle of this civil war. These feelings were not shared by Holmes and Canterel, who were seized by a cold fury at the turn events were taking.

"Damn, it's really over," said Holmes.

"So it seems, old chap."

Busy trying to stimulate Verity through all kinds of movements recommended by Dr. Mardrus, Lady MacRae did not appear affected in the least. Grimod bit his cheek, reinforcing the impression he gave of champing at the bit.

Seeing their crestfallen faces, Prince Svechin came over to inquire kindly as to what was causing their obvious unease. Holmes and Canterel looked at each other; despite the feelings of friendship that this figure inspired in them, they hesitated to confide in him. Grimod made up their minds for them and began to summarize the real reasons for their journey. When he was finished, the prince scrutinized them one by one, as if trying one last time to reassure himself, then took the leap.

"I know how to get you to Peking," he said in a low voice, "but I'm risking more than my life here. Not a word to anyone! In Slyudyanka, you will retrieve your bags, and you will wait for me. We will not get back on the train."

They agreed with slight nods of their heads, but with sparks of hope and gratitude in their eyes.

When the train stopped at Slyudyanka, a happy surprise was waiting for them: almost none of the luggage that they had stored in the baggage car was missing. Questioned by Holmes, a station employee told them that a little man with blue glasses had taken it upon himself to get everything checked and sealed up together in the storeroom where they found it. Dr. Mardrus pranced with joy at finding his instruments and manuscripts, but there came a moment when he noticed that, alone among all the passengers, neither Canterel nor Holmes nor Lady MacRae showed the slightest interest in picking out their effects so they could be placed in the wagons. Meeting Canterel's indifferent gaze, he suddenly understood that his new friends had no intention of leaving, and his face fell. Clawdia saw him, bewildered in the middle of the hustle and bustle, bowled over by his initial reaction. Overcome with remorse, she went to him, quickly informed him of the opportunity that the prince had afforded them, and invited him to stay with them.

"There's nothing left for me back in Irkutsk," said Mardrus, suddenly beaming with gratitude. "How can I ever thank you? Together, we are going to help your daughter pull through, I promise you!"

Prince Svechin had gone to say his goodbyes to Baron Ulrich. Upon learning that the prince and his friends were not continuing on with him, the baron cracked a half-smile.

"Always the same, isn't it? The widow and the orphan . . . But that's why I respect you. Can I do anything for you?"

"An escort to Listvyanka . . ."

"Listvyanka? You never cease to surprise me . . . But consider it done. Thirty of my best Buryats will accompany you."

"And six sleighs."

"And six sleighs . . ."

"Thank you. I wish you the best of luck in the coming times."

"The day you realize that it's better to die trying to change the world than to grow old watching it collapse, you'll join me."

"You'll already be dead, I'm afraid . . ."

"I hope so! Remember the words of our philosophy professor at Pavlovsk: 'He who does not die young regrets it sooner or later . . .' That stirred you at the time, if I remember correctly."

They looked at each other deeply with the affection and irony of old lovers, snapped their heels together smartly, and set off down their separate paths.

The armored train was just moving away when the prince reached the place where they were waiting for him, followed by six covered sleighs; Clawdia did not have to explain herself: Svechin met her eyes, turned his head toward Dr. Mardrus, looked back at her, and blinked in consent.

The crew loaded the luggage, huddled up under the warm covers, fastened their hoods, and then set off at a gallop over the ice of Lake Baikal, accompanied by Baron Ulrich's horsemen. It was twilight once again; bits of ice flew up from under the blades of their runners and traced behind them long lines, whose phosphorescence faded slowly.

Halfway to Listvyanka, which he had only mentioned to cover his tracks, the prince gave the order to turn north, toward Polovinka.

The first light of dawn gradually drew the outline of a fin-shaped opening that ended in a rocky inlet. This opening in the mountain was so narrow that it could only be seen from the lake from a certain angle of approach. The sleighs went in far enough to reach the gate and the launching ramp of what appeared to be a large boathouse carved into the mountain.

Svechin went up to a small door fitted into the gate and, with the butt of his pistol, gave it three quick raps, followed by three more widely spaced knocks, then three quick ones again. He was about to start over again when a peephole in the door opened, only to close again almost immediately. Keys clanked in locks, and the door opened to reveal a robust man in an ill-fitting leather jacket, his features puffy with sleep. He faced front, saluted, and then threw himself into the prince's arms.

"Sergeivich Svechin," he said, hugging him tightly, "heavens above, you haven't changed!"

"I can't say the same, Ivan Yevgenievich, you look like a muzhik! All you're missing are the baggy pants . . ."

"It won't be long," said the man, rubbing at the white bristles of his three-day stubble. "I shave, and I look ten years younger!"

"How is the Caspian sea monster?"

"It's getting old, too, but you can count on it."

"Then it's time, Vanya. We'll leave as soon as you're ready."

Ivan Yevgenievich adjusted himself, his face lit up with happiness; he hopped up and down for a moment, then disappeared, closing the small door behind him. After the sound of drawbars being removed, the heavy metal panels of the gate parted just enough to let him through; assisted by the Buryat horsemen they began to slide the gate open completely.

More and more intrigued, Canterel and his friends approached. What they saw inside the hangar made them take a step back.

In the half-light of the cavern, the muzzle of a huge, cold beast fixed them with its soulless stare: a mix between beetle and tarantula, with two batteries of multiple pupils protruding from its chitin armor. Their eyes growing accustomed to the light, they saw a streamlined machine, a metal vehicle covered in rivets from which rust was seeping like running mascara.

Canterel was the first to react.

"A pteroship!" he said, sounding like an old man seeing his first bicycle in a childhood photo.

"Not just any pteroship," clarified Grimod, with the enthusiasm of a connoisseur, "it's an Ekranoplan . . . A KM60 ground effect vehicle!"

"It looks like one," said Vanya, as he busied himself under the apparatus' wings, "but this one has been modified, it's a Tolstoy 1239. It doesn't just glide, it flies! At least, I hope . . ."

"We all do," said Canterel, raising an eyebrow.

"There have been that many models?" asked Holmes, astonished.

"It's the only one of its kind," Prince Svechin replied. "Vanya is a big romantic: 1,239 is the number of pages in the abridged edition of *War and Peace*."

"But what about fuel?" asked Grimod. "Don't tell me those engines run on methane or something, it's unfeasible."

The prince smiled and, shifting a few meters, showed them a stack of barrels marked with a red flame on a black background.

"Kerosene. We have enough for two or three flights, then it will be grounded for good."

"Unbelievable!" exclaimed Holmes. "Might as well put liquid gold in the tank of a wreck . . . Where did this godsend come from?"

"I'd explain, but for the moment there's no time to lose."

While they were talking, Ivan hitched the machine to two teams of horses. On his order, the Buryats pulled the cables taught and gave it the necessary momentum. Barely shaken, the vehicle slid smoothly down the inclined plane until it stopped of its own accord on the ice, about thirty meters from the hangar.

Set free, the monster was even more astonishing. Seventy meters long and forty wide, with the profile of a Chris-Craft hull, this blend of aircraft and seaplane had two sets of four adjustable turbojets immediately behind the cockpit. Its T-tail and short, forward-swept wings were bewildering in the immensity of their sails.

"Devil take me if this thing takes off!" said Holmes, raising his eyebrows.

Vanya was finishing climbing the ladder treads mounted to the fuselage; he clambered up to the door, unlocked it, and climbed into the cockpit; several minutes later, the whistling of the reactors swelled through the bay, echoing off the mountains. A hatch on the side dropped open almost immediately. Prince Svechin loaded up the bags, then invited his guests onto the craft, helping Canterel transport his daughter himself.

When this was done, the prince checked that all the elements necessary to the airship's preparation had been brought into the hangar and that, in front of the duly resealed panels, no evidence remained of their passage through this place. He then released Baron Ulrich's men, having first rewarded them generously, and hurried to rejoin his companions. The hatch closed behind him.

The Ekranoplan's eight reactors ramped up to produce the cushion of air it needed to move. Rising a few centimeters from the ground, the machine began to glide over the frozen surface of Baikal in a whirl of wind and vaporized ice.

In the cockpit, Ivan Yevgenievich was monitoring the dozens of trembling needles on the dials of the control panel. When one of the needles indicated they'd reached the speed necessary for takeoff, he lightly reared the vessel up and revved the engines. The Tolstoy 1239 rose up, right into the sun, with the slow majesty of a whale rising out of the sea.

Having reached the altitude of five hundred meters, Vanya stabilized the machine and allowed himself a long sigh of relief.

"It's in God's hands now!" he said, having knocked back a tiny bottle of vodka.

Sitting in the copilot's chair, Grimod was mopping at his forehead. "We're not going any higher?"

"It's not so bad, my friend! This thing is designed to fly just above the waves. Without my system of inversing the turbines, we would only be able to cross the lake. You know where we're going?"

"Peking, I think."

"Good. There aren't any mountains around there, at least not that I know of. If you can get out the maps and give me a route, it would be very kind of you. Navigation is not my strong suit."

XXVI

Giving the Finger to the Iron Locker

Despite the late hour, Monsieur Wang is still in his office. He is in a foul mood, combing through various listings, trying to forget what is bothering him: Free Legs Diamond has not returned. He knows pigeons never fly at night, but he is determined not to leave the factory, waiting, despite himself, for the loud signal that will announce the bird's return.

Louise Le Galle has also stayed. More of out compassion than professional obligation. She doesn't really care about the pigeon, but it makes her sad to see Wang in such a state. So she has gone back to reading the thick file on "lean management" that he asked her to synthesize to learn how to make it work at B@bil Books. The "lean" part is nothing complicated: this "bottom line" management really just means applying the rules of common sense, economy, and efficiency that were her bread and butter in the army. The 5S approach, for example, which is used to create an optimal work environment (*Seiri, Seiton, Seiso, Seiketsu, Shitsuke,* Japanese words that can be translated as sort, straighten, shine, standardize, sustain), seems modeled on the maintenance procedures for an assault rifle or a barracks. Devised and implemented in the postwar period by one of the founders of Toyota, these techniques have been part of a deliberate strategy to restore the Japanese economy, while also acting as a counteroffensive aimed at fighting the Americans on other terrain—manufacturing.

This approach, the file's author says, "must be piloted by a team of non-conservative people who are open to change and innovation, and who are familiar with the operations at each work station." Louise sees herself in this statement. She knows how to spot black sheep, shirkers, people who are unembarrassed by dirt or clutter, for the simple reason that these deficiencies are just a slightly distorted reflection of their mental structure. These were the same people who stole ammo or vials of morphine without thinking for a second about the repercussions that this could have in combat.

Same with 5G, the simple steps to solving a given problem. *Gemba, Gembutsu, Genjitsu, Genri, Gensoku*: put yourself in the real place, observe the real thing, collect the real facts, refer to procedures, and re-establish good practices—or else come up with better ones. What else had she done in Afghanistan? Louise remembers a particularly enlightening incident, at Tora, in a division of the "Advisory Team" that she had been asked to take command of. A mutinous atmosphere prevailed among the soldiers. Several of them had refused to participate in training operations with the members of the Afghan army they had been charged with instructing. Disciplinary sanctions had been redoubled but this had not curbed the wave of disobedience.

"Lieutenant Le Galle?" the base commander had said, surprised that such a task had been entrusted to the young man he was back then.

Louise once again sees the suspicious look the commander had given the lieutenant's slightly odd, effeminate appearance, imagines his face if the situation were to repeat itself today . . . She smiles. Barely six days later, this same ass-kisser had warmly congratulated her.

She had insisted on accompanying a squad—the Dantès Division—into the Uzbin Valley, ten kilometers from the outpost at Tora, followed by about fifteen soldiers from the Afghan army. The first rocket had exploded thirty meters from their convoy right as they were entering a village in the area. The troop had taken cover, fighting back toward the ridge, while the inhabitants hid in their huts. Called to the rescue, a Tiger from BatHélico had flown in an hour later and cleaned out the hills. At the end of the fight, they lamented one severely wounded soldier among the French, a sergeant who had taken several slugs to the legs. A volley from a FAMAS fired by one of the Afghanis he was instructing and who had managed to escape. This was what was going wrong: the French troops were being shot in the back on a regular basis; on top of the fear of ambush, they had to cope with the fear of being targeted by the men they themselves had trained in the art of war. Regulations wanted French soldiers to always go in front of the Afghan recruits on the ground, because this was their mission: to lead and guide. Louise recommended that this procedure be modified. From the moment the rumor went around that the Afghan soldiers would now be moved to the front line, the mutinous sentiment evaporated.

A singular mixture of pride and nostalgia pushed her back in her chair. She regrets nothing, but she misses the straightforward excitement of combat at times, such as now.

And 3M, *Mura*, *Muda*, *Muri*: waste, inconsistency, overburden. The three evils that a business must eradicate in order to attain excellence, "Zero Defects." Satisfying this requirement means that if even one in a hundred products is defective, it counts as accepting deliberate waste, and thus foregoing a great deal of profit. To explain how *Muda* comes into being, the manual gives the example of a machine that began to use more oil than usual. The error was the choice to increase the supply of oil to prevent the risk of a breakdown, rather than first seeking to eliminate leakage. And indeed, a month earlier, they had a problem with toilet paper here, the employees began to use twice as much as usual, so much that the question was posed of increasing the supply. Pondering the possible causes of this overconsumption, Louise thought "food," "cafeteria," and noticed that the head chef had altered the menus to lean more heavily on spinach and prunes, foods that are natural laxatives. Once the balance of the meals was restored, the overconsumption of paper subsided.

Louise feels that she has mastered all these techniques, and she should finish up this file and go to bed. But she has a niggling suspicion this evening: Wang is interested in someone else. These last few weeks, she has noticed how he has paused for longer behind Charlotte Dufrène during his daily inspection, but this afternoon he asked outright to look at her file.

"That girl radiates intelligence," he said, "I would like to see if we can entrust her with more responsibilities within the company."

Intelligence my ass! Everyone had seen how he squinted at her rack . . . That, too, was a dysfunction, a perfect example of *Muri*, of a useless operation, labor that is unnecessary, misspent, underutilized.

Doubtless there was a little bit of jealousy in what she had just decided to do, but it was first and foremost for the the sake of the company. The idea that such an action could seem reprehensible did not even cross her mind. She put the file in a drawer, grabbed her things, and cracked open the manager's door to let him know she was going home.

Too busy scrutinizing the night, Monsieur Wang did not bother turning around to say goodnight. He was imagining Free Legs Diamond perched somewhere, perhaps injured, at the mercy of a cat or a falcon. His bird had left Biarritz in optimal weather conditions: wind from the southwest, perfect visibility; he did not understand what could have delayed him. This waiting was driving him up the wall, he felt the feverish helplessness of a hunter deprived of his weapon; really, he was telling himself, it was like sitting next to a tree and hoping for a rabbit to smack into it and stun itself.

When his iPad gave off a loud signal, he jumped, thinking his pigeon had returned, then, disappointed, he glanced at the screen. It was his personal surveillance system: someone had just entered the women's locker room. Louise, in this case. Wang watched her mechanically: he saw her snoop along the lockers, reading the DYMO labels glued to each one; having located the one she was looking for, the Director of Human Resources opened it with a master key and busied herself under a shelf, working to fasten something to it with the help of a fat roll of tape. She relocked the door, made as if to turn away, changed her mind; as she turned back around and paused for a second, he saw her give the finger to the iron locker. The camera was placed in such a way that he had the very disagreeable impression that this gesture was meant for him.

XXVII

Too Well Hung to Impregnate a Girl

Once the Ekranoplan had reached its cruising speed, Prince Svechin made a point of clarifying the mysterious aspects of their extraordinary escape. Alarmed by the situation in his country, the Archimandrake had charged him with hand-delivering a message to the Protodeacon of Port-Arthur. It was a distress call: in it, the Archimandrake painted a dark picture of the uprisings that were devastating Russia and for the first time asked for the help of the Powers. Without their aid, he did not think that he was likely to survive, nor that they would outlive him by much, such was the fanaticism currently menacing the very structure of the civilized world. The Archimandrake had granted him the broadest powers to complete his mission, including the use of the vehicle in which they now found themselves.

"It is Ataman Semenov's plane," said the prince, "the one he once used to flee Siberia, leaving his troops behind. His Highness had it restored years ago, anticipating a time of need. Ivan Yevgenievich is the engineer who dedicated his life to revamping the machine, altering it, then maintaining it meticulously in order to have it ready to serve a noble cause when the time came. It so happens that this admirable man is also my uncle."

Holmes, who was just opening up a bottle of Tulamore drawn from his reserves, proposed a toast to Ivan's health, in which everyone gratefully participated.

Once the prince had returned to the pilot's seat, they all stretched out and tried to get some rest. Busy with his notes, Dr. Mardrus was soon nodding off over his notebook; Clawdia and Verity went peacefully to sleep, followed shortly by Kim and Miss Sherrington. As for Holmes, he seemed determined to sip at his scotch until it was all gone.

Canterel swallowed another dose of Chlorodyne and tried in vain to get to sleep. Besides the unbearable humming of the motors, a thought was bothering him. He chewed it over for several long minutes without managing to unravel it, got himself worked up, then opened his eyes, overwrought.

"So who is he, really?" he asked, in a tone that did not allow for any more evasions.

"Damn!" said Holmes, surprised. "You frightened me! Who are you talking about?"

"Grimod, of course! If we are to remain friends, I implore you to tell me who this fellow is."

Cornered, Holmes relented. We will summarize, to avoid the length and embellishments that the number of single malts—which it would be dishonest not to mention—caused to tarnish the clarity of his tale:

Perhaps the reader remembers the awful story that once cast a pall over Falconhurst, Alabama. There, Warren Maxwell had a slave-breeding plantation whose success was envied as far away as Louisiana. Weakened by rheumatism, the master of Falconhurst was now pushing his only son, Hammond, a young man who was simple, honest, well built despite his lame leg—he had fallen off a horse at the age of five—a true Maxwell whose sudden passion for slave-fights his father condoned. Did he not himself have an infatuation with pure Mandingos, the strongest, the most docile Blacks, the ones who made the best slaves if you took care not to crossbreed them? All things considered, the only thing Maxwell's son was missing was a wife capable of giving him an heir, a union that he had recently begun working to promote.

Anxious to obey his father, Hammond went off to ask for the hand of a cousin who lived some sixty miles from Falconhurst. A silly young sixteen-year-old named Blanche, whose parents handed her over without a fuss, all too happy to pocket the dowry of three thousand dollars that was about to pay off their debts.

On the way back home, Hammond stopped off at the house of a friend of his father, Mr. Wilson, a scatterbrained man of culture whose advanced age seemed to have carried him to the shores of senility rather than wisdom: also a slave breeder, this extraordinary person lived in such harmony with his slaves that he refused to sell them, in defiance of the most elementary laws of economics, preferring to multiply the mortgages on his abode rather than separate a negress from a single one of her children. Beloved patriarch of his population of serfs, the fellow was waiting for death quietly and with a great many swigs of an excellent Madeira. It was at this house, in the person of Ganymede, a superb Mandingo who had just reached maturity, that the father's hobby combined with the son's: Hammond immediately saw in Ganymede the "fightin' nigger" he dreamed of, as well as the studhorse that would enable his father to continue his racial breeding.

Out of friendship toward Warren Maxwell, and after having asked Ganymede what he thought of the idea, Mr. Wilson consented to let him go with Hammond. He warned his guest, however, that Mede, as he called him, was much too well hung to impregnate a girl without tearing her open first. To which the young Maxwell replied that he had already been confronted with this problem and that there was no member so thick that a little suet would not allow it to enter even the tightest female.

Returning to Falconhurst with Mede, he immediately began training him hard, preparing him to face the country's champions.

After their marriage, Hammond honored his new wife with a single night, then abandoned her bed to continue sleeping with his favorite slave, Ellen, with whom he was so infatuated that he gave her a gift of earrings. Mede won all his fights; as for the elder Maxwell, he seemed rejuvenated by having a daughter-in-law to keep him company. Everything appeared to be in order.

This, as you may guess, was only an illusion. Forsaken by her husband, jealous of Ellen, Blanche took to drink, then plotted her revenge. One day, when Hammond was out, she made Mede come to her room and forced him to couple with her. Satisfied by this first experience, she repeated it as often as possible. To make his father happy and to provide him the grandson he desired, Hammond came to lie with his wife from time to time. When Blanche became preg nant, no one doubted, not even she, that the unborn child was the fruit of these conjugal visits.

The announcement of this pregnancy brought the two Maxwells great joy. They carried her to term as best they could.

Blanche's mother, Beatrix, came to Falconhurst two weeks before the expected due date. When the moment came, Hammond went to get Dr. Redfield, the estate veterinarian, and his new assistant, Widow Johnson, who had served as the region's midwife for ages. She officiated upstairs, assisted by Beatrix, while the men, a little anxious, drank toddy after toddy as they awaited the result. Girl or boy? The answer was of the greatest interest to Hammond, who would very much have liked to cease all physical relations with Blanche once his line was assured.

When the baby appeared, and the women saw that it was black, it was Beatrix who took it by the feet and smashed its skull against the marble fireplace. At the announcement of this, the elder Maxwell said that she had done what was necessary, and called for another toddy. For Hammond, the thing was simply impossible to swallow. Cuckolded by his fighting slave, ridiculed in front of all the blacks on his plantation, and affected in his very standing as a white owner, with his father's consent he took the only steps that seemed to him likely to restore his honor. He began by poisoning his wife, giving her a remedy supplied by Dr. Redfield, a foolproof powder used to "shorten negroes' suffering," and ordered that same doctor to get rid of the little corpse. Blanche was buried that very evening. In the early morning, Hammond forced the Mandingo into a huge cauldron of salted water set over a blaze. He had already "salted" Mede several times to harden his skin for fighting, but this time he boiled him until his flesh and bones were completely dissolved. Bucket after bucket, he then had this human soup poured over the still-fresh grave of his wife.

The next day, he left Falconhurst to start a new life in another state, and no one ever heard from him again.

And that is the tale of Hammond Maxwell and his Mandingo, such as it has come down to us and such as he himself, in spite of his terrible vengeance, hoped it would be spun. He did not know that it had a sequel—certainly a happier one, but one that remains no less worthy of being told.

As he was getting rid of the newborn, whose features and sturdiness pointed to Ganymede's offense better than any denunciation, Dr. Redfield realized with horror that the child was still alive. Despite the blood plastered to its face, the infant had opened its eyes; it was trembling in the doctor's hands. Redfield could not say why he did it—out of veterinary instinct, he would say to silence the midwife when she reproached him in action—but he brought the little one home, clothed him, fed him, and kept him by his side until the baby, with his abnormally hardy constitution, had recovered. He named the child Jason, and gave him to a negress from his plantation to raise.

Aside from the scar across his forehead—the exact imprint of the marble molding his head had struck—the child was good-looking. He was quick-witted, strapping, and endowed with uncommonly manly attributes. When he was old enough to be sold, Dr. Redfield got a thousand dollars for him from a traveling slave trader, who brought him to New Orleans and traded him for five times that to Monsieur Roche, a Frenchman who introduced himself as the natural son of the old governor, Baron de Carondel. A notorious pedophile, Monsieur Roche flaunted him in front of his friends and used him for three years as his catamite and personal bed warmer. It was this man who rechristened him Grimod, in memory and mockery of the famous Grimod de La Reynière, whose gastronomic excesses—such as those funereal meals where only the color black was allowed—Roche took as a challenge.

When the child became reluctant to serve as his candlestick-holder and grew impertinent, even aggressive, Roche chastised him by locking him in a pigsty for a night. Grimod came out horribly mutilated, with three fingers missing from his right hand. Disgusted, his master sold him to an English lord who was on his way back to his own country.

This was Grimod's chance. On top of having a large fortune, Lord Edward Glenarvan, Laird of Malcom Castle, a beautiful family estate on the shores of Loch Lomond, was a good and generous man. Ardent defender of Scotland—only a Frenchman would have taken him for an Englishman for even a second!—avowed abolitionist, member of the very exclusive Royal Thames Yacht Club, he publicly adopted the child, attracting the reprobation of his peers in the Chamber of Lords.

Grimod benefited from the best education; he proved so brilliant in his studies at the Edinburgh Academy that he entered Magdalen College at Oxford two years early. Fitted with a prosthesis whose clever machinery voided his hand's disability but forced him to wear a glove, he showed a certain talent for watercolor and excelled at tennis and rowing. He graduated at the age of twenty-three and went to London to pursue his research as an anatomist, all while frequenting the most avant-garde literary circles of the era. A juvenile but pleasant undertaking, which consisted of extolling great aristocrats of the mind that Oscar Wilde, Baudelaire, and Jules Barbey d'Aurevilly were of their time.

It was during this period that Lord Glenarvan registered his yacht for a prestigious regatta, hoping that his victory would once again serve the honor of the Highlands. To the grief of his friends, he disappeared in the Irish Sea when the *Duncan* was wrecked on the Maidens. In his will, he left his adoptive son the entirety of his riches.

"By the Holy Foreskin of Chartres," Canterel exclaimed, "are you going to explain to me what such a man is doing in your employ?"

"That," said Holmes, with palpable unease, "is another story entirely . . . You wouldn't by any chance go find me another bottle, would you?"

XXVIII

An Extended Fly

Her legs are nestled against each other, folded, welded into a mermaid's tail beneath the comforter. Her left arm is resting on the thick pillow she is holding tight against her chest. Nearby, the mirror on the wardrobe reflects the unmade bed. Carmen has just woken up. But she has to get up, Dieumercie left for work a long time ago, and Madame Lemercier is expecting her ironing at ten. The hum of an insect brings her out of her semi-coma, she cracks her eyes open to see a strange fly has just landed on the pillow. An extended fly. Focusing her gaze, she realizes that it is actually two flies in the process of mating. They are still, but with careful attention one can see the male's abdomen pulsating, and his back and forth movement inside the female. Fascinated, Carmen observes the metallic luster of this tiny coitus. The muscles of her thighs copy its rhythm. Extremely slowly, she walks the fingers of her right hand across her skin, first around her navel, then her lower abdomen. She touches herself, surrenders herself to the matte smoothness under her fleshy parts. The flies' performance excites her. Images come to her, of orgies and proliferating erections. The dirty old man whose house she cleans every Thursday morning buys porn magazines, he leaves them lying on the tables, open to certain pages, as if he has just stopped reading, but she can see that he arranges them in strategic places where she can't help but come across them. The kind of perverse messages meant to fluster her, as he behaves normally toward her, acts like the very soul of discretion and kindness. So she reads, she reads and she learns. The records held by certain porn stars: Annabel Chong, 251 men in ten hours; Spontaneus Xtasy, 551 partners; Candy Apples, 721 lovemaking sessions in a row, stopped in her attempt at a "kilobang" (1,000 men) by the intervention of the police. So many stiff cocks, some long, some thick, some curved, so many warm squirts onto her breasts, into her mouth, between her wide-open legs. Madame Bonacieux moans, she tries to imagine the volume of semen that such a feat would produce. Two or three liters? Enough to fill the sink? A bathtub? She read that a certain Trucula Dukon used sperm cures to lose weight. Ten tablespoons per day for a month, consuming no other food. How many daily blowjobs did it take to keep up that diet? Did it nourish her even a little? Was there a process, seasoning tips, a recipe book? "Snow balls" with salmon roe, ejaculate over minced ginger, jellied semen served in an oyster shell and sprinkled with Espelette pepper? She also remembers that ad for a dildo shaped like a Doberman's member. A penis distorted by a double hump in its middle, with a glans the shape of a red quince, the right color for that organ but striated with opaline streaks; an alien mess that she wants to feel spasm deep inside her. Her middle finger quickens its motion on her clitoris. Why not buy a dog now that Pile-poil is dead? Her vision blurs, a black cloud limns shifting swirls: hundreds of mating flies cover a face. A murmur of pleasure escapes its lips, and as the ink of insects thins, she recognizes the features of Jean-Johnny Hercule, her husband's friend.

XXIX

The Three-Jeweled Eunuch

Vanya landed his machine on the lake at the Summer Palace, long enough to unload the passengers and their luggage, then took off again for Port Arthur.

They dropped Clawdia and Verity of at the Grand Hotel Peking, leaving them in the care of Miss Sherrington and Dr. Mardrus. Focused on their objective, Martial, Holmes, and Grimod rushed to the address that had led them so far into the East. They brought Kim with them, sure that his knowledge of Mandarin could be useful.

Hugh Palmer's boutique was located at 97 Morrison Street in Liulichang, the antiques district of Peking. Its façade of newly re-painted wood, decorated with *Sang de Boeuf* columns and scrolls of sky-blue clouds, was only one story tall, at the heart of a labyrinth of alleys swarming with pedestrians, wheelbarrows, and rickshaw runners; countless lanterns with golden tassels swayed above their path under the eaves of the buildings. These sorts of shops were everywhere, their windows cluttered with curios, paintings, and cal-ligraphy. Brushes of every size, some as big as flyswatters, hung from walls of gray brick. Beneath them scurried huge rats.

This *hutong* was not ten years old, but it was dilapidated enough that it looked a hundred years older.

Above the door, two ideograms stated the store's name: "Three Jewels"; to the right of the entrance a gleaming copper plaque read: "Mr. Hugh Palmer, art dealer accredited by Messrs. the Ambassadors, great Chinese art connoisseurs."

The proprietor was a man more pudgy than plump, a Shanghai native who looked like a Benedictine monk, with the eyes that looked like Buddha's, but dull, and the smile of a complicit grandmother. The most anxious of customers were reassured after talking with him, and even his presence seemed to guarantee that they would be dealt with fairly. Listening to him discourse on any of the works in his boutique was a delight.

An hour earlier, he had begun by explaining to them how a Muslim eunuch of the fifteenth century, Admiral Zheng He, had brought back from one of his voyages a boatload of ivory, tortoiseshell, and rhino horns, which had earned him the glorious title of the Three-Jeweled Eunuch; a nickname with which our collector liked to adorn himself, though he was not lacking anything—he insisted on making clear—in that department. In truth, everyone called him "Bunny," an insulting soubriquet that played off his assumed taste for pederasty.

The interior of the shop was arranged like a curio cabinet. The walls were of cherry-pink damask with an acanthus-leaf pattern. An amber-hued cabinet stood facing the doorway; on its shelves were arranged a stack of scroll paintings, two decorative-tile mouthpieces from the Ming tombs, several snuffboxes decorated with birds on flowering branches, and, in its original case, an enamel watch made by François-Louis Stadlin, engraved with the name of the Kangxi Emperor. On other stands as precious as the objects they displayed, one could see a Nile-green bronze wine vessel, a Dunhuang manuscript, a piece of pottery with a three-colored glaze featuring a horsewoman aiming her bow at the clouds; blue and white porcelain from the Yongle era sat near priceless spittoons of beige sandstone; ancient ivory contended with cups made of rhino horn. Other rarities left one speechless: an autumn fan painted by Osaki Tanako, two pieces of jade from Princess Dou Wan's burial suit, an intact sheet of the *Lantingji Xu*, written in 353 "in the drunkenness of joy and pure words"; among the ventral shells of turtles carved with oracular inscriptions, a *penzai*—a "garden of little nothings"—simulated an island. There was also a Cremona cello.

Upon seeing this instrument, Canterel spun around and looked down: seated on the floor, his arms bound behind a pillar of old mahogany, naked as a blanched pig, was Hugh Palmer, his eyes staring, bulging with surprise more than terror. His guts stretched out from an incision in the crease of his lower abdomen to reach a mechanical spit two meters away, around which the rest of his intestines had already been wound. Only now did they finally register the sound of the mechanism jangling and rattling with repeating jolts. In the slatted light that fell through the windows, this capstan of organs looked like yet another ivory wonder.

"Too late!" said Grimod, bending over the tortured man.

"The poor man!" Holmes gasped, having stopped the mechanism.

"Sweet Christ!" said Canterel, a cambric handkerchief over his nose.

"This suggests that the monster who did this just left," said Holmes. "He got nothing for his trouble: the safe is untouched."

"Who's to say he didn't close it again before leaving?" Grimod said, approaching the heavy, red-lacquer cabinet that his friend was examining.

It had a combination lock with a line of four knobs with numbered dials; two safety locks, each covered by a protective plate, flanked the device. Above it, in fine calligraphy, an inscription read:

施氏食獅史
石室詩士施氏, 嗜獅, 誓食十獅
氏時時適市視獅

十時, 適十獅適市

是時, 適施氏適市

氏視是十獅, 恃矢勢, 使是十獅逝世

氏拾是十獅屍, 適石室

石室濕, 氏使侍拭石室

石室拭, 氏始試食是十獅

食時, 始識是十獅, 實十石獅屍

試釋是事

"Lucky we thought to bring you with us," Holmes said to Kim. "Are you able to read this text?"

The valet complied, translating line by line without apparent effort.

"The Lion-Eating Poet in the Stone Den.

"In a stone den lived a poet called Shi, who loved to eat lions and had decided to eat ten.

"He often went to the market to look for lions.

"One day, at ten o'clock, ten lions arrived at the market.

"At that time, Shi had also just arrived.

"He saw the lions, and killed them with his arrows.

"He brought the corpses of the ten lions to his stone den.

"The stone den was damp. He asked his servants to dry it.

"After the stone den was dry, he tried to eat those ten lions.

"When he ate, he realized that those ten lions were in fact ten stone lions.

"Explain this."

"Thank you," said Holmes, doubtfully. "I rather fear that we are no further along."

"Yet these old lions are hiding something," Grimod exclaimed in frustration, "I'd stake my life on it!"

Looking pensive, Canterel repeated to himself the words that had just been spoken; seized by an idea, he snatched up the cello and shook it, making a metal object inside it ring. He upended the instrument, then contrived to slide the object toward the F-holes.

"And here, perhaps, is the start of a solution," he said, seeing two little keys fall to the floor.

Holmes immediately tried them in the safe's locks: they fit perfectly.

"There's still the combination," said Canterel, "but I've got nothing. It should, however, derive from the characters that we have before our eyes, since the text itself invites us to decode it."

"The story of these lions does not seem to make any sense," said Holmes. "I have no doubt of Kim's abilities, but maybe we should have it translated by someone else?"

"If I may," said Kim, "there's no point. I know what this is: an exercise designed to demonstrate the limits of pinyin. I was taught it when I was very young, when I started to learn Chinese."

Taking a deep breath, he reread the text aloud.

"Shī Shì shí shí shì:

"Shíshì shīshì Shī Shì, shì shī, shì shí shí shī.

"Shì shíshí shì shì shì shī.

"Shí shí, shì shí shī shì shì.

"Shì shí, shì Shī Shì shì shì.

"Shì shì shì shí shī, shì shī shì, shì shì shí shī shìshì.

"Shì shí shì shí shī shī, shì shíshì.

"Shíshì shī, Shì shí shì shì shíshì.

"Shíshì shì, Shì shí shì shí shì shí shī.

"Shí shí, shì shí shì shí shī shī, shí shí shí shī shī."

"It all becomes clear . . ." grumbled Holmes, looking defeated. "If I didn't know you so well, I'd be inclined to think you were mocking us."

"God forbid," said Kim calmly. "As you heard, the characters chosen to compose this text are all pronounced the same way, with some differences in intonation. The point being less their meaning, than to show how ridiculously incomprehensible it becomes when transcribed."

"Certain ideograms repeat fairly often, don't they?" Canterel noted, bent over the inscription.

"Yes," said Kim, "of the ninety-two characters, there are only thirty-three that don't recur."

"So then, let's try this," he said, turning the dials one by one: nine, two, three, and three.

He drew back, turned the two keys at the same time, and, to everyone's astonishment, the safe opened.

"Hats off, my friend!" said Holmes.

"Unbelievable!" Grimod added admiringly.

They hurried to look inside. The safe was empty, alas, except for a central tray where two objects were in evidence: a poorly printed pamphlet and a hemispherical mirror.

In a quick gesture of vexation, Holmes punched the palm of his left hand.

"If the diamond really did make it here, the Straddler got to it before us . . . How did he do it, by God?"

Kim took advantage of this moment of disappointment to look inside the safe for himself; a vague smile on his lips, he hastened to comfort them.

"No one opened this cabinet before you," he said, confident, "I've seen these objects before. They were with the diamond in Lady Mac-Rae's safe."

"What?" said Grimod. "Why wouldn't she have told us about them?"

"Ask her," replied Kim, "but I imagine she did not lend them any importance. As little, in any case, as you just did."

"This changes things," said Canterel. "For a reason we are not aware of, the diamond continued on its way even before the Noh

Straddler arrived; these objects attest, therefore, not only that we are following the right trail, but also that this poor man let himself be gutted rather than see them pass into other hands."

Placed on a pedestal with a mother-of-pearl inlay, the pamphlet and the mirror, on examination, only served to increase the mystery. The booklet was entitled *The Breviary for Lottery Players*, it was two hundred twenty pages long and gave only this information regarding its provenance: "10th Edition, Les Ateliers Fardin, Port-au-Prince, Haiti." The mirror was mounted on a smaller nickel-plated screw thread impeccably set into the surface of the glass. It was eight to ten centimeters in diameter as far as could be guessed without taking precise measurements; etched in almost imperceptible italics around its base, just at the start of the curvature, were reproduced the words of St. Paul in his letter to the Corinthians: "For now we see through a glass, darkly; but then face to face."

All of a sudden, they heard a noise like the scrabbling of a dog slipping across a floor. A finger over his mouth to call for silence, Grimod drew his revolver; he approached a folding screen whose panels were still shaking in their frames when a terrified creature escaped from behind it. It was a chimpanzee, its arms raised protectively above its head. Rigged out in a costume of yellow silk, like Sun Wukong in *Journey to the West*, the added absurdity was the fact that he was fitted with a black-lacquer prosthetic leg. On his left shoe, they immediately recognized the Ananke brand.

"Another one!" said Canterel, perking up.

Seeing his master, the animal overcame his fear and hobbled over to him. He lifted one of the cadaver's arms, was astonished to see it fall, tried again, then began to utter heartbreaking wails while inspecting the man's mouth. He found a wad of paper, which he extricated delicately; having sniffed at it, he threw it behind him.

Holmes picked it up. It was a snippet of a black-and-white photo that the collector had obviously tried to keep from his attacker.

Unfolded, it became apparent that the entire right side of the image had been torn away. The remaining half showed a pretty young Asian woman sitting cross-legged on a bed, her bent knee giving a narrow, suggestive view onto the curve of her thigh. Dressed in a revealing nightgown, she was inclining her torso in the pose of the Boy with Thorn, with whatever she was fussing at hidden from view, her left leg and hip cut off by the tear. Her eyes half-closed under dark brows, mouth painted, hair woven in a braid that fell to the top of her breasts, she looked like a stage actress. An impression confirmed by the signature written in white across the photo.

"Sarah Bernhardt?" read Holmes, incredulous.

"Looks like it," said Canterel. "This time, we know exactly what we're looking for."

"A Chinese woman who goes by the name of Sarah Bernhardt?"

"No, my dear: a woman with a wooden leg."

XXX

The Cigar Makers' Bible

In 1835, well before the introduction of reading in the Caribbean tobacco factories, people were reading aloud in the nascent capitals of the industrial revolution, in London, Edinburgh, Glasgow. Not in the mechanized factories where the noise of the steam engines would have prevented hearing anything, but in the workshops of tailors, watchmakers, and cabinetmakers. The craftsmen would chip in every morning to buy the newspaper, and one of them would read it aloud during the workday. For the most part, this was all the education they received, but it was from among these people who had been read to that the pioneers of the labor movement in the nineteenth century emerged.

In Cuba, certain readers had forged such connections in progressive circles that they managed to get news first hand and pass it along to the workers before the stories appeared in the papers. Unsurprising, then, that one José Martí had immediately foreseen the good that could come from such a platform: it was in the factories of Tampa and Key West, through the voices of the readers who recited his speeches to the Cuban tobacco rollers, that he had succeeded in triggering the war of independence. "Some write on the bark of trees," he had said, paying tribute to them, "others roll the leaves of tobacco; on one table ink, on the other filler and wrapper. With the tobacco leaf, all that remains is the courage of the worker, but with the written page there sometimes lingers the reason for its right and the means to achieve it."

Dulcie knew these beautiful formulas by heart, but kept them in their context. If the reading of newspapers and political propaganda within the workshops had indeed served Martí's cause at that time, they still shouldn't be taken for a panacea. The raising of awareness was owed first and foremost to literature.

"Marx," she would say, "Proudhon, Stirner, and others, their texts were chosen in defiance, to annoy the bosses a little; just extracts, most of the time, they were good in small doses. The papers, it must be confessed, were boring, apart from the news. No, it's really novels that opened our minds . . ."

And a madness for learning, thinks Arnaud, remembering.

The madness of Edmond Dantès, abandoned in his cell, save that the voice of a fellow sufferer managed to save him from suicide and darkness. This prisoner, Abbé Faria, is an unjustly imprisoned scholar; like a castaway on a desert island, he has recreated everything he has missed over the years: he makes paper from his shirts, dip pens from fish bones, ink from his blood and sweat; the high window in his cell serves as his sundial, the fat from his meager rations a candle that he lights with two flints. Prison has reduced him to a kind of primitive animality, but unlike Dantès, whom seems to be on the verge of letting go, the abbot has managed to find the resources to rebuild an embryo of civilization, to try to remain a man to the bitter end.

This strong character works out a foolproof escape plan, concocts the ruses that will allow them to blind their guard and escape from the crypt where they are held captive.

He also proves to have a prodigious capacity for deduction. From a few elements furnished by Dantès, he reconstructs the mechanism that led to his incarceration, names the traitors, identifies the informants. Equal to the best armchair detectives, he deciphers a mysterious message in which the coordinates of a buried treasure are inscribed!

Ingenuity, cunning, pure logic: Abbé Faria is Robinson Crusoe, Ulysses, and Chevalier Dupin at once. But this combination is not the result of mere chance; the man is a living library, a reader who stays standing thanks to certain select books. One hundred fifty works, to be precise, read and reread so many times that he knew them by heart before his arrest; a digest of science and philosophy that he is still able to recite aloud in the hostile silence of his jail. This is the real treasure, the source of life that Abbé Faria will orally pass on to Dantès, day after day for years, until his disciple also manages to escape mentally, to walk free on the paths of knowledge before hoping to do so outside his prison.

A humanist education program, the promise of an oasis that does not preclude vengeance or farewells.

Arnaud has just realized why *The Count of Monte Cristo*, more than any other book, was always the cigar makers' bible.

Last Telegrams of the Night

Things that make the horrible sound of castanets without indicating the presence of a Spanish woman.

In a short time, the unfortunate woman was reduced to a little heap of ashes in which her charred bones crackled from the heat. A doctor confirmed her death.

Things that defy all comparison with reality.

Armed with a fake gun, a fake police officer attacks a mail truck. A fake postman stops him.

Things with neither head nor tail.

Losing his marbles, the legless Spaniard kills his rival.

Things that make one favor cats as pets.

Clos-des-Mésanges. Punched by a neighbor because of her dog's barking, a woman loses her glass eye. A magpie swallows it and flies away.

Things that attest to the magic power of logos.

Monsieur Adrien Bougrillé, a resident of Reims-la-Brûlée, intentionally set himself on fire.

Things that make one assume the worst.

The porn star disposes of the circus director. The autopsy shows that he was subjected to sexual assault. One of the animals is missing from his menagerie.

Things that are difficult to hear.

As if true zeal had flowed into his fiber, he kept silent, howling out the Song of Solomon.

Things that are more humiliating than deterring.

Endowed with thirty thousand deutsche marks, the Karl Kraus prize will be awarded to a writer who commits to never publishing another line.

Things that seem deeply unjust.

Juan-les-Pins. He slips a finger into her anus while she is sleeping; his wife gets upset and files a complaint.

Things that keep one up at night.

"He was snoring like a dead man," said the police.

XXXI

The Infernal Sausage

Against all odds, identifying the woman in the photo proved astonishingly easy. Immediately upon leaving the boutique where the late Hugh Palmer still lay, they started showing the picture to the nearest vendors, hoping without really believing that someone would remember having seen the young woman in their neighbor's shop. The first one they asked recognized her without the slightest hesitation. This Chinese beauty was a celebrity: an actress of great talent trained in the strict Peking Opera School, Indisputable Whiteness—as she was really called—had gone to Shanghai, more precisely to the Éden-Théâtre in Tianducheng, where her show was drawing crowds.

The chimpanzee had followed them. Distraught, he had chosen a new master in our dear Holmes, to whom he glued himself, trying by any means necessary to climb into his arms. Holmes took the animal out of pity and, having consulted Canterel, decided to adopt him. He named him Darwin, for the striking resemblance he saw in him to the famous naturalist.

It was with this new companion that they hastily made their way back to the Grand Hotel.

"Well," said Lady MacRae, once she had been brought up to date, "what are we waiting for? If he wanted to hide the photo of this young woman, it's because she is an important link to what we're looking for."

"Without a doubt," said Holmes. "And, anyway, it's our only lead. Your diamond will end up taking us all the way around the world!"

Questioned about the objects retrieved from the collector's safe, Clawdia confirmed the report given by her servant. Yes, the curious mirror and the pamphlet had been stored in her safe, but she was ignorant of both their purpose and their origin. Souvenirs her husband had kept, at least that was what she had thought until today.

"Remember Chung Ling Soo's message," said Canterel, pensive, "'the diamond and its reflection' . . . It was not a figure of speech, but rather an allusion to the mirror that has fallen into our hands."

"So, off to Shanghai!" exclaimed Holmes, with Darwin hanging from his neck, hooting with excitement.

"Ah!" said Dr. Mardrus, taken aback. "Well, I should say my good-byes, then . . ."

"Not a chance," said Lady MacRae, taking his hand affectionately. "If nothing calls you elsewhere, I pray, come with us. Verity needs you, and I have faith in your methods. What would you say to becoming her personal physician?"

Mardrus did not even pause to consider.

"I accept with great pleasure, my dear lady. With very great pleasure!" he added, his eyes misty with emotion.

Two days later, once the steamship *Salam Express*, captained by Dalla Chiesa, had deposited them on the docks of Shanghai, a junk took them as far as the Tianducheng gates.

Imagine their surprise when they found themselves dropped off by a curb somewhere between the Place de l'Étoile and the Trocadéro! Canterel puffed out his chest; it suddenly seemed to him that they had never left Paris.

Dr. Mardrus having assured them that a walk in the fresh air would do the greatest good for Verity, they set the girl in a kind of bamboo wheelchair and took turns rolling her down the pavement.

Nothing was missing from this life-size replica of the city: not the Eiffel Tower, which rose above real Haussmann buildings, or the metro entrances, or even the Wallace fountains. Upon closer inspection, however, something offended the senses, triggering a feeling of vertigo: not one of these structures was in the right place. Everything was designed, in fact, to provide Chinese sightseers with the ideal view of such and such a part of Paris, to the point that it was enough to turn a corner to change arrondissements and come across a new postcard view: a vista of the Champs-Élysées gave way to the steps of Montmartre, the Champ de Mars opened onto the Palais Garnier, and so on, as if some genie had fulfilled a weary tourist's wish to shrink the city. The typical details that ordinarily satisfy travelers' meager appetites were also there, distorted by magnification. Police officers wearing kepis, Parisians sporting black berets with baguettes under their arms, pairs of lovers kissing passionately. At Les Deux Magots, a drunk with a prominent forehead was writing poems before a glass of absinthe; at a table at the Café de Flore, one could engage in conversation with a philosopher identifiable by his lazy eye.

Hundreds of white-skinned extras thus contributed to the authenticity of this immense garden of acclimatization, the designers having spared no expense. Among all these exhibitions of outdated and lost scenes, one display invariably provoked contemptuous chuckles—that of a bookstore reconstructed according to the best sources, in the image of those that existed before the digital divide that had finally stamped them out. Inside were fake readers around fake spindly booksellers who sorted piles of fake books.

Throngs of Chinese tourists were coming here on holiday, hotels and apartments were turning people away. And, because it was a fashionable honeymoon destination, brides in long trains saturated every overlook.

Along their way, they learned of the existence of many other similar exhibitions throughout the country: a Venice in Wuqing, a Dutch village on the banks of the Yangtze, a little London in Songjiang adorned with Yorkshire cottages and Gothic churches, a Great Pyramid of Giza in Hunan, and in Tianjin, on the estate of "Dynasty Wine," a Château de Montaigne that was three times larger than the original.

It was thus that they arrived, almost without realizing it, in front of the Éden-Théâtre. *L'Aiglon* was playing, with Sarah Bernhardt, alias Indisputable Whiteness, in the title role. The few images from the play posted around the entrance showed her as hieratic, in the style of the famous actress, taking the likeness so far as to have, like Bernhardt toward the end of her life, only one leg, shod in an ankle boot.

"You were right once again!" said Holmes, addressing Canterel.

The latter had a vexed expression on his face.

"It's not her . . ."

"What do you mean? She's perfectly recognizable."

"Yes, but that's the wrong leg. In our photo, it was the right one that was visible, while the left was hidden by the tear. Look: in these images, it's the opposite. This woman is missing her right leg, not her left!"

"Perhaps the image was inverted?" Clawdia suggested.

"It's possible," replied Canterel, "but not likely. We would not have recognized her so easily. And then there is that beauty mark, there, on the side of the nose, which is in the same place."

"There's only one way to make sure," replied Grimod, leading them inside the theater, "we have to meet her."

The interview cost so exaggerated a sum that we hesitate to reveal it, but it took place, which is the important thing, even if this amount would have enabled the real Sarah Bernhardt to stay in bed for an entire year. The Chinese actress received them in her dressing room, in costume, and winced when they showed her the image retrieved from Hugh Palmer's safe.

"That's not me," she said coldly, "it's my sister."

She rummaged through a box and eventually produced the same photo as the one they had in their hands, this one complete. It showed twin sisters in the process of binding the stumps at their knees, one her left leg, the other her right.

"That was two months after our operation, I haven't seen her since."

With patience, and once she had gotten them to leave her alone with the woman, Lady MacRae succeeded in reconstructing the full story. The person they were looking for was Reverse Waterlily, her conjoined twin. They had been connected by a shared leg when they were born, which had allowed them to work for a circus until they were eighteen. Her sister's frenzied sexual appetite and a grim romantic rivalry had separated them more irremediably, she made clear, than the surgical procedure that had freed them. Lien-hoa Ló—Reverse Waterlily—had gone to the Shanghai Club, first as a singer, and later as a stripper. Now, as far as she knew, her sister was a courtesan at Lady Be Good, a brothel in Sydney.

"To tell the truth," Lady MacRae finished, blushing, "'courtesan' is not the word she used."

On the junk that took them back to Shanghai, the difficulty of continuing their journey became evident, so much so that there was a long moment when everyone was silent, lost in his own thoughts. Kim had started talking to the driver of their boat, who seemed to be responding to him with onomatopoeias, until the moment when he lifted his head and pointed at something in the sky.

Kim jumped up.

"Luck is with us!" he said, jubilant. "Look, look!"

In the direction he was pointing, an airship was just coming out of the clouds.

"By Jove!" said Canterel. "Is it coming or going?"

"It's coming," replied Kim, "but it's leaving again tomorrow for Australia."

"Hip, hip, hooray, boys!" shouted Holmes, dancing a rigaudon with Darwin.

Built in the workshops of the Zeppelin Society in Friedrichshafen, the *Plectrum* was on its way to completing its first circumnavigation of the globe. As large as St. Peter's Basilica in Rome, the body of this aerostat was built around twenty-one circular duralumin frames, linked together by a complex web of longitudinal struts. This structure housed giant cells manufactured of waterproof canvas that contained the four million cubic meters of hydrogen capable of holding it all up. That is, as the booklet distributed to the passengers said, "three hundred fifty tons of luxury floating toward the Empyrean." The canvas of the casing had been coated with cellulose, aluminum powder, and iron oxide to make it waterproof and to protect the balloons from the adverse effects of the sun's heat.

Three hundred fifty meters long and 65 wide, as tall as a twenty-story building, this airship looked like an astounding *Monte Cristo* fitted with propellers. Powered by six Postel-Vinay electric motors arranged two by two on each tier of the body, it was carrying 90 tons of Fulmen accumulators, just as much iron and nickel, 20,000 liters of potassium hydroxide solution for electrolysis, 30 tons of freight, and 60,000 liters of water for ballast.

The passenger areas being fitted to the inside of the casing, all spectators could see on this elegant cigar was a little pilot's pod set at the very front.

When she saw it that morning, her eyes fixed on its mooring mast, enormous, with two sets of folding stairs inviting passengers to enter into the black hole of its bowels, Miss Sherrington cried out, "You will never make me ride in that infernal sausage!"

It is true, in her defense, that the *Hindenburg* disaster remained present in everyone's memories.

Canterel, then Lady MacRae tried to reason with her, but no one would have succeeded in getting her to board without the incident that disrupted their embarkation and forced her fear into second place. A movement in the crowd made them all turn: in the group of passengers waiting for permission to progress toward the *Plectrum*, Grimod recognized the sly face of Scummington. Darwin had grabbed the inspector by the neck and, teeth bared, was shaking him like a rag doll.

XXXII

If He's Talking to You, It Means He's Breathing!

She's no longer aware of anything apart from the raucous beating in her arteries. Fabrice's face, enlarged, carved in a giant mask, tumbles through her dreams. He comes toward her to the sound of timpani, accompanied by an unyielding bassline of cellos, between two rows of huge refrigerators floating in the depths of the heavens. Sparks are escaping from their seams, as if the doors are just barely holding in the blaze that is distending them from inside. But a slate-colored cloudiness has just darkened this view, disturbed it, corroded its enameled perfection, while the beating of the drum intensifies, assaults her ears to the point that she yanks out her earplugs. Someone is knocking on her door, battering it in, as if all life depended on it. Charlotte rushes to open it. Marthe is there, her eyes bloodshot, a merciless sybil of nightmare.

She is wearing slippers, but with a black skirt with white polka dots and a greasy blouse like the gauze on a burn victim. A curling ribbon serves as her belt.

"You can't break down my door like that! Really, Marthe!"

"Can you help me get Chonchon up?"

"But he's dead drunk and weighs a hundred and twenty kilos, Marthe!"

"I know . . ."

"We've tried to get him up when he's been drunk before, and you know it's impossible."

She tilts her head, raises her eyes to Charlotte with the pleading look of a sick dog.

"Can you give him a hand?"

"I can't, Marthe, he's completely drunk, just like every night. It's his own fault."

"Can someone call the fire department?"

"And what would the fire department do? He's going to sleep it off on the floor, no big deal."

"Can you give me a hand?"

"No, there's no point. Listen, Marthe, no. I already know I can't. It smells bad in there, anyway. It smells bad everywhere! He'll get better, just like every other time."

"He's gonna die."

"He's not going to die, come on . . ."

"I know, don't you wanna help me out a little?"

Charlotte slowly exhales. In her panties, her breasts bare under her T-shirt, she follows Marthe into her hovel.

Her husband is on the floor between the bed and the table, lying in an indescribable heap of disgusting garbage.

Charlotte approaches Chonchon.

"Give me your hand, will you?"

"It's fine," says Chonchon. "Softly, so gently . . ."

"Yes, yes, gently! Go on, try, sit up!"

"Pull, by God!"

"I can't do it, you weigh a hundred and twenty kilos! I can't."

"I don't need anyone's help!"

"Well, then let go of me! You say you're drunk, you want to be left alone? Too bad, we're not going anywhere. So quit your whining and let us help you."

Charlotte has grabbed one of the jars lying around him, he holds out his hand, threatening.

"You can go back home," he mutters, squirming around like an invalid fallen from his bed.

"What are you doing with this mayonnaise?" Addressing Marthe, she says: "Listen, he's still drunk. He doesn't want anyone's help."

"Gotta call the fire department . . ."

"The fire department! When he sobers up, he'll get up, just like everyone does, and then it'll be fine."

"Can you call the fire department?"

"We're not going to bother the fire department with this, Marthe. They have other things to do!"

"You don't wanna help me out?"

"I helped him, he yelled at me! I can't lift a hundred and twenty kilos, Marthe!"

"You know anyone?"

"In five minutes he'll be standing. He pulls through every time, just wait a little . . ."

"He's gonna choke, his head's too low."

"No, he's sitting up, it's fine."

"He's gonna choke, dear . . ."

"You know, you know that you're . . ." They go back in.

"Leave me alone," Chonchon grumbles.

"See, it'll be fine . . . You see, he's sleeping it off. There's nothing to worry about, let's go."

"He's gonna choke . . ."

"Monsieur, are you choking? No. See, he's fine. Well, goodbye, Marthe. Let me go, I want to go back to my place."

"Is he gonna choke?"

"I'm leaving because it smells so bad. The whole building smells bad. He's piss drunk, Marthe."

"But is there a chance he'll choke?"

"He's not going to choke, he managed to talk to you. If he's talking to you, it means he's breathing! Alright? Go on, close your door."

"Is Chonchon gonna die?"

Charlotte closes her eyes, deliberates, says carefully: "If I say he's not going to die, he's not going to die."

She goes back into her apartment, slamming the door behind her.

XXXIII

A Fish With Human Hands Grabbed My Breasts!

Designed like a luxury liner, the *Plectrum* had three decks located in the middle of the ship, just behind the steering pod. The interior architecture and design of the passenger areas gave such an impression of spaciousness that it was difficult to believe that only a twentieth of the aircraft's total volume was devoted to them. The passengers enjoyed five-star service, offered by crewmembers whose smiles, military stripes, and impeccably pressed uniforms dispelled any apprehensions. They welcomed the passengers from the moment they boarded, forming an honor guard up to the place where Francisco Scheletro, the airship's commander, was waiting for them. Affable, but never letting his pride slip for an instant, he shook their hands and with the same movement positioned them to stand beside him in front of the waiting lens of a photographer, hunched behind his tripod, who suddenly straightened up, brandishing a flash that splashed them with an intense light. This preliminary dazzle left a thousand and one stars in their eyes; it foreshadowed and emphasized the wonders to come when they would have the chance to explore the vessel. Even before the end of the voyage, they would be able to buy gold-edged cardboard prints of this amazing moment, when their dream of flight had become a reality.

A steward then led them to their cabins, pointing out the layout of the ship as they went along. The lower deck was reserved for the kitchens and crew quarters. On the main deck were the reception desk, with its three nickel-plated clocks showing the time in London, Moscow, and Peking, the dining room, the smoking room, and a large panoramic lounge. This room was equipped with a duralumin Steinway, specially lightened to weigh only a hundred eighty kilograms; its pig-leather lining nevertheless guaranteed its perfect tone.

The cabins were all located on the upper deck, on either side of a central compartment occupied by bathrooms. Each cabin contained a double wicker bed, a retractable Bakelite sink with hot and cold water, a wardrobe, and a bell pull for calling the maid.

As the *Plectrum* started to pull away from the telescopic mast, the passengers hurried to the portholes to witness their departure; leaning against the slanted windows, they saw the ballast water spray those careless enough to stand beneath the machine. At the order to drop everything, which was proclaimed by the captain through the loudspeakers, the mooring lines suddenly went slack, then were hoisted back up into their respective hatches as the airship gained height. The six motors got underway in perfect unison, and the *Plectrum* turned its prow toward Australia. Below, the buildings of the airfield seemed no more than an anthill disturbed by mysterious movements.

"Pfff!" said Scummington, closing the official brochure. "This machine's crawling along, we need to go faster . . ."

"A hundred twenty-five kilometers per hour is not bad," Holmes retorted, bringing a glass of Lagavulin to his lips. "There are 7,756 kilometers between Shanghai and Sydney, we'll be there in less than three days!"

Perched on his stool at the counter of The Icarus, the bar on the main deck, Scummington shook his head and ordered a second Fernet.

He had just told the story of his adventures since the attack on the Transsiberian, and how he had followed the Noh Straddler's trail without faltering for a single moment. Despite the difficulties of this pursuit, he had seen to their luggage, alerted the Sleeping-Car Company so that they would be rescued as quickly as possible, and striven to catch up to his opponent. But in vain. The one he was pursuing so stubbornly was always a step ahead of him. While keeping what information he had to himself, Scummington did concede that his investigation had directed him to Sydney, and that it was perhaps time to join forces for the likely showdown with their mutual adversary. As he looked to be in such low spirits, Holmes acquiesced, offered a clean slate, and graciously informed him of the objects in their possession.

"This is a good thing," Scummington admitted, touching the scabs that had begun to harden on his neck.

The violence of Darwin's attack had left marks. Now caged in the cargo hold, the cursed beast could no longer molest him. Not understanding his sudden aggression toward the inspector, but sharing it in his own way, Holmes was sympathetic. That was how humans would act if they had gumption. This monkey had the ardor of youth, his fierce intransigence demanded admiration.

Entering the grand lounge where he was to meet his friends, Canterel grimaced. Although it could not compete with that of the *Normandy* or the *Île-de-France*, the aesthetic of the place left nothing to be desired—and for good reason, since it had been entrusted to Bouwens and Vaillat, who had decorated those same ships—but the display of a dozen coral-red statues was in manifestly bad taste. He couldn't help but go over to inspect them.

On display exclusively for the occasion of this crossing, these statues were examples of the work of the famous visual artist Gerhard Reutlinger. His exhibition *Behind Appearance* had taken Shanghai by storm for the last three months and was sure to become a great success in Sydney. It was made up of a hundred skinned bodies, in everyday positions, preserved and plasticized through a secret process. A quiet hell where people continued to ride their bikes, play tennis, and even fornicate, but without their skin, in the ultimate nakedness of muscles and organs.

On board to oversee the relocation of his work, the artist had agreed to offer his most beautiful pieces for the passengers' delectation. So they could enjoy the sight of a man sporting his own skin in his right hand like Hercules with the Nemean lion, a seductive woman squeezing the fatty masses on her chest, a basketball player frozen mid-dribble, a woman, eight months pregnant, whose open belly revealed a shriveled baby, and a Santa Claus with his wife.

Despite the systematic skinning of the bodies, it was still evident to the viewer that all the corpses were Chinese. How had the "artist" procured them? At what price, according to what contract? Could anyone in the world have really agreed, in exchange for money, to see a family member thus skinned, then fixed for eternity in the immodest flesh? These questions created a dark aura of mystery and revulsion around Reutlinger.

The man himself was at the center of a small group of passengers, including Clawdia and Grimod, who were listening to him defend the philosophy of his methods; he had a silver tongue and easily fended off all criticism.

"Have you visited the Capuchin Catacombs of Palermo?" he orated. "Have you seen all those poorly mummified bodies, standing there, suspended like rags from meat hooks? Their families came to see them once a year, they brought their children, no one was shocked. What I'm doing is no different, aside from the fact that my subjects, these here, are perfectly preserved. My master, the late Dr. Auzoux, used to say that through his services he offered naturalized bodies a kind of immortality. I believe I have surpassed him: by ridding them of their casings, I sublimate them into their innermost truth. I pull off masks, I unveil!"

"This man is sick," Canterel whispered in Clawdia's ear.

"No more so than others," she retorted, examining the cutaway of a "Rodin's Thinker," its brain in the air and its testicles hanging from the ends of its spermatic cords, looking like those balls that children clang together for the simple pleasure of the repetitive noise.

Canterel shrugged and joined Holmes, whom he had just spotted in the smoking room. Next to the salon, but separated from it by a revolving glass door, this area was another of the *Plectrum's* oddities. The architects had pressurized it to avoid any possible risk of explosion in case of a hydrogen leak. Inside, an officer offered to light your cigar or pipe with the only lighter on board, a Döbereiner made of Meisser porcelain that only he was allowed to use. This same keeper of the fire was then in charge of putting out every last ember before allowing the smokers to leave the room.

"I was waiting for you," said Holmes. "What are you having?"

"Nothing, lunch should be served soon."

"Precisely, my dear, precisely . . . We have to whet our appetites!"

Sitting a few meters away, Grimod was smoking a cigarette. He looked gloomy and showed little desire to hold conversation with anyone.

"What's wrong with him?" asked Martial.

"I think he's sulking," Holmes replied, embarrassed. "He blames me for telling Scummington about the brothel we're on our way to."

"Did you?"

"I'm afraid so . . ."

"At this point, it doesn't seem to make much difference, but you should have thought about . . ."

"About what?" Holmes cut him off, defensive.

"About finishing your glass, old chap, it's time to go sit down."

The hands of the clocks at the reception desk turned with astonishing speed. Trained to break the monotony of the ship's voyages, the crew kept up a nearly constant state of activity, to increase the chances of keeping the travelers entertained.

So, at the welcome dinner, with crayfish and fine wines, there was an interlude among the tables with a clairvoyant Sikh in a red turban; after an hour of rest, all of the passengers had to put their life jackets back on to go along with a mandatory "abandon ship" drill that brought them to tea time. Only a little later, the *Plectrum* floated down until it was skimming the waves to allow them to better admire the evolution of a colony of blue whales charting a course across the surface of the Pacific. By the time this was done, it was already time for "Captain's Cocktails."

The passengers barely had time to get changed. For two days, they lived in a continuous celebration, their astonishment at the abundance of "magnificent buffets" competing with the hushed romance of the evening dances. Kim, who had managed to sneak down to the lower deck and get a fellow cook to buy him a drink, saw the other side of the coin: there, under their feet, were a hundred and fifty people of all nationalities, sweating blood for the convenience of seventy privileged persons.

If our companions had decided to enjoy these benefits, no one could have blamed them, but they were uninterested. Canterel barely left his cabin, where he played chess with Grimod, relentlessly trying out a personal variation on the *Gambit Camulogène*; Clawdia and Dr. Mardrus devoted themselves body and soul to reeducating Verity, while as for Holmes, his elbow seemed to be welded to the bar in the smoking room, where his eyes browsed tirelessly over the labels of the hundred and twenty-three scotches that blazed under the lights of the mirror.

In response to numerous complaints, the "works of art" displayed in the salon had been relocated to the hold some time ago. Upset, Reutlinger was no longer showing himself. No one, truth be told, missed him, aside perhaps from Dr. Mardrus who, as a scientist, had proved fascinated by those frightful anatomies and had pestered their creator with technical questions.

The morning of the third day, the captain informed his passengers that the Australian coast was in view, an announcement that was met with cries of joy from the whole airship; then he gave the weather report: the line of black clouds in front of them indicated a low-pressure area and signaled some turbulence, but the *Plectrum* had come through others just fine, and their arrival in Sydney was still scheduled for 6 P.M. Finally, he would be waiting for them at the farewell banquet in half an hour, and he urged his guests not to miss the concert by pianist Saténik Karaboudjan, who would be singing the world's most recent hits in French, including "Boom ladda boom boom," "One, two, three, four times" and "Shoobidoo bidoo pwa pwa."

Inside the airship, the passengers' applause sounded like a flock of partridges suddenly taking flight.

When Martial sat down at the table, he saw Clawdia's empty seat and felt a dull disappointment. A feeling that clearly showed on his face, since Dr. Mardrus, grinning, put a hand on his shoulder.

"She won't be long, my dear. I was supposed to wait for Lady Clawdia to tell you, but we have a bit of good news, very good news, to share with you."

He was unfolding his napkin when there was a commotion at the front of the restaurant. The doors opened, pulled back by two out-of-breath maids, and Lady MacRae made her entrance, rolling Verity's chair before her.

"Our daughter has something to say to you," she said, beaming. "Go on, my dear, show him!"

Verity's lips trembled, opened. As she looked at her mother disconsolately, Canterel saw her fingers tighten on the chair's armrests.

"She also moves her toes," Dr. Mardrus couldn't stop himself from saying.

"It's very emotional for her," said Clawdia. "You have to give her time . . ."

"Of course," said Martial, both moved and annoyed by this staging, which he found too theatrical.

At that moment, the *Plectrum* entered the storm clouds with a jolt that made the glasses clink on the tables. Behind the bay windows, the blue sky gave way to bubbling reddish-brown ink, curling on itself in tangible swirls. Bright bursts of yellow light pulsated at its center.

"Is Devil?" Verity articulated.

"No," replied Canterel. "It's just a storm, it will pass."

"How do you think I stop myself talking?"

Surprised, Martial shot a questioning glance at Mardrus. The latter made a face to show that the girl had not yet recovered all of her faculties.

"Oh, my dear," said Canterel, going over to hug his daughter. "You'll be better very soon, you'll see."

"I broke my age," she replied, her voice shaking.

Fat drops of sweat at her hairline attested to the terrible effort that speaking cost her.

"Horses," she breathed, "speed. It's too hard . . ."

Behind her, Lady MacRae sobbed silently.

Taking the matter in hand, Grimod pushed aside the chairs to allow Verity to sit at the table with them. A steward passed out flutes of champagne. Outside, the tempest raged. The airship pitched slowly as hail rattled against the windows.

At the staff table, no one seemed concerned about these abysmal conditions, but the captain took it upon himself to stand and raise a toast.

"A drink to this cruise, which is coming to an end," he said in a loud voice, "and to all of the passengers present here! With my apologies for the inconveniences we are experiencing: I may be the captain of this ship, but I can do little about the weather. That being said, I can confirm our on-time arrival in Sydney, and I wish you all a pleasant stay in that city."

He wet his lips with champagne, turned around, glass in hand, and sat back down to pounce on the milanesa that had just been served.

"Greeting, sleep," said Verity, "therefore ships know not much, but I think we've been destroyed."

There was an embarrassed silence, while a few people plunged into their meals.

"Look!" exclaimed Clawdia, pointing at the windows.

Coming out of the mass of clouds, as if followed by spotlights that filtered through it, the airship found itself in a blue clearing transfigured by the sun. A dense flock of albatrosses crossed it, then swooped toward them, overwhelmed by an aerial current. Clawdia leaned against the bay window to follow the birds' movement; horrified, she saw the *Plectrum*'s propellers shred them to bits in a ruffling of bloody feathers.

The motors coughed, then seized up in the influx. Immediately, the airship veered to starboard and, listing like an ailing fish, started to turn in a circle.

The captain and his second in command had hastily left their table to return to the steering pod. As the stewards tried to help up passengers who had lost their balance when the ship tilted, even before the order came over the loudspeakers, Grimod followed his instincts.

"Help me," he said, lifting Verity from her chair. "We have to get out of here and find the life vests!"

The port motors having been shut off, the airship had regained its equilibrium, fortunately, but now it was no longer maneuverable and was drifting toward the coast at the mercy of the wind. When it became apparent that the vessel was losing altitude and would soon be forced to make a water landing, the passengers panicked. We will leave to others the description of what a panic on board an airship that is crashing into the sea might look like, but it was in this context that our friends were thrown into a maelstrom where neither reason nor faith was any comfort. They were separated in the stampede.

The officers worked hard to minimize the destruction; deftly manipulating the ballast and gas releases, they kept the *Plectrum* in the air, all while keeping it from being taken by the storm that was raging above them. When this became impossible, they released the front third, in order to preserve the ship's buoyancy, which caused the pod to skid over the water like a seaplane's floats. Designed for smooth landings on runways, the passenger compartment did not bear up well. The waves shattered the windows, flooding the switchboards and sending sparks flying; two men were injured, but the airship finally came to a stop and floated on the swell.

The first to escape was Captain Scheletro. He was seen floating away from the *Plectrum*, flat on his stomach on an air mattress that he was propelling with his arms, heedless of the Neapolitan insults that were gushing from the pod.

Charged with Verity's safety, Grimod and Canterel found themselves next to an emergency exit, all three of them wearing life jackets. Despairing at having lost Lady MacRae at the beginning of the panic, Canterel wanted to wait a little longer, but Grimod unceremoniously pushed him out, then jumped into the water with Verity, keeping a tight hold on the waterproof bag in which he had taken care to gather all of their passports, as well as all the cash in his possession.

The others had, in spite of themselves, obeyed the whimsical logic of the chaos. Hampered by the long, thin skirt she had chosen to put on that morning, Lady MacRae could not get back to her cabin. Kim had rushed to the lower deck to warn his new friends of the imminent catastrophe. Miss Sherrington had gotten held up fighting with Reutlinger, who had been jostling to get in front of everyone else. As for Holmes, he had gone to the bar to save a priceless bottle—a seventy-year Mortlach—then worked his way to the hold to free Darwin.

Scummington and Dr. Mardrus had disappeared, swallowed by the mob that was surging toward the upper deck.

Hurled into the water without really understanding how it had happened, Clawdia was swimming, half-naked, her survival instinct having gotten her undressed. Around her, on the smooth surface of the ocean, were half-submerged men and women, their faces eaten away, skulls burned, eyes lidless, a host of the damned whose hands stretched toward her. Terrified, she panicked and swallowed a mouthful of water, not realizing that these were Gerhard Reutlinger's skinned corpses floating in the sea. At the very moment when she began to think about the sharks and other aquatic monstrosities that haunted these shores, she felt two hands plant themselves directly to her chest.

"Oh my God!" she screamed, hysterical. "A fish with human hands grabbed my breasts!"

"Calm yourself," said Canterel, his face appearing behind her, "calm yourself, I beg you!"

"What are you doing?" she said, realizing that it was Martial who was holding her to his chest.

"I'm saving your life, my dear," he replied calmly, "and mine, too."

XXXIV

Under the Belly of a Fox

The countryside passes beneath him at full speed, like the view from a plane at low altitude when it is taking off or landing, a relief map with minutely rendered details patiently chiseled in, hills carved from solid oak, blocks of lime for the houses, fields and prairies flocked with dyed silk; there are trees, vineyards, groves of fine chenille where strands of taffeta intertwine with twists of brass wire, lakes and rivers gleam like oil paintings, roofs, stones, walls, the warm hues of watercolor paper. Monsieur Wang whizzes through the sky, clinging to his bird's collar. He would like to guide him, to instill in him a route back to the pigeon loft, but he himself is lost, disoriented by his flight over this infinite model where all roads are muddled into one.

Free Legs Diamond has still not returned. It's over. Almost forty hours have elapsed since his departure; even if he came back now, he could no longer be relied on in competitions. Wang hopes he is dead, struck down in all his glory, rather than diminished by some failure: a shard of jade is worth more than an intact porcelain tile.

That morning, he had kept his anxiety at bay by solving a supply problem. The Indian factory in Florange was behind in delivering the memory cards needed for the last step in the tablet's assembly. He had had to listen to their poor excuses, shake them up, and threaten to cancel the order and talk to their Korean competitors in Montargis.

In truth, this was a bluff. The delays were too short compared to the overall timetable. The B@bil Book absolutely had to come out before Christmas or it would face becoming a commercial failure. But it was fine, the matter seemed to have been resolved.

At the end of the afternoon, Wang was confronted with a new problem; he learned from his head of HR that a number of CPUs had disappeared, but that she knew the name of the man—or in this case the *woman*—responsible and offered to reveal it.

"A denunciation," Louise told her superior. "Charlotte Dufrène, someone saw her do it."

"I can't believe it was that young woman. She doesn't have a thief's mind."

"If you will allow me, we can find that out here and now."

Leaving the office, the Director of HR called a security guard to come with her to the workshop. She swept down the wide alley in military step and stopped behind Charlotte's seat.

"Will you follow us, Mademoiselle?"

"What's going on?"

"Just an inspection . . ."

Getting up, Charlotte gave Fabrice a look to say she had no idea what they wanted her for. Under Louise's watchful gaze, the little group went into the women's locker room.

"Is there any reason you wouldn't want to show me the inside of your locker?"

"Not at all, I don't have anything to hide," Charlotte replied, taking the key from her pocket, "but I don't understand what you're looking for . . ."

"Open it, please."

Charlotte opened the door and stepped aside. Used to conducting this kind of search, the security guard combed through her things carefully, striving to disturb them as little as possible. This inspection having turned up nothing, he began to feel along the underside of the shelf until his hand touched something. He cleared his throat, gave the head of HR a look, and started to detach the object using an X-Acto knife.

"What's that supposed to be?" said Charlotte, seeing him hand the director a bubble-wrapped package.

Louise borrowed the guard's knife to rip open the packaging.

"You're sure you don't know?" she said, showing Charlotte the contents. "CPUs . . . Enough for quite a bundle of cash!"

Panic-stricken, Charlotte opened her eyes wide.

"I didn't put those there. I swear! I'd never do something like that!"

"Well, they were found in your locker, so you'll have to explain it to the manager."

"But why? I'm telling you, it wasn't me!"

"Let's go. The less you make a scene, the easier this will be."

The security guard made as if to take Charlotte by the arms to lead her away, but she shook him off sharply.

"Hey you, you let go of me, okay? I haven't done anything."

The bell sounded the end of the workday as they were climbing the stairs.

When they entered his office, Monsieur Wang simply raised his head and listened. Louise had the security guard make his statement and then, triumphant, set the eviscerated package on the manager's blotter.

Sometimes a crushing blow can make everything clear, thought Wang: it was not until he saw the bubble wrap that he made the connection to the nocturnal scene witnessed on his iPad. He looked the head of HR right in the eye, trying to understand her motives. Taken aback, Louise felt her face redden. There had been precedents, other thieves caught red-handed; each time, Monsieur Wang had proved merciless, swiftly dismissing the guilty party and handing the matter over to the police. Punishing one to terrify a hundred, he had explained to her, that was his take on the subject. This time, he seemed to waver.

"Thank you, you may leave," he told the security guard. "I'll rely on you to remain discreet about this."

As soon as he was out of the room, Louise tried to speed things along.

"Well, then. I'll call the police, as usual?"

"No!" cried Charlotte. "I'm innocent, someone else did this. I swear, it wasn't me!"

At the age of fifteen, she had been caught at the exit of a department store with a ring on her finger that she had thought she could steal. It had gotten her sent to the police station, then juvenile court. The lesson had stuck. She saw herself once again hustled, accused, disgraced; the vision filled her with terror and shame.

"Not the police, please . . ."

"That depends on what you say, girl."

Wang freed the CPUs from the plastic one by one, slowly lining them up on his table, then finished counting them out loud.

"Thirty-one, thirty-two, thirty-three . . . Do you know what we say in China? Stitched together, little scraps from under the belly of a fox eventually make a fur coat. At a hundred euros each, these come to thirty-three hundred euros. A pretty sum. What price were you hoping to get for them?"

"But I'm telling you I didn't steal them! I'm begging you, you have to believe me!"

"And why would I, Mademoiselle? These CPUs were found in your locker . . ."

He had come right up to her, his eyes fixed on her chest, enjoying seeing her fear seep out from under her armpits. Louise, perplexed, was watching him; she had thought to get rid of Charlotte easily, but

Wang had decided differently. All she could do was add further to the accusations to try to stay in control.

"And I bet there were others. It may even be a whole network . . ."

"Listen, girl, if you give me names, I can be quite merciful. We'll forget this ever happened, I promise."

"I didn't do anything," Charlotte whimpered, wringing her hands, "I don't know anything . . ."

Wang stood, looking annoyed.

"Like a broken record . . . We'll see about that, but for the moment, I'm afraid you'll have to undress."

"Are you joking?"

"Certainly not. I have to make sure you haven't hidden anything in your underwear. Madame Le Galle will be the one checking, of course."

"No way," Charlotte stammered. "You don't have the right . . ."

"Too bad, then. Louise, please phone the police station. Let's have done with this business!"

The director of HR was still dialing when Charlotte began to remove her clothing, furious, challenging Wang with her eyes. She dropped her clothes on one of the chairs and stood facing him, holding her forearms against her chest, one hand forming a shell over her pubis.

"There's nothing," said Louise, having checked the clothes with her fingertips.

Charlotte sneered: "Do you want to do a cavity search while you're at it?"

"That won't be necessary," said Wang, trying not to let his eyes wander from her face.

"Then I can get dressed."

"No, Mademoiselle, I don't think so. Sorry, but that would be too easy."

He turned to open the wall safe.

"Madame Le Galle, if you will . . ." he said, holding out an empty basket. To Charlotte: "You'll get them back once you've told me everything."

"This can't be happening! You don't have the right! My god, what do you want me to tell you?"

"You'll have all night to think about it. Until tomorrow. Madame Le Galle, you may go home. I'll thank you to turn the heat up a little before you leave."

In the middle of closing the safe, Louise froze; a surge of bile burned her throat.

XXXV

Dr. Mulbach's Snake Oil

How our friends found themselves lying unscathed on the shores of Melville Island, off the northern coast of Australia, and by what means they succeeded in continuing their voyage to reach their destination, we will allow ourselves to omit in order to avoid making our story unnecessarily long.

Having just arrived in downtown Sydney, that city by the sea, they rushed to the Union Club, where Holmes got himself recognized as a member of the Athenaeum in London and a personal friend of the governor, Lord Macquarie, whose recommendation got them in the door of the club's lovely building on Bent Street and instantly smoothed away all of the material difficulties they were facing, having lost their belongings. This meant that they could give out promissory notes and set themselves up at Petty's Hotel, the sober palace where Louis d'Orléans, Prince of Condé, had spent his final days.

As for Scummington, he was set up with lodgings in Cadmans Cottage by his colleagues in the New South Wales Police.

The intelligence they provided stated that the Lady Be Good was located not far from there, on the Rocks, the harbor district across from the promontory where the Government House stood. It was the most famous of the numerous brothels that flourished on Cambridge Street—formerly called Bladder Row.

Holmes, Canterel, and Scummington made the trip, as Grimod had been appointed to run the various errands necessary to the continuation of their stay.

Once they had passed through the heavy red hangings at the entrance, a hostess led them into a cabaret whose *opera buffa* décor endeavored to evoke the mysterious ambiance of a Khmer temple. Nothing was missing, not monumental Buddha faces, not pagodas laced with roots and creepers. Piercing through the dim light in places, gas-powered torches shone with the light of an Indian camp. In these halos of trembling light, Asian strippers—Thai, Chinese, Filipina—pole-danced while doing a strip tease, then stretched their naked bodies out on circular platforms, competing in skill and obscenity to show off the contracting power of their vaginal muscles. One was launching bursts of ping-pong balls, another was peeling a banana and then propelling it several meters, yet another was blowing out a candle using those same muscles, and the next, with a harmonica jammed between her thighs, was producing a sweet melody while accompanying herself with a Tibetan singing bowl.

The hostess seated them at a table right next to a young woman who was squatting down over a glass of scotch.

"*Kabazzah*," said the hostess, "snapping pussy, is good for men!"

The performer gripped the rim of the glass between her labia and, contorting herself, managed to pour the contents into herself.

"What a waste!" said Holmes, revolted.

"What are we waiting for?" said Scummington, impatient. "Do you think this girl is going to come up and introduce herself?"

"In the land of the legless," Canterel replied laconically, "one must begin by sitting on the ground."

Thrown, Scummington shot a questioning glance at Holmes.

"We don't know anything about this place," he explained. "Let's try to get a sense of it before we act."

Having taken their order, the hostess returned with their drinks. She passed out the glasses, then knelt down between the inspector's knees and started to open his fly.

"What are you doing?" he exclaimed, shrinking away. "Stop that!"

"Is included," she said, astonished. "Is free . . ."

"What the hell does she want? I don't understand."

"She's saying it comes with the drink," replied Holmes, sniggering.

He explained to the young woman that they did not require her services and, glass in hand, focused on what was happening around them.

By observing the other clients' conduct, they got a better grasp of how it all functioned. Once you had chosen a girl from among those who were making a spectacle of themselves, all you had to do was signal a hostess and point at the one you wanted, though certain regulars merely whispered a name in the hostess's ear. When the girls switched out at the end of their numbers, the hostess would come find the client and accompany him to a giant cobra head whose jaw opened as if to swallow him. Before the serpent's mouth closed again, there was time to glimpse a red staircase lined by soft lights.

As they had just seen two men climb the stairs together, Holmes and Canterel judged that their initiative would not appear too suspect. They consulted for a moment, then Holmes signaled one of the servers.

"Reverse Waterlily," he whispered, impassive, with a quick gesture to indicate that it would be the three of them.

She acquiesced, though with a grimace that made it very clear what she thought of the infinite and mysterious perversity of men.

When the time came, they went with her. Into the serpent's mouth, first, then following the throbbing slit of her long satin dress up to the second story. There was an elegant reception desk up there, in the neutral style of international hotels, which transitioned seamlessly into a hall of the same type, the whole thing decorated in stainless steel and pale wood, from which radiated three long hallways with lavender carpeting.

An elderly Chinese woman, her features sadly bloated with silicone injections, attempted a smile at them, while the hostess summarized the transaction for her in Cantonese.

"Ah, ah," she said, fixing her black eyes on them, "foreigners very like gang bang, but much more money, much, much!"

"How much?" asked Holmes.

"Much, much, much! Reverse Waterlily, beautiful person for jig-jig, very much money, priceless!"

Canterel got out his wallet and, without counting, threw down a wad of banknotes that made her eyes widen. She grabbed them and immediately regained her professional demeanor.

"You want Victor Hugo ducal room, Admiral Nelson cabin on HMS Victory, Torquemada torture chamber, or old Soviet submarine command post from first age? Only rooms free tonight, but you gentlemen, you want Victor Hugo, yes?"

"Victor Hugo ducal room," Canterel confirmed, smiling. "It's the least we can do."

The madam activated two pneumatic levers before her, uttered some incomprehensible orders into a copper funnel connected to a large tube of the same metal, raised her voice, threatened, then, suddenly content, invited them to follow their hostess.

"Victor Hugo room," she said with the Goyesque grace of a gossip. "'Making all my love from Paris,' as they say in your country."

"Sending all my love to you, as well," said Canterel with the insulting preciseness of mockery.

The room they entered was like a new world. Under a green and white canopy festooned with stars stood a big bed with spiral columns and suggestive gothic figures. Despite the low quality of the trompe-l'oeil frescoes on the walls, they could recognize the Notre-Dame Cathedral with its gargoyles, Cosette with her bucket, Jean Valjean in his wooden shoes. As far as furniture, the only thing in the room was a tall military drum.

As naked as can be, Reverse Waterlily was waiting for them, sitting cross-legged on a garnet velvet bedspread. She was the mirror image of her Siamese twin. The stump of her right leg was wrapped in a tight bandage, deliberately stained with merbromin to give the impression that it had just been amputated. She was wearing an Ananke shoe on her left foot.

"And a third!" said Canterel, triumphant.

At that instant, a dart—a thin needle fitted to a paper cone—flew into the door beside his neck. The young woman had shot it, using the same method employed in the shows downstairs.

Holmes hurried to explain the motives behind their visit. Once she learned that they had come from Shanghai, where they had spoken to her sister, she proved willing to cooperate.

"Where did that shoe come from?" Canterel asked, covering her shoulders with his jacket.

Her response to this question alone will clarify many aspects of the mystery with which we are concerned.

She took up the story where Sarah Bernhardt had left off. The man with whom she had fallen in love was called Giorgio Triskelès; he worked with them at the Martyrio Circus back when they were still being exhibited as Siamese twins. He himself was also a carnival freak: the "man with three right feet," the "human footstool." In spite of his extra leg, he rode horses, played tennis and soccer; his tap-dancing drew crowds. As each of his feet was a different size, he was forced to buy three pairs of shoes every time. The extras he offered to the one-legged performers who had the right shoe size. A magician, a trapeze artist-monkey who had had an accident, and her, after the operation that had freed her from her sister.

"Our affair was a happy one," she continued, "but I let myself cheat on him a few times. When some good soul showed him the evidence, he left the circus to found his own troupe, and I never saw him again. After he left, he continued to have his left shoes sent to the three of us on a regular basis, no matter where we were. Do you know what became of him?"

Canterel and Holmes looked at each other, embarrassed.

"Always that same brand?" asked Scummington.

"No. They've only been Anankes since he left. I've never seen them in stores."

Holmes pulled the mirror from Palmer's safe out of his pocket.

"Have you ever seen this object before?"

The young woman looked less surprised than disappointed.

"Oh, you're with those people . . ." she said, her tone changing. "Of course I've seen it."

Having stretched herself out to rummage under a pillow, she took the mirror and nonchalantly screwed it into a double-humped dildo.

"It's an anal jewel," she said. "There are people who bring it, sometimes, to have me show them."

"To have you show them what?" asked Canterel.

"Would you pass me the gel, there, behind the drum?"

Disgusted, Canterel held out a little bottle whose label read: "Dr. Mulbach's Snake Oil," an elixir made of half cade oil, half rattlesnake venom. She poured a little on the tips of her fingers and, without any shame whatsoever, started massaging her anus, taking care to get some of the viscous fluid inside her. After which she cautiously inserted the device, then turned over, arched up, her head thrown to the side, displaying her buttocks. Tattooed on her fleshy bits, deformed marks stretched out around the mirror in large concentric circles.

Canterel immediately saw what was going on. It was one of those mirror anamorphoses, like the ones people used to keep in curio cabinets: painted backward and mathematically distorted, these pictures seemed to suggest only crude aberrations or abstract shapes; they were presented flat on a table and sparked little interest until the moment when the spherical or cylindrical mirror for which they had been designed was placed in their center. Restored by the curvature, the image then appeared in all its perfection on the surface of the glass.

Canterel knelt down: on the mirror exhibited by the young woman, two lines of text rendered the meaning of the incoherent tattoos that surrounded it. Martial read them aloud:

"A dead cockroach in my beer 19 38 57

A monkey's arm in my ass 15 26 69"

"Well then!" said Scummington. "We're wasting our time with this shit."

The young Chinese woman pulled out her dildo and returned the mirror to Holmes.

"There," she said. "Are you satisfied?"

"Not really," he replied, smoothing his whiskers while contemplating the incomprehensible nature of the message. "Do you have any idea what it means?"

"I have no idea, and I don't want to know. Giorgio was the one who tattooed these things on my buttocks. People come here with that mirror, they pay a lot of money to look, and then they leave. That's enough for them."

Despite Holmes's insistence on the identity of these clients, or on the reasons her lover had had for giving her these tattoos, Reverse Waterlily could not tell them anything more, and they had to resign themselves to leaving her be.

Scummington having decided to go to the Australian authorities to denounce the scandalous pornography of Lady Be Good, Canterel and Holmes found themselves back in the lounge at Petty's Hotel without him.

"My God, will this never end?" Clawdia sighed, once briefed on the new riddle they had brought back.

Grimod turned to Canterel, begging him to admonish them not to give up hope.

"This is like nothing I've seen before," Martial said, annoyed. "Too much sense and not enough. Plus that series of numbers . . . It's a key cipher, not a combination cipher. Even if we found the key, we couldn't learn anything from it without the source that was used to encode it. A novel, a railroad timetable, an encyclical for all I know, it could be anything. This time, we are well and truly stuck."

"Come now, my dear," said Dr. Mardrus, raising his head from his notebook, "I thought you were tougher than that. All rivers eventually lead to the sea. So the truth evades you? Be even more real than reality, that is the secret to success."

Canterel merely snorted in response.

Fortunately, the arrival of Verity, pushed along by Kim and Miss Sherrington, defused the situation and smoothed some of the lines from his face.

XXXVI

What Kind of Dog is It?

"Carmen . . ."

"Yes?"

"I don't know how to say this . . . Do you love me?"

"Of course, *doudou* . . . What's wrong?"

"A cripple, that's what I am. How can you love a guy who can't give you pleasure?"

"I'm happy with you, that's what matters, right?"

"I want you to know: if you want to see other people, just to get what I can't give you, I'm fine with it."

"You mean sleep with someone else?"

"Yes."

"Are you serious?"

"I am. I've thought about it a lot, I can't ask you to be faithful under these circumstances. It's very hard for me to say these things to you, but I don't have a choice. You'd do it eventually, so it might as well be with my consent."

"And who's to say I haven't already done it?"

"Have you?" Dieumercie muttered, swallowing his words.

"Of course not, wise guy! I'm joking. But I'm sure you wouldn't have noticed anyway."

"Don't count on it . . ."

"Listen, you're the one I love, you're the one I want to make love to, not someone else. One of these days you'll get better, and we'll laugh about this whole thing."

"Maybe, but I'm serious. If you do it, I just want you to talk to me, tell me . . ."

"But why? You're crazy! Even if that happened, I'd keep it to myself. You wouldn't be able to help it, you'd resent me, get jealous."

"You've already thought about this? Imagined you were cheating on me? Just like that, in your fantasies?"

"Stop it!"

"Please . . ."

"Well then, answer me first. Have *you* ever done it?"

"In my dreams, maybe . . ."

"With who?"

"I don't remember. They were just erotic dreams, all I know is that it wasn't your body, your face."

"What kind of body?"

"My memory's fuzzy, a pretty big girl."

"Big how?"

"A fat girl . . ."

"Oh good, and here I've been killing myself trying to stay in shape! What kind of fat girl? Tall, short? A girl with big tits, a big butt?"

"A very, very fat girl, with a double chin."

"You're kidding me! You slept with the lady from the butcher!"

"Only in a dream," said Monsieur Bonacieux, reddening, "I'm not even sure it was her . . ."

"And did Madame Porky get you up? What did you do to that mountain of lard?"

"Don't get upset, sweetheart. You're the one who wanted me to tell you about it. It never even happened! Why are you making such a huge deal out of a dream, anyway?"

"I'm not getting upset, it's just that I'm just finding out that you've been sleeping with that bitch of a butcher, and even in if it's in your dreams it makes me feel bad. After everything I do for you . . ."

Dieumercie is about to reply when the doorbell rings. He rushes to the door, looks through the peephole, and goes out onto the landing, closing the door behind him. When he returns, hardly two minutes later, he is smiling the wide, silly smile of a herald angel.

"Happy birthday, my love!" he says, handing Carmen a shoebox tied with a bow.

"It's not my birthday," she says, her eyes shining.

"Every day is your birthday, my dear. I love you!"

She undoes the ribbon, lifts the lid, and pulls from the box a puppy with glazed eyes. It can't be more than four or five days old. It squeals, it stinks of newborn shit, urine, curdled milk.

"You told me the other day that you'd like to have a dog, so here. Its name is Kiki."

"Kiki?" said Carmen. "He's so cute! Oh, I adore him!"

"You're going to laugh, but the butcher brought it, her bitch just whelped. I told her I'd take one. It's still nursing, but I got a bottle! She explained everything to me."

"What is it?"

"What do you mean, what?"

"What kind of dog is it?"

"A toy poodle. It won't get big, you'll see. As an adult, it won't be any taller than a rabbit."

"Are you sure?" said Carmen, tears in her eyes.

"Sure," said Monsieur Bonacieux, moved. "She'll give us lots of little . . ."

"She?"

"It's a female, my kitten. If we need to, we'll have her spayed."

Carmen puts the dog back in its box and bursts into tears.

"Oh, my love," Dieumercie whispers, taking her in his arms. "What's wrong, why are you crying?"

"No reason," Carmen lies. "No reason, don't worry, it must be from happiness."

XXXVII

The Big Bloop

The reader will recall how flabbergasted Grimod had been by the absence of logic in Martial Canterel's approach to solving the most complex of riddles. Knowing that the latter had not stopped mulling over the two lines that had appeared in the mirror, and certain that he would not fail to decrypt them soon, in spite of his doubts, Grimod pored over them, looking for the smallest detail that could serve to unlock the lines by some means.

What happened in the hotel lounge provided him an exemplary opportunity to examine the process involved. Afterward, he identified several crucial steps.

First there was the picture—one of the many canvasses decorating the room's walls—that was facing Verity's chair and that seemed all of a sudden to hypnotize the girl. On this canvas, a nice enough copy of a Jan Matsys, was a young woman, naked from the waist up, sitting in the lap of an old man and embracing him amorously. On their left, another young woman, whose features showed her kinship with the first, was holding a plate of apples and grapes and offering a dish of wine to the same man. The subject couldn't have been more indecent; it evoked Lot's daughters getting their father drunk in order to couple with him, thus thwarting the divine punishment that had kept them deprived of men since the destruction of Sodom and

Gomorrah. Disturbingly, the half-naked elder sister was laughing, all the while looking at the viewer complicitly.

Clawdia was trying to gloss the painting for her daughter when she realized that it would be inappropriate to explain what the details implied. Trapped, she blurred her explanation behind a veil of discreet phraseology.

"It's a parable," she had simply continued, "that all at once denounces drinking, incest, and whoring . . ."

Seeing Lady MacRae's embarrassment, Holmes distracted Verity's attention by showing her a different painting that was less difficult to explain. This was the second step of what had not yet emerged as a meaningful sequence of events.

The picture in question, a *Beggar's Dream* inspired by Fragonard, featured a poor wretch half lying on a flight of stairs. The Queen of Spades at his feet showed him to be a card player ruined by his vice, but his closed eyes and vague smile indicated that he was dreaming of bygone days and the short period of time when he had won more in the game than he had lost.

The third and final phase was instigated by Verity, when, in her cryptic way of expressing herself, she synthesized the two images that she had just been shown. Replying to Clawdia, who was asking her what these paintings made her think of, Verity shook her head bleakly.

"The brief yesterday," she stammered, searching for words and dissatisfied with each one she pronounced, "the brief yesterday thwarts Lot and laughs . . ."

In the shocked silence that followed, Canterel repeated the phrase aloud, as if seeking to penetrate its significance, then jumped up, lips dry, nostrils flared.

"By the scrotum of Saint Perpétue, how could I have missed that bit of common sense? The pamphlet, Holmes, we'll find the solution in the pamphlet!"

And, as his friend seemed not to understand: "*The Breviary for Lottery Players*! Remember Chung Ling Soo's message: 'the diamond and its reflection.' Its 'reflection,' Holmes! The mirror was traveling with its decryption key!"

Just a few moments later, once Grimod had retrieved it from the hotel safe, they bent over the pamphlet.

It was a Dream Key that associated a number with the notable elements of certain dreams; a toolbox intended to predict the winning numbers in the Haitian State Lottery. Listed in alphabetical order, these oneiric elements appeared thus:

> Abandoned (by one's family, self) 03
> Abandoned (by the rich and powerful) 01
> Abandoning (one's country) 33
> Abandoning (one's home) 03
> Abandoning (one's wife) 40
> Abased (feeling oneself) 11
> Abasement (someone else's) 27
> Abandonment 46
> Abattoir (empty) 51
> Abattoir (seeing something killed) 16

This list ended with "Zebra (enraged)"; in its terrible succinctness, it expressed, better than any study, the endless nightmare that haunts the nights of Port-au-Prince.

Turning the yellow pages, Canterel looked up the words revealed by the mirror on Reverse Waterlily's buttocks one by one. The word "cockroach" corresponded to the number 48; "beer (dead in one's)" was number 50, and so on. On page 7, the *Breviary* listed connections between the alphabet and "numbers by threes." The group 19 38 57 was for the letter S, and 15 26 69 referred to W.

Canterel read the result:

"48 50 S for the first line," he said, frustrated, "and 123 20 W for the second. It breaks my heart to say it, but I'm afraid we're on the wrong track . . ."

"That's impossible," said Grimod. "It's all linked together, these letters have to mean something."

"License plate numbers?" Holmes proposed half-heartedly.

"Or street intersections?" said Mardrus.

There was a pause, and in the muffled silence of Petty's, a deep voice with a heavy accent from the south of France was heard: "What would you say to geographical coordinates?"

As heads turned toward the stranger who had just inserted himself into their conversation, Canterel rejoiced.

"Of course! Which quite logically gives us 48° 50' South and 123° 20' West . . ."

"That is, the coordinates of Point Nemo, dear sir, and which is in many respects quite extraordinary! But, excuse me, I must introduce myself: Alcide Sanglard, professor of marine biology at Miskatonic University."

"Sanglard?" Mardrus exclaimed, elated. "The Sanglard of 'A Blow to the Blind: Confused Sexual Behavior in Deep-Sea Squid,' the brilliant article published in the Royal Society's *Biology Letters*?"

"The same, in fact. I'm flattered that you know that little work. Very honored. I mean absolutely thrilled. Never did I dream that my study on the *Octopoteuthis deletron* would secure me such renown!"

The man was colorful, short-legged, but solid and square like a pilaster; his long, thin white hair, tied with a ribbon at the nape of his neck, looked like a wig. He inspired feelings of friendship.

Canterel got up to shake his hand and make the introductions.

"'Point Nemo,' you said?"

"Yes, it's the pretty little name scientific types have given to the 'oceanic pole of inaccessibility,' the point in the ocean that is farthest from land. A wink at Captain Nemo, and his extreme and fascinating misanthropy. Because even the hoariest geographers know to remain true to the enchantments of their youth."

"Just a point in the sea . . ." said Lady MacRae, dismayed. "It's not possible, Martial, there must be some mistake."

"No, alas, I'm sure of myself, or at least of my transcription."

"A false trail, then? This one is leading us right to the end of the world . . ."

"It's true," said Sanglard, "the point is located in the Pacific, 2,688 kilometers south of the Pitcairn Islands, and even farther west from Chile, very far from any shipping lane."

Grimod looked at him warily.

"We were cavalier enough to ponder this matter aloud, dear sir, and I do not know exactly what you caught of our conversation, but can I ask you what seemed to you so extraordinary at the moment you stepped in?"

"Rest assured, I was quite lost in thought, my brain merely reacted to the coordinates that have been my obsession for months now. You will understand. Do you know about the NOAA? No, of course not, I'd be astonished if you did. It is the acronym, very well chosen, by gum, of the National Oceanic and Atmospheric Administration, an organization charged with understanding and predicting climate change, but also with managing marine ecosystems. There are some million of us researchers associated with the program. Among the observations in which we engage, the continuous monitoring of low undersea frequencies is one of the most exciting and useful, insofar as it allows us to log seismic activity in the Earth's crust, the breaking up of icebergs, whale migrations, etc. It is a vast network of underwater hydrophones, a kind of radio telescope that transmits even the most remote sounds from the abyss. Indeed, last year, we picked up a sound that was extraordinary, unique, unacceptable. I'll show you . . ."

Professor Sanglard rummaged through his pockets and pulled out a sheet of paper, which he unfolded on the table. There were two graphs drawn on it, one above the other.

"These are spectrograms of ultra-low frequencies. On the first, what interests us is that the sound rises sharply up to an amplitude of fifty hertz, produces a kind of enormous 'bloop'—from which we got its name, the 'Big Bloop'—then disappears almost immediately into the background noise. The signal is so powerful that it could be picked up more than five thousand kilometers from its point of origin. And, more astounding still, it does not overlap in any way with the acoustic signature of an earthquake or volcanic eruption, but rather that of a living creature. Compare it with the other, isn't it staggering?"

Before the patent incomprehension of his audience, Alcide Sanglard flared up, raising his arms to the sky: "That's the sound profile of a blue whale, which means that the Big Bloop corresponds to an animal ten, maybe even fifteen times larger! You see? A never-before-identified creature, an unprecedented monster from the deep! The sensors recorded it several times over the course of last summer, always in the same place, near Point Nemo. I only came to Sydney in order to get there and try to observe it. You understand why my heart skipped a beat when I heard you state, almost in spite of yourselves, the coordinates of that location!"

They understood, but without succeeding in making their expressions appear any less dazed.

"When are you leaving?" Canterel managed to ask, nervously scratching at a bit of dead skin by his left nostril.

"Alas, I have no idea," replied Sanglard, sagging a little. "You know what American universities are like: anything is possible, as long as you can find sponsors . . . The International Fortean Organization subsidized my expedition up to a hundred thousand drachmas, which allowed me to get this far with the necessary scientific equipment. The American Visionary Art Museum in Baltimore invested nearly the same amount for me to charter a ship, for two hundred million thalers I sold the eventual rights to the story of my discoveries to a docudrama producer, and still I have met an insurmountable obstacle . . ."

"Which is?" asked Grimod.

"Imagine, I found a two hundred-eighteen ton schooner, with its whole crew, ready to leave for the destination of my choice. I loaded my instruments, my bags, and then the shipper, in light of my navigation plan, turns pale, starts babbling nonsense, and finally demands three hundred thousand more Australian pounds before he'll weigh anchor. When I have hardly a sou left in my pocket!"

"That's very unfortunate, and unfair," Grimod continued. "I can imagine your disappointment. But, if it's not indiscreet to ask, can you tell us more about your itinerary?"

"Oh, there's nothing confidential about it. I would simply like to reach Point Nemo, conduct my observations for a few days, then continue on to South America, cross the Panama Canal, and return to Toulouse, where my wife and children are waiting for me."

"Don't you teach at Miskatonic University?" asked Dr. Mardrus, surprised.

"Of course. But there, too, it's a professorship à l'américaine. I offer my courses intensively for two months of the year, and the rest of the time I'm free to work in France, at Mirail, in my lab."

"Forgive my incompetence," said Canterel, "I have some trouble with maritime jargon. What kind of a ship weighs two hundred eighteen tons?"

"A *big* boat," Grimod replied.

"By some standards, yes," Sanglard acquiesced. "It's a 138-foot yacht, which makes it more or less forty-two meters long and eight wide. Two masts, ten cabins, it's more than enough."

"What are you drinking?" Holmes asked, putting a hand on his shoulder.

"Oh, I don't know. A glass of red wine would be perfect, but I wouldn't want to . . ."

"Waiter!" cried Holmes. "Refill the scotches for those whose glasses are empty, one tea, three apple juices, and a large glass of red wine for Monsieur. The very best!"

"Ten cabins . . ." said Canterel, tapping on the table with his finger.

"Yes," said Sanglard, "not counting those for the crew."

"And how much do you need?" asked Holmes.

"Three hundred thousand Australian pounds, unfortunately."

Dr. Mardrus glanced at Lady MacRae, who turned away, annoyed, pulling Verity's chair closer. Holmes frowned, and Canterel was about to speak, when Grimod once again took the initiative.

"Professor Sanglard, I do not know how much this proposition will agree with you, but what would you say to bringing a few passengers with you? Paying, of course. There would be eight of us, and with the few bags we couldn't do without, plus the inconvenience our presence could cause, it seems to me that the sum of five hundred thousand pounds would cover our expenses and contribute not only to your research, but also to our well-being? What do you think?"

Alcide Sanglard looked him right in the eye. He adjusted his ponytail, slapped his hands down on the table, and clenched his fists.

"You," he said, his voice trembling, "you . . . Oh, Mary full of grace! What I mean to say is, you may come to Toulouse anytime, there will always be food and shelter for you there!"

XXXVIII

The Apocolocyntosis of the Barnum Museum

Reading the news, thinks Arnaud, you'd swear that reality produces more fictions than literature could possibly absorb. But sometimes, like tonight, looking at the *New York Times*, a troubling inversion occurs that strongly suggests that reality is, on the contrary, only a subservient mirror of what has already happened in novels. A mirror that is frightening in every respect.

Between 1841 and 1845, an enterprising young man, Phineas T. Barnum, bought the collections of Scudder's American Museum and the Philadelphia Museum, which had just gone bankrupt. He gathered them up, added his own innovations, and opened his own museum, Barnum's American Museum, on Broadway. On the four stories of a huge building on the corner of Ann Street, he had an incredible number of colorful advertisements painted, magnificent badges that alternated with the windows across the whole façade, announcing the place's mission: to offer the public an exhaustive, splendid, and "expensive" visual encyclopedia of all the marvels of the world.

Above a basement dedicated to steam engines—boilers, tanks, and various mechanisms allowing the whole thing to work together—the first floor housed the ticket windows, several souvenir shops, restaurants, and the monumental marble staircase up to the second floor. Here, all the walls were pierced with peepholes or windows that looked in on sensational dioramas. These scenes explored the intimacy of the most beautiful royal palaces, transported viewers to Istanbul or Venice; in less than a second, the visitor could plunge into the heart of the Siberian countryside, fly over the Great Wall, attend the decisive battles of the Revolutionary War, rub shoulders with Christopher Colombus in the gradual discovery of the New World—"Savage scenes of mutiny aboard the *Santa Maria*, terror of the natives," the panels read. Among the countless historical scenes, the transfer of Napoleon's ashes to Paris was bewilderingly successful. In the halls, a large, steam-powered model of Niagara Falls provoked cries of admiration. There was also the "Fiji Mermaid," comprising a monkey's head and torso and the back half of a grouper, Joice Heth, General Washington's mammy, "one hundred and sixty-one years old," blind and paralyzed, but still able to state that she had nursed the Father of the Nation. Further in, a "tattooed Greek noble" danced the sirtaki to the sound of an orchestra of Ethiopian minstrels.

On the third floor, the main hall was occupied by an enormous round aquarium, nine meters in diameter and six meters tall. There, a white whale from Labrador moved peacefully through seawater brought via aqueduct from the North River. Objects from Nantucket were displayed all around, engraved sperm-whale teeth, harpoons, ropes, barrels, all the trappings of a whaling ship. In the adjoining room, probably for the sake of comparison, the skeleton of a mammoth stood next to a live elephant with its mahout. Then came forty aquariums showing fish from all the world's rivers and seas, as well as an electric eel, an alligator, and dozens of turtles. At the heart of this "water garden," Unzie, the Hirsute Wonder, got a sea lion to juggle. Leaving the aquariums, visitors entered a cabinet of curiosities that contained masterpieces of glassmaking—include a crystal steam engine—distorting mirrors and other anamorphic processes, nested ivory bowls, and even American whistles made of pig tails. There, Dotty and Flo Carlson, the Half Ton Twins, told fortunes;

Miss Swan, the Scottish Giant, would palpate your skull according to phrenological principles, and Zerubby, the Circassian beauty with natural curls, would calculate the answer to any math problem in a flash. Passing by great aviaries filled with island birds, you entered a wax museum featuring, among others, a young Lord Byron, Queen Victoria, and Robert C. Kennedy, the "pyromaniac of luxury hotels, wearing the same clothes he wore in life"; the highlight of this collection indisputably being the effigy of Jefferson Davis, the president of the Confederate Army, disguised as a woman to escape the Union soldiers. In the uniform of the Army of the Potomac, Captain Abigail Khab, a Pequot Indian who had survived the Battle of Gettysburg, acted as his caretaker. With a terrible scar across his face, Khab had distinguished himself on Little Round Top, where a bullet had taken his leg; with the end of his prosthesis, he would lift Jeff Davis's skirts to show the public his boots. On the other side of the room, life-size robots reproduced the Last Supper; a glass of wine in hand, Christ turned his gaze toward Judas, making him hang his head. Further along, an Indian chief lay eternally dying, surrounded by his most valiant warriors. Then came a gallery of oil paintings by Rembrandt Peale: popes and emperors, saints and courtesans, famous pirates and assassins on the same picture rail, sharing a shining posthumous eternity.

From there, visitors went up to the fourth floor, almost completely occupied by the "conference hall": a veritable theater fitted with the most modern equipment where, twice a day, there were performances of morally irreproachable plays such as *Uncle Tom's Cabin* and *Narcissus Fitzfrizz, The Dancing Barber*, for the edification of the social classes that were most exposed to the contamination of the contemporary repertoire. Soprano Jenny Lind, the "Swedish Nightingale" over whom the great stages of Europe were fighting among themselves, sang there for several months. Without ever having heard her, Barnum had offered her a contract for a whopping thousand dollars per performance for a total of a hundred and fifty concerts. "But how can you consider hiring me without having listened to my voice?" the astonished singer asked before accepting. "I have more confidence in your reputation than my musical judgment," the entrepreneur had replied. His repartee was soon on everyone's lips.

In the main hall and the foyer, there were a horse and his rider petrified by the attack of a boa constrictor, insect display boxes, rare puzzles, exotic weapons, jawbones of sharks and narwhals, shirts taken from the corpses of heroic figures, Jim Bowie's knife, Davy Crockett's hat, the autographs and personal effects of George Washington, Benjamin Franklin, Thomas Jefferson, three authentic Egyptian mummies, the Sacred Cow of Benares—"the only one Buddha's high priest allowed to leave the temple"—and, surrounded by brightly colored birds, all the animals of the earth artistically stuffed and arranged to showcase their uniqueness. Among them, the most impressive of all were two zebras whose three hundred sixty-five stripes had been numbered on their coats by a savant, in order to demonstrate that every one of their species invariably bore the same number; but also a dodo from Mauritius (*Raphus cucullatus*), which the most recent evolutionary research placed in the Columbidae family, demonstrating that it was descended from none other than the rock pigeon.

The fifth floor ended in a kind of apotheosis, or, Seneca would have clarified with a smile, "apocolocyntosis," a transfiguration of the museum into a fairytale pumpkin. The staircase led to a professional seamstress who was sewing away at the most recent model of Singer sewing machines, all surrounded by the latest inventions intended to prepare for the advent of the twentieth century. In contrast with this marvelous example of modernity, ethnographic displays dedicated to the Indians and the Pacific tribes, featuring one of the twenty clubs that had knocked down Captain Cook, testified to the victory of progress over primitive times. Immediately after, a pungent odor of wild animals and acetylene caught in the throat. The next exhibit was the largest zoo ever assembled on earth in human memory. Cages arranged in exotic panoramas offered a Bengal tiger, a Transvaal lion, a hippopotamus (the "Great Behemoth of Scripture!"), a crouched giraffe, a kangaroo, an anaconda that was ten meters long, fifty poisonous snakes straight from the Amazon Jungle and the Libyan Desert, drowsy eagle owls, porcupines, hyenas, wild pigs, gorillas, chimpanzees, straight-backed bonobos, monkeys, monkeys, and more monkeys, whose screeching made any conversation impossible. After this menagerie came a quieter room displaying an incredible collection of shoes, from the first Egyptian thong to the latest fashionable styles; nickel meteorites that had recently fallen on Johannesburg; and knives and colts belonging to famous outlaws in the West. Continuing on, another room cluttered with dim displays claimed to be rescuing from oblivion the final remnants of a collection once gathered by an obscure German Jesuit; there the speechless visitor would find a Mandarin Chinese costume "made of coarse blue gauze," boots, a cap, and a paintbrush made of wolfskin; sixty-six dried fish, all labeled, enclosed under glass in gilded frames; the headless skeleton of a hunchback; two other skeletons of fetuses that were totally separate except for their skull, which had developed only one face for the both of them; shrunken female heads; two boxes containing human teeth of different ages and colors; a rope of spermatic vessels injected with wax, along with the matching testicles; a box containing several engorged male members; a tuft of hair and a tooth found in an ovary; a whale penis that was two meters long; a chicken bone found inside a negro's head; a series of thirty eyeballs displaying different maladies; a folding knife with a mother-of-pearl handle ornamented with a silver head of St. Ignatius, which opened abeam and contained poison; an embalmed cyclops that had lived for nine months, and whose whole eye had been organically preserved; different progressions of silkworms; a double coconut from the Maluku Islands.

Whether or not the spectacle of these curiosities prepared them, visitors then entered the chamber of phenomena to witness the "great ethnologic congress of the planet's peoples." Passing in front of a series of boxes, they would see in turn an Ubangi woman "with a mouth and lips as wide as an adult crocodile's," the Siamese twins Eng and Chang who were married to two sisters and had fathered twenty-two children, the "living Venus de Milo" who played the harp with her feet, the dwarf Tom Thumb dressed as Napoleon, the hairy family of Burma, the Seven Sutherland Sisters whose hair measured more than fifteen meters long end to end, Eko and Iko the "Ecuadorian Cannibals with the Heads of Sheep," two African-American albinos who began their career thus, but ended it thirty years later as "Ambassadors from the Planet Mars Discovered Near the Wreckage of their Spaceship in the Mojave Desert"; there was also Gabrielle, "half a wife with three husbands," stating loud and clear that women don't need legs. "I can appreciate life and do what I want," she would say to anyone who would listen, "I don't envy those who have them!"

Right before the exit, they finally encountered the "What is it?"— a being of simian appearance so named because of Charles Dickens's reaction the first time he saw it. "A lower order of man," a placard read, "or a higher development of the monkey?" Missing link or not, everyone agreed that it was the most interesting of the eight hundred and fifty thousand curiosities on display inside the establishment.

On this day—July 13th, 1865—at half past noon, a faulty boiler caught fire in the museum's basement; an employee immediately alerted the fire department, but hardly twenty minutes later the fire had set the first floor ablaze, escaping all control.

Last Telegrams of the Night

Things that make us wonder why they fascinate us.
Trie-sur-Baïse. Having lost his voice, the world champion of imitating pig cries slits his own throat.

Things that disturb the senses and make one's member swell behind one's fly.
The blind seer prophesied while sucking his clients' breasts. His future is in Fresnes Prison.

Things that leave one speechless.
His wife kisses him, leaving him mute. With a bleeding tongue Leonardo Vitale checked himself in to the hospital in Enna (Sicily). He'll never talk again, swears Toto Riina, his employer.

Things that are disconcertingly cold.
Chicago. Young thieves kill the goldfish so there won't be any witnesses. "It wasn't fair, he never would've exposed them," lamented the couple who had been robbed.

Things whose form, if cubic, would make the lives of chickens unbearable.
Among slow-moving objects, the egg is a marvelous example of aerodynamics.

Things that endear Apollinaire.

"Evil has not changed over the course of the centuries," Monsieur Paul Reynaud sighed. "The same cowardices prolong the same mistakes, and then one day you wake up with your head chopped off."

Things that suddenly make one's genitals hurt a little.

He is paraded before two hundred people with a cinderblock from a mosque hanging from his testicles. This, along with a caning, is the punishment that was imposed upon a thirty-year-old man by the local assembly of a village in Bangladesh for kidnapping a twelve-year-old girl and forcing her to marry him.

Things that divide opinions.

The mystery of the woman who was chopped into pieces remains intact, but it does seem she was leading a double life.

Things that one is reluctant to taste in spite of their semantic richness.

Gringuenaude. 1. A little bit of filth that sticks to your insides and other unclean places. 2. Left-overs that are still good to eat (*Dictionnaire Littré*).

Things that are darkly silent.

Blinded by jealousy, a deaf-mute kills his happy neighbor.

XXXIX

Strong Homerin

Driven by a stiff breeze from the west, under full sail, the *Black Orpheus* was in broad reach, its long, black hull, sitting well on the waves, leaving behind a bright white wake that sparkled in the sun. At the exact boundary where it trailed away, terns were skimming the waves.

In the five days it had already been sailing, the schooner had traveled the nearly 800 nautical miles that separated Sydney and New Zealand. At the moment we return to our story, it had just passed Auckland and was continuing east-north-east to reach the thirtieth parallel. The captain had explained that although this route was not the most direct, it allowed them to sail in the best conditions; they would not go back down toward Point Nemo until the last possible moment, in order to put off encountering the "Roaring Forties," those terrible winds that constantly plague the Southern Hemisphere. Not that the *Black Orpheus* wasn't capable of measuring up, but still, there were women aboard who had not paid to be manhandled.

Wedged among the rigging, at the starboard corner of the poop deck, the upper part of his face disappearing in the shadow of a wide Montecristi Panama hat made of real straw, Canterel was daydreaming. It was nice to hear the eddying of the water behind him, to contemplate the swelling of the sails and their way of catching their breath at regular intervals, but all this could hardly dispel his deep melancholy. From time to time, he would raise his photographic talisman to the sun, examine it, then return to his pose of a stricken dandy.

At this stage in their investigation, the situation was catastrophic. They had certainly unraveled the mystery of the three right feet, but they had not traced Giorgio Triskelès—or what was left of him after his triple amputation—and they had not figured out how this man was linked to the theft of the diamond. The Noh Straddler was nowhere to be found, as if he had given up the chase. And here they were, on their way to what might turn out to be an imaginary location in the Pacific, for lack of any other trail, and because none of them dared to admit that the evidence showed they had failed.

Scummington alone had felt the full measure of their defeat. Briefed on the decryption of the coordinates of Point Nemo, he had protested that they were crazy and mocked their wild imaginings. He had stayed in Sydney to finish his work: thanks to his efforts, Reverse Waterlily was behind bars.

"We'll interrogate her," he had added, "and I swear to you that that trollop will end up telling us a great deal more than you supposedly spelled out on her buttocks!"

At least they were rid of that odious character.

The other good news was that Verity was gradually regaining the use of her legs. She was now able to take a few steps, as long as she was supported. More and more often, she could be seen practicing on the deck, held up by one or another of the passengers, working hard to try to speed her progress.

The *Black Orpheus* was a gaff schooner with a topsail, which means that three yards and two square sails extended from its mizzenmast. A hunting ship, built for speed, what the Americans who had developed this type of boat called a "clipper." Driven by its 480 square meters of sails, it moved at an average speed of six knots, sometimes reaching ten. If the winds kept up, with the 1,450 miles that remained for them to cross, they would be at their destination in less than ten days.

The crew consisted of five men. Four sailors was enough, all of them Maoris from New Zealand with tattoos from head to toe, plus one Togolese chef, whose provenance was somewhat of a mystery. To make life easier, the captain had dressed them up with nicknames to which they responded immediately, without seeming the least bit offended. Spade, Heart, Diamond, and Club for the sailors, Smalls for the cook. No name could have suited him less: though still young, he was a potbellied man who panted like a seal when he moved. On his chubby face, scars in the shape of claw marks left the passengers wondering. No one had ever seen him smile, and in tasting his cooking they couldn't help but think that his dishes, though well prepared, were affected by this melancholy.

No complaints about the sailors, either, thought Canterel, even if they were overdoing their Maori performance. Always grimacing, showing their muscles, and gazing lecherously at Clawdia every time she came up to the deck for some fresh air. The captain kept an eye on them, however, and intervened whenever he caught a menacing glance or heard one of those ribald compliments that they loved to come up with in their language.

"Mr. Heart, please," he would say, "trim the topgallant!"

And he would send them up the masts or to go take care of some suddenly urgent task.

A strange fellow, this captain. He had introduced himself as Captain Abner Jonathan Ward, and made it clear from the outset that he always preferred to be called simply Captain Ward. Protruding ears, white hair cropped very short, aquiline nose over a large mouth with well-defined lips, he displayed the musculature of a gladiator in the prime of his life. Under the brim of his cap, his eyes had the leaden hue of an oncoming storm.

Despite his size and his assertiveness, however, the man suffered from an uncommon defect that is difficult to explain. It will be best to relate how it manifested itself the first time they encountered it. When they had shown up for their departure, at the end of the plank that was serving as gangway to the *Black Orpheus*, the captain was on deck, his back to them, inspecting the tension pulleys of a lower shroud.

"Captain Ward?" Holmes had said.

At these words, though they were pronounced calmly and courteously, the man had jumped so abruptly and so exaggeratedly that he had almost gone over the handrail. This might have seemed comical, if his features had not, in that moment, shown the wildest terror. It had only taken him two or three seconds to recover and immediately impress upon them his calm determination. This eccentricity would have been inconsequential if it had not consistently been repeated throughout the hours and days that followed. As long as you were within his field of vision, you could have threatened Captain Ward with a loaded pistol and not a muscle in his face would have trembled, but if you caught him off guard, if the dinner bell rang out of sight, if you came across him in a corridor when he wasn't expecting it, all his limbs went suddenly slack and he jumped as if from a strong electric shock, always with that brief but unfathomable terror in the depths of his eyes.

The fact that during these outbursts he would let out several heartfelt oaths was less astonishing, in the end, than the fits themselves, especially coming from a seaman accustomed to using strong language when giving orders. The night they cast off, however, there was a scene that puzzled them all deeply. When they had gathered in the wardroom, around a large anti-rolling table that was set for dinner, Lady MacRae bent over to pick up a napkin, accidentally presenting the captain a plunging view down her cleavage. Ward, who was in the middle of extolling the virtues of his schooner, suddenly fell silent, his face flushed as if he were suppressing a sneeze, then began to spout a stream of profanity, featuring "shithead," "motherfucker," and "cocksucker" as the most favored expressions.

At the start, Canterel had stood up, ready to intervene, but the clearly pathological nature of this verbal slip had left him as paralyzed as everyone else.

Looking frightened, his head and torso twitching, the captain struggled with all his might to resist the uncontrollable flow of oaths that was befouling his lips, only managing to lessen it by whispering these horrors more and more quietly until they were inaudible. Only then did he stop. Regaining his composure, he stood to address Lady MacRae.

"I beg you to excuse me," he said, red with shame, "it's not my fault. I, I have . . . It's an illness, a kind of reflex that happens against my will every time I feel an unusual emotion. I had thought I was rid of it."

"You're from Maine, aren't you?" Dr. Mardrus asked gently. "And your family has French roots?"

"How can you know that?"

"Perhaps they even lived for a time in Greenville or Rockwood, near Moosehead Lake?"

"Rockwood . . . This is sorcery!" said Ward, turning white.

"Of course not," replied Mardrus. "It's medicine, more precisely neurology. It so happens that I tackled neuroscience in my studies, and I was very intrigued by a study by George Miller Beard that described a rare neurosis, geographically limited to the farthest northeast of the United States. Have you ever heard of the Jumping Frenchmen of Maine Disorder?"

"Never. What is it?"

"It's the affliction from which you suffer, dear sir."

Sinking back in his seat, Dr. Mardrus savored the effect, smiled at Lady MacRae, then continued: "At the end of the last century, a small group of Quebecois lumberjacks was working on harvesting precious woods around Moosehead Lake. Spending months secluded deep in the woods, subject to the stress of solitude and the daily dangers of a hostile environment, these woodcutters developed an extraordinary nervous disorder. They all began to jump, pathologically and disproportionately, at any change, no matter how small, to their environment. They seemed overcome by that primordial fear we imagine prehistoric man must have felt, in a time when the smallest rustling of a leaf, the slightest clap of thunder could have deadly implications. The pathological terror of the 'jumping Frenchmen' became an attraction in Maine. People organized treks to go scare them and roared with laughter at their simian response!"

Lady MacRae interrupted him.

"This conversation is nothing short of embarrassing, I'm not sure it is to Captain Ward's liking, at least not with us present. Perhaps it would be preferable to explain all this to him in private?"

The captain ducked his chin at her, showing that he appreciated her delicacy.

"Carry on," he said, authoritatively.

"Among the affected subjects," Mardrus continued, "this primal fear causes at the same time a contraction reflex in the larynx, which first translates into onomatopoeias resembling a yell—'ho,' 'ha,' 'hum,'—certainly this is the case with children, and then when the subject gets older, into cursing. The latter acts as a decoy meant to mislead the invisible assailant, to delay the threat of attack, even for a moment. It is an incantation, it is smut, and it is—subconsciously, of course—perceived as effective."

"But I'm aware of the obscenities that are coming out of my mouth," Captain Ward corrected. "That's what makes my attacks so unbearable . . ."

"Honestly, the whole thing is very mysterious, but the fact remains that it is a disorder listed by Charcot and his school, and we should be very forgiving of its manifestations. The divine Mozart himself suffered from this, I could read you letters to his cousin next to which your latest tirade would appear quite innocent . . ."

"Is Sunday he cure the fucking shit one day?" asked Verity, earnestly.

"They tried arsenic, Mademoiselle," Mardrus replied, as if the girl had asked a perfectly intelligible question, "but the effective dose is too harmful to the body to be worth the benefits. Instead, I would recommend calm, seclusion, an avoidance of overstimulation, but I don't mean to cloud the issue: 'once a ticker, always a ticker,' as they used to say." Addressing the captain, he continued: "I do, however, know of a simple but sovereign remedy, and with your permission I will be happy to write you a prescription . . ."

Without waiting for Captain Ward's response, Mardrus scribbled on a sheet of paper, applying himself to writing a signature that would doubtless have interested handwriting experts, then carefully tore it out of his notebook. Searching through the inside pockets of his jacket, he finally pulled out a little metal box, which he offered Ward along with the paper.

"Here," he said in reassuring tone, "it's less dangerous than arsenic, and it should solve your problem."

What he said was true, even if, in reading this unusual prescription you might rightfully think he was joking:

DR. CHARLES-JOSEPH MARDRUS
Hyperesthesia, spasmodic dysphonia, coprolalia

STRONG HOMERIN

But the boat that charges over the waves does not escape the sirens' gaze; they sing their song, their voices clear: Come to us,

great Ulysses, stop your boat, come hear our voices. No black-
hulled boat has ever passed these shores without succumbing to
the spell of our melodious song.

Charles-Joseph Mardrus

As for the box, whose spun aluminum lid showed an Egyptian vulture with outspread wings, it contained wax earplugs; Captain Ward could thus put them in when he wanted to conquer his malady completely, and take them out when he judged that it was essential to the running of the ship.

And so our companions had gained the presence of a deaf man at their table, and the leisure to converse freely in front of him.

Clawdia's voice brought Canterel out of his reverie.

"Have you seen him?" she said, pointing up at something. "He's priceless, isn't he? Watch, watch how he flies!"

Left free, Darwin was playing ape-man in the rigging. There was indeed a great deal of skill and fluidity in his manner of moving from rope to rope.

Clawdia's face was lit with golden hues by the setting sun, her thin dress of white linen seeming to stir of its own accord in the supernatural light.

She knelt down unceremoniously next to Martial.

"But really, what have you been looking at all day long?"

"Your rib cage, my dear," he said, his voice sounding strange. "I've been looking for your heart, and I haven't found it."

Lady MacRae suddenly became the Madame Chauchat he had once known. Recognizing the small X-ray preserved in glass that she had thought was lost so long ago, she seized it and softly tossed it overboard.

Still looking Canterel right in the eye, she took his hand and brought it inside her bodice, placing it right on the skin above her left breast.

"It's just that you don't know how to look," she said, as if speaking to a child.

Despite what this gesture might have appeared to suggest, Clawdia allowed Canterel nothing more; she turned away and left him in a state of frustration that did very little for his peace of mind.

XL

Tourette's Virus

Dear mama, thank you for your pakage, the pritty pencil that I reseeved was verry nicc and I cant livc without it, and the sky blue swet-
ter looks good on me, I am splendid. The beutifull ten-franc coin, I
play with it, I look at it, I felt so happy whcn I saw thccs gifts. Granny
is well, she is helthy. Grampa is fixing the windo. Granny fell down
the patio stares, when I herd that funny story, I started laffing! Ha ha!
thinking of the day of anuther acsident, wich was not so bad, when
she tripped on the rug in her room trying to put on her underpants,
she took a noesdive! I saw she was hurt and her hair was messed up, I
called Grampa who got jellus, he picked her up all out of breth. Rite
then, on the street, I saw a dog wearing glasses, but it was a girl . . .

Granny Vitrac had worked in a SEITA match factory for a while.
She chopped sticks of poplar using "the Glutton," a cutting machine
that automatically pulled your arms back to keep your fingers away
from the choppers. But it would eat you up anyway if you fell asleep
out of boredom or exhaustion. Hortense had gotten caught once, now
she only had a thumb and index finger on her left hand. After the
accident, she had been sent to roll Gitanes in another factory. She had
worked herself to the bone there until she retired.

Grampa and Granny have finally sold their tires, not to the jipsy who bargined for the sossages but the guy who bot back the Aronde. While Grampa was getting the best deel of his life—40 francs!—Granny was calling him a sukker behind his back. I will be happy when I have my weekly allowince, because there is a fair at Domme or Castelnaud, I don't no yet, and I get my mony for the cherrys all at once. Today I asked Grampa what he was going to do to fite pollution, and you no what he said? I'm gonna change my socks, that's alreddy a small step.

As for Eugène, he slaughtered pigs for a living. He would get called to some farm, and he'd show up at dawn with his instruments. He would knock the animal out with a club of his own invention, a bludgeon made of a metal shaft screwed to a *boule* ball, which was enough to indicate its Anjou origins. By the time he left, at sundown, the swine had been fully broken down into its various cuts. People enjoyed listening to him hold forth on his art, while he stirred his fetid broths, insisting that water, or even grease, could not replace blood in a good boudin.

I reseeved your letter this morning with the menu from La Pérouse, thanks a lot. Really, mama, your letters don't brake the record for being long! Anyway, I forgiv you. This morning at seven, I started my job picking cherrys, I'm sending you my pay because I'm worried I'll spend all the mony, I'm gonna work the other days to, when it's not so bad, but tomorow if it's not raning like today I ekspect I'll make 100 or 120 francs, you'll see. It pays well, I worked for 4 ours, tomorow if the wether is good I'll work 9 and a haff, I really have the soul of a <u>gatherer</u>! (the dictionerry helped me find that) Yesterday, I made Granny say sorry because she let out this eksplosive fart, so bad it was hard to see the TV for a few minutes. Grampa farted to a cupple minutes later. It's crazy how hard it is to write and tell you new things every day . . .

My search for information about you has turned up nothing. You must not be using Dad's name anymore, or even your maiden name, otherwise I would have traced you by now. It's unbelievable how many Petitbouts and Lemestres there are on the Internet! I've spent several Sundays looking. Last week, I talked to Charlotte about you, it hurt her.

The other day, Granny had made her speshul mash. I didn't want to no what's in it. I cudn't eat it, I don't like cucumber soss with my mash, it makes me choak. Grampa scoalded me and made me cry. Blow your noes! he told me. I can't, I said, the water jug is on top of my hanky. I cant wait til I'm an adult so I can order peeple around! The gypsy (I looked it up!) came back looking for the tires, but Grampa alreddy sold them to the guy with the Aronde. He made a huje fuss! Granny chased him out, she scaired him with her to fingers and her rooined hand.

Last night, I dreamed about witches with sticky hands. And right after, I had a dream about an algorithm hiding within the very makeup of the phrase, unstoppable and beautiful: Tourette's virus. From a hidden set of instructions, the machine took a given text and made it into a series of anagrams of quotes from *Vice Amply Rewarded*, trying to restore the text's licentious vocabulary. The screen showed nothing but an endless list of dirty words and filth.

I got unorganized in my mail, you didn't get a letter Monday, a thowsand apologees, I'll catch up, because the fair was Saturday night, so I waited til Sunday morning. At the fireworks Granny took anuther tumble. While she was on the ground, a little gypsy was running around everywhere, and a lanturn fell off it's hook and cot fire right in front of her noes. She was yelling so loud that Constabull Cole (who was a marry old soul and a marry old soul was he, hee hee hee!) ran over to see what was going on . . .

It's been two days since Charlotte's been at work. I miss her, I'm worried. Some people saw her leave the factory after her meeting with the director of HR, others swore she never came back down. One of her friends is going to go by her house after work, we'll know more tomorrow morning. B@bil has become unbearable, but nobody's moving. It's like they're all hypnotized by that bullshit coming over the speakers. I'm sick of it, can't wait for the bell to ring so I can get the hell out of here.

Wow, I wrote you a whole reem! I hoap you folow my example . . . Sending you all my love, goodby now, til tomorow for the next episode.

Fabrice

XLI

The Strangers of Morning

As you can imagine, Sanglard had not remained idle during these days at sea. With the help of Grimod and Dr. Mardrus, he submersed a hydrophone capable of recording low frequency sounds at great depths. The sensor transmitted information in the form of a curve that was displayed in real time on a domed, green screen in a mahogany case. Connected to this was another instrument that looked like a barograph with a pen, for keeping a written record of interesting events. As he manipulated various potentiometers, the professor explained to them that he was adjusting his device in order to exclude any frequencies whose spectrograms did not resemble the signature produced by whale song.

He also set up a device that would allow him to convert captured ultrasounds, then amplify them to make them audible to the human ear. A loudspeaker with a voicecoil would broadcast this noise at an adjustable volume; to avoid inconveniencing anyone, they could also listen to it individually by putting on what Sanglard called a "topophone," a kind of pilot's headset made of leather, with earflaps connected to the machine by two copper coils. All of this equipment was electrically powered by a wind turbine set up on the sterncastle, and, when the wind was insufficient, a Cabirol diving pump that had been modified into a generator.

No zoologist would have crossed so many miles of ocean without trying to collect new species during his passage. Sanglard was no exception, and he had the *Black Orpheus* dragging a three-meter-wide trawl whose cable was hooked up to a dynamometer. As it filled, the net got heavier, moving the needle of a dial indicating its weight in kilograms. As his snare was being dragged through the deepest depths, a zone that was not hospitable to an abundance of fish, the professor gave the order to pull it in every three hours, after first activating the system that would close the trap, so that they would not take in anything else as it came up. As soon as the men started hauling at the windlass, the passengers were sure to appear and, along with those members of the crew who were not currently busy with some other task, they would gather at the stern, where the net would dump its secret contents from the chasms of the Pacific.

These meetings left them amazed; the net teemed with monsters every time. It was not their size that was impressive—they were almost always small, if not tiny—but rather their excessive and extremely varied aberrations. In the gelatinous mass that was spread out on the deck, they could make out an intermingling of jagged mouths attached to spindly bodies; gaping mandibles lined with pointed little teeth, clamped tight inside or protruding out like boar tusks; hatchet-fish with telescopic eyes; sea devils with lanterns on their snouts and branching gills under their chins; pelican eels with their triangular jaw-pouches; a whole hodgepodge of slimy antennae, blind creatures with missing or degenerated eyes whose luminous organs shot out as they gave off their final glows.

They seemed like demons from hell, dreadful and terrifying, like something from St. Anthony's dreams.

Sanglard would dissect them, finding other horrors in their stomachs, and still more in their half-digested waste. Next he would wash them, then place them in bottles filled with formol, which he would carefully label.

"Everything you bring to the surface is one of the worst creatures from our nightmares," Clawdia said that morning, jokingly, but in a tone that exposed the disgust she felt toward these unnatural animals.

"Perhaps that's true," replied Sanglard, his voice serious. "Perhaps all we're doing is flying over the secret reservoir of our fears. Do you know how deep I've been sending the trawl? Five thousand meters down . . . Given that not a single photon is visible below five hundred meters, the beasts that you see wriggling before you come from a world of total darkness, of a blackness so thick, so extreme that we can't even imagine it. The pressure is so great that it lowers the freezing point of water well below what it is on the surface; the temperature there is always between 0.5 and 1.5°C. Add to that the absolute stillness of the liquid medium, unmoved by even the worst storms or anything else that can shake our world, and you get a nightmarish universe, a black sorbet of hallucinatory neurons."

He shook his head as if to shake off this vision.

"It is an underworld that from its beginnings lost contact with ours, as my old friend Adrian Leverkühn used to say. And in this world, famine prevails, hence these extravagant ploys in order to find food, to reproduce, to try to survive at any cost. For millions of years, the processes that led to us being the way we are worked on them in the same way, with results that are just as eccentric, just as horrible, just as ridiculous, but just as perfectly adapted. In that general darkness, predators are equipped with an arsenal of sophisticated little lights that attract their prey. Red and green lamps in the corners of their mouths, Chinese lanterns at the tips of dorsal fins that extend like fishing rods in front of their mouths, long strings of bright points that pulse with different colors or, in some cases, rows of yellow windows that twinkle, reignite, and burn out like ships sinking. There is nothing like it, it draws curious victims like flies! Things are more complicated for the prey, as always. We imagine them navigating in the utter darkness, to avoid being spotted, but they too need light in order to attract the male or female necessary to the continuation of their species. So they light up their silhouettes, or the intricate pattern of their ovaries or their reproductive appendage, and, most of the time, get themselves gobbled up before they've even had time to mate. Which sometimes leads them to try extremely risky strategies . . . Like the giant Pacific octopus, which haphazardly releases spermatophores that are more than a meter wide, drifting mines of semen that will perhaps never come anywhere near a female's reproductive tract."

"What a mess!" Canterel muttered. "Though not too far off from the behavior of some of my friends."

"These animals," Sanglard continued, not noticing the interruption, "are merely optimizing their chances of reproducing, and in this matter nature always chooses the path of least resistance, as chaotic or deviant as it may appear to us. This is the case with my *Octopoteuthis deletron*, the squid I studied. The male only reaches sexual maturity a short time before his death, so he only has one chance in his life to procreate. When mating season arrives, the males hurl themselves at anything that moves and implant their spermatozoa on both females and other males. Since members of that species live alone, in absolute blackness, they have not developed the ability to recognize their congeners' sex, a solution that would doubtless cost too much in evolutionary terms, and they prefer this strange but effective boondoggle of sperm. And the fact remains that they are still here."

"That's horrible," said Clawdia. "That relentless estrangement, that awful distance from other beings . . ."

"Not always, dear madam, nothing is systematic. Among ceratioid anglerfish, for example, which are just four to eight centimeters long, encounters must have been so difficult that nature fixed the problem in a totally different way: as soon as a male meets a female, who is ten times his size, he bites her, just about anywhere; his jaws and tongue graft themselves to her tissue so tightly that he remains fixed to her body for the rest of his life."

"Ironclad fidelity," Canterel laughed, "Othello's dream!"

"That is far from certain . . . Doubtless the female gets something out of it, but the male is in permanent hell. He becomes a parasite on the thing he has bitten, his circulation is melded to hers, to such an extent that he receives all his nourishment by this means. In addition, most of his organs—his digestive system, his eyes, his brain—atrophy, as they no longer serve any purpose; his reproductive glands, on the other hand, inflate to enormous size and, swollen with gonads, he ends up dangling like a shrimp fritter under the female. And the worst part, for your Othello, is that others come! It is not uncommon to find ladies with three or four of these gentlemen embedded in their bellies. Or their backs, or on their cheeks, their faces . . . As I said, they hook on wherever they can at their first encounter, and lay their roots there until they die."

Alcide Sanglard had hit his stride. As he sorted hideous specimens from the last load, he continued monologuing on his favorite topic. In order to survive, the proletariat of the open ocean had developed tactile filaments, supersensitive fibrils, a whole network of extracorporeal perception meant to warn of approaching danger. The universe in which these creatures lived was a perpetual ghost train: they felt shadows brush against them, never knowing whether it was time to light its strings in the hope of copulating, or to ball itself up to avoid being eaten. They lived and died with fear in their hearts. Instead of black ink, he said, panicked cuttlefish spit out a haze of light.

"The opposite of our world," Clawdia whispered, impressed by his evocative rendering.

"No, my dear," Sanglard replied, "it is a *different* world, strange, frightening, beyond all human understanding. An image of what our planet might have been reduced to had not land emerged in the distant past, and of what it will look like when we have pushed our foolish desire for power to its very limits."

Jostled by a stronger wave, the *Black Orpheus* yawed slightly, causing the professor to lose his balance.

"Why this fascination with monsters?" asked Dr. Mardrus, helping him back to his feet.

Sanglard looked troubled; evidently such a question had never occurred to him, and it took him several seconds to respond.

"You are a doctor, so you know that you can learn the most about health by observing an ailing body. Anyone who has ever dismantled a stopped clock knows this as well. Perhaps we will only understand something about the secret order of the world once we have earnestly and patiently indulged its inconsistencies?"

At that moment of palpable and already unusual gravity, a long bellow was heard. The grave sound of a Tibetan horn, followed by echoing laments. All eyes, frightened, turned first to the loudspeaker, then to Sanglard, who had rushed to his instruments.

"The Big Bloop?" asked Holmes, nervous.

"No, humpbacks," he replied. "A whole pod. Listen to this! Hear how they sing, the darlings, how they talk to one another!"

It would take a passion like Sanglard's to hear songs in these deep groans interspersed with gurgles and abrupt stridencies, in which they seemed to recognize the anxious cries of young girls startled by nightfall. Terrified, Darwin had taken refuge at the top of the mizzenmast, mingling his own howls with those that were enveloping the ship.

Only Captain Ward noticed that the crewmen had also been struck with a holy terror. Legs set wide, hands holding tight to the wheel, he gave the order to trim the sails and congratulated himself for having put his balls of wax in his ears.

The whales had not surfaced, but they were close enough to the boat that its hull reverberated with their sorrowful modulations.

Between their moans, the background noise reemerged, sounding like hoarse breathing.

During one of these pauses, Verity's voice gave them all a start.

"Yes," she said, concentrating, her eyes fixed on a spot on the sea, "forward from the schooner. Is there reason that me?"

She listened to a sequence of low notes, then continued.

"Well, lots, strangers of morning! Almost as if fire. It comes from above, beyond the stars . . ."

Then came still more motifs that sounded like growls, which grew louder, intertwined, and waned in feverish repetitions.

"Neither true nor false," said Verity, "just devoid of meaning. You have an advantage, we are less than reality."

She had closed her eyes and begun to tremble all over.

"My darling," exclaimed Clawdia, shaking her, "wake up, I beg you, my darling!"

"She understands them," said Sanglard, stunned, "she understands them and is answering them . . ."

XLII

The Tiger's Bite

Anyone who remembers Monsieur Wang will tell you that he was a tyrant, a scumbag slant-eye obsessed with profit, but in the end not a bad guy. They will talk about him like an invalid, their voices using the inflections of pitying excuses reserved for those with mental disabilities. That is how Charlotte sees him in this moment, tangled up in his desire for her and his despair at having lost his pigeon. Amazing how much he has been telling her for hours about the mess birds make . . . She pretends to be listening, sitting here, stark naked on the office chair where he invited her to take a seat. A vague uneasiness, a mixture of shame and anticipation, has paralyzed her. This clown holds her in his power, but she is not afraid of him, knowing instinctively that he is not prepared to risk everything to give in to his impulses.

In Monsieur Wang's head, the situation is much less clear. Charlotte has the most beautiful breasts he has ever beheld, two marvels that he can only compare to doves with milky, platinum coats. He has to force himself not to go kneel before them, give them the honor they deserve. The rest of her body is uninteresting to him, but he recognizes that it is certainly admirable, not an ounce of excess fat, no bulges or stretch marks, the body of a young woman in which the fresh forms of adolescence can still be seen in all their natural suppleness.

"They are a kind of angel," he says, glancing at his pigeon loft. "When they fly off bearing a note, their wings carry the message across the sky like an annunciation. They are envoys, arrows of fate. Do you know how Nathan Rothschild increased his fortune twenty-fold? Thanks to a carrier pigeon. One of his spies, who was at Waterloo, managed to send a pigeon to inform him of the English victory. Tipped off before anyone else, the prudent man manipulated the London Stock Exchange in such a way as to bring down the exchange rate of the pound, then bought up that currency at an unbeatable price. Once news of Napoleon's defeat reached London, it caused a huge rise in the pound, and enormous benefits for those who had had the intelligence to make the right choice."

These are the words coming out of his mouth, but his eyes show something else entirely, and Charlotte still feels threatened. Sitting behind his desk, Monsieur Wang is playing with a roll of brown packing tape. *Here's what we're going to do*, his eyes say, *I'm going to tape your ankles and knees to the legs of the chair, then I'll bind your outstretched hands behind the backrest. Next I'll walk around you with the tape, pulling it tight, and once I'm done the only thing left showing will be your bulging bosom, turning blue and purple.*

"An ancient historian told of a pigeon that crossed the space separating Babylon and Aleppo in forty-eight hours, a distance that would take a person a month on foot. They also say that gladiators released pigeons after combat to announce to their friends that they had emerged victorious from the arena."

Monsieur Wang feels his heart beating like fifteen buckets on a waterwheel, seven of which rise while the other eight fall. In his mind he brushes against Charlotte's breasts, touches them with the tips of his fingers, pats them, trills his tongue against them, he rubs, compresses, flattens them in order to watch how they slowly bulge out again, then he pinches her nipples, stretches them, twists them slightly to firm them up. One by one, he squeezes the raised bumps along the pink-brown smoothness of her areolas, returns to the fleshier parts, coaxes them, makes them wobble, fondles them gently; only then does he knead them, alternating between his palms and his fingertips, he grasps them, feels them, manipulates them. He considers himself a past master of these caresses; in reality, all of this could be summarized by simply saying he gropes them.

"For lack of homing pigeons, they used to use swallows as well. An impresario who organized chariot races brought them to Rome. He would send them back to announce the success of such-and-such a charioteer to provincial gamblers: they would return to their point of origin, and the color he had painted them—blue, red, green, or white—indicated the victor."

Wang is looking at Charlotte more and more strangely. His hands are invisible, hidden under the desk. He is staring so fixedly at her chest that it starts to tingle. His twisted mouth really frightens her. She is not sure what she has just heard, as it is so incongruous, but it seems the bastard has just farted.

His lips curling back, Monsieur Wang seizes the skin of one breast between two canines and clamps down with the full force of his jaws. She screams. Two red dots appear, resembling a snake bite. He imagines himself continuing—ignoring the girl's wails—imprinting other marks in a curve to create lines that he then examines with his mind's eye. On one and then the other, according to a plan that seems to owe nothing to chance, he varies the shapes of the bruises by changing how he inflicts them. She screams. He bites. Upper teeth against lower lips to make "the coral and the jewel," the reverse for "the monkey's smile," using all the teeth while breathing in for "the tiger's bite." He licks up beads of blood as they form. At the end, when he steps back to enjoy his work, his nips and brands have formed Chinese characters, which he pronounces vehemently: *"wànsuì, wànsuì, wànwànsuì"* (万岁 万岁 万万岁), the formula once used to wish the emperors long life.

"And if I told you pigeons sometimes get hard, little mammillated tumors that come up on the surface of the skin, especially on their fleshy membranes? These mounds are sliced off, then the wounds are cauterized with silver nitrate."

On the three chrome-plated clocks that tell the time in Paris, New York, and Beijing, Charlotte sees that it is already five in the morning. She is numb with exhaustion.

"I'm cold. Give me my clothes, please. I haven't stolen anything, I swear!"

"I know," says Monsieur Wang, standing up, key in hand, to open the safe.

She gets up too, furious.

"Then why am I here? What are you playing at?"

Wang offers her the basket containing her clothes. It would be good to confess, he thinks, watching her hastily get dressed, but it's too hard to take the first step.

"Louise engineered this whole scheme."

"The head of HR?"

"Yes. She's jealous. That is, 'she,' 'he,' who really knows anymore . . ."

"What the hell are you talking about?"

"Oh, you'll have to ask her, but she has not always been a woman, if you know what I mean. She resents you because I have plans for you. A promotion within the company."

"By which you mean keeping me here all night, naked in your office? This is unreal! You're nuts, all of you! I'm the one who's going to file a complaint, I'm warning you . . ."

Wang does not appear at all impressed by what she's saying. It looks like his mind is elsewhere.

"Come now, don't act more stupid than you are: it will be your word against mine, and I don't have a criminal record."

"I'm getting the hell out of here!"

"No one is stopping you, Mademoiselle. The door was open the whole time, you know. I very much enjoyed spending this time in your company."

As he shoves his hands into his pockets, in a dominating pose, Charlotte notices the dark stain that is dampening the area around his fly.

"Pig!" she says, her chin trembling, overcome with disgust. "Fuck you!"

She left, slamming the door behind her as hard as she could.

Alone, Monsieur Wang retrieved the keychain camera lying on his desk and pressed the button to stop recording. It was only after having transferred the file onto his iPad that he lay down on the couch. Sleep overtook him as he watched the tablet replay the sad film of his night.

XLIII

The Infernal Cyclist

The singing had stopped at Verity's last words. Sanglard, who had already started work on an experimental design for decoding the humpbacks' language, did not appear at all discouraged. He carefully recorded the girl's words, noted the chart recordings that preceded each of her responses, and stood by in case another opportunity presented itself.

As interesting as it was, this adventure would have come to nothing, except that it marked the beginning of a significant change in the crewmen's attitude. All of them, including the cook, seemed overwhelmed by the unearthly voices that had reverberated through their ears. The Maoris held long confabulations in the forecastle, their faces grave; from their way of indicating a particular direction over the sea, and from their fingers that sometimes pointed at the scientific instruments, it was clear that they linked the two, the singing and the course they were on. They started incessantly drinking an island ratafia, which caused them first to chant sadly, then made them aggressive or crudely lecherous. It now took a certain amount of time, and a certain amount of swearing, to get them to follow through on the captain's orders.

As for the cook, Smalls, he was suddenly spending more of his energy on praying than cooking. At all hours he could be heard reciting psalms or reading aloud from the Book of Revelation. Kneeling in his galley before thin spermaceti candles, he would work up a sweat, crossing himself, his eyes rolling, a little froth at the corners of his mouth. What little he was still willing to cook was homogeneous and unidentifiable.

These disturbances soon created an unhealthy and oppressive atmosphere on the ship—an uneasiness that came to a head two days later, in the middle of the night.

Around three in the morning, Canterel, unable to sleep, came up to the deck to get a little fresh air. The full moon, rather high on the horizon, was shedding a ghostly light on the *Black Orpheus*. Martial lit a cigarette and nodded at the watchman rooted to his spot next to the wheel. As the latter did not return his greeting, he walked away, heading off toward the bow.

He had just reached the base of the mizzenmast when a peculiar movement caught his eye. What he saw left him stunned: upside down on top of the cuddy, her skirts up around her neck, Miss Sherrington was about to be sexually assaulted by Mr. Club! Grabbing a fishing bludgeon that was lying next to him, Canterel rushed over; right as he was about to intervene, something about the housekeeper's passivity stayed his arm. Looking toward him, she displayed the kind of fake smile normally associated with the mother of a toddler who has just urinated in your arms. "It's not so bad, no harm done," she seemed to be saying, indulgently. The man took advantage of this brief hesitation to thrust forward and penetrate her; at that very moment, Canterel saw him throw himself back suddenly, fall to his knees, then start bawling, his two hands grasping a sort of bloody funnel that was clamped onto his penis.

It had taken Miss Sherrington only a second to straighten her clothing and run off to get Dr. Mardrus.

Awoken by the yelling, everyone was soon on deck. After a quick examination, the doctor had Mr. Club moved to the wardroom. It took him two hours of patient effort to cut away the terrible mechanism and to extract, one by one, the steel hooks that had driven into his penis. The patient needed several stitches, but in the end Mr. Club, knocked out by the anesthetics, fell into a peaceful sleep. Despite the extreme pain and a few barely visible scars, he did not experience any aftereffects from this procedure and, for better or worse, he retained his virility.

Miss Sherrington recounted how she had come up for some air and how the sailor, clearly drunk, had attacked her. Luckily, she never went out without her anti-rape device, she had summarized, or else God knows what would have happened to her! The apparatus in question was a vellum sheath, inside of which the housekeeper had sewn six rows of little harpoons, their points turned in such a way as to allow something to slide in, but prevent it from coming back out.

Called upon to explain himself, Mr. Club gave a rather different version, claiming that the old lady had made such obvious advances on him that he had felt justified in approaching her. Besides, she hadn't protested at any point, he swore.

Miss Sherrington has, up to now, only been described from a perspective that is not conducive to showing the Victorian subtleties of her personality. It is time to add a few brushstrokes to a portrait that has doubtless been too cursory. A single anecdote will suffice, one that is still told with a shudder in the bars of Biarritz, and that was reported in the papers under this headline: "The Infernal Cyclist."

Martial Canterel's housekeeper had not always been the tetchy old lady we know. In her youth, at a time when young women from good families were emancipating themselves willy-nilly by taking on jobs or getting into charity work, Alice Margaret Sherrington had committed herself body and soul to Louise Michel's Guild of the Slaves of the Immaculate Heart, the revived lodge of "Universal Fraternity." A native of Manchester, she had worked there for several years as a "knocker-up," a profession that consisted of waking the workers at dawn so that they would arrive at the mills on time. Along with a number of colleagues, she would sweep through the city between the hours of five and six in the morning, knocking on the doors and windows of the two hundred people with whom she was charged. Three knocks of her fist on lower entrances, three raps with her stick on the shutters it could reach, and above that three chickpeas from her peashooter against the windowpanes. She had developed the fist of a blacksmith and the lung capacity of a Murano glassblower.

Later, during the terrible armed conflict between Lancashire and the Highlands, she had taken part in the war effort by getting a job at a heavy machine-gun factory. It was at this point that she had become passionate about mechanics and developed a unique creativity in that field. Lancashire owed her the invention of the "sticky bomb," a spherical grenade that was loaded with nitroglycerin, then slathered with glue before being isolated in a glass ampoule. Extremely effective against tanks, this "candy apple," as she had christened it, had not been successful in preventing the Scottish victory, however, or the digging of the canals that now separated that country from the rest of England.

Among many other innovations, she had come up with the double-ended cigarette holder, the anti-splatter skirt-lifter, and the "apparatus to prevent projecting ears," a flattener so comfortable to wear while sleeping that Miss Sherrington never went to bed without this elaborate chin-harness.

These biographical details are only included here to make it clear how this same person, when she was already in Canterel's service, one day came to develop a rather remarkable bicycle antitheft device. Once she had fitted the contraption to her personal bicycle, Miss Sherrington left it ostensibly unprotected, wherever she stopped. Concerned about her apparent carelessness, Diribarne Arostéguy, the grocer on La Place Clemenceau, spoke to her about it several times, even offering to lend her a padlock and chain to secure her bicycle while she was doing her shopping. Miss Sherrington systematically refused, arguing fatalistically that nothing would ever dissuade a thief determined to commit his crime.

It was in front of the window of the colonial goods shop that a vagrant had the misfortune of trying to take it. He had barely mounted it when the housekeeper bounded outside, as if she had not ceased to monitor her vehicle for a second. With a firm hand, she stopped the grocer from running after the thief.

"Not worth it," she said, excited. "Ten florins he won't get more than thirty meters!"

The man, however, gained speed, rolled about fifteen meters, then thirty; all seemed lost until they heard him squeal like a pig, before watching him zigzag and then fall down in a clatter of scrap metal and bell fragments.

It was not until she had gotten her ten florins from the grocer that Miss Sherrington consented to explain the principle behind her antitheft system. Each turn of the pedals made a gear located near the shifter move a notch. After a certain number of turns, a cotter pin activated a powerful spring inside the tube, which shot a ten-centimeter-long metal spike out of the saddle. A hidden push-button made it possible to disengage the system, of course.

The unfortunate thief having failed to kick the bucket, the idea had made a big splash. Miss Sherrington could safely dismantle her device; no one came within three meters of her bicycle.

The memory of this incident left Canterel skeptical about the truth behind Mr. Club's guilt; everything led him to believe that his dear housekeeper had provoked him solely in order to test her new invention. This was not voiced in so many words, but the fact was that Captain Ward did not judge it necessary to punish him, or to record this incident in the ship's log. From that day on, however, he never appeared on deck without a holster on his belt.

The next morning, Captain Ward took some measurements with his sextant and gave the order to steer due south and invited the passengers to join him in his cabin. Armed with a compass and a ruler, he calculated for them their bearing on his nautical chart of the South Pacific, which he had pinned to a large table secured to one of the bulkheads.

"That," he said, indicating the three arcs that intersected on the thirtieth parallel, "is where we are, almost directly above Point Nemo. I have adjusted our course; if we don't run into any foul weather, we'll be there in two or three days."

Grimod leaned over the chart. It showed their route from Sydney, precisely marked in a dashed line traced in graphite. Lower down, on the forty-eighth parallel, five centimeters from the place where this line stopped, a red X marked Point Nemo.

Between the two, to the west, under a question mark, he managed to read a set of coordinates that had been penciled in almost invisibly: 47° 09' S – 126° 43' W, followed by the words *Hic sunt dracones* ("Here be dragons"), the Latin expression that appeared on ancient maps in areas that had not yet been explored.

"And there," he asked, "what is that?"

" . . ."

The captain looked at him, smiling, as if he had not heard a word.

Pointing to his own ears, Grimod signaled that the captain should unblock his.

"Sorry," he said, having taken out his earplugs, "they're so comfortable . . . You were saying?"

Grimod repeated his question.

"It's nothing important," replied Captain Ward, "just a personal note. I enjoy hearing old legends, and I mark them on the chart each time they are specific enough to figure out a geographical location. On other documents, I could show you the alleged positions of Atlantis or El Dorado. The spot you pointed out came from the story of a certain Johansen, first officer on the schooner *Emma*; he claimed to have discovered the cyclopean city of R'lyeh. Pure fiction, of course, since no one else has ever seen anything around there, but still fascinating in many respects. Did you know that it is in that same place that the Melanesians situate their underworld and the dwelling of the Great Douk-Douk, the spirit of retribution? You must have noticed, I imagine, how perturbed my men have been since we started to approach it."

"Absolute drivel," said Canterel, annoyed.

Sanglard squeezed his shoulder in a calming gesture.

"Doubtless, my dear, doubtless . . . But all this forms a series of coincidences that are at least unsettling. One of my colleagues at Miskatonic, Professor Harry Armitage, has shared with me certain data that I am sure would excite your curiosity. Do you know of the Great Old Ones, Yog-Sothoth, the Crawling Chaos?"

Canterel did not have the chance to respond, as at that moment they heard Dr. Mardrus's urgent summons from the deck to come look at the instruments. They hurried to join him. On the trawl's control dial, the needle kept climbing; it showed a hundred twenty kilos, that is, three times as much as they had brought up to this point.

Sanglard gave the order to haul in the net; as the crewmembers nonchalantly ignored his orders, he took up the winch himself, immediately relieved by Grimod. Their eyes fixed on the dial, they had a moment of panic when the needle reached five hundred kilos, the maximum level that indicated a traction approaching the breaking point. For a few long seconds, the capstan appeared to be stuck, then it freed up, the needle going back down to the seventy-kilo mark.

When they opened the net to dump out its contents, it was Darwin's body that flopped down on the deck. His head and several parts of his body showed circular bruises, wide as saucers, giving them impression that poor creature had been horrifically mauled by suction cups.

Despite the inhumanity of this sight, the strangest thing to see was that he was holding a strangled pigeon in his right hand.

Liquefied by terror, the crewmembers went into a morbid trance in which the name of Cthulhu was repeated with abject submission.

XLIV

Name Is Bond

It is Sunday. Monsieur and Madame Bonacieux have just arrived at the "German" farm. The owners of the operation have been French for several generations, but, as they have a Germanic-sounding last name, this makes it easier to identify them; and it's only been eight years since they bought back Father Moulard's lands. Carmen managed to convince her husband to bring her to the little agricultural festival that they organize every year during breeding season. The Roetgens raise horses. *Everyone's* raising horses these days. It must bring in more than corn or rapeseed, Jean-Johnny had said to her. The other day, she had gone by the bakery again, and this time they had chatted a little. The fair had been his idea. "Come with Dieumercie," he suggested, "it won't be a problem, I often help out at the stables on weekends; they're nice, I can invite whoever I want. And there will be wine, snacks, a bite to eat."

Everything is happening outside, in the meadow that extends out behind the barn toward a thick line of walnut trees. Canopies, open trucks, tables mounted up on trestles, displays—it looks like a mixture of a market and a fairground. Local producers have come in droves, there is honey, meat, goat cheese, heaps of earthy vegetables, homemade jam. Rummage sales, stands selling beignets or kebabs. In an area marked off by rebar and white and red plastic tape, a dozen animals are being showed off, lined up between bales of straw. There is a crowd around a Percheron and a prize bull with a curly coat. A sign announces the schedule for the various highlights of the day, tractor races, a bale-cutting exhibition, hand breeding.

Carmen was not expecting such a large gathering; she is even more frustrated that Dieumercie is already showing signs of impatience.

"We won't hang around here too long," he sighs, looking melancholy. "It smells like grease."

She is just telling him that it would have been better if they'd stayed at home when JJ's voice booms out behind them.

"*Bonzour*, everyone! *Byen kontan* to see you!"

It's funny, the way he mixes his language with ours. No one knows how much he does it on purpose. Kisses on the cheek, hugs, Monsieur and Madame Bonacieux are smiling again. Talking all the while, JJ leads them toward the farm. The owner lends his field to the township to set up the fair, it's friendlier and it brings people in to see the stud.

They walk past the barn, pass the wide-open gate. In the huge yard bordered by the farmhouse and the stables, some visitors are watching the horses, others are scattered around a long table set up at the entrance to the house. This is where Jean-Johnny brings them. Regularly-spaced thin skylights open in the gray roofing stones that extend in a canopy above paired walls. To the right, the turret of a pigeon loft rises up between the barn and the stables. On the paved walkway that surrounds the central area of clay, the stored equipment looks so new that it gives evidence of its meticulous care.

"Hi JJ," says Roetgen, "you came with friends, how nice!"

Jean-Johnny makes the introductions. The man is amiable, beaming; he invites them to help themselves and feel right at home. On the table, there is a wood pigeon terrine with porcinos, summer sausage, cured ham, various quiches, an abundance of cakes, and several unlabeled bottles of red wine.

"From Anjou," Roetgen clarifies in response to Carmen's questioning glance. "I know a good winemaker over there."

And, winking at Jean-Johnny: "You know where the bottle of perry is, have them try some as an aperitif . . . Excuse me, I have to go unstitch Marouchka, the meeting is in twenty minutes."

JJ doesn't need to be told twice. With a conspiratorial glance, he brings Carmen and Dieumercie into the kitchen and goes to get the perry out of a cupboard.

"He makes it himself," he says, lining up three shot glasses, "it's *extra*."

Carmen is amazed to see a Bartlett pear in the bottle. It looks like it has just been picked, but its color is off, like that of a fetus in a jar.

"It dates back to his grandfather's days," JJ explains, "but they have to keep the bottle full enough to make sure the pear is always covered."

They taste, exclaim, taste again, drink the rest down. Jean-Johnny refills their glasses. Carmen swallows hers in a single gulp.

"Who's Marouchka? What did he mean, unstitch?"

"A mare," replied JJ, laughing. "Purebred Arabian. Their pussies get sewn up so they don't take in air or germs."

Dieumercie frowns and serves another round of hooch: "Their-pussies-get-sewn-up?"

"Yessir! But they don't feel it at all."

Carmen sets down her glass, banging it a little too loudly on the table.

"Easy for you to say, I'd love to see you survive that!"

"No, I swear, you give them a little prick and they don't complain a bit. After they're unstitched, they're sewn back up, they're full of little holes, like lace-up boots."

"And when do they get unstitched?" asks Dieumercie, his eyes wide.

"When they're nice and hot, just before they meet the *souval*. They get a little bit of lube, and there they go. *Bonzour* love!"

"The *souval?*"

A whinny is heard, followed by shouts and the sound of hooves clacking on pavement.

"There's the *souval*," says Jean-Johnny. "He's Name is Bond, an Anglo-Norman."

They go out into the yard. Roetgen is there, holding Marouchka by her harness. Another rope, connected from her bridle to a ring in the ground, limits the animal's movements. The mare is quiet, responsive, her back arched, her rump spread open slightly. She lifts her tail, reveals her spasming, licorice-colored vulva; her labia open, close, reveal the pink of her vagina.

"She's flashing," says JJ, as if to himself, "it's going to work."

The stallion has a chestnut coat and a surfer's mop of hair with a washed mane. Straining at his lead, he pulls the stable boy along more than the boy manages to lead him, turns about, approaches the mare, sniffs at her rear, neighs, twirls away again. His penis hangs between his legs. Stiff, astounding, discolored as if with vitiligo. Dieumercie does not dare look away from this scandalous virility. It leaves his neck and ears marbled with red splotches, humiliates him. He senses his wife's excitement, sees it even in the way she is holding her breath, perfectly still next to him.

The mare squirts out little jets of urine. Name is Bond puts his nostrils to her damp vulva, sniffs, draws back, his eyes rolling at this influx of hormones and genital fragrances. After another half turn, he lays his head on Marouchka's rump. His member arches, becomes taut, grows even larger in its excessiveness. A young woman in blue overalls has come right up to the horses; in her hand she has a black cylinder fitted with two handles, a rubber vulva at one end, a sterile bag at the other. When the stallion stands up on his hind legs to mount the mare, the woman diverts his penis and inserts it into the artificial vagina. He pushes, she resists, sheathes him up to his testicles. And here she is, feet planted, ass thrust back, while he thrusts between her hands. The motion of his haunches accelerates, a geyser of piss and semen spurts out of the cylinder, splatters the farm girl. She winces, alarmed, arms extended to keep this milky churning away from her face, but there is something ancient and sacred about this continual shower.

It's over, the stallion gets off the mare, his sex shrinks. The girl is smiling uneasily, she totters, the sloshing sheath in her hands.

Dieumercie finally manages to turn his head toward his wife. Carmen realizes that she is still holding Jean-Johnny's hand, she drops it immediately, her gaze pleading. He meets JJ's eyes, drowns in them for a second, then gives a slight nod of consent.

Jean-Johnny Hercule begins to walk toward the barn; Carmen follows him.

XLV

Hic sunt dracones

"Those marks are from suction cups, aren't they?" Grimod said.

"Yes," replied Sanglard, as he finished measuring them, "from an *Architeuthis dux*. Fourteen centimeters . . . According to the usual proportions, the diameter would suggest a squid fifteen to twenty meters long, with tentacles double that length. It must have attacked the net, then let go at some point, doubtless because of the strain from the winch."

"How horrible!" said Lady MacRae. "I thought those monsters were just myths."

"Indeed, for a long time that was believed to be true, until certain irrefutable proofs of their existence were uncovered. The largest ever found had a span of eighteen meters. But several years ago, inside a Tasmanian whale's stomach, there were indications that confirmed the existence of much larger specimens: a sixty-centimeter eye, cross-sections of tentacles as big as plates . . . This would correspond to an animal of fifty meters, perhaps more!"

"By that account," Grimod remarked, "it sounds like you've found the party responsible for your 'Big Bloop,' doesn't it?"

"Disabuse yourself, my dear. Producing a sound requires air and a membrane capable of expelling it or moving it from one organ to another. A capacity that marine mammals have, but that cephalopods are utterly lacking."

"A gigantic whale, then?"

"Also impossible," replied Sanglard. "Cetaceans, however large they may be, must come up to the surface to breathe. If such a whale existed, we would have detected it long ago."

"Neither Leviathan nor Kraken," said Canterel. "You are running after an invisible creature, professor."

"Laugh if you like, Martial. But everything is possible in nature, and some nights I pray to heaven not to encounter what I seek . . ."

Stricken by the chimpanzee's death, Holmes shook his head: "This doesn't explain how the poor beast could have wound up in the net."

"I don't know," replied Sanglard. "Perhaps he fell into the sea . . ."

"Or perhaps someone deliberately put him in the trawl," said Grimod, giving a meaningful glance toward the crewmen.

"Impossible," Dr. Mardrus protested, "I supervised the last launch myself."

"An accident, then?" said Holmes, looking far from convinced.

"Why not," replied the professor. "Look at this pigeon, no one could doubt that it ended up there by accident."

As he was speaking, he picked up the bird's body to examine it.

"I don't know much about them, but this looks to me like a champion pigeon. He has rings around both feet. I will pass along his registration number to the Museum so they can alert his owner."

"How did he find himself way out here in the middle of nowhere?"

"Updrafts, then jet streams in the upper layers of the atmosphere. It has been shown that windspeed there can reach one hundred meters per second, fast enough to allow one to move from one part of the world to another, as if one were inside a suction tube. I assure you, the animal died of asphyxiation well before it could have perished in the Pacific."

So the bird was thrown back into the sea, though Holmes insisted on giving Darwin a less hasty funeral. Miss Sherrington agreed to sew his remains into a sailcloth sack, and it was thus, with a cast iron ingot as ballast, that he was slid overboard. With all the more emotion because Verity was crying, which she had never done before that moment.

As it was now necessary to sail upwind, Captain Ward had to go to great lengths to bring the crew out of its lethargy. When it came time to tack, the passengers watched him berate them, get out his weapon, aim carefully, and then shoot at the mast a few centimeters from Mr. Heart's face. Between the fear they felt at their proximity to the Great Old Ones and the way in which the bullet exploded through the wood, the men quickly returned to the automations of the maneuver. They became active and listened, and on Captain Ward's order the *Black Orpheus* veered proudly to starboard, immediately regaining its course in the wind.

That evening, Holmes got himself deliberately drunk. With half a bottle of scotch in his veins, he sang a few bawdy songs while pacing the deck; cursed the heavens, the ocean, and all those who go to sea; then gave notice that he was going to climb the mast. Canterel followed him, concerned by his obvious clumsiness on the rope ladder. The *Black Orpheus*'s heel was so pronounced that his friend, had he let go, would certainly have fallen into the ocean.

Holmes had barely reached the platform on the mainmast when Martial joined him and hurried to secure him with a bit of rope.

They remained there, suspended between sea and sky; Holmes smiling sadly at the stars, Canterel suddenly disconnected from the world. The neck of a bottle was sticking from the old drunk's pocket, Canterel took it and drank a long swig before holding it with both hands above the waves, watching for the right moment. Once released, the bottle spurted magnificently through the rigging, then disappeared into the sea without a splash.

"Well played, old chap!" said Holmes.

"Not too bad," Canterel conceded. "And now, what would you say to going back down?"

"Out of the question! I'm staying here . . ."

"Then I'm staying, too. But you have to tell me."

"Tell you what? Why I got so attached to that damn monkey?"

"No. I need to know about Grimod . . . What is he doing in your service?"

Holmes scowled.

"You remember the Eden Life and Insurance Company . . ."

"The huge bankruptcy from last year?"

"I lost my whole fortune in one night. I'll spare you the details, but Grimod was the only person who could come to my aid. I'm the one in his service: I play the master and he plays the servant, holding the purse strings all the while."

"Madness! What does he get out of it?"

"Anonymity. He has put himself in the place where people would like him to be. The 'colored' Glenarvan heir offended polite society; he gave rise to hatred and contempt. As Grimod again, the 'simple negro,' no one distrusts him, he is accepted in all circles as long as he is in my company; this enables him to work on all sorts of projects that I don't really understand."

This confession having sobered him, Holmes agreed to come down from his perch soon after.

The next day, a strange sensation woke them in the early hours of the morning. The wind had fallen away completely. Sitting motionless on a large swell, the schooner was rolling slowly from side to side in a seesaw motion. Captain Ward had backed the sails to spare the rigging, but the sails would crack from time to time above them like huge, unfurled sheets. Instead of the stormy seas that they had been promised, they found themselves utterly becalmed. To the south-south-east, toward Point Nemo, a massive fog bank, rather low on the horizon, formed a mountain range of menacing clouds.

"You'd think we were on the Sargasso Sea," said Captain Ward, noticing Grimod. "Sleep well?"

"Fairly, thank you. Any chance this will change?"

"Not right away, I'm afraid. The barometer is stuck in the high pressure range. But there's a strong current, which is keeping us drifting in the right direction."

Grimod appeared satisfied. He returned to the little group that was forming around Sanglard, Holmes, Canterel, and Lady MacRae, who seemed to be experiencing an irritating technical difficulty.

"Nothing to be done, it doesn't work anymore," she said, indicating the object she was holding in her hands.

It was a Bradbury 451 in its plated brass case, with its little, immediately recognizable green screen and Bakelite external generator; a reading tablet that had had its hour of glory, but that now seemed quite worn out.

"Let me take a look," said Grimod.

He pulled the little crank out of its groove, turned it several times, checked the connections between the corrugated conduits, then tested the device. As nothing happened, he disconnected the generator from the casing and placed his tongue on the two contacts.

"It's not the battery," he said, puckering his lips at the shock. "Perhaps it's the screen or the circuits, but there's nothing we can do about that here, I'm sorry to say. Too damp, most likely. Try leaving it out in the sun . . ."

"Thank you," said Lady MacRae. "It's so silly, I only had three chapters left . . ."

"What were you reading?" asked Canterel.

"*La Spirale*, by Gustave Flaubert. The story of a man whose dreams gradually take the place of real life. Have you read it?"

"No," said Canterel, "but with a title like that, the plot must end by eating its own tail, I'd guess."

"So much the worse, then," she said, with a mocking smile. "I suppose I'll have to ask Miss Sherrington to lend me some knitting to do . . ."

Around ten o'clock in the morning, Professor Sanglard's dragnet brought up a large amount of multicolored particulate and garbage that they identified as plastic. Sanglard was still lost in conjectures about the presence of this residue at such a depth, when Captain Ward rang the dinner gong.

Once they were reunited in the wardroom, however, they waited in vain for their lunch. Dispatched to the galley, Kim returned with bad news: it appeared that the cook had gone mad.

They found him, naked and scantily covered by mosquito netting, kneeling before a cross that he had made by nailing two smoked sausages from Melbourne to the wall. His eyes yellow, he was chanting an endless prayer.

"*Ph'nglui mglw'nafh Cthulhu*, mighty God! *R'lyeh wgah'nagl fhtagn!* Oh, Dreamer, have mercy! *Iä Iä, Cthulhu fhtagn!*"

"Mr. Smalls," Captain Ward interjected, "kindly pull yourself together and make our lunch!"

"*F. nye Cthulhu, me zi ne togbui kple mama o, galokpo, me zi ne miawo kpata yi ke da dje be gbadegbe so gbadegbe pu anyi*, damned may he be, for he who dreams forever is not dead!"

"This man has gone mad with terror," said Grimod. "He needs help."

"I'll go get a sedative," said Dr. Mardrus, heading back up to the deck.

"God, God, God," the cook continued in the voice of a priest, "drive out the demons that have besieged us, oh yes, drive them from our bowels!"

There was a pause—and then they heard the belching sound of vomiting coming from inside the cook's cabin. Then once again that same sound of convulsing of viscera, this time followed by a barely audible cry:

"Help! Help me! I'm dying . . ."

They hurried into the room. Imagine their surprise at finding

Scummington spread out on the cook's bed, his face ashen, suffering from the worst case of seasickness ever beheld.

"Help me, I don't want to die!" he repeated between two outpourings of revolting bile.

Grimod was furious.

"What are you doing here? How did you get on board?"

It was no use pressing him; the inspector was too delirious to reply.

Two hours later, after Captain Ward had given the order to tie him to a mooring line and plunge him into the ocean to negate the effect that the rolling swell had had on him, they finally received some explanations.

Before leaving Sydney, Holmes and Canterel had interceded with Lord Macquarie to have him get Reverse Waterlily released and placed under his protection. Furious at losing his chance to interrogate her, Scummington had decided at the last moment to follow their trail. Knowing he was not welcome aboard, he had bribed the cook to let him hide in his cabin and to bring him food in secret. For reasons that were beyond him, the bastard had stopped bringing him food and drink; helped along by the seasickness, the inspector had been watching himself die by inches for almost three days now.

No one knew what remedy Dr. Mardrus gave the cook, but the latter began to feel better almost immediately, though without recovering the faculties necessary to complete his duties. It was Miss Sherrington who took charge of the stoves, and no one had any complaints regarding the menu during the brief period when she assumed this post.

That afternoon, the net brought up such a quantity of imputrescible refuse and amalgamated jellyfish that they decided not to drop the trawl back into the water. Captain Ward measured the sun's height, checked the log, and returned to his cabin, looking troubled.

A kind of ennui settled over them, which was the direct result not so much of their inactivity as of their profound discouragement.

Clawdia and Dr. Mardrus held a series of endless séances using tarot cards, trying to interpret their successive draws as if their lives depended on it. Grimod paced incessantly up and down the deck, his face grim, but mindful of Verity's balance as she clung to his arm. Still greenish, Scummington brooded in his corner.

End of game, check and mate, thought Canterel, watching Holmes set his empty bottle on the gunwale.

Sunset provided them a magnificent distraction. Aflame with glowing red rays, the cloudbank toward which they were moving floated low on the horizon. There was a brief moment when the light trembled and turned cloudy before them like a mirage, tracing the fictitious outline of a devastated atoll, the vague flotsam of a shipwreck.

The morning of the next day, the swell of the waves had given way to a mercury mirror furrowed only by the ship's drifting. The bitter cold turned their breath to vaporous nebulae, the sails hung stiff with frost. This dead calm stretched up to the sky, and in the whiteness there was something of a pitiless warning.

At the stroke of noon, Captain Ward tried in vain to measure the sun's exact height. He expostulated at his crew for form's sake, prodding them to polish the deck with more conviction, then returned to his ephemeris, having first requested that Grimod regularly tell him the ship's speed.

He came out again around three o'clock, his expression grim, and asked for the passengers' attention.

"48°50'S 123°20'W," he announced. "If my calculations are correct, we are there, or not far off, within a few seconds."

"Point Nemo?" asked Lady MacRae.

"Yes, Madame. The human beings who are least far from us are 2,600 kilometers from this ship. Living ones, that is. There are some who are closer, but their mummified bodies have been floating 410 kilometers above us for thirty years."

"What are you talking about?" said Canterel, annoyed.

"The astronauts of the International Space Station," he replied, crossing himself quickly.

They were all silent for a moment in memory of that catastrophe. Then Sanglard said: "I've done everything humanly possible from a scientific point of view." He looked over his instruments, vexed. "If you gentlemen will agree to it, I propose that we set our route back toward the north once the winds turn favorable once again."

Holmes and Canterel did not need to consult each other to agree with slight nods, but Grimod suddenly seemed desperate, scanning the ocean around him and looking miserable.

It was at this exact moment that the ship heeled, scraping its hull against an invisible shoal, then gently settled in a few degrees, as if it had just run aground on a beach.

Almost simultaneously, the phenomenon observed the evening before occurred again. Sea and sky were seized by a slight rippling, the image split into fringes; it quivered, shimmered and became distorted, then stabilized.

There was a flash of violet light, and where a few seconds before there had been nothing their eyes discerned the contours of an island.

A hundred meters from the *Black Orpheus*, the coast rolled in eroded, fog-covered hills. Beneath the shifting flocks of birds, they could make out seals and penguins. Closest to the shore, dark scaly creatures were moving slowly, their forked, pink tongues darting out at the ship.

"Dinosaurs!" cried Holmes, his eyebrow raised above his telescope.

"Sadly not," said Sanglard, looking through in turn, "they are lizards, enormous lizards. Komodo dragons, more precisely, which have no business being here, believe me . . ."

"Well then, at least we have something in common," said Canterel, striking a match in front of the half of a cigarillo that was threatening to burn out between his lips.

XLVI

The Most Massive Harpoon

When the first fire engines arrived at the scene, the flames were already licking the big sign on the third floor, *"ALL, ALL, ALL CAN BE SEEN FOR 25 CENTS AT BARNUM'S AMERICAN MUSEUM."* Rolling in from all sides, the fire department's Silsby fire engines had just pulled up to the building, while squads of helmeted firemen rushed to unroll the hoses, then hook them up to the fire hydrants, before bracing themselves to project their powerful jets onto the façade.

Behind the police lines, the Broadway crowd was clumping together, eager not to miss any of the show.

Warned by the employees in time, most of the visitors had been able to evacuate, but there were still people trapped upstairs, who could be seen gesticulating in the windows. The comedian who played the title role in the *Dancing Barber* was recognized by his red hair, elbowing people out of the way to be the first to get down the ladder that had just been raised up to his window. Since he was holding an unconscious woman in his arms, the firefighter in charge helped him get a foothold on the rungs; he was starting to climb down when a gust of wind lifted the lady's skirts, revealing his deception: the actor had merely rescued the wax mannequin of Jefferson Davis! As soon as the mannequin reached the ground, the crowd seized the Confederate president and, having hanged him from a lamppost, gravely sang the Northern anthem.

Inside, the guards opened all of the cages to give the live animals a chance to escape the fire, adding to the general confusion. There was a great deluge of terrified beasts, monkeys, snakes, and mixed-up creatures flowing down the stairs, right through the middle of the people trying to escape or contain the fire. While the man-eating alligator let itself be devoured by the flames without reacting in the slightest, the others took refuge en masse on the top floor, where they suffocated to death; nevertheless, the firemen had to defend themselves against the Bengal tiger and shoot it with a revolver. A panicked lion took off down Fulton Street, its mane singed.

What appeared to be a kangaroo jumped from the third floor, but it turned out to be Rising Shadow, a Comanche chief who landed safely on a trampoline held out by the firefighters. Those of them who had made it into the building strove to save as many things as possible, but with a marked preference for the curiosities from the wax museum, as if the fragile material from which they were made lent them tremendous value. Hastily deposited on the sidewalk on the other side of the street, the wax figures of Ravaillac, Jesse James, and Catherine the Great appeared to be contemplating the disaster with the unflappable calm of hardened stoics.

By one o'clock in the afternoon, the whole building was in flames. In the bilious sky over New York, the plumes of black smoke from the steam pumps were rising on all sides, joining with the convulsive swirls from the conflagration. Fanned by the breeze from the southeast, tongues of fire roared out of every window; the copper balconies were melting; the bronze decorations, steel frontages, and zinc roofing were dripping profusely, spurting and hissing at the touch of the firefighters' water. Beneath the stench of burnt rubber, an unbearable odor of charred animal fat caught in the throat.

At 1:15, the fire spread to the nearby buildings, despite the preventative measures kept up by the firemen; by 1:20, the rupturing of
a steam pipe rang out like a tromba marina, which the crowd that
had gathered on Broadway thought was the sound of stampeding
elephants: people trampled one another trying to flee from this imaginary herd; and when, at 1:30, the side of the museum facing Ann
Street collapsed, followed shortly after by the Broadway side, releasing
an opaque storm of dust and smoke, the general panic reached its
height.

By the time the fire was mostly contained, ten buildings adjacent
to the Barnum Museum had burned down, several of them having
disappeared as if they had sunk into the earth, swallowed up by some
subterranean power. Dozens of stores were destroyed, notably those
of Mr. Anderhub, producer of paperbacks, Mr. Swift, bookbinder,
and Messrs. John Ross and Subring, tobacco dealers known for the
quality of their Cuban cigars.

Not a single animal escaped both the fire and the police's bullets.
Despite the hundreds of injuries, both major and minor, there was
only a single human death to mourn, that of Captain Abigael Khab,
the Pequot Indian who was a Gettysburg survivor. Seeing the fire
progress, Khab was getting ready to leave the floor where he officiated to take refuge on the upper floors when he came across the big
aquarium where the white whale, alerted by some sixth sense, was
showing every sign of extreme agitation. Reflected in the glass of
the tank, the flames were rising in the hall, painting a picture of
the hell that promised to be their fate. The man stopped, then went
up and put both hands against the aquarium wall, as if seeking to
reassure the animal, to speak to it. The whale dipped toward him,
soothed, fixing its wrinkled eye upon him. It was at this moment
that he turned around and hobbled as fast as he could over to the
tools used by the whalers of Nantucket. Grabbing the most massive

harpoon, he limped back to the aquarium and struck the glass with it as hard as he could, again and again in the same spot, until it cracked and then exploded in a crashing flood. Seized with fear, a firefighter who witnessed the scene saw the whale burst forth from its prison, sweeping the Indian away as it passed, dragging him with it into the midst of the blaze; heroic to the end, the witness stated, the veteran had sacrificed himself in unleashing the water from the tank in an attempt to curb the fire's growth.

But we, thinks Arnaud as he archives the clipped-out article, we know very well that it was not true, that something terrible played out on the third floor of Barnum's American Museum, because it is impossible that a Captain A. Khab, scarred and one-legged, could have been wiped from existence by a white whale without recognizing a contamination at work in the world around us. Not fifteen years after the writing of *Moby-Dick*, and when the horrific sinking of the *Pequod* was still on everyone's minds.

Every sentence written is a presage. If events are replicas, more or less faithful reconstructions of stories already dreamed up by others, then of what forgotten book, of what papyrus, of what clay tablet are our own lives the grimacing copy?

Last Telegrams of the Night

Things that make one raise one's eyebrows and fart silently into one's pants.

The colonoscopy he was performing on a patient having revealed several benign polyps, the surgeon decided to cauterize them. For an as yet undetermined reason, a spark during the electrocautery caused an explosion of the patient's intestinal gases, which were abnormally concentrated inside his colon, as well as the death, ten minutes later, of Monsieur Camille Maloriol, the famous contortionist.

Things that make one wonder whether or not they confirm the principle that the fluid levels of connecting vessels will always balance out.

When my husband drinks, my breasts flow freely, the instructor confesses to her students at Saint-Mamet.

Things that make one understand abstract art.

A shepherd is found dead around his sheep.

Things that stir feminine curiosity.

In his underpants they discovered an object with which he blinded his adversary.

Things that make one look suspiciously at the person saying them.

Yes, Simone killed her husband, but she acted alone, declared the latter, the owner of a café in l'Oise.

Things that have the refined grace of the beginnings of aviation.
She was light, and she was flying. One year's suspended sentence.

Things that militate against the use of baby bottles.
When the child has finished feeding, you must unscrew it and put it in a cool place, a cellar or refrigerator.

Things that make one hope the aliens are coming.
Two Norwegian sisters swear that they saw a strange man with a tool shaped like a spinning top.

Things that warrant a self-portrait.
Arles. On the operating table, they noted that the wounded party had had an ear ripped off during the accident. The ambulance immediately returned to the scene, and the nurse was lucky enough to find the ear in the car. Brought back immediately, it was able to be grafted back onto its owner.

Things that momentarily disturb the calm of the countryside.
He sneezes, his tractor explodes.

XLVII

The Island of Point Nemo

Captain Ward's focus, understandably, was on extracting his schooner. After he had the launch dropped into the sea, he went out in it to take soundings around the ship until he encountered a depth of more than triple his draft. He dropped his heaviest anchor, turned the boat around, and climbed to the top of the mainmast to thread the hawser to a pulley. Back down on the deck, he tied the rope to the capstan. His men set to work, and the *Black Orpheus* straightened up before heeling over to the other side. Extracted from the mud little by little, it floated off and was steered back into deep water. Captain Ward had a second anchor dropped forty-five degrees from the first, and it was not until his anchorage had firmed up that he consented to see to his passengers.

After their initial emotions, a wild hope had spread through all of them; some had different reasons for this than others, but all showed the same demonstrative enthusiasm. Professor Sanglard exulted: he had before him an unknown world to map, hundreds of observations to make, and new species, certainly, to describe and classify for the first time. Also very excited, Dr. Mardrus was peering at the coast and making sketches. As for our friends, the existence of the island alone vindicated the coded message that had brought them here, offering them, against all odds, one final chance to give meaning to their odyssey.

Even Scummington seemed cheered at the prospect of stepping on dry land again.

They desperately needed to disembark.

Captain Ward carefully tempered their impatience. The afternoon was too far gone for them to be able to go ashore under the proper conditions. Better to stay on board for the night and prepare for their expedition with the necessary rigor.

Sanglard proposed exploring the coast in one of the boats, even if only for a few hours, but the captain categorically refused to allow that either: there was nothing so deceptive as the calm of the Pacific, especially at this latitude. How would they get back to the ship if the weather suddenly turned? No. The *Black Orpheus* would remain just off the island for as long as her passengers chose—after all, they had paid for this service—but visits to the shore would be undertaken according to his orders, and with respect for the basic rules of safety.

So the rest of the day was put to use in gathering their explorers' kits. Sanglard's equipment soon obstructed a great deal of the deck. He was bringing his magnifying glass headset, of course, but also three pickaxes, a spear-shaped trowel, various knives and pruners, a number of corked metal bottles filled with alcohol, two large boxes for collecting plants, reams of paper and heavy cardboard, latticed wooden frames, clamp boards, a press with leather straps, rope and string in various sizes, as well as tarpaulin for protecting his harvest; it being understood that this was simply the portable equipment necessary to any naturalist! He added to this baggage several topographical instruments—tape measure reels, a collimator, a bearing compass, target plates—and was satisfied.

Canterel, for his part, made an effort to bring only a single large steamer trunk in which, he swore, he had packed nothing beyond what was strictly necessary to his preservation.

Lady MacRae packed up boots and warm clothes for herself and Verity, an example that everyone else followed.

Grimod added several weapons and their ammunition. As for Holmes, all he was bringing was a small crate in which he had wedged six bottles of scotch and some bags of little pancakes stuffed with cheddar.

When this was done, it took one of Miss Sherrington's acerbic remarks to make them realize that they had thought of everything but the most important thing: food. She was charged on the spot with outfitting them, and to their luggage was added a barrel of water and substantial provisions.

Alarmed by the magnitude of the outfitting, Ward nevertheless got it all packed up, though not without regretting his decision to postpone his passengers' disembarking.

After dinner, they once again consulted the nautical chart of the South Pacific, then *Findlay's Directory*, page by page, to make absolutely certain: the coast on which they had run aground was not mentioned anywhere. There was nothing at all besides a note from Naval Lieutenant Bawn Assyew that mentioned with a very *British* humor the position of Lincoln Island as being 34°57' South and 150°30' West, that is to say much farther north, with the qualification that "it was, thank God, purely imaginary."

"Hence the delightful paradox," said Canterel, "that we know exactly where we are, without having the slightest idea of where we find ourselves. Good evening, everyone, I'm going to bed."

The next day Ward sounded the morning bell at 5:30, as they had agreed the night before. He had hesitated to come with them, fearing for his ship and brooding over this predicament for much of the night, but in the morning the temptation of setting foot on an unknown land carried him away. He would accompany his passengers, at least for this first day, in order to ensure that their expedition was running smoothly.

As his sailors were reluctant to obey him, more out of fear than malice, the captain attempted to cajole them by assuring them that afterward they would wait on board to watch over the ship; he then offered them a gold thaler in pledge of his word. This argument won them over, the men dropped the dinghy into the sea, transferred over a first load, and, Mr. Club still being in recovery, Ward replaced him at the oar. It took them no less than five round trips to offload the whole cargo.

After the last unloading trip, the "Sanglard mission" finally boarded the boat, while the crew, visibly relieved, hurriedly climbed back onto the schooner.

It was almost eight o'clock when they started to move toward the island.

The ocean was still just as calm, but it had merged with the sky in a dreary grayness with pewter glints. Very low on the water, the coastline suggested an atoll darkened by an approaching cyclone. The barometer had fallen during the night; standing at the tiller, his eyes fixed on the shore, Captain Ward had the good taste to keep his uneasiness to himself.

An icy air settled like frost on their lips.

Canterel, Holmes, Kim, and Grimod were at the oars. As they paddled forward, with a strange feeling of reverence, Sanglard, leaning on the ribband, examined the seabed through a glass hatch.

"Polystyrene, nemopilema, rhodoid," he stated aloud, while Mardrus, who had accepted the tedious task of clerk, noted down his words in a notebook as fast as he could, "nemopilema, ethylene, I believe, carybdea, *Chironex fleckeri*, polysterene, again, nemopilema, everywhere . . . No coral, none at all. It's unthinkable, there's nothing but plastic and jellyfish!"

Above all there were jellyfish, among them the most venomous known to man.

As they approached, they could see a shore that looked just like what the professor was observing under the water. Twenty meters beyond, the view extended over a grassy plain, barely elevated by a gentle slope. A sad and monotonous steppe, puckered with yellow-green mounds, where neither trees nor scrub were visible. Scattered sparsely across the beach, several seals and a colony of penguins watched them with perfect indifference.

As they landed, the deafening noise of the sea birds—they recognized petrels, sterns, and cormorants—seemed to grow even louder.

They disembarked without too much difficulty, slipping on the decomposing jellyfish, and as quickly as they could returned to the heap of crates and bundles that were waiting on the heath. Despite their efforts, they had only managed to draw up a third of the launch, so Captain Ward secured it by hooking two grapnels to it, as far away as the length of the ropes allowed.

Their plan was to explore the island all day, then go back aboard before sunset. During this excursion, Kim and Miss Sherrington would set up the camp and see to the meal. As he put together his equipment, Sanglard gave some advice on how to behave around the animals. There was nothing to fear, as long as the human visitors did not get in their way. Not even the Komodo dragons, even though they could reach speeds of twenty kilometers per hour and their bite was poisonous, rather like a moray's, because of the bits of putrefied flesh that remained between their teeth.

"Although," he said, offhandedly, "that's how it was with the ones I got to study in Indonesia, but I don't know anything the ones around us now; it's very possible that they have developed different patterns of behavior."

"What kind of behavior?" asked Lady MacRae, sounding a bit worried.

"Oh, certainly nothing much. Maybe they run a little faster, or a little slower. Same with aggressiveness, it all depends on how difficult it is for them to procure food."

"In any case, we have guns," said Miss Sherrington, as she finished unpacking a bundle of repeating rifles.

Located about four kilometers ahead of them, the highest mound they could see was no more than twenty meters tall. They resolved to climb it as soon as possible in order to get a better idea of the scope of the island.

Their journey proved more difficult than expected. Even though it gave the visual impression of firm ground, the terrain concealed unexpected treacheries. Where it seemed certain that the ground would bear weight, their feet would sometimes sink down half a meter, each step revealing new pitfalls. Under the thin film of mosses and lichens, the humus released whiffs of stagnant water. They walked over a woeful mass of more or less agglomerated refuse—shreds of plastic bags, bits of net, frayed rope, eviscerated tins, putrid scraps of algae and jellyfish—from which protruded the ossuary of driftwood that the ocean leaves on coasts.

They reached the summit after an exhausting three-hour climb, slowed less by Verity, as one might have feared, than by Sanglard, who was constantly squatting down to inspect the ground more closely. Certain details produced cries of admiration:

"Sphagnum, my friends, we're positively walking on sphagnum!"

Among other astonishing properties, he shared, including the ability to absorb up to twenty-six times its weight in water, this moss grew indefinitely, drawing its nutrients not from its roots—simple structures of dead cells whose slow dissolution ultimately produced peat—but from its highest branches, exposed to the dust carried along by the rain. This spongy carpet sheltered a number of small carnivorous plants, droseras with rounds leaves, utricularia, pitcher plants, but also mauve-petalled orchids specific to this biotope. The professor collected certain ones in the pouches he had brought, and planted pennants near those he was planning to come back for later. He seemed ten years younger, so much did his joy transform every muscle in his face.

Despite showing signs of an identical interest, Dr. Mardrus quickened his steps like the others, anxious to take in the full extent of the island.

At the top of what did not even deserve to be called a hill, they finally had the overview they were hoping for. The island—because it was definitely an island, none of them had ever doubted it—had the rough form of a spiral, its outer end starting at the south, where they were standing. From the spot they had reached, the terrain rounded off toward the north for about twenty kilometers before turning back south to curl in on itself in a short helix. This form thus delineated two lagoons, one, almost enclosed, that was located behind the central tip, and another that formed a large bay directly below them. If the breeze that had just picked up continued to rise, thought Captain Ward, it was there that they would soon need to bring his schooner for shelter.

Sanglard having quickly taken a few measurements, it appeared that the island as a whole had an external circumference of 35 kilometers and an approximate surface area of 95 square kilometers. Its width varied between 1 kilometer, in the narrowest sections, and 3.5 kilometers in the broadest. In the southeast, the channel measured barely 300 meters. As the wind had now cleared the sky, Ward could also take the sun's elevation. His navigation was not so bad, he announced proudly, Point Nemo being located 6 kilometers in front of them, right at the center of the spiral.

With its gently rolling hills, among which white scrapes opened at intervals, the whole thing looked like a vast golf course, or, more exactly, a landfill that someone had toiled in vain to rehabilitate as a golf course.

Ever excessive in his sarcasm, Canterel summed up this distasteful impression by saying that the island looked like a swirl of junk around a sink drain.

In the minute that followed, there was change in the wind from the northwest to the southwest that put Ward on alert. He was about to speak up to warn the others that they urgently needed to get back on board, when Scummington suddenly appeared:

"Look!" he exclaimed. "A ship!"

Every head turned in the direction he was pointing. They did in fact see a two-masted ship flying gracefully toward the north, but it had taken all of the inspector's incompetence, some might say his remarkable stupidity, not to have recognized the *Black Orpheus*, which was moving away from the island under full sail.

"What a bunch of amateurs!" said Captain Ward, his fists clenched. "They've let out far too much sail for what's awaiting them . . . Tighten the foresail, you wretches," he yelled by reflex, without the slightest chance of being heard, "reef the topsails, or you'll run right into that storm!"

XLVIII

When the Tigers Broke Free

When his doorbell rang, when it was her, with her face crumpled and wearing that flowery dress he didn't recognize, he let Charlotte cry on his shoulder. Words only come to Fabrice in dreams, so he used the appropriate gestures to quarantine her grief, finding for her the same bustling kindness that Granny Vitrac had displayed each time he closed a letter from his mother: the old woman offered to have him help her make a clafoutis, or to go up and check the attic for the old gramophone that she'd promised to give him, with the Carlos Gardel records, or some other incongruous thing whose retrieval was suddenly imperative. He even suspected that she had engineered some of her most spectacular falls as diversions.

Fabrice wanted to make a Nescafé, but as he squirmed to try to plug in the kettle, his elbow knocked over a pile of printed circuit boards, and like dominos all of his stacks collapsed on his head. She laughed, asked if she could take a shower and sleep here, burst out laughing at him again as he lunged over to rummage through the drawer under the bed, then at his relieved look upon miraculously unearthing a clean towel. As soon as she stopped smiling, however, a mask of sorrow disfigured her.

Only once she was clean and dressed did she recount in detail, as if to better untangle the memory, the humiliation she had just undergone. Then, they ate a package of Haribo bears, lying side by side on the bed, and she fell asleep at once, hugging her pillow.

Silently, Fabrice has gotten up. Sitting in front of his computer, he is drumming away on the keyboard as fast as he can, headphones over his ears. The gradual crescendo of *When the Tigers Broke Free* fills his head with a great volley of pink flames.

A thousand and one mutinies are jostling behind his eyes in shifting mists. He would like to be able to calmly piss all over Monsieur Wang's body, laugh from the underworld, deface the shadows of his cave. Live without the worry of having to pay for the simple act of living, warm himself with the wood of his forest, eat the fruits and vegetables of his garden, plug his computer into the power of wind, water, and sun. Live in the woods, if need be, no longer need to tremble before an envelope bearing the seal of the National Treasury. Breathe. Fill his lungs with the beauty of the world, be ready, taut, heroic.

Were someone to give him a patch of land, he would build a dwelling on it. Like an Ancient Greek, a trapper, a Papuan before the Whites. Restore meaning to each of his gestures. Come out of his shock. So what? A lightship anchored in international waters? A far-off land, an island?

What they did to Charlotte has changed him.

The longest task was masking his signature, in order to stop anyone from being able to trace it back to him after the attack. This is not as easy as "n00bs" think, but he knows how. As for the box itself, he is surprised to note how poorly secured the server was. He managed to infiltrate it in less than fifteen minutes! And now, he is trolling around in the system, completely at home, probing tree structures, opening certain files, modifying them, putting them back. It was Verity's manner of speaking in the story that gave him the idea for the virus that he is now inoculating.

This is war, a secret and merciless war against B@bil Books.

XLIX

A Blaze of Black Feathers

Transfixed with astonishment and powerlessness, they could only watch the schooner until it disappeared from view, each of them realizing what the ship's flight signified: in the space of a few seconds, they had just been demoted from explorers to castaways.

Their first reflex was to go back down to the camp. If Kim and Miss Sherrington were alarmed by this twist of fate, they did not let it show, distributing the sandwiches that they had prepared to their companions. They ate in silence, their eyes distant, sitting where they could among their odds and ends.

Captain Ward was the first to break the silence.

"It's two o'clock in the afternoon," he said, with the self-possession of someone who has weighed his words carefully, "four hours remain until sundown. Or whatever we'll have in its place," he qualified, his head turning toward an overcast sky streaked with swiftly moving clouds. "A squall is approaching, a bad one. The first thing to do is try to shelter ourselves as best we can before nightfall. The sailor's craft teaches you this kind of thing, so I propose to work on it along with those of you who would like to lend a hand."

"Here? But that's crazy!" said Scummington. "Why not go inland? There must be a cave somewhere, a more suitable nook or cranny . . . We'll all freeze to death if we stay here!"

"The 'nooks and crannies' you're talking about might exist," replied Ward, "but you saw the layout of the island as well as we did. There isn't anything promising nearby. We just walked for three hours without seeing a single rock, and it won't be possible to go any farther today. It would jeopardize our safety."

"You really think we could find shelter?" asked Lady MacRae.

"I have no idea. Perhaps toward the center, where the hills are the highest. In any case, that's where we'll be the most protected from the wind, which is what matters. We'll go in the boat once the weather becomes manageable again."

As everyone was nodding, he continued. "Secondly—and on this point I share this gentleman's concerns—we must urgently consider building a fire."

"That may not be so simple either," said Holmes. "The branches lying here and there aren't enough to last us long . . ."

"That's why one of you is going to shoot some penguins. The fat from those animals makes an excellent fuel; whalers use it to feed their boilers. Five or six of them ought to last us the night."

Like those who suffer from the most terrible stutters but who, in moments of action, are able to express themselves without embarrassment, Captain Ward seemed to have stopped experiencing his affliction.

"The third and final thing," he continued. "We won't lack for food, hunting will provide amply for us. On the other hand, I haven't seen a single stream. As it is uncertain when we will find any more, we can only count on this barrel of fresh water, which will be enough for two days—four or five, if we start limiting our consumption now. After that, we'll have to depend on the rain. And that goes for the scotch, too," he said, addressing Holmes, who was getting ready to uncork one of his bottles.

Holmes halted, looking sheepish, and put it back in the crate with the others.

"Can we still have a little glass tonight?"

"Never fear, we'll all need a pick-me-up. Well. Enough said. Anyone up for the penguins?"

Everyone lowered their gazes, trying to avoid meeting his eyes.

"If it really must be done," came the hesitant voice of Dr. Mardrus, "I can take care of it."

"Make sure you conserve the powder," said Ward, holding out a rifle. "Our survival depends on it."

Mardrus took the Winchester and started walking toward the place three hundred meters away where the motionless penguins, standing shoulder to shoulder, were engaging in their plaintive gabble.

As soon as he had gone, Ward got to work, handing out tasks as if he were accustomed to spontaneously bivouacking every night. He spread the big tarpaulin that had been covering their luggage and, while some of them held it flat, had the others arrange their heaviest equipment in the middle. Canterel's trunk alone formed a sufficient base—it took four people to lift—but the captain also added the crate of ammo for more weight. He then folded the rest of the tarp over this central ballast and attached it to Professor Sanglard's sights, which he had sunk deep into the ground and bound with rope stays, in order to create a kind of canopy. What protruded from the tarp was stitched around the horizontal brace, then steadied with cast iron pincers dating from the Third War, an item that the captain always had on him and which he used not only in brawls, but for also cracking nuts.

After this, the captain clumped the rest of the bundles onto the sides, securing those that seemed too light with ropes, as a way of caulking the whole structure together. In the end, this den, a little over a meter tall, looked like a large animal immobilized by Lilliputians.

In the meantime, Mardrus had brought four penguins over one by one. He dropped each body by the entrance, then went off again, focused on his task.

They put up more sheeting, mostly made up of the professor's pennants, behind the nearest mound.

Miss Sherrington was finishing up her supply inventory when Mardrus returned, dragging his sixth corpse. He laid it next to the others and wiped his forehead, surveying his work. Lined up on the ground, they looked like a group of musicians shot in their tuxedos.

Everyone felt ashamed at this massacre by proxy.

It was only then, as the canvas of their hut snapped loudly in a gust of wind, that they realized that the doctor had not fired a single shot.

"I was told to conserve the powder," he said in excuse, "and that's what I did. These birds are so stupid they let themselves be bludgeoned to death."

So saying, he displayed the bloodied butt of his rifle.

"These poor creatures are no stupider than you or I," said Sanglard, "it's just that they have never learned to fear humans. Two or three days from now, you'll see how they avoid us like the plague . . ."

No one dared to voice the sad corollary to this observation, namely that they were well and truly stranded on a desert island.

Backs to the wind, numb with cold despite the thickness of their coats, they watched Captain Ward light the fire. If certain readers have needed to ignite a dead penguin in the course of their lives, there is hardly any doubt that they can be counted on the fingers of one hand. So, for the vast majority of the others, we will detail how to proceed.

Having made an incision from the anus to the throat, the captain emptied the animal of its entrails and threw them onto the beach below, attracting hundreds of relentless gulls to fight over them. He then crumpled several pieces of paper lifted from Professor Sanglard's stock and inserted them into the body. These wads soon being lit, the flame spread to the penguin's fat, which immediately flared up, producing an intense heat, its only downside being a terrible stench of rancid fat and rotten fish.

As he was asked what occasion he had had to acquire this set of skills, Captain Ward explained that in his youth he had worked on a ship charged with harvesting penguin oil along the coast of Patagonia. Men worked year round, skinning them, passing their hides through a press, and extracting their precious liquid. It took two hundred fifty thousand of these creatures to fill a vessel of a hundred thirty tons. During migration periods, the same men mined the birds' guano to make up for the loss of income. It was one of these men whom he had seen warm himself in this way. The hunters even used it to light their shacks. These birds were so soaked with oil that it was enough to insert a wick into their beaks to make them into candlesticks.

Ward prepared the other corpses, then they all had a bite to eat around the fire, warming their hands on this blaze of black feathers.

"A puffin oil campfire," said Holmes, "no one will want to believe me when I tell this story at the Athenaeum!"

"Penguin oil," Sanglard corrected. "Puffins live on the other side, in the Arctic."

The wind was still rising, spraying their faces with seawater. Huge waves rolled in the dusky light, stirring up masses of phosphorescent gelatin on the beach. It was only seven o'clock when they slipped into the hollow of the shack.

Canterel had saved a surprise for them. Hardly had they settled in when from inside the tent came Archibald Joyce's "Autumn Dream," a waltz for orchestra whose harmonies matched the evening's melancholy. This music was coming from a little travel phonograph that he had pulled from his trunk just before it was requisitioned by Captain Ward.

"I only have one record, unfortunately," he said at the end of the piece.

"What's on the other side?" asked Lady MacRae.

"'Nearer My God to Thee.'"

"Under the circumstances, I think we'll do without, if you don't mind . . ."

Canterel put away his device, but the damage was done. Far from instilling courage in his companions, the wistfulness of the music had left them feeling more overwhelmed. Holmes halfheartedly proposed a game of charades, darkness fell, and there was no longer anything but the cries of the petrels, so like the wailing of children, to disrupt the monotonous rhythm of the surf.

Around nine o'clock, the tempest unleashed its full fury. A heavy and terrible rain began to patter on the tarp, accompanied by hail, lightning, and rolls of thunder. The fire sizzled, choked and coughed like a white fumarole, rekindled for a few seconds, then went out again. Despite Captain Ward's precautions, water was leaking in everywhere, trickling in rills that the wind was driving inside the shelter. In a few minutes, they were soaked to the bone. An icy cold made them clump up against one another, defying all decency.

At Holmes's suggestion, the bottle of scotch began to be passed from hand to hand. A real MacKay from Glasgow, he stressed, as if doling out words of encouragement. After her second swallow, Verity fell asleep, curled up in her mother's arms. The others found the alcohol small comfort. Worn out, overcome by the power of the elements, they were lost in haggard and delirious insomnia. At certain moments, when the squall resurged, they had the impression that the island was shuddering, and that what they were hearing was not the wind, but rather the screaming of ghosts.

So passed the whole night, terrible and helpless.

At the break of day, the storm died away as quickly as it had come up. They came out of their shelter as out of a tomb, looking gaunt, some of them going off behind the banks. Scummington, for his part, had judged it more convenient to piss his pants.

The effects of the storm turned out to have been disastrous for their belongings, now for the most part unusable. Still more upsetting, because of what this loss implied, the wind had carried off their boat during the night.

When Ward tried to start relighting the fire, they realized that the matches they had brought, dissolved by the rain, were totally useless.

"It's not so bad," said Sanglard, "once the sun comes back out, we'll use my magnifying lens. Until then, I know a good old-fashioned method that should get us out of this mess."

He just had to dig a little cavity in a piece of wood and unearth a slightly straighter stick, and he began to explain how to make a fire in the manner of those whom, he said professorially, we must never call savages, as they show more resourcefulness and shrewdness than we do. Half an hour later, however, he was still twisting the stick between his palms without having produced the slightest hint of an ember.

Returning to camp, Canterel found him kneeling before his contraption, his face crimson, on the verge of apoplexy from his vain attempt to kindle his dead branch.

After a period of reflection over what the poor man was trying to do, Canterel leaned down toward him.

"Perhaps this would serve you, my friend," he said, holding out one of the boxes of waterproof matches which filled his pockets.

Sanglard cursed for form's sake, then hurried to help the captain light the fat of the last three penguins. Gathering soon after in front of a roaring inferno, they began to take an interest in life again, postponing the clean up of their devastated encampment.

Gradually, as day broke, all of the island fauna reappeared. The mellowed sea was still undulating in a heavy swell. There, through the mist, a reddish half-sun could be seen on the horizon.

Grimod, looking around, suddenly seemed puzzled.

"Captain Ward," he asked, "which way would you say is east?"

Surprised by the question, the captain pointed first at the sun, then turned his head from side to side and, noticing the hill that they had climbed the day before, hastily pulled out his compass.

"It's not possible," he said, showing every sign of fright, "we've rotated a quarter!"

In the absence of an earthquake, and excluding the belief that the configuration of the stars could change by some miracle, this could only mean one thing: in some way or another, the island was floating.

They did not have time to examine this new folly any further, as a cry from Lady MacRae suddenly turned their attention elsewhere.

"Verity, my God, what's she doing?"

The girl had walked right up to the edge of the moor, in the direction of the channel; motionless, shoulder to shoulder with two penguins, she sat peering toward the center of the island from which, in the distance, was rising a thin column of smoke.

L

The Dream of Alexandria

Louise Le Galle had had a terrible night, her sleep broken by night-mares in which she relived in magnified and distorted form Monsieur Wang's affront from the night before and what she imagined of his relations with the creature abandoned in his paws. Arriving at the factory early in the morning and before everyone else, as was her habit, the feelings she bore toward her boss were divided between rancor and contempt.

When she entered the manager's office and found him asleep on the couch, his iPad on his stomach, however, her first reaction was a burst of tenderness. She decided to let him rest a little longer and picked up the tablet to spare it an unfortunate fall. Brushed by her fingers, the screen lit up, showing a photo of Charlotte Dufrène in the state of nudity in which Louise had left her the night before. Her resentment rekindled; she shut herself up in her office to see how far Monsieur Wang had gone with his sequestered delights.

She fast-forwarded through the video, glad to see that it showed only the young woman and that Wang, therefore, had never come close to her. When she saw her get dressed, she scrolled back to the beginning to watch the scene at normal speed. What she heard come out of the manager's mouth turned her to stone, then brought blood rising to her cheeks. As far as her gender reassignment went, he must have investigated at one moment or another; but how could he know about the CPUs? He didn't have eyes everywhere!

Her fingers moved faster than her ability to understand: minimizing the active window, they revealed the list of folders where Monsieur Wang kept his videos. Dumbfounded, Louise uncovered licentious images, insulting nicknames, the river of mud of which we are already aware. Unfortunately for her, she opened a file entitled "The Afghan Sow" and, drinking the cup of bitterness to its dregs, recognized herself pulling down her pants in the bathroom reserved for the administration.

Scarlet with shame and anger, she plugged a flash drive into the tablet and began copying its contents.

That day, Monsieur Wang woke up around ten. His iPad had slid between his body and the back of the couch. Remembering what he had been doing when he fell asleep, he hurriedly locked it before splashing water on his face. In the hall, he glanced at the loft, still hopelessly empty of Free Legs Diamond. He felt sad and alone, body and shadow consoling each other.

That afternoon, the technical director and the fags from marketing came to show him the final B@bil Book simulation. "The Dream of Alexandria: A Whole Library in a Single Book!" They showed him the graphics that went with this slogan, the media and press kits, online spotlights. They had an ad campaign planned for train stations, and above all a televised commercial showing a muscular firefighter escaping from a burning library, cradling under a shawl what appeared to be a baby; out of danger, he lifted the cloth and smiled contentedly as he revealed the B@bil Book, "The Library!" As he rocked it gently, the ghosts of books flew out of the tablet: Balzac, Hugo, Zola, Flaubert, Maupassant, Dumas, Jules Verne, Montaigne, "Preloaded with Two Hundred Classic and Modern Books" that slid into place on virtual bookshelves to form "B@BILBOOKS.COM, the Honest Man's Library!"

The whole team had been working for months to achieve this result. They looked enthusiastic, convinced—and not without reason—that they had found the best approach to selling this new product, revolutionary in its promise to promote free access to our literary heritage rather than in its mercantile approach. Monsieur Wang congratulated them, had the bottles of champagne opened, and gave his green light to launch the whole operation. The technical director was authorized to implement the CompactFlash drives as soon as he arrived the next morning, while the others were to go all out on the advertising and commercial side. There was no turning back, they were off!

The truth, thought Wang when he was finally alone, was that it was all hype; war does not balk at any ruse. That is, if the texts included on the e-reader were all in the public domain, no one should count on finding on it *La Comédie humaine* or *Les Rougon-Macquart* collected in a way that was complete, annotated, illustrated, and pleasant to read. That would have given the historic publishers of Balzac and Zola cold sores. Those versions would still need to be bought for a few euros on dedicated platforms. It would be out of the question to put them directly on the B@bil Book. Among the two hundred available books, every single one was very famous, chosen for its resonance with popular movies. Hugo? *Les Misérables.* Zola? *Germinal.* Balzac? *Colonel Chabert. In Search of Lost Time?* The first volume, not the rest. And so on. If they had not already read them several times, people could catch up on the complete adventures of Sherlock Holmes, La Fontaine's *Fables,* or *Twenty Thousand Leagues Under the Sea.* It reminded him of China under Mao, when the whole body of literature and philosophy was more or less limited to the works of the nineteenth century.

From the publishers' point of view these were simply loss-leaders used to increase sales on their latest books. For the e-reader developers, this was not useful in the least. By the time the customers opened their ebooks, even just to flip through them, they would already have upgraded the tablets and the file standards three times. The important thing was not even that they purchase the most recent ebooks, but that over and over they buy the *possibility* of purchasing them. The same system that was used everywhere else, and that was running dry, like the rest of the economy. The digital library was just a modern variation on the sin of pride, the sin of upstarts anxious to show off their prosperity, surrounding themselves with flashy books—even just empty bindings—that they had never read and never would read.

In the parent company's research offices, people were already working on "one shot" readers, disposable B@bil Books that would only hold a single title and would be shrunk down to just a single sheet of flexible plastic. They had the technology, all they needed to do was develop the communication strategies that would make this device essential. Another project, just as far along, aimed to get rid of writers altogether. Monsieur Wang had been able to test a beta version of the software, a miracle of artificial intelligence that combined the well-established mechanics of "storytelling" with several generators for texts, situations, and characters, in the desired style. He could already see what it would grow into in a few years. "Disappointed by Contemporary Literature? Take a Stand, Only Read Books Where *You* are the Author!" Or your kids, your friend, your dog.

A little later, when Louise Le Galle came in to have him sign a few papers, she was friendly and smiling. Her mouth is laughing, but it doesn't reach her eyes, thought Monsieur Wang. It would take more than that to fool him, but he was in a good mood and decided to appease her.

"Thank you for letting me sleep," he said. "I was up late."

"Please, it's perfectly normal. On that subject, what are we doing about Charlotte Dufrène?"

"She didn't confess anything, but when in doubt, fire her. Let's just say that I don't like her attitude."

Taken aback, Louise hesitated a moment before replying.

"Me neither, Monsieur. But perhaps she should be given a second chance?"

"Do as you wish," he said, immersing his head in his files once more, "this subject no longer interests me."

He watched her back away, a smile on his lips, proud of his maneuver.

It was the next morning that things went to hell. The technical director asked to be received as a matter of urgency: they had been hacked, it was beyond comprehension, a catastrophe! He was shaking.

"Calm down," said Wang, "and explain from the beginning, please."

"Someone's made a mess of the operating system, it's everywhere, even in the epub files."

He turned on a B@bil Book and handed it to the manager. Instead of the home screen, there was a Guy Fawkes mask, the sneering emblem of Anonymous. Like aggressive warning lights, phrases flashed across the screen:

KNOWLEDGE IS FREE!
WE ARE LEGION.
WE DO NOT FORGIVE.
WE DO NOT FORGET.
WE ARE COMING.

"But that's nothing," he continued, opening a random title from the catalog, "look what they've done, it's a huge mess in here!"

Wang read a few lines that were supposed to come from *Les Misérables*:

"He immediately offered his intervention, as an obliging friend. But she refused. Then he noticed that she was crying. She pointed her finger

at Mademoiselle de Verneuil: 'In Lapland, in Tartary, in America, it's an honor to prostitute one's wife to a stranger.' Hearing this, he began to tremble like an adulterous woman under her husband's gaze."

"So?"

"You don't see?" choked the technical director. "It's mixed everything together! Zola, Hugo, Balzac, Flaubert . . . Every time you open a book, the machine pinches random phrases from all the others and reconstructs a totally nonsensical page. I've tested every one, they're all infected!"

Monsieur Wang centered himself, repeating the precepts of lean management. *Gemba, Gembutsu, Genjitsu, Genri, Gensoku*: put yourself in the real place, observe the real thing, collect the real facts, refer to procedures, and re-establish good practices or come up with better ones.

"Have you tried downloading a book?"

"Yes. It's the same. Whatever they put in here takes over the file and shreds it to bits before it's even opened. There must be at least two viruses. Trojan horses; one in the bootloader, another in the reading software. I've halted implementation and the CF duplicators, but we have eighty thousand readers on our hands."

"Any solutions?"

"Reformat everything; no way out of it. But before reimplementing the system, we'll have to secure the network completely, otherwise the people who did this can just start over again. It's going to take weeks!"

Wang turned toward the window, frowning, looking off into the distance. A little muscle was twitching in his cheek.

"I'm going to tell you this straight, Monsieur Cabrol, the campaign is launched as of this morning: if our products are not shipped out of here within eight days, neither you, nor I, nor anyone else will have any work at this factory. How much time do you need to reset the home page?"

"That's not the hard part. All I need to do is replace the boot-loader that was tampered with, but I'm telling you, that won't solve the problem."

"I know, but that's where you're going to start. I want you to restore the home page on all the defective products so that we will be able to send them out as planned."

"Wait a second, you mean to say . . . It's unthinkable, people will notice right away!"

"Meanwhile," Wang continued, "you are going to get me ten thousand functioning readers, and those and only those will go out to the specialized press and the vendors as demo copies."

"This won't end well . . . Can you picture the chaos when the buyers notice?"

"It's already a disaster, Monsieur Cabrol, thanks to your errors in the management of our computer network. I'm just trying to minimize the consequences. When the time comes, we'll offer a patch to update the system or an alternative solution, based on what we find. Remember the launch of the ePsilon 4: a telephone that couldn't make phone calls! That didn't stop them from selling millions before addressing the problem with the antennae."

"If I may," the technical director ventured, "it's not quite the same . . ."

"Goodbye, Monsieur Cabrol. You have a week, and not a day more."

LI

There's Whiskey in the Jar!

Because it indicated a human presence on this barren soil, the smoke they had seen transported them with joy. If the island was floating, as had been shown a little earlier, said smoke could not be coming from a volcano, or even a sulfur spring. Everything suggested that there were other people over there, most likely whalers or seal hunters who could rescue them. Sooner or later a ship would be coming to get these men, perhaps it was even already anchored in the central bay hidden from sight by the hills. Their own penguin fire had certainly attracted their attention—surely they would send someone over soon.

It took all of Captain Ward's experience to temper their hopes once again.

"Nothing is certain," he said, "and we can't wait here for someone to come get us. Just imagine, what if they're castaways, even more helpless than we are? Or if it's just a fire started by the lightning . . . We'll have to go to the center of the island, even if only to find a better shelter for the next storm. Without a boat, this will be extremely difficult. We'll only be able to move very slowly, with little or no water, without any way of protecting ourselves against the cold . . ."

"Far be it from me to accuse anyone," Scummington interrupted, "but it's too bad the launch wasn't berthed more reliably."

"You could have spent the whole night watching it," said Canterel.

"Why not a raft?" Holmes suggested, then realized that they did not have enough material to build one.

"We're wasting time," said Grimod. "Here's what I propose. Kim and I will go out as scouts and walk as quickly as possible toward the center of the island. If we find a better place along the way, Kim will come back to get you and move the camp while I continue on. As to what this smoke means, I will return, in time, to report."

Despite the risks it entailed, this proposal was endorsed right away. Kim and Grimod were unquestionably the most athletic of the group, and they would move much faster alone than with the whole troupe trailing behind.

Miss Sherrington packed them up a bottle of water, dried fruit, and biscuits. Canterel added one of his matchbooks and, rifles on their shoulders, the two men headed off toward the north, walking as quickly as they could over the sodden ground.

Once they were gone, there was a moment of uncertainty at the magnitude of the damage done by the storm. The contents of some of the bags were scattered across a hundred meters. Their first concern was, therefore, to gather up and sort everything that still seemed usable.

An hour had ticked by when Canterel was suddenly heard cursing himself.

"By the Holy Head of the Sacred Gaucho, what a fool I am! Holmes, your idea for a raft was perfect, I should have thought of it immediately rather than letting our companions go off . . ."

"And how are you planning to make your raft," asked Sanglard, "from penguins?"

Without paying any attention to this retort, which was said with more astonishment than mockery, Canterel set about extricating his trunk. He pulled from it two metal suitcases stenciled with an inscription in red letters: "Stoner's Patent Life Saving Apparatus."

"Don't tell me you also packed a raft!" said Clawdia mockingly.

"Alas, no," Canterel replied. "After our compulsory swim in Australian waters, however, it seemed to me that this survival suit might prove useful to us. I bought two in Sydney, thinking of you and Verity."

As he spoke, he unfolded the contents of the suitcase.

The apparatus consisted of a large drysuit made of gummed cloth, protected by articulated brass plates. Circular and concentric, these metal bands nested together, allowing the casing to fold in on itself and holding everything together in the largest of the circles. Under the arm openings, an impressive air chamber ensured its buoyancy, while at the top, near the head, was attached a hemispherical hood fitted with a rectangular visor. This could stay open when desired or, in rough seas, it could be closed up like a sugar bowl. In the latter case, two bent tubes, coming out of the dome like antennae, provided ventilation. The wearer got into this getup by slipping on the legs, then pulling the rest of it up around him before adjusting the straps. He could then have his hands free to, for example, blow his nose, smoke, fire a pistol, or fold back his sleeves in order to move—the arms of the suit ending, in fact, in rigid gloves in the shape of duck feet.

The advantage of this aquatic armor was that it could be worn over clothes; one of its (major) faults was that the wearer immediately felt like dying of absurdity.

"Now I understand why your trunk was so heavy," said Captain Ward, approaching.

"What the devil do you mean to do with this device?" Holmes asked, concerned.

"To cross, of course! The channel is only two or three hundred meters, it will be child's play. Once on the other side, we'll be right near the center of the island."

"We?"

"Who else, my friend?"

"You know very well that . . ."

"Holmes, the whole idea of this apparatus is to provide perfect safety to people who don't know how to swim. What do you think, Captain?"

"What do you want me to say? Go ahead, but your equipment does not inspire my confidence. At least take this," he said, unhooking his holster, "you never know."

"Which means we're going to have to get through reorganizing the camp without them . . ." grumbled Scummington. "Well played!"

"Rest assured, Inspector," Canterel replied icily, "we will be back before you have even gotten around to lifting a single crate."

They carried the suits to the place on the beach where the distance between this part of the island and the opposite shore was smallest. As the Stoner apparatus was equipped with a hand pump, inflating the floats took only a few minutes. After this, they put the suits on and, like knights entangled in their armor, advanced toward the water.

Once they were afloat, Canterel shot a smile at Lady MacRae, giving her a slight wave of farewell.

"Onward, old chap!" he said, leading by example.

They began to swim clumsily and, with a great deal of splashing, got about twenty meters; then came the moment when they could no longer do anything but turn in circles before being swept away by the current.

As they drifted, carried toward the island's inner harbor, Canterel displayed the tight-lipped look of someone who has just seen his plans thwarted by circumstance; less fatalistic, Holmes was wriggling around inside his suit in search of the bottle of scotch that a careless movement had sent sliding down to one ankle.

Tears in her eyes, shouting herself hoarse calling for Martial, Clawdia ran along the coast until they disappeared from view.

During this episode, Kim and Grimod, unaware of the drama that was playing out behind them, had moved north with less difficulty than expected. After half an hour of bogs similar to the one in which they had left their companions, the moor had firmed up under their feet, so much so that they had been able to speed up to a slow trot and get across fifteen kilometers in three hours. During this stretch, they had not, unfortunately, encountered a single rock or landform that would make a suitable place for their camp.

At the moment we return to them, however, they had just come across an area of land so flimsy that it was impassable. However much they would have liked to traverse its whole breadth, to explore the slightest bend that might conceal a passage, even right up against the ocean or the inner lagoon, there was no practicable way. Undermined by the tempest, this part of the island had been loosened so much that it was now merely a dangerous swamp, impossible to skirt. They would have to turn back.

It was on their return trip that they discovered the dinghy. The craft had run aground at the bottom of a deep recess formed by the inner shore of the island. Their hearts pounding, they got to it as fast as possible. Although it had water up to its rowing benches, the barque was intact, the oars still in place, stowed on the floor. They bailed it out as well as they could, then put the boat back in the sea, hurrying to rejoin their friends and share the good news.

Kim and Grimod had been rowing for a few minutes when they heard a voice at their backs that sounded like it was coming from the depths themselves. Turning, they saw two webbed monsters, equipped with antennae, which the current was carrying straight toward the boat. Frightened, Grimod sat up and cocked his rifle. He was shouldering it, ready to fire, when he recognized the nasal timbre of Holmes from every time he, returning from some carousal, had intoned his favorite air:

Well shirigim duraham da
Wack fall the daddy oh,
Wack fall the daddy oh,
There's whiskey in the jar!

The two floating divers were hoisted aboard in a trice. There was a great deal of congratulating and explaining and, rowing with eight arms and singing heartily, they continued on their way back to camp.

They were welcomed with as much surprise and joy as you may imagine. Lady MacRae clasped Canterel to her chest for a long time. The words she whispered in his ear did not reach us, but they were effective, as Martial remained as if electrified, radiant with happiness. Holmes later swore that this was the first time he had ever seen the man blush.

Captain Ward cut these outpourings short. Under his orders, the dinghy was loaded with the bare necessities for a new settlement; the rest of their things were sheltered under tarps, and everyone embarked.

Sped along by the same current that had interrupted Holmes and Canterel's crossing, the boat slid effortlessly into the channel. The farther they went toward the interior of the island, the more the swell abated, the oars only needing to brush the surface of the water to make the barque move. The sky broke through in tatters of ultramarine among the clouds, the banks passed by, gradually getting closer together.

Sanglard was conversing in low tones with Mardrus. The results of his deductions regarding the nature of the island were staggering. A thousand and one things had begun to make sense once he realized that it was floating. Its spiral shape, its base of more or less firmly amalgamated refuse, all these elements had put him in mind of the vortex in the North Pacific, a whirlpool created by the Coriolis effect in which all of the plastic scattered through the oceans of the globe had gathered. Certain eccentrics had spoken of a "gyrovague continent as big as Texas" and had situated it off the coast of California, thirty meters down. The problem was that this continent did not exist. After several expeditions, the scientific community had formally refuted this rumor. There was plenty of plastic trash adrift on all of the seas, far too much, certainly, but it wasn't concentrated anywhere, Coriolis effect or no Coriolis effect.

"In any event," said Sanglard, "that's what I believed until now."

"So you suppose . . ."

"Yes, my dear. Everything leads to the conclusion that we are entering for the first time what should be called a 'metaphor.'"

Two hours later, they rounded the promontory around which the island coiled to discover, dumbfounded, the cove it protected. Coming in closer, they made out large greenhouses whose ribbed domes, curved roofs, and hexagonal towers recalled both the Crystal Palace and the Jardin des Plantes.

Supported by pontoons, a long landing stage jutted out perpendicular to the coast.

A figure appeared and started down the platform. It walked slowly, matching its gait to the boat's pace. When they landed, a man was waiting for them; he held out a mooring line to them and introduced himself.

"Cyrus Smith. Ladies, gentlemen," he said, nodding. "I bid you good morning, and welcome to Port Nemo."

LII

Leave this page, children, and you as well, readers whom immodesty offends!

They ate the pizza together, all three of them, on the coffee table in the sitting room, between the sofa bed and the TV. When night fell, Carmen had pulled the curtains, lit a few candles. Now, the bottle of perry that JJ brought is half empty. Their cheeks are burning, their voices a touch too high, their gestures slow.

"He read us a good bit, at the factory this morning!" said Monsieur Bonacieux.

"Which one?" asked JJ.

"The one about the world sauna champion."

Carmen's eyes opened wide: "There's a championship for that?"

"Yes, in Finland. Imagine, these guys lock themselves in cabins that are heated to 110° C, and the winner is the one who hangs in the longest! Last year, the winner lasted three minutes and forty-six seconds."

"They're crazy!" said Carmen. "How could they survive a heat like that?"

"Well, that's kind of the problem . . . This year, there was a Russian who tried to beat the record. No one knows if he succeeded, but six minutes later, he was dead. Cooked through!"

"*Kwi vidé!*" JJ snickered.

"That's awful . . . More like world championship of bullshit!"

As the poodle was trying to climb into her lap, she pushed it away brusquely.

"Get the hell off me!"

"She wants to play," Dieumercie reproached her gently, "why do you hurt her?"

"I don't hurt her. She's always there rubbing herself against me, it's annoying."

I know someone else who's always rubbing herself against everything, Monsieur Bonacieux wanted to say, but he swallowed this remark, knowing how easy it would be for his wife to turn it against him. He is the one who made the extravagant gesture of offering her her freedom, even giving his permission for the meeting! Carmen has slept elsewhere five or six times since that day. He's no longer keeping count. Always with JJ, at least so she claims. She has changed. Against all expectation, she has soured a little, as if she resents him for this new situation. It is to mollify her that he has agreed to what is going to take place this evening. She has been asking him for this from the beginning, to sit in, to watch them making love. This idea embarrasses him and arouses him at the same time. He knows it's dangerous, that he's risking polluting his memory with it forever. But it won't be worse than imagining it.

Jean-Johnny hasn't said anything. Not a word. At work, he merely looked at Dieumercie with his puppy eyes from time to time. JJ has just given him the same long look, before finally making up his mind to speak.

"How about a dance?" he suggests, standing up.

Dieumercie is grateful to him for pushing back the deadline. He's out of anecdotes, he no longer knows how to fill the painful silence that is obliging them to keep mindlessly multiplying the glasses of perry. Carmen has rushed over to put a disk in the clock-radio CD player, moved into the living room for this occasion. Their song, the song from when they met eight years ago. It's obvious that she didn't choose it by accident. A tightness in his throat, Dieumercie watches his wife dance with JJ. She glues herself to him, but he holds her back, forces her, for better or worse, to preserve a shred of decency. He's an honest guy, this situation makes him uncomfortable, it shows in the fold of his lips, each time their eyes meet. As if to say: it's not my fault, what can I do, a girl like this is impossible to resist, any Morisycn who's not a *kouyon* would do the same . . . For the second slow song, Carmen comes and gets Dieumercie to bring him into their measured dance. All three of them are dancing like this, hugging one other.

At the end of the song, they go sit down again on the sofa. Carmen seems drunker than the men, but she pours herself another round of perry.

"So," she says, grabbing JJ's crotch, "are we gonna get down and dirty or what?"

And here it goes, we're off, Monsieur Bonacieux thinks. Leave this page, children, and you as well, readers whom immodesty offends! Because Jean-Johnny is boiling hot, he unzips his fly and pulls out an appendage whose bulging immensity comes straight out of a science fiction movie. Dieumercie wavers. He sees images of Grimod, of what he imagines a Mandingo's sex to look like. Everything goes so fast, he sees them undressing each other, devouring each others' mouths, grabbing at each other, writhing and groaning, and finally the penetration. But it is Carmen who is on top of JJ, gripping his brawny paddler's pectorals. She closes her eyes, shaking her head, focused on her personal journey, the rocking of her pelvis. As for JJ, he is acting like a sumo wrestler at the moment of combat, he grits his teeth, breathes in, and bellows, all while laying heavy slaps on her buttocks.

"Take off your clothes," says Carmen, continuing to bounce on top of Jean-Johnny.

"Uh, I don't know if now's the right time. I think I'll wait a little, dear . . ."

"Fuck, *doudou*, you could try to pleasure me, at least once, couldn't you?"

She says this choppily, as if sitting on a spin dryer.

She awkwardly unbuckles his belt, JJ tears his shirt as he tries to unbutton it, Dieumercie ends up taking off his own pants and finds himself naked, in his socks, on the sofa bed that has been transformed into a trampoline.

Carmen uproots herself from JJ, gets down on her knees on the couch.

"Be the mare . . . Go for it! Please, do it for me!"

She looks totally insane, the dog has come wriggling into the middle of things, trying to find a place for itself, but Dieumercie is no longer able to think, he gets down on all fours, closes his eyes, and accepts the catastrophe.

They must have prepared for this, because JJ immediately moves behind him. Monsieur Bonacieux feels the touch of his fingers, the icy wash of an oily substance, very pleasant around the rim, then without delay Jean-Johnny's dick sliding into his anus. He goes in gently, like a good friend, pulls out, sinks back in with more urgency, turns his attention to the walls of Dieumercie's rectum, his prostate. It's flexible and hard, gentle and painful, but no more than a hard workout. However, it's not until the moment when JJ thrusts into him up to the hilt that the miracle occurs. Carmen begins to shout, to stamp her feet like she's just won the lottery: Dieumercie is swelling, he's arching up, his erect penis wagging! Infused by his bum-gut, as Gargantua would say, this new sensual delight is miraculously transmitted to his balls, then to the seized-up springs of his arquebus, oiling it and reloading it so well that he now has several bullets in his barrel. And as the Mauritian slides in and out of the dampness of his entrails, Carmen arranges herself under their bodies to put her mouth around her husband's glorious sword.

In brief—you can come back, children!—Carmen sucks on Dieumercie while Jean-Johnny fucks him. Oh, oh! says Papa Bear, how will this story end?

LIII

A Single Green Creature

The man who had introduced himself as Cyrus Smith was wearing a heavy sealskin coat, but his appearance was not that of a hunter or sailor. His manicured hands, his slightly stiff elegance, and something authoritarian in his way of speaking instead recalled an officer of the Royal Navy, an impression that soon vanished in view of the extreme kindness of his gaze. He looked to be about forty-five years of age, perhaps three or four more, despite his perfectly white hair and the slight limp that also added a certain martial air to his figure. They later found out that he had just celebrated his sixty-fifth birthday, and that his hair had turned white upon waking after a certain black night stained by the confessions of a dying man.

"God be praised," said Captain Ward, setting foot on the wharf, "we had believed the island to be uninhabited . . ."

He stated his rank, the name of his schooner, and, having given a brief account of the circumstances of their abandonment, presented his companions as he held out his hand to each of them to help them out of the dinghy.

After the first moment of joy at the prospect of their deliverance, the view of the buildings erected before them, their displaced and anachronistic beauty, provoked another question. It was Sanglard who voiced it.

"This island is nothing more than a floating sponge; how does all of this remain standing?"

"If you agree to be our guests," said Cyrus Smith, "I will explain in detail. For the moment, I invite you to follow me, it will be more comfortable if we converse inside the base. Leave your things in the boat, I'll have them sent for."

Without any other comment, he turned his back on them and retraced his steps back along the dock.

Lady MacRae and Grimod followed suit, as if they found it quite natural to be thus awaited and greeted after so many misadventures. Their friends' hesitation lasted only a second; they had no choice but to follow their lead. But Sanglard and Mardrus never stopped whispering, losing themselves in speculation.

"He used the word 'base,'" Dr. Mardrus was saying. "Doubtless this is a place of study, one of the stations like the ones on the Kerguelen Islands and by the poles."

"A 'scientific base' we've never heard of? In a 'land' unknown to maps? It's inconceivable. There's some mystery here that surpasses my understanding."

"And what I find rather worrying," added Holmes, "why haven't they made any effort to take an interest in us. They can't have missed seeing our fires since yesterday . . ."

"A little patience, Messieurs," said Canterel, "we'll find out soon enough."

They were now arriving at the structure's porch. Coming closer, they noted that they were not in the presence of a single edifice, but of several buildings linked together by glass tunnels. As far as they could see, the whole thing consisted of a huge central glass roof in the shape of a rectangular mastaba, flanked on each end by a step pyramid, one higher than the main body, the other lower and recessed; to the right of this complex, another glass roof rose up in a series of arches upon which three extended apses rested. Above the biggest one rose a cylindrical tower topped with a faceted dome. Isolated from these perpendicular constructions, two enormous cupolas formed the tips of a right angle.

All of the architecture used the same geodesic principle: the domes and polyhedrons were all formed from the multitude of triangles of a light duralumin lattice. Up close, they could see that the covering on this frame was not made of glass, but a kind of plexiglass that was transparent in some places and opaque in others—and here, tinted white—according to the nature of the buildings.

Green reflections glimmered on the closest pyramid.

Once they had entered an empty room, Cyrus Smith closed the door behind them and turned the hatch wheel several times, making sure it sealed completely. This done, he opened the valve on a pressure gauge; a hissing sound made them look up. Several nozzles attached to the ceiling had begun to let out a dry, odorous steam that soon had their throats prickling.

"Rest assured," said Cyrus Smith, "it will only last a few minutes. Nothing and no one enters here without this preliminary decontamination."

"What is this substance?" asked Sanglard.

"A powerful antibacterial, totally harmless to us. It eliminates one hundred percent of germs capable of harming our internal environment."

"Such precautions!" Scummington scoffed. "Where are we? Some kind of secret laboratory?"

Without deigning to respond, Cyrus Smith stopped the spray and opened the second hatch. He preceded them into the corridor, took two forks, then ushered them into a compartment containing half a dozen bunk beds.

"I've had your beds prepared. You will excuse the lack of privacy, but we are hardly in the habit of receiving visitors." He pointed out the doors to the washroom and the toilets and, sliding aside the panels of a large wall cupboard, continued: "Here you will find towels and what you need to get changed. You will be served a meal in a few minutes, then I will return and show you the premises. Until then."

He slipped away, leaving them bewildered.

Grimod went up to the cupboard.

"It's incredible," he exclaimed, "they have our names on each of the piles!"

Each of them saw these labels, then looked at them in silence, disturbed by this inconsistency and what it suggested regarding premeditation.

Holmes rushed over to the door.

"It's not locked," he said. "At least we're not prisoners."

"What purpose would that serve?" Canterel disparaged. "On a round world, there's no option but to go around in circles."

"Indeed . . ." said Lady MacRae, sounding doubtful. "I'm going to wash my face. Going in circles doesn't mean we can't presentable."

She took two stacks of linen and locked herself in the bathroom with Verity. When she came out, the others followed her example, and everyone reappeared dressed in the clothes chosen for them: petrol-blue cotton coveralls with red bands around the armholes and a zipper up the front. Although these garments were in their sizes, they became them differently. Although Clawdia, Verity, Kim, and Grimod wore them quite naturally, their companions looked like novice transvestites at their first costume ball.

A little later, a young man appeared, decked out in a spangled jerkin, his beard short, his hair cropped—the tonsure on top of his head was in the shape of a star. He set out baskets of fruit, water, and, on plates marked with three interlacing R's, an assortment of little tarts garnished with a mixture of onions, tomatoes, and peppers sautéed in olive oil.

"He's a Donghak," Kim whispered in Holmes's ear. "The Korean sect devoted to eastern doctrine, I recognize their mark."

When he turned around to go out again, they saw with alarm that actually *she* was a Donghak, as the right half of her body was that of a woman, beautiful and long-haired, whose masculine half one could not imagine being on the other side of that profile.

This strange person left without speaking a single word, and Sanglard explained that they had just encountered a "half-and-half," like George-Ette "the double-bodied Venus," whom he had had the chance to observe at Arkham during a run of the Barnum and Bailey Circus.

"They are rarely true hermaphrodites, but men who decide to stage their androgyny. They only build muscle on one side, and on the other they accentuate their femininity by all kinds of methods, from local injections of silicone to breast implants. In the end, they make for very convincing Amazons . . ."

Scarcely had they finished their meal when Cyrus Smith returned. Rid of his coat, he appeared in a lion tamer's costume, including epaulettes and a vest with gold frogging on his chest.

Their questions gushed forth. How had he known their names, their measurements? Where were they? What was the meaning of all this? Why had no one helped them earlier?

Cyrus Smith chose to answer only this last question.

"It was only because of your fire that we found out you had landed. Even if we had wanted to intervene, the storm would have prevented us."

"Even if?" exclaimed Holmes. "You mean to say that you wouldn't have come otherwise?"

"When one is playing a game, one must not change the rules at the last second. We sent you a sign, but it was essential that you reach the goal you were pursuing by yourselves. As for the rest, everything will be explained in due course."

"Who's playing anything here?" Sanglard spluttered, getting worked up. "You, I don't doubt, but certainly not me or any of my companions!"

"Calm yourself, professor, you will soon understand. If you will follow me . . ."

"Who do you think you are, you fucking mime, no one has ever spoken to me in such a manner!"

Mardrus led him by the arm while he continued to choke with indignation.

Cyrus Smith brought them down other translucent corridors where the light seemed to come both from outside and from the glassy material itself. Having passed through a door made of PVC flakes, they came out into the biggest pyramid. The spectacle before them took their breath away. There was a thick tropical forest, an eruption of trees tangled with lianas that the setting sun pierced with long, slanting rays. Blistered with cryptogames and parasitic plants, the dense undergrowth gave off pungent smells of fermentation. In the wet heat, a thousand invisible insects buzzed in their ears, like tinnitus amplified by a single flitting fly. Some of the most gleaming butterflies, Morphos, Ulysses, and Mormons moving erratically, Dryads mating before them, motionless on lower leaves, wings embroidered with a double yellow circle.

A single organism, a single green creature was enclosed here, sweating life from all its pores.

As he plodded along, Cyrus Smith provided them with figures that forced their admiration: this pyramid spanned 1,900 square meters; within its 22 meters of height and 35,000 cubic meters, it sheltered 1,833 different species of plants, chosen for their resilience and their superior abilities with photosynthesis.

"This farm of ours is a veritable lung," he continued, "this forest produces ninety percent of the oxygen you are breathing."

"In a closed system?" asked Sanglard, his tone softened.

"No, that's not the goal. As you know, any closed system is doomed to entropic death. Nature, like society, is an open system, it can only survive through exchange with the exterior, the constant intake of new information, crossbreeding. We're trying to maintain, as much as possible, a natural equilibrium between oxygen production and carbon dioxide emission, but it's necessary to inject air in regularly."

"How about water?"

"Same thing. Although they are recycled infinitely, the 1,500 cubic meters of fresh water that we use must be supplemented every month. Which is not a problem, since we have reverse osmosis desalinators."

"How do you make them work?" asked Dr. Mardrus, astonished. "The irrigation pumps, the other machines, the lights? You must use some kind of energy, wood, gas, oil, something!"

"Just electricity. We have several oscillating-foil hydrokinetic turbines submerged to the depth required to make use of ocean currents. They are made of copper sheeting and we use ultrasound to protect them from algae, barnacles, and other organic colonizations. We also have a two-megawatt fuel cell in one of the domes that you must have glimpsed, the other serves as hydrogen storage, and all of the panels that cover our biosquare can collect solar energy and emit it at will, in the form of heat or light, thanks to bioluminescent bacteria. I'll add that we have recently been experimenting with a piezoelectric network installed on the waterfront, under the humus layer; it transforms the penguins' waddling into electrons and is producing excellent results."

"Great God of Thunder!" murmured Sanglard. "How is it that we've never gotten wind of such a site? Are you the one in charge of this wonder?"

"I am only its chief engineer. Come, we have only scratched the surface of the surprises in store."

They came out of the jungle and with no transition entered the quadrangular greenhouse linking the pyramids. Their amazement, artless and dramatic, caused Cyrus Smith to smile.

A vast terrain stretched out before them, taking elements from the savannah and the landscape of Provence. A rolling plain, planted in some places with pines and eucalyptus, in others with fruit trees, grapevines, and olive groves, opened into large clearings covered with yellow grass and coppices, through which a river wound. Scattered along its banks, a whole menagerie was grazing peacefully: elephants, giraffes, lionesses, llamas, giant tortoises, all of whom, it could be seen, were suffering from some greater or lesser infirmity. If a number of these animals was missing a paw, replaced by carbon steel protheses—one tortoise was even moving itself along on two streamlined rear wheels—the majority were blind and rambling, guided only by habit or smell.

In this artificial paradise, a mechanical tiger, reduced to a steel musculature riddled with cables and circuits, paced through the area with the sound of connecting rods and perfectly oiled pistons.

"What hell," said Canterel in a tone of infinite sadness.

LIV

The Donkey Killer

Awakening from long comas, certain miraculous survivors assert that, despite all appearances, they could hear what was going on around them. Arnaud has chosen to believe this, and continues to address Dulcie as if nothing has happened. He shares with her his impressions, his fears, his unbroken hope, the wish to one day see her come out of her relentless sleep and return to her life. The fiction sessions destined to be read the next day he writes only for her; love's medicine, a desperate treatment that he administers, page after page, in the silence of the grotto: to name something is to give it the chance to exist.

He has put her to bed on her side, just now, curled up to vary her points of contact with the sheet. God she's beautiful, and how this coiled position softens her. Dulcie, goddess of water and earthquakes, her eyes laughing every time she lay down like this, inviting him to join her.

Recollecting this, he sometimes gets the impression that she's responding to him.

When a reader climbed up to his platform, no one ever looked at him. The workers would listen to him religiously, focused more on the work of their hands than on his voice, but when he stumbled on a word, when he held a pause for a few seconds too many, how their anxious eyes would rise toward him. The smoke of the cigars—all of them, men and women, smoked them—would stagnate in the workshop like a cloud of incense; they held back their throat clearings, even the clattering of the knives seemed to quiet a little. This churchly silence, a precise measurement of their attention, turned the reading lectern into an altar of truth.

The only benefit of a repetitive job, Dulcie used to say, at least when it is still craftwork, is that it lets the spirit roam free. You can be elsewhere, dwelling in memories or the fantasy of a better life. Only the practice of reading aloud could keep us all in a single plot, make our dreams uniform. Another of the powerful moments was when the reader closed his book. At once the workshop began to hum with words, people would comment from table to table on what had just been read, they would approve of one character's attitude and criticize another's, questions would burst forth regarding the novel's events, a historical point, or even the meaning of an obscure word. In cases of doubt, there was the *Mataburros*, the "donkey killer"; one of the workers who knew how to read would be sent to check in the dictionary or encyclopedia, the only two books kept in the workshop. Whatever the result, everyone benefited from it. "That's how I learned about Dumas, and how everyone started howling with joy when we learned that his grandmother, Marie-Zézette, had been a slave in Santo Domingo."

In Villers-Cotterêts, she had discovered much later, the tobacco shop kept by Marie Labouret, Alexandre Dumas's mother, still stood on the Place de la Fontaine. This information had almost frightened her, so deeply did the author of *Monte Cristo* seem linked in some secret manner to the destiny of the cigar makers.

She knew that sooner or later the modern world would do away with the practice of reading in the factories, that radio and television would carry through with their deadly work, but she hoped for a surge, an opposition, a revolt. How could he tell her that the battle was lost? The president of the Union of Writers and Artists of Cuba had just proposed to UNESCO that it classify the office of the reader as part of humanity's intangible heritage. The application justified the high cultural value of this tradition by underlining that, thanks to this practice, "Cuban cigar makers focusing on a novel, a poem, a newspaper article, or a simple classified ad, but most often on works written by great authors, achieved a refined and superior quality of cigar; they had transmitted to the tobacco their passion for what they heard, for adventures and dreams, so that the other great pleasure in life, smoking, might be converted into a supreme ecstasy."

All that just to arrive here . . . Not content to simply endorse the permanent erasing of the readings—upon examination, UNESCO's lists contained only fragments of lost or dying worlds—this epitaph, using all the lyricism of promotional flyers, reduced the cigar makers to simple flavor enhancers: after a century and a half of readings in the tobacco workshops, only the cigars had come out improved, not the people who rolled them!

To increase their chances of securing their place in world heritage, the Cuban authorities had begun to bring tourists to the few platforms that still remained, and this, more than anything else, was a sign of death.

He would not share these horrors with Dulcie. Nor the dismay that forces him to rest his forehead on his folded arms for a moment. Abandonment would be a better word to describe the loneliness that enfolds him; like the sailor Selkirk, who was Crusoe's mirror image, left—"abandoned," as it were—on a desert island.

It's strange how the imagination works, and how it is akin to dreams. We take a beak from here, a paw from there, some feathers, gleaming scales, and a machine inside us reconstructs it into a new creature, a monstrous collage of scraps, glimpsed fragments, forgotten readings, childhood fears that return, that agglomerate in the night to form islands, black continents. Randomly programmed, artificial.

Absolutely nothing that is not born of recycling, of a watermark on the strand. We are acted upon by tides that we don't control, but from time to time a bit of driftwood arrives on them whose riddle seems to have the power to change the world.

This afternoon, behind the glass of the radio booth, Arnaud felt his heart go to pieces, with brief, arrhythmic pauses following oppressive accelerations. Forced to stop his reading to regain his breath, he noticed the silence that descended, panicking more at its persistence than at the reasons behind his faintness. Images had begun to float behind his eyes, colors overlapping one another as on a washed-out watercolor: Dulcie, Barnum's museum, a sperm whale on fire. It had lasted less than a minute, but it was inside this whiteness that a final defense had yielded. With the awful sensation of an obvious and irreversible fact, he had admitted that his beloved would never wake up.

This doesn't change anything about what he promised himself; he has only three or four chapters left before facing a similar ending, but in the countdown that has just started ticking away, Arnaud feels for the first time how inexorable, how distressing, how vain a book can be.

Last Telegrams of the Night

Things that measure time with the regularity of a clock.
Marcel Blancpain, seventy years old, killed himself with five pistol shots to the temple, fired at fifteen-minute intervals.

Things that miraculously return the power of speech.
Alaska. Her tongue frozen to the railing of a metal bridge, a little girl is freed by a whiskey massage.

Things that leave a taste of blood in the mouth.
The man with the severed hand speaks . . .

Things that definitively take away all pleasure from playing with dolls.
Pedophilia: A Californian man becomes sexually aroused by swallowing Barbie heads. After having evacuated them into the toilet, he puts them through the dishwasher before gulping them down again.

Things that make one want to blow one's nose properly.
Hit from behind while he is picking his nose at a red light, a motorist sinks his index finger in up to his eyeball and dies of a hemorrhage.

Things that are no longer useful but that bring back fond memories.
I've been killing for seven years, the cannibal farmer from Wisconsin stated. One body, five women's heads preserved on ice, four human skulls, and ten masks made of skin were found in his home.

Things that demonstrate how little the handicapped differ from others.
The blind man, having received treatment, went to file a complaint at the police station. According to the description he gave to the officers, the attacker was a thirty-year-old man, short, rather stout, with a round face, a dark complexion, wearing a charcoal Loden cape and a checkered cap.

Things that make the shrewdest of detectives jealous.
The postman's body was found, though all that remained, alas, were his boots.

Things that fall from the sky and make one's nose wrinkle in disgust.
It's raining s*** in Saint-Pandelon. The deputy mayor is not hiding his concern: "We can't eat fruits or vegetables from our gardens anymore. And I don't even want to talk about our swimming pools." The neighboring town's gendarmerie is on full alert.

Things that make a conversation bounce back.
A roofer, Monsieur Olive Gaillard, fell twenty-five meters. Luckily, a pile of bricks cushioned his fall.

LV

Martyrio, the "Woman Cannonball"

They walked behind Cyrus Smith, hypnotized by the strange beauty of their surroundings. Quashing Canterel's first impression, the animals they met did not seem unhappy in the least. Despite their handicaps, they were in good health, and the engineer could not walk by them without them immediately coming over to rub themselves against him or lick his hand in greeting. A tangible softness emerged in these silent demonstrations, which were even more astounding in that they were also addressed to Verity. From the beginning of their crossing, the animals had been coming up to her just as much as Cyrus Smith. The girl stroked them without showing any surprise and, by the strange miracle that had allowed her to speak with the whales a few days earlier, she called each one of them by its name, petting them with the familiarity of a shepherdess in the middle of her flock. Brave Rajah! she would say, or Shere Khan, or Sultan. There! There! The elephant was named Harriet, the tortoise Gustave; naturally fascinated, neither Lady MacRae nor Canterel thought for a second to protect her from these touches, even when she teased a lioness by blowing in its ear.

Without giving them time to take stock of what they were experiencing, Cyrus Smith led them to the end of the gallery, then faded away to allow them time to appreciate the wonders of the second pyramid. They all stood frozen at the sight of the phantasmagoria spread out before them.

It was the inside of a circus tent. Confused by the profusion of simultaneous images, their gazes first registered the geometric shapes enclosed under the glass structure: the intersecting circles of three arenas bounded by noisily painted boxes, the concentric rings of benches that surrounded them, the vertical sweep of the lattice towers erected around the circumference, the oblique lines of the guying. Then suddenly the focus sharpened, they had the impression of beginning to see. A thousand and one scenes were unfolding, magnified by turns, as if by a zoom effect. They could make out the swaying of a dozen trapeze artists performing high above like hair-raising constellations. They flew up under the spotlights, twirled and spun in defiance of gravity and danger, focused on the catching of hands from which— you could feel it in the bristling of your skin—the harmony of these heavens came.

Hanging on a long ribbon of yellow fabric, a young woman in a corset was making statue poses; she pretended to let go, fell, barely caught herself with a section wound around her ankle or fist. Then she smiled, waving gracefully, though her flesh could be seen turning blue and swelling from the torsion.

At the same height, spinning through the air, acrobats were performing strings of perilous jumps in order to trace the curves of a single broken-down movement.

Two tightrope walkers balanced on cables, competing in madcap pirouettes. On the ground, a horsewoman, tethered by one foot to the collar of a galloping Frisian, was sweeping the track with her long blonde mop of hair; contortionists in flesh-colored singlets were walking on their hands, their legs twisted up around their necks; under the iron rule of a Mother Christmas, molded into a mini skirt with red frills and smiling impishly, rabbits were leaping through a flaming hoop while a magician in tails pulled kilometers of illuminated string lights from his mouth. There was also a gorgeous brunette in Oriental dress, with a lamé bikini bottom and bra upon which rustled the suggestive coilings of a python; indifferent to her presence, whiteface and auguste clowns were throwing buckets of glue at one another, shouting.

It was only at this point that they noticed the caravans set in the back, the clotheslines where bloomers were drying, and, scattered throughout this rest area, the freaks going about their business. Her makeup removed, next to an armless Indian who was practicing archery with his toes, they recognized the half-and-half who had so surprised them earlier.

An orchestra was accompanying the acts; it played a tune by Mozart, the Andante from the *Sinfonia Concertante*, whose offbeat sorrow emphasized the extreme enchantment of these tableaux; this music stopped short, replaced by ten drums mutedly imitating a heartbeat. When all of the artists came to a standstill, a floodlight illuminated a huge cannon straight from one of Jules Verne's dreams. A woman in black climbed the rungs of a ladder in order to insert herself, feet first, into the tube. An assistant lit the fuse, and the cannon thundered, propelling its human arrow toward a net hanging in the heights. The acrobat grabbed onto it, arms and legs spread wide, simulating a spider in the center of its web. At the moment when this image took shape, a series of bulbs flashed above her, giving the illusion of a surge, in a luminous signature that read: Martyrio Circus. The woman then came back down, at the end of a glittering tether.

A jungle, a paradise for cripples, the Martyrio Circus . . .

"And here we are, back where we started," Holmes whispered in Canterel's ear, as Cyrus Smith led them through a new tunnel. "What we're looking for must be here, it can't possibly be otherwise!"

"I don't know a damn thing," replied Martial, "this place is an insane asylum. It's making my head spin."

They had entered new, lower greenhouses dedicated to intensive farming. Perfectly kept fields of grain that alternated, under the mist of the automatic sprinklers, with vegetable patches arranged along gardener's lines and separated by narrow aisles of raked sand.

Coming back into the residential sector, Cyrus Smith quickly showed them the kitchens, then ushered his guests into a laboratory staffed by men and women in white coats. A colony of horrible, hairless little animals with exaggeratedly long incisors stirred inside a wall vivarium made of clear tubing.

"Naked mole-rats!" exclaimed Sanglard. "I don't believe my eyes!"

"My congratulations," said Cyrus Smith, "few are familiar with this animal. So you also know what distinguishes them from rodents of the same size, like moles or mice?"

Sanglard made an effort to recall and recited: "Muscles of the jaw represent twenty-five percent of the total musculature, resistant to atmospheres rich in carbon oxides, adapt their body temperature to the surrounding air, skin immune to acid . . . As far as I remember, they're also the only mammal known to behave like ants or bees: in a colony of three hundred individuals, there is only one fertile female, a queen who, until she dies, gives birth to the totality of the offspring necessary to the population's survival. Which implies, of course, that for her whole life she copulates only with her brothers, her sons, or her grandsons. As with social insects, she is surrounded by a court of servants of both sexes, who nourish and protect her. Here I'm quoting the works of Professor Rochelle Buffenstein."

"Certainly," replied Cyrus Smith, "but it gets better. Not content with enjoying exceptional longevity—they live for up to thirty-five years, which in human years would correspond to an age of a hundred and fifty—these animals do not experience any cell damage for almost the entirety of their lives. No decrepitude, no cancer. They die young, whatever their age."

"Fantastic," said Sanglard, reflecting on the possibilities of this new information, "absolutely fantastic! If we can come to understand this mechanism, can you imagine the prospects for humanity?"

"That's what we're working on."

Before leaving the area, they had time to glimpse aquariums in which various species of jellyfish were floating; they aroused the professor's curiosity, but Cyrus Smith had already turned his back and was starting up the stairs.

"But where are you taking us?" Holmes called, beginning to feel his fatigue. "I can't stand it anymore."

"One last effort, I beg you, we are nearly there."

Each of the three landings they passed opened onto corridors like the ones on the first floor; they seemed likely to open onto other lounges, other laboratories.

Cyrus Smith ignored them, continuing to climb. He then led them up a spiral staircase, and the little troupe came in behind him to a large circular room topped with a geodesic dome. Through the diamond-shaped glass openings set regularly in the opaque structure, they could see only the sky, flushed with the glow of the setting sun. At the center of what was evidently the base's control tower sat an octagonal console surrounded by straight-backed chairs; each of its sides had switches, LED lights—some green, some red—and a number of screens twinkling with figures and graphs.

"Everything is controlled by computer," said Cyrus Smith, "ventilation, gas exchange, wastewater recycling, temperature, humidity . . ."

He went up to a terminal, typed several lines on a keyboard, and tapped sharply on the "Enter" key. The image that had appeared on the screen was suddenly projected before them, significantly enlarged, on the wall of the dome.

"Here is the map of the island," he said, in a tone that signaled that they would finally get answers to their questions. "As you have doubtless noticed for yourselves, it is in the shape of a spiral, which is

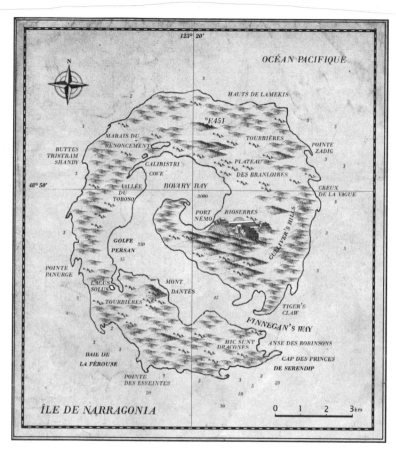

"'Here is the map of the island,' he said, in a tone that signaled
that they would finally get answers to their questions."

due to the vortex that caused its formation. Initially, it was simply a matter of plastic and marine herpes amassed in this place by the currents, a cloud of particles that were impressive in mass—we're talking thirty million tons of plastic—but unusable. At least until we found a way of amalgamating these particles to one another."

"But how, what miracle allowed this?" asked Dr. Mardrus, astonished.

"Serendipity, as is too often the case . . . Meaning that we found the solution by chance, while looking for something else. A biophysicist who was working on osteoarticular infections accidentally discovered that a proteolytic enzyme was capable of coupling the collagen in cartilage to certain molecules in plastic material, with the effect of polymerizing these two agents and producing a functional regeneration in damaged tissue. When this same scientist noticed that the collagen in jellyfish, which is similar to that in humans, reacted better than others, the link was soon made. The implementation was not as easy as my account might make it sound, but that is the technique we used. The results have been spectacular."

Irritated by all this jargon, Canterel played the Philistine.

"It seems to me, however, that we waded across your island like a swamp."

"Indeed. While the center of the island is solidified over ten hectares and forty meters deep—which we allowed in order to construct the buildings where you are now—the process is still ongoing, it is far from complete."

"Hence the bogs, I imagine?" Sanglard asked.

"Yes. We're trying to accelerate the consolidation by all kinds of additional means, the specific biochemistry of certain lichens, or guano, for example. But we are still far from mastering things. In some respects, the island behaves like a living organism."

"That's wonderful!" said Lady MacRae. "How many times I pictured this in my childhood dreams, sailing on the back of a whale!"

"Let's not exaggerate," said Cyrus Smith. "The island is passive, it is content to float. I would say, rather, that it reacts like an epidermis that is having trouble healing. The cells repair themselves and proliferate without anyone being able to predict the scope of the repair. Look at its geography: the surface should be perfectly flat, but the storms we experience at this latitude are constantly altering it." He aimed the beam of a laser pointer at the image. "Mount Dantès, here, Fahrenheit 451 Hill, all these hillocks were formed by breakers heaping up refuse on the outer edge. This explains why the polymerization process is slower on the periphery of the spiral, and also, alas, why we are obliged to draw up a new map after every meteorological upheaval. The one you see before you dates from this morning, it incorporates a rotation of ten degrees in relation to magnetic north, which does not often happen, luckily."

Captain Ward took a deep breath and jumped in.

"Forgive me, I don't understand much of what you're saying, but I'm a sailor, I know when I'm seeing things and when I'm not. We were not three miles from Point Nemo, and your island rose up as if by magic, since we should have seen it long before . . ."

"You weren't seeing things, captain. In the same way any sound can be cancelled out by sending back to the listener the same frequencies from an opposite point, it is possible to erase images by artificial means. It's simply a question of waves, of dosage, obviously. We set out visual reversal mirrors, the exterior of this dome is covered in them. Again, it's a little difficult to describe without resorting to mathematical language; simply put, it comes back to project, in 360° around the island, photons that are modified as we please. In the eyes of those who receive them, they create the reflection of a real ocean, but one from which the island has been expunged. Diminished reality, sort of."

"You are visible or invisible at will!" exclaimed Dr. Mardrus. "It's not viable!"

"And yet . . . You see this switch?" He activated it as he spoke. "Up, we become visible again. Down, we disappear from all human pupils. I triggered it myself when I was sure that it was indeed your boat."

"Unbelievable, utterly unbelievable!" said Sanglard, though it was unclear which of these revelations he was thus extolling.

"Our boat?" asked Canterel. "How could you have known?"

"Nothing could be simpler, you were proclaiming your destination to the four winds. We have informants, our survival depends on it."

"This method doesn't stop your island from existing, even invisible. What's there to stop a ship from running aground by chance?"

"Nothing arrives here by chance," came a deep voice from the room.

As they were looking around to see where this voice was coming from, one of the chairs at the control center swung around, revealing a pleasant-looking woman who examined them with an unsettling gaze, her head slightly tilted to the side.

"Only dreamers and madmen take such an eccentric route," she continued, "and those will always be welcome."

Cyrus Smith presented her: "Martyrio, the 'Woman Cannonball,'" he said, smiling warmly, "and also the person in charge of this station, and our Reverend Mother."

She was sitting down, her chest upright, her hands resting on the arms of the chair. Her black silk dress, tight at the waist, flared out in wide pleats that were hitched up above her knees, revealing calves clad in fishnet stockings extending up from patent leather boots. Between her thighs, which were a little further apart than they should have been, hung two other similarly attired legs, short and slender, as if there were a little girl hidden in her skirts.

Lady MacRae let out a moan of fright then, reddening, tried to apologize.

"No matter," Martyrio interrupted her. "With time, I've grown accustomed to it."

LVI

Butter Cookies

Charlotte spent three nights away from home, taking the time to pull herself together. During the day, while Fabrice returned to the factory as if nothing had happened, she cleaned up his studio, careful not to disrupt the disorder of his things, but taking trips to the laundromat on the corner to clear away the dirty laundry that had accumulated. She had acted without asking any questions regarding the young man's apparent negligence, merely obeying her own desire for order and cleanliness. Upon his return, Fabrice had thanked her half-heartedly, apologizing for having taken her in under such conditions, uncomfortable about the fact that she had handled his dirty boxers.

The morning of the first day, he had gone out to buy her some bread and ham before leaving for work. On his way home, he took the time to pedal up to the pizza truck to grab them some dinner. In the following days, Charlotte took care of cooking simple dishes on the two hotplates that had been so much work to scour: pasta with canned tuna, reheated ravioli, tins of lentils with bacon from Leader Price upon which they feasted. Fabrice recounted his battles, told of his obsessions, named his enemies, trying to make her understand the urgency of saving the world from the profiteers who were sucking the marrow from its bones.

"It's going to explode, don't you see? A unique cocktail, kind of like if you mixed the Crusades, the Market Crash of '29, and the

Russian Revolution. There will be blood, but that's the price of re-birth. At last, maybe . . . What's certain is that we must stir things up if we hope to make everything good!"

An expression that came from Grampa Vitrac.

He had brought her news from the factory, described the damage done by his attack and how Wang, the vile chink, had more or less remedied the situation. She would need to find the courage to file charges against the bastard, to bring him down! Evasively, she had insisted on seeing the letters he was writing to his mother; he had read her a few, and they had gone to sleep against each other, bathed in tenderness.

On her way back to her apartment to grab some clothes, seized with chills, feverish with hope, Charlotte felt herself come back to life; it seemed to her that happiness had become possible, that Fabrice loved her. She walked, looking straight ahead, breathing free, noticing for the first time the changing colors of the Dordogne, the relief of green groves overhead against the slate scales of the roofs. Arriving at her door, she was surprised not to see Marthe coming out onto the landing. She felt so strong, so full of compassion, that she rang at the woman's door several times before noticing the bit of red and white adhesive stuck to the doorframe near the lock. The voice of Monsieur Jargeot, the upstairs neighbor, made her jump.

"You can ring all you like, you won't get an answer. They've both kicked the bucket. One of 'em killed the other and then died, too. The disinfection service is supposed to come by tomorrow, but I wouldn't want to be in the landlord's shoes: it's gonna take a lot of work before he can rent it again!"

Charlotte had trouble opening her door, her heart pounding, her eyes blurry with tears. There was an envelope on the floor, a sum-mons to the Sarlat Police Station. She walked back out, determined to go immediately.

For the whole bus ride, Marthe's last words looped through her head. She had heard them several times before that night, but nothing had come of it, since the old drunk had woken up the next morning, in a hurry to leave his den and go back out to get drunk again. Plus, there was nothing to suggest that this tragedy had unfolded immediately after she'd left. She tried in vain to remember the next day, unable to picture Chonchon other than on the floor, aggressive, mayonnaise in hand, or even to remember how much time had passed between that terrible encounter and the moment she had found herself a prisoner.

At the police station, an inspector received her. He took the trouble of reassuring her, beginning by summarizing everything he knew about her interventions to help the couple, her notification to the Regional Health Agency, her two phone calls to their welfare officer, but here they were, misery is not cured as easily as might be hoped.

Chonchon must have spat out one insult too many, and Marthe had killed him, smothering him on the floor under half a mattress.

"She was heard tapping on your door, making a racket. Then nothing. The autopsy showed she'd swallowed two bottles of Chancellor, her husband's anti-diabetics. At some point, she picked up the phone and called the fire department, but she didn't manage to say anything. By the time they managed to get to her, it was too late. She had died of a heart attack."

Now. According to what they had told him in the building, Charlotte was the person closest to the deceased. Neither of them had any family, so if she wanted to keep some of their personal effects, as keepsakes, he didn't see any objection. She would simply have to sign a receipt.

Charlotte shook her head, her throat tight, but the inspector had already gotten up to rummage through a metal cabinet.

"There's not much," he said, setting a cookie tin down on the desk.

The place where Marthe kept her treasures, a rusty circular vault with a snowy landscape, infinite blurry flakes, and *Butter Cookies* written on the lid in garish faux gold. Only now did she discover its contents: ID cards reduced to lace, a tatty family record book, a tarot card from Marseille—*The Wheel of Fortune*—two five-franc pieces, a baby's slipper, keys, a bundle of letters in a child's handwriting, held together by a black ribbon that was pinned with a little medal bearing the image of St. Anthony of Padua. Opening the family record, Charlotte already knew, as we ourselves dimly sense, that she must expect the worst. She read and began to cry. Not for Marthe, not for Fabrice, but out of panic and almost terror at the abominations that prowl around us.

Charlotte signed, shook the policeman's hand, got back on the bus.

Now she is sitting on a railing above the Dordogne River. Her legs over the void, the box balanced on her knees. She is crying off and on, her eyes puckered, as Marthe's had been a few days earlier. *Lucette Marthe Jalabert, née Lemestre, widow of Petitbout*. Fabrice's mother. We would like to be able to help her, make her understand that, once opened, this kind of box cannot be closed again, that she has here a capital of misery to share with Fabrice, the hope of a real foundation for their love. She is going to barge in on his world, break his magnetic coating, all the defenses behind which he protects himself, and tell him. Tell him that she loves him, that all the nuclear plants in the world can blow up, and the planet too for all she gives a damn; that she's not afraid to die, as long as she's in his arms when it happens.

But she doesn't know. She has no idea if something viable can happen beyond the ambiguity where she is now, between silence and revelation. To be honest, neither do we; and it is doubtless for this reason that the tin is trembling harder and harder on her knees.

LVII

A Slow Atlantis

Nature's quirks are never so surprising as when they come to bear on humans, as if the deviation from the physical norm revealed in them a distortion of another order, a supernatural eccentricity. A goddess with supernumerary legs, Martyrio mesmerized our companions.

"This island," she said, indifferent to the uneasy hypnosis that she had brought on, "we call Narragonia, in honor of Sebastian Brant and his *Ship of Fools.*"

"A land of plenty, then?" Canterel interrupted.

"A lucid dream, rather, a vision . . ."

"All these literary place names on the map, I imagine, are yours?"

"They emerged spontaneously over the course of our installation. I would say that they were deduced. There is no reality that is not rooted in some prior fiction. These are dedications, as they almost always are, lighthouses, seamarks; this is the bewitching power of maps, and perhaps their only justification."

She closed her eyes for a few seconds to pick up the thread of her thoughts, then continued.

"Cyrus Smith was good enough to take you by the biosquare we built. It can be considered the third of its kind. The first one—the only one, in truth—is the Earth itself, an ecosystem in perfect equilibrium, at least until these last few years. The second was a fake; it was a project developed half a century ago in Arizona by a bunch of charlatans and an enlightened billionaire: a complete simulation of self-sufficiency meant to reproduce the living conditions of a human colony on Mars. Lamentably, it failed, so much so that today it is no more than an amusement park with scientific pretensions. Despite its limitations, "Biosphere 2"—the name by which you have doubtless heard it called—nevertheless provided the data behind the problem, which explains why we keep it in this genealogy. Our station, here, claims only independence. It is a refuge, a rational utopia for a community of researchers, men and women 'of good will,' as they used to say in a time when that still made sense."

"With what money?" asked Sanglard, puzzled. "It must have taken hundreds of millions . . . Who funds you, some sponsor or university?"

Martyrio looked at him almost tenderly before responding.

"Everything relies on my own funds," she said, smiling.

"Excuse me," Mardrus intervened, "I don't mean to give offense, but I have trouble believing that the circus business could have left you so rich. Where does such a fortune come from?"

"Even if you underestimate what one of the performances from our glory days could bring in, it is true that I've benefited from a certain legacy, as generous as it was unexpected. You will allow me, for the moment, not to speak of it further. There is nothing about it, in any case, that would make me blush or that anyone could reproach me for."

The half-and-half whom they had already encountered suddenly reappeared and went up to whisper in her ear.

"Dinner is served," said Martyrio. "Let's go down, if you will, our discussions will go better with glasses in our hands."

She stood and walked over to the stairs without any apparent difficulty; slowly, however, and with a precision of gesture that betrayed how much this learning must have cost her in effort and perseverance.

At this point in our story, the reader will be surprised that neither Holmes nor Canterel has brought up the Ananke, the diamond whose trace they had been following with so many complications. After their hostess's ambiguous response on the origins of her wealth, it occurred to them that she could have taken possession of it, but it took only a little common sense to reject this hypothesis. If that were the case, it would have been easy for this woman to dispose of them—something in the way she crinkled her eyes suggested that she was capable of it—instead of welcoming them as she had. Furthermore, everything indicated that she was affluent enough not to need to lust after the precious stone for which they were searching. As for the thief, if he had sought refuge on this island, better to remain cautious and not alert him by revealing the reasons for their presence. Even Scummington, whose eyes revealed his suspicion, managed to keep quiet.

That the Noh Straddler had not appeared for so long did not stop bothering them, either. This demon never gave up the chase; it was impossible to believe for a second that he had turned tail.

A buffet had been laid out for them two stories below, in the grand salon. Adapting to the darkening sky, certain coated panels had begun to diffuse a golden light, similar to that in a Grand Siècle ballroom. On the white linen over the oval table gleamed silver place settings and those porcelain plates marked with three interlacing R's that had intrigued them earlier. Artfully arranged, dishes and plates offered up simple and varied food, Belle de Fontenay gratin with stuffing, smoked fish, and a colorful assortment of Asian appetizers. Holmes raised an eyebrow, however, noting that the carafes contained nothing but fruit juice.

Cyrus Smith pulled out the chair at the head of the table and invited Martyrio to sit.

"Reverend Mother," he said ceremoniously, "please."

She thanked him and, once seated, addressed her guests.

"Be so good as to forgive me, I have a little trouble remaining standing for too long. Sit where you will, there is no seating plan."

Leading by example, she began to serve herself.

They were still in that state of perplexity of diners hesitating to begin their meals when Sanglard began to speak. Brow furrowed, fingers interlaced above his empty plate, he voiced a thought that had clearly been bothering him.

"I would like to buy into the idea of an independent research center," he said, his voice grave, "and even, as you said, a 'rational utopia'—a contradiction in terms whose legitimacy, or at least poetic character, I believe I nevertheless grasp. What little of your work I've seen, I confess, has left me flabbergasted: the rainforest, the savannah with its animals, the naked mole-rats . . . The fact that these labs are located in the middle of nowhere, that I can accept as well, but, by goodness, what does the circus have to do with anything? Entertainers, far from anywhere, without an audience . . . It doesn't make any sense!"

Martyrio looked at him enigmatically, then replied.

"Let us say that it is the island's heart, its umbilicus. The arena where we stage the game of the world, with its rites of survival, death, and resurrection."

Sanglard lifted his hands toward the sky in a gesture of pique and annoyance.

"Allow me to repeat," he said, "I'm not judging you, I'm trying to understand. What is the point of this masquerade? Where are we? In a cult? A phalanstery?"

"I told you, my dear sir, this is a haven, a non-place where all of our society's rejects are gathered. A brotherhood of castaways, wanderers of the South Seas."

"Or an insane asylum!" grumbled Scummington, low enough that only Lady MacRae heard him.

As he listened, Canterel was observing his companions' behavior; he couldn't quite believe their apparent casualness. Though Holmes was sulking, which was understandable, the others were pecking at their food as if they were at an embassy cocktail party. Ward, Mardrus, and Scummington, however, kept their eyes down.

He was grateful to Sanglard for not dropping the subject.

"Our world is in a bad way," he continued, "I'll give you that. That's no reason to take yourself out of it, to deny it. There are other solutions . . ."

"What solutions, professor? Continuing to act as if God hasn't been dead for two hundred years? As if science alone could be enough to call us to an ethical code? As if the States still offered an ounce of hope? As if capitalism, Marxism, and other global ideologies had not shown their inability to ensure people's happiness? As if ecology could be anything more than a simple individual awareness? As if war and peace had not dissolved into a continuous malice?"

"So cynical! How can you feel this way?" Sanglard rebelled. A nervous tic was making his left eyelid quiver. "It's not so bleak, so hopeless as that!"

"I'm simply telling you that the lifeboats remain systematically stuck on their davits, that it is always the biggest, the strongest, the stupidest who trample over the women and children to save their own pitiful lives, and that the captain is not even required to go down with his ship. We are living a slow Atlantis, Monsieur Sanglard, a sinking so subtle that only the most vulnerable of us notice it. Not a tsunami or cataclysm of any kind, but a tenuous, everyday infiltration that makes the sponge of our planet a little heavier each day. This world is impossible to live in, and that is why we have chosen not to be content with it."

"We? Who are you talking about, now? Your team of tumblers?"

Without appearing offended by this remark, Martyrio replied in the even tone that she had been using throughout the whole conversation.

"Rest assured, we are legion. Myriad scattered 'tumblers,' independent agents who are known to each other and for their work: the UX, for Urban eXperiment. The principle is the very simplest: to take over a micro-zone and try to improve it to the best of their abilities. This is the team Untergunther, who were the first to enter the resistance. Half a dozen Parisians who took it upon themselves to repair the Pantheon clock. The Authority had let its mechanism deteriorate, out of negligence and incompetence, so that it had not worked for years. Untergunther entered the building in secret, and every night for two years, they carried out an exemplary restoration, all the while enjoying the place and managing to remain invisible. When the clock was fixed, they set off again and evaporated into the wild, leaving not the slightest trace of their passing."

"Indeed," said Canterel, stirred by this sudden recollection, "I remember one summer evening, on the Rue de la Montagne-Sainte-Geneviève, where I checked the time on that clock and noted that it was correct. I had a drink in the neighborhood to let a few minutes pass and make sure it wasn't a coincidence. It was astonishing, and it put me in a good mood for the rest of the day. Two days later, alas, the clock was broken again . . ."

"A youthful mistake," said Martyrio, "and one that has not been repeated. Untergunther was so proud of their work that they notified the Powers of the mechanism's repair. The result was swift. They were charged with 'entering a public place without permission'; the next day, the Authority mangled the clock, intentionally, this time, so that it would not be said that anything about the way of things could be changed without its permission. Had they not told anyone, it would be running still."

"Tragic," said Sanglard, "tragic and petty."

"I've given you the example of Untergunther because they were the forerunners, I could have told you of other actions that would appear less anodyne. It's simply a matter of arranging things where the dysfunction can be dealt with on an individual level, where it is immediately feasible. Under siege by a horde of Naturopaths, twelve of our people chose to die of hunger in our Pavlovsk base rather than touch a single one of the millions of seeds over which they had custody. For all that, it's not necessary to go to such extremes. Everyone does what he can, according to his abilities and the situations in his city. You're a clockmaker? You restore the Pantheon clock without asking anything of anyone. Electrician? You fix that street lamp whose bulb the township hasn't changed in three years. Banker? You refuse to transfer the sum that passes through your hands to a tax haven. Cashier? You direct your customer away from some product that has been cunningly advertised to him and instead to another that is exactly the same for half the price . . . If you're a soccer player, worth millions thanks only to the cleverness of your feet, you take a homeless person under your wing, you offer him housing, a job, you do whatever is needed to get him back on track. The 'Mexican Consolidated Drilling Authority' organizes free showings under the Palais Garnier for penniless film buffs. Members of the 'Gardening Amazonian' plant trees and vegetables in vacant lots and public spaces under cover of night, they throw soil grenades stuffed with seeds of ivy, poppies, and marigolds onto roofs and into the smallest brownfields. There is no plot, no conspiracy, just men and women who are trying to reclaim their space, their power, their food . . . Their existence."

"You're dreaming, my dear lady," said Sanglard, sadly. "Reality is not to be manipulated so easily."

"This is not irenicism, Monsieur. We are realists, politicals in the first sense of the word. Every individual is fully in command of the realm he occupies, however small it may be. Remember what Pericles said in his discourse on Athenian democracy: 'Poverty does not bar the way to advancement, if a man is able to serve the state, he is not hindered by the obscurity of his condition.'"

Mardrus raised his gaze from his plate. "To which one could respond," he said archly, "with Machiavelli's terrible words: 'There is no republic, however governed, in which there are more than forty or fifty citizens who attain positions with authority to command. Now, since that is a very small number, it is easy to insure oneself against them, either by having them done away with, or by granting each one an appropriate share of honors or offices.'"

"Murder or cronyism, a pretty agenda! Republics have died of it, beginning with the Florentine. We repair, we replace a part here or there, in such and such an organization or government; we intervene whenever possible to stay the world's sinking, but never would a single one of us bring about another man's death, except in self-defense. We are recusants, Monsieur Mardrus, and poets, not assassins."

Although this brief exchange was formulated politely and in a tone of mutual respect, it was followed by a long, embarrassed silence. They noticed, during this pause, that Verity had fallen asleep, her elbows on the table.

"I think it is time to retire," said Martyrio, getting up. "It has been a long day. Cyrus will accompany you back."

As they copied her, standing up one after another, Captain Ward asked the single fundamental question that was on all of their minds.

"I hope you won't think me ungrateful," he said abruptly, "but when are you expecting the next ship, on which we might return home?"

"We are indeed expecting a ship," she replied, leaning on Cyrus Smith's arm. "I don't know when it will arrive; sooner than we hope, I'm afraid."

LVIII

The Terrible Vengeance of the Afghan Sow

Since she had learned what kind of behavior she could expect from Monsieur Wang, and what a pitiful opinion he had of her, Louise had been living in a mortified hell. Certain that she had lost all credibility with the employees—even if she had not shown herself at the factory since that infamous night, Charlotte must have spread the secret details of her private meeting—and dying of shame whenever she glimpsed a smile or a conniving wink at her passing, she thought she could hear the smutty taunts that were being whispered behind her back. Summing up all the insults that were jostling about in her head, the outrage of being called "the Afghan sow" made her forehead burn like a stigma.

The morning of the sixth day, after yet another night of terrible dreams—awful scenes populated by obstetricians with pig snouts who pursued her with forceps—she decided to regain control of the situation. In any case, this was how she formulated the thing in her mind. She had not hatched a plan, thought anything over; no strategizing, no scheming: this just needed to end. After a long bath that did not succeed in relaxing her, she waxed, washed her hair, and while it was drying, smeared her body with a moisturizing lotion that she was trying for the first time, careful to rub it into her chest, massaging it in thoroughly. When all the cream had soaked in, she got ready, taking particular care in choosing her clothes, then matching her makeup and shoes to them.

Once outside, thus equipped, she regained the watchful poise of someone heading into combat, assault rifle over her shoulder. It wouldn't have taken much to make her break into a jog.

At the factory, Monsieur Wang had remained on deck almost night and day, his only guests being worry, suspicion, and alarm. To speed up production, he had had to institute round-the-clock shifts, despite hostility from all sides. Even the breaks had been drastically reduced, to the point of causing complaints from a staff representative. On that occasion, Wang had outdone himself.

"They have only to put on diapers," he said seriously. "I'll make sure we order some."

No one had complained about it again. These French people were so funny! Why not reinstate the unions, while they were at it! On the other hand, when he had brought up the idea of taking away their reading time, he had had to backtrack in the face of threats to strike. All these measures had produced the desired effect: T-minus three days before the B@bil Book's release date, and the operational e-readers had been sent to the specialized journalists and the test labs; the others, duly cleansed of their hijacked home screen, were currently being shipped. Doubtless desiring to redeem himself, the technical director and his team were scrambling. A system update patch was practically in sight, and he did not doubt the network would be completely secured within the week: even shot by a powerful bow, every arrow gives out at the end of its arc.

And yet, a shadow of sadness kept him from rejoicing fully. The story of his vanished pigeon undermined him. It wasn't a question of money: he had taken care to mate Free Legs Diamond with a sublime female of the same breed, a gem; their offspring would go for exorbitant prices once they were raised and trained. No. Rather, a feeling of loss, mixed with the absurd impression of having been betrayed. And with that, the obsessive hope that the bird would return.

It was incomprehensible, but some pigeons reappeared three or four months later, often in the spring, without anyone knowing where they had nested during that time. Something temporarily disrupted their homing instinct, a storm, another pigeon, the lure of another loft, then whatever it was reversed and they came back. If Free Legs Diamond came back, his racing days would be over; he would be set to breeding and treated to a quiet old age.

When Louise Le Galle came in, around two in the afternoon, he was dozing in his chair, threatening to fall asleep. He didn't hear her turn the key. She moved forward, smiling, decked out like a Christmas turkey.

"Yes, Madame Le Galle?" he said, pleased to see her in such good spirits.

Louise had come up to the desk and was standing in front of him, trembling.

"These last few days have been difficult, I thought you might need to unwind . . ."

Her gaze never leaving his face, she undid her blouse, then with a quick movement her bra, which she pulled up over her breasts. Taking hold of them from underneath, she stroked them and made them bulge out, twisting her torso suggestively.

Pleasantly surprised, Monsieur Wang stood and went over to her.

"If this is what you want . . . you know I can't refuse you anything . . ."

Hastily bending over her, he pinched her nipples, very quickly, then fixed his lips to one, sucking at it in short gulps; and as he suckled, the texture of a button appeared to him, enormously enlarged, as if looked at through a microscope, and this budding, grainy hardening excited him, and he wanted to burst it with his teeth; and though he resisted the desire to bite and rip and hurt, there was an extreme violence in his mouth, his apparent calm only the result of the ritual with which he constrained his pleasure, the meditation that allowed him to enjoy it. Wang never paid any attention to Louise's reactions, but he felt her hands pressing more and more firmly on his nape, guiding his lips over her chest, crushing them, smearing them into moist flesh and softness; because he had not done this with her in so long, or perhaps because of the session with Charlotte, he was boiling over with sensitivity, suppressed tension, almost suffocation. Volatile, claustrophobic, a sensation he had felt before, but when, where? No way to remember. He was still licking at her breasts, swallowing their heavy sweat, his anus dilated, releasing a long salvo of strangled wind, when he was forced to catch his breath. He opened his mouth, trying in vain to take in the air he needed. Something had swollen inside him, was continuing to expand, obstructing his airway, breaking loose, superabundant. Falling to his knees, Monsieur Wang brought his hands to his face, pressed down on his tongue to try to flatten it, flailed about, screaming silently. His eyes were bulging, his skin burned, his throat swelled as if being garroted. It was as he raised his head toward Louise, a pink froth at the corners of his mouth, clutching at her skirt in a desperate gesture of supplication, it was as he met her gaze that everything came to him, even the smell of wet dog that had nearly killed him twenty years earlier. He rolled at her feet, rocked with spasms; a hissing rattle escaped his swollen mouth, making him resemble a fish suffocating out of water, an over-dilated bladder. Her breasts still out, Louise knelt in turn, making them dangle in front of his nose. "You bastard, little shit! You getting a good look? You want to suck on them again? I prepared them specially for you: bio-firming skincare by 'the Afghan sow,' yours truly, to feel young in a firm body. The cream is 'rich in plumping ingredients,' makes your skin do the work, gives it a nice spring, makes it look tight and perky, it's called the 'trampoline effect.' The cream's smooth, satiny

texture envelops you like a blanket: an iron fist in a velvet glove."
Swinging her torso, she slapped him violently with her left breast.
"Elastin, allantoin, primrose oil, and . . . the deadly peanut butter.
Massive swelling—the ultimate fall skincare regime, you little prick!"

And, coming right up to his ear, "This is the last time you'll ever
fart, you motherfucker . . ."

Louise Le Galle stood, refastened her bra and blouse, fixed her
hair in front of the bay window, then left the office without a glance
at the prostrate body of Monsieur Wang. Returning to her computer,
she turned it on for a moment to access the video control center,
plugged in her USB drive, and uploaded its revolting contents onto
the factory's internal server. It was not until ten minutes later, when
she was sure she could hear the angry rumble of furious workers coming up from the workshops, that she called emergency services from
her BlackBerry.

LIX

A Thousand Vain Jihads

They had gone to bed without delay upon returning to their room, pleading fatigue to defer having to discuss on their conversation with Martyrio. If we have not failed to render Martyrio's words, the reader will understand the uneasiness prompted by her profession of faith. In the pessimism of her worldview, as much as in her humanistic undertakings, it was the outrageousness of it all that rankled them. That this strange woman was in many respects unconventional, no one would have doubted, but the certainty of having been confronted with an exceptional being was tempered by the uneasy sensation that she had staged their talk, that nothing had been improvised.

Despite the jumble of their thoughts, it did not take them long to find sleep.

The night ran its course, punctuated by Holmes's snoring and the quiet reboots of the ventilation system. The wall panels gave off only a soft glow, hardly enough to distinguish the outline of the room and the greenish forms of the sleeping bodies.

It must have been five in the morning when one of them—male or female, it was impossible to tell—sat up in bed, observing the silence. Reassured, the figure got up and furtively left the dormitory. The station was immersed in a darkness broken only by the red glow of the emergency night-lights and, here and there, diamond-shaped patches of moonlight. The shadow slipped down the corridors, careful to remain unseen. At every junction, it wavered, doubled back, trying to find its way. Arriving at the main landing, it entered the laboratory that Cyrus Smith had shown them. There again, the figure seemed to rummage randomly through the bottles of reagents and chemicals arranged on a laboratory bench top. It gave a sigh of satisfaction as it grabbed a demijohn marked with three X's and a skull and cross-bones. Armed with the fruit of its theft, it quickened its step, entered the stairway, and mounted the steps four at a time until it reached the command post.

Twitching in his sleep, Canterel had fallen prey to night terrors. He was crawling through an underground tunnel that was just wide enough to allow him to move forward by wriggling, his arms against his body. His headlamp—or perhaps it was his vision itself—illuminated only damp clay walls. He realized that he would soon be stuck, without any possibility of turning back, when an inscription appeared to him, traced by a finger in the clay: *Nomen est omen*, Cicero's lovely phrase, according to which every word spoken must be heard as a prediction of good fortune or woe. At the same moment, a pallid multitude swarmed toward his face, a teeming horde of naked mole-rats whose incisors were already cutting into the flesh of his neck. He began to yell, surprised at the strength of his own voice.

A deafening alarm resounded through the station.

Jolting awake, everyone got up, panicked. Only too happy to have escaped his nightmare, Canterel was the first to rush over to the door to find out what was going on. It was bolted from the outside. A commotion had broken out in the hallway. He called out, banged on the door with all his might. To no avail. Aided by Grimod, he then tried to break down the door with his shoulder, but it quickly became apparent that this method would not be successful.

Looking around for a piece of furniture that could serve as a ram, Grimod froze at the sight of the little group gathered in the center of the room.

"Scummington!" he cried.

He ran over to the bathroom, opened the door to the toilets. The inspector was no longer among them.

"What can that fool have gotten up to now?" said Holmes, associating him by the same token with the alarm that was drilling into their ears.

At that moment the din ceased. They were still in a state of expectation and relief at the restored silence when the door opened onto Cyrus Smith, accompanied by eight burly men.

"Please follow me," he ordered, his voice firm.

"What's happened?" asked Holmes.

"I am not authorized to tell you," he replied, starting to walk. "Come, hurry."

"We were locked in," Lady MacRae remarked, "one of us has disappeared."

Sanglard refused to leave. "Where are you taking us?"

In reply, one of the men gripped his arm and pulled him along.

"I protest!" the professor squawked. "You can't treat us like this! It's outrageous!"

"I share his objection fully," said Canterel, as another man grabbed him, forcing him to move.

Ward and Grimod struggled, but an armlock compelled them to obey.

"Help!" cried Miss Sherrington.

"Let us go!" Dr. Mardrus was saying to the men leading them.

As for Kim, he was visibly controlling himself, but seemed to be on the alert, ready to intervene at any moment. Clinging to her mother, Verity followed along, smiling, as if she were watching a bit of boulevard theatre.

They were led unceremoniously to the circus they had glimpsed the night before, then gathered together under guard in the middle of a track. The station's lighting had dropped in intensity since the alert, all of the lights now relying on generators. It was enough, however, to reveal part of the bleachers and their occupants. The whole population of the biosquare was convened, artists and researchers mingled together, all looking at them with frightening severity.

At a signal from Cyrus Smith, a spotlight singled out the Reverend Mother, sitting in the front row. At her feet, a man was writhing on the floor in a pose of petrified suffering.

"Scummington!" Holmes exclaimed, rushing toward him.

"It's no use," Martyrio said gently. "He's dead."

Holmes backed away slowly, afraid.

"This man," continued Martyrio, "entered one of our laboratories tonight, where he stole a demijohn of sulfuric acid, then went up to the command center with the intention of sabotaging it. To a large extent he succeeded. Doubtless you know that this acid has the property of dissolving almost all metals; so all he had to do was inject small quantities of it into our computers to render them inoperable."

"What happened?" asked Canterel. "Who killed him?"

"His own ignorance. The welding of the printed circuit boards was made of tin; when it made contact with the metal, the sulfuric acid produced hydrogen sulfide, a highly toxic gas with effects similar to cyanide's. When our regulating system stopped working, it triggered the alarm. Surprised, Scummington then hurried to leave the area, but he had already inhaled a lethal dose of the poison. He collapsed right here."

"How do you know all these details?"

"Cyrus Smith neglected to tell you that we have surveillance cameras all over. I watched the recording, it doesn't leave any doubt."

"But good Lord, what got into him?" Holmes swore, overwhelmed by this turn of events. "Why would he have done such a thing? It's insane!"

"Did someone come to this island before us," Canterel asked suddenly, "people from outside?"

"No, you are the only visitors we have ever received. As for the people living in the biosquare, the most recent addition arrived three months ago."

"You must know that we are not here by accident. A priceless diamond was stolen from Lady MacRae, and in following its trail we reached you. The one who stole it must be in this station, or have passed through it. Scummington, like us, was searching for it. Perhaps he only acted under the pressure of the circumstances?"

"Impossible," said Marytrio, authoritatively.

"How can you be so adamant?"

She nodded toward Lady MacRae, inviting her to respond.

"Because there never was a diamond," said the latter. "Or rather, it's still in my safe, at Eilean Castle."

"In your safe!" cried Canterel. "But it was empty . . ."

"I told you it was empty, and you took me at my word. In which you did well"—she pointed her chin at Scummington's body—"since that trash ended up here."

Canterel felt his reason falter.

"For the love of heaven, you owe me an explanation!"

"I was about to give you one," Martyrio replied, her voice even. "You know, at least by reputation, the one called the Noh Straddler, do you not? Our goal was to lure him here and neutralize him. We knew that such a diamond would stir his lust, at first, then his hatred, once my name was mentioned."

"What does he have against you?"

"Those whose plans we have once thwarted have a hard time forgetting us . . . It was my husband, Giorgio Triskelès, the 'man with three right feet,' who simulated the theft and planted the clues necessary for the practice of your talents. According to the initial plan, you should have found only his shoe prints in front of the safe."

"But then . . ." said Canterel, suddenly understanding.

"Yes," continued Martyrio, "Lady MacRae is a part of our organization."

"'Astonishing Bourgeoisie,'" Clawdia supplied, smiling, "Highland division."

"I can't believe it," Canterel blustered, "you have used m– us, Holmes and me! All these puzzles that almost drove me mad, you knew the answers in advance! I'll never forgive you . . ."

"You would be mistaken, Martial, I was not in on the secrets. We had to make sure my reactions were genuine."

Martyrio continued. "The Straddler was much craftier than we had thought: he managed to capture Giorgio, he mutilated him horribly to try to make him talk, then he left him for dead. We saved him *in extremis* and brought him here, where our engineers looked after him." She waved her hand. "Giorgio, please."

Every gaze turned toward the place she was indicating. With a mechanical rattle, a man, equipped with half a motorized exoskeleton, came forward into the light.

"Rest assured," he said, with a thick Italian accent, "he cut off my feet, but I still have my two penises."

Holmes almost choked. "Two . . . You mean to say you have two . . ."

"Why yes," said Martyrio, "and substantial ones at that, I can assure you. Which is especially valuable when you have two vaginas."

There was a silence pregnant with a strong force of fantasization, everyone trying in spite of themselves to visualize what a coupling between two such freaks of nature could look like. Confronted with a new challenge, Miss Sherrington frowned, already imagining a double-entry anti-rape device.

"Grimod is also one of ours," Martyrio continued. "He acted as steward and was responsible for relations with several of our correspondents throughout the course of your journey."

"You, too!" said Holmes, stunned.

"'Haitian Penetration,'" Grimod whispered, winking at him.

"And it worked," continued Martyrio, "the Straddler rushed into the trap, though he left numerous casualties, unfortunately. He killed our old friend Chung Ling Soo, tried to make that poor Yva talk on the Transsiberian, then managed to reach Hugh Palmer's place in Peking before you, without you discovering his identity until now."

"Viper!" Miss Sherrington grumbled, addressing Scummington's corpse.

"Yes and no, dear madam. This one here was venomous, but he merely performed his master's dirty work. The Straddler himself has stuck to you like glue. He integrated into your little group so well that no one suspected him for an instant. Is that not so, Dr. Mardrus?"

A second spotlight came on, revealing a face that was now beyond recognition, flushed with rage.

"Lies! Lies!" cried the professor, indignant. "You don't have the slightest proof!"

"Oh, but I do! More than enough. Before he died, your friend Scummington was generous enough to answer a few of our questions. You played your trump card by sending him to destroy our security system, but you omitted telling him that he would not come back from it. And this, would you believe it, made him quite loquacious."

With surprising agility, Mardrus suddenly sprang into action. In less time than it takes to write it, he grabbed Verity by the waist, pointing the barrel of a revolver at the base of her skull.

"I have other cards in my hand," he said, stepping backward. "Anyone moves, and I blow her brains out!"

"Let her go, I beg you! She's only a child!" cried Lady MacRae.

"You vile, loathsome bastard!" said Canterel, his lips white with anger.

"The Powers have your coordinates," Mardrus continued, paying no attention. "By now, a whole fleet is zeroing in on the island . . ."

"Indeed," said Martyrio, without losing her calm. "Three battle-ships: the *Thénardier*, the *Hyde*, and the *Harkonnen*; two battle cruisers, the *Kurtz* and the *Iago*. They set a course for us as soon as the alarm sounded."

This omniscience seemed to disconcert him for a second. His eyes darted around, as if the thickness of the air hid some threat, then headed for the exit. In his arms, Verity looked like a marveling dancer. As soon as he had left the big top, Canterel, Grimod, and Captain Ward set off in pursuit. Reaching the biosquare's airlock entry, Mardrus abruptly turned around to command one of them to open the doors.

"You take one step outside, and I kill her," he said in a tone convincing enough to freeze them on the spot. "Ward, you're coming with me. I need your arms for the boat."

He began to run at a gentle trot toward the landing stage, carrying Verity more than pulling her along, frequently throwing quick glances behind him. Ward preceded them, staggering with rage and powerlessness.

Dawn was breaking over a heavy gray sea riffled by icy gusts. Petrels were falling from the sky with showers of spray.

Five minutes later, they stopped directly beside the boat, which was tossing against the beams of the dock. Mardrus turned around one more time. Through his hair, which the wind plastered against his face, his eyes shone like shards of obsidian, frightening in their ferocity and triumph.

"Untie the mooring lines," he said to Ward.

At the same moment, Verity sagged, weighing down on his arm in a sudden collapse. She had not fainted, however—she was talking, gaze distant, eyelids flickering.

"Come! Come! Come!" she was saying. "I know you, lead me where I'm going . . ."

Then, from a wide swirl that stirred the sea, burst a deep sound, plaintive and menacing, the roar of a stadium rumbling with a thousand conquests, a thousand slave trades, a thousand vain jihads.

The "Big Bloop" that Sanglard had so longed for.

Cthulhu, urgency, the Jumping Frenchmen of Maine disorder . . . This terrifying hiccup threw Ward into Mardrus with such violence that he sent him rolling three meters from Verity.

Mardrus got back up; revolver still in hand, he aimed at the girl.

Behind him, in a continuous boiling sound, something monstrous emerged, a porcelain dome of gigantic proportions, flamed with red spots. From a plastron of brown flesh, which abruptly retracted, shot out long, conical appendages, which met at their base around a terrible black beak.

Warned by what he read in Verity's eyes, Mardrus turned half way round; just far enough to appreciate the horror of what was happening: the bundle of tentacles stretched out above him snapped him up, lifting him off the pier like a fly; immediately after came the sound of cracking bones from the creature's jaws.

LX

The Ohio Giant

There had been no drama, no yelling, no reproach. When she had opened her eyes, after that crazy night on the sofa bed, they weren't there anymore. Carmen had spent the rest of her Sunday doing housework, as much out of necessity as to try to get round her hangover. Fuzzy images of their lovemaking came back to her, short pornographic sequences that oozed from her bashed-up memory, surprising her in their frenzied obscenity, leaving her with a vague feeling of guilt. She hadn't burst into sobs until sundown, when the night had slid into her like a dagger.

Dieumercie had gone to live with his friend JJ. They had taken the dog with them.

After the first days of self-pity over the injustice she felt herself to be the victim of, came the cold hatred, contempt, then an urge to remake her life that had less to do with the mitigation of her distress than with a furious desire for revenge.

Looking at him more closely, Monsieur Morini, the retiree from her Thursday mornings, was not so old, and was rather a handsome man; he gave into her advances in under ten minutes. Before starting the ironing, she had browsed through his porno magazines, feigning curiosity, at first, and then a sudden and incomprehensible excitement. "It's making me feel things, seeing what they're doing," she had confessed, simpering. "Do you think that's normal?" And as he was asking her where these feelings were coming from, she had said down there, where it was wet between her "patties," and there, too, look, they're all warm and pointy. She had gotten him to touch her breasts to check, and they had ended up naked. On this point, alas, Morini resembled her husband: if he had ever gotten it up, it was merely a memory from his school days. His fixation was fruits and vegetables: eggplants, leeks, carrots, cucumbers, zucchini, avocados, bananas, papayas—it was crazy the things he had managed to cram into her! It seemed like he was sticking strictly to the orders of modern dietetics: five fruits, five vegetables a day. Not all at once, of course, but what hefty goods organic farming could produce. He spent a fortune at the market gardener's.

She had soon had enough of minestrone and fruit salad. There was nothing so good as a duck neck enjoyed alone in front of the TV.

It was as she was doing her shopping at the poultry dealer's, appropriately, that she heard news of her husband.

"Madame Bonacieux?"

Turning around, Carmen saw a fat lady with a red face.

"Hello, I'm Nadège Morteau, I work at B@bil Books. You don't know me, but your husband used to show us photos of you often. What a story! I can tell you, we all fell on our asses!"

The two of them had gotten coffee together, and the woman had hurried to tell her the little she knew regarding Dieumercie. Everyone had been gossiping about him and his friend, so they had both tendered their resignation three weeks after the manager's death and the placing of the factory into receivership. Wicked tongues claimed that they were whoring themselves out in Valencia, but the director of HR had received a postcard from them from Mauritius, showing a thatched hut on the beach and coconut palms. Which proved nothing, because, well, they could be doing the same thing there.

"What did they write, on the postcard?"

"Nothing. There was the letter R three times, and their signature. No one's gotten what that meant."

Carmen didn't understand either, but that very night, she shoved an Ohio Giant into her vagina.

The Ohio Giant was a potato. One of those overlooked varieties that had recently come back into fashion. Among the motivations behind this gesture was doubtless the force of habit from her time with Monsieur Morini, but also and especially a kind of defiance, the vegetal caulking signaling that she was done with men. All that mattered was that these four hundred grams of smooth fullness, a secret weight that she was aware of at every second, filled her well enough.

She had continued to work for one week, carefree, until a steady itch, pleasant and irritating at the same time, forced her to grab a mirror to identify the cause of the trouble. Emerging from her labia, three purplish rhizomes were twisting their hooked tips toward the light. The tuber had germinated! Madame Bonacieux had not expected such a phenomenon, but she took it as a blessing and devoted all her attention to the growing of this plant. Panties were banished, and when it became too difficult to walk without damaging the stems, she decided to stay home. After one last trip out, during which she stocked up on heaps of potato chips, Carmen settled in on her sofa bed, legs open, and watched the Ohio Giant sprout.

It is in this position, vigilant reader, that we see her for a few moments before leaving her to her fate. We would have to count up the empty packages and apply a certain divisor to deduce the number of days that have passed, but that would have only an anecdotal interest. The fact is that she is here, half naked, numb, with the Miss France contest on the television. Carmen has the impression of being concealed in tropical undergrowth. Even the smell adds to this misconception. Through the leaves, she watches the Mauritian competitor, who is strutting along the white sand in a low-rise bikini. She grabs another fistful of chips and crosses her fingers so that slut won't win the competition.

LXI

To the Andaman Islands

Scarcely had Mardrus disappeared in the horrible way we described, when those who had witnessed the scene had broken into a run. Neither Verity nor Captain Ward, however, had appeared to flee; facing the sea monster rising above them, hand in hand, they looked like a Harlequin and a Columbine getting ready to bow.

An egg-shaped dome was now floating alongside the quay, the top of a colossal ammonite, with, it seemed likely, two-thirds of its body still submerged. The living cap that housed the tentacles had closed again; beginning as dark brown mottled with white, this mass of flesh quivered, traversed by waves of changing colors, like the skin of a horrified cuttlefish. At the nascence of this operculum, an eye with the texture of a tendon, perfectly expressionless, was pierced with a small dark pupil that stretched downward in a comma.

As he neared his daughter, Canterel's first reflex was to get her away as fast as possible, but Cyrus Smith held him back with a firm hand.

"There's no danger," he asserted, "trust me."

"But that thing just swallowed a man!"

"A man, you say? Mardrus didn't deserve the name, and that 'thing' knows how to tell the difference."

Sanglard had just joined them, out of breath, ready to faint.

"*Nautilus pompilius*," he breathed, falling to his knees with exhaustion and shock. "I don't believe my eyes! Do you grasp the significance of what we're seeing? It's a nautilus, my friends, a cephalopod that shouldn't be able to grow beyond a handspan, and that we have here before us, as tall as the Capitole de Toulouse!"

The visible portion of this enormous spiral showed signs of age. Its surface, in places, showed deep, horny fissures onto its black insides, with flakes of pearl and scarred wounds from collisions or assaults that were difficult to imagine, given the creature's size. A closer examination, however, uncovered certain details that were surprising, at first, then frightening: glints of glass encircled with bronze, crooked metal clamps that looked like ancient repairs to precious Chinese porcelain, adornments, embedded copper and brass.

When a door opened in the shell, five meters up, and sailors were seen preparing to lower a gangway, Sanglard was so greatly traumatized that he lost consciousness. Cyrus Smith leaned down and slapped him methodically until he regained his senses.

"Now is not the moment, professor," he said in a tone of amiable reproach. "Time is short, we have decisions to make."

He had not yet finished speaking when a spray of foam rose up in the middle of the bay, followed some fractions of a second later by the far-off rumbling of a cannonade. The briefness of the salvo—a dozen shots, at most—and the way in which the projectiles scattered over the water and the moor made it seem, for a moment, like a volley of warning shots, but the last two blasts hit the center of the station: in a crash of fireworks, the space between the pyramids and the biosquare seemed to evaporate.

"Get in," said Cyrus Smith, "quickly! I'll be back as soon as possible."

And he began to run toward the soup of sulfur-yellow smoke that was soiling the sky.

"They need help," said Canterel, pulling his daughter and Lady MacRae toward the gangway. "Holmes, Sanglard, go with the women; Miss Sherrington, I entrust them to you!"

Escorted without a shadow of hesitation by Grimod, Kim, and Captain Ward, he set off after Cyrus Smith.

As soon as they were on board, they were brought into a room furnished with brown leather club chairs and elegant coffee tables. A spiral staircase indicated the presence of an upper floor. On the curved wall, a porthole formed of the same material as the hull gave a view back out toward the biosquare. Despite the thickness of the glazing, they soon saw the crowd that was gathering at the entrance to the structure, then everybody from the station hastened toward the nautilus in good order.

A quarter of an hour later, they saw their companions among the last members of the procession and, bringing up the rear, Cyrus Smith, Martyrio, and Triskelès, who was carrying an unconscious woman.

Curled up in a ball on a cushion, Verity seemed to be in the grip of another fit. Rocking back and forth continuously, she was stammering out unintelligible words punctuated with the names of some of the animals from the day before.

Lady MacRae had embraced her daughter and was stroking her hair, looking disconsolate. They heard the gangway folding back in, then the sound of vacuum suction from the door as it closed. Soon after, Canterel, Grimod, Kim, and Captain Ward entered the sitting room. They were still wide-eyed, dazed by their discoveries, when the sound of an organ rose up, a powerful seventh chord that made the floor of the room vibrate. This was followed by the roar of a waterfall somewhere below them, and the nautilus began to descend.

"We're sinking!" Holmes exclaimed, panicking as he saw the water rising outside the porthole.

"We're not sinking," Sanglard retorted enthusiastically, "we're diving!"

"Now's not the time to play with words, we have to get out of here!"

"It's a controlled immersion, my friend. The miraculous mechanism that allows this still escapes me, but all indications are that we are inside a submarine, a biological machine. Nautiloids are really at home below four hundred meters, even though they emerge once a day to make another layer of shell through contact with the sun. As huge as it is, ours is obliged to do the same, but it is a creature of the abyss, like sperm whales and squid."

The porthole was already no more than an azure circle swirling with strings of bubbles. With a slight bump, they felt the enormous vessel leave the surface and find its trim, then its terrible slowness in the thickness of the ocean. Muffled detonations reached them; the cannonade had started up again.

Martyrio and Cyrus Smith came to find them. They learned from the latter that all of the animals in the biosquare were dead or dying, which explained Verity's distress.

"Mustard gas, it seems, or something similar. We were already in the sealed-off area, it's a miracle that none of us breathed in the poison."

"And that woman?" asked Grimod.

"Dulcie Présage, our archivist. She has suffered a nervous shock, but she should recover shortly."

"Why? Why are they doing this?" asked Lady MacRae.

Marytrio replied, her voice calm.

"Some of them would like to bring the world to such a point of decline that it will have to either fade away or regenerate. They destroy out of the goodness of their hearts, so to speak. Others see only the deposit of plastic and its commercial value, but what they all have in common is their passionate hatred of dreamers. The Powers don't need any justification, they're in charge, and they're quick to remind anyone who shows the slightest indication of forgetting it. I am heartbroken not to have been able to offer you the choice, for here you are, on board, at least until our next stop."

"Which is?" asked Ward.

"The Andaman Islands in the Bay of Bengal—North Sentinel, to be exact."

"I understand better now," said Grimod.

"You understand what?" asked Holmes, a little shortly.

"Sentinel Island is a sovereign entity, officially under Indian protection, but *de facto* uncontrollable; it's only seventy-two square kilometers, and no one knows anything about its inhabitants or what's happening there: no visitor has ever been welcomed by anything other than a volley of arrows."

"True rebels against tourism," said Martyrio, smiling, "despite their slightly overenthusiastic side. They know about fire, though they don't know how to make it; that is their weakness, and their glory. We have a fallback base there. It goes without saying that we will unload those of you who would wish it in Sumatra or Malaysia."

Lady MacRae turned to Canterel, her gaze anxious.

"I go where you go, my dear. But only if I can smoke a cigar from time to time."

"Please, help yourself," said Martyrio, opening a cedar box. "These are *Jean Valjean*s, high-end cigars from a small producer in Périgord, you'll see that they rival the finest Havanas."

Despite their importance, these considerations were Sanglard's last concern. The nautilus's anatomy was perfectly familiar to him, he knew that the shell comprised forty consecutive cells, left empty as it grew, the mollusk inhabiting only the largest, the one that opened to the outside. When the animal wanted to move up or down, it filled the unoccupied chambers with water or gas.

"I am a man of science," he said. "I can imagine that you have set aside some of these chambers to serve as ballast and that the ones in which we find ourselves are supplied with air by some artifice of your contrivance. This creature's gigantism is not a real hindrance either; these cases of hypertrophy may be rare, but they nevertheless occur in nature, and I know of other examples. There is only one thing, one single thing that is niggling at me: how do you steer it? How can a human brain dictate orders to a cephalopod?"

"We no longer have any reason to hide anything from you," Cyrus Smith replied. "Is the name Captain Nemo familiar to you?"

"Of course, at least if you are indeed speaking of the man who perished with his submarine in the eruption of Lincoln Island."

"That's the story I told, at his request and for his protection."

Sanglard gaped in amazement.

"You mean that . . ."

"You are on board the actual *Nautilus*, my friend. The captain is still at the controls. Would you like to go down and see him? It will be easier to explain."

Through a little door at the back of the room, Cyrus Smith brought them to a staircase that descended into the bowels of the ship. As he walked, he summarized certain events that had once brought him together with Captain Nemo.

"If you have in your memories the story of my adventures—such as I've relayed them, at least—you know that after we flew away from the siege of Richmond in our balloon, my fellows in adversity and I landed on a desert island, Lincoln, where we would have had the greatest difficulty surviving without the mysterious aid of Captain Nemo. I then told how this admirable figure died in my arms, from loneliness more than from any disease, and how the *Nautilus*, imprisoned in an undersea grotto, served as his tomb. I also said that he had left me his whole fortune in pearls and diamonds, with the mandate of using it for the good of humanity."

"Which you did," said Canterel, "by building the biosquare and its laboratories . . ."

"Which 'we' tried to do," he corrected. "As you can see, the *Nautilus* hardly matches the strictly mechanical description I gave. Nemo's genius was that he demonstrated how we can take control of an animal by implanting remotely operated microchips on some of its neurons. The very elementary brain of a nautilus is the best suited in the world to this system, so much so that for years, the captain piloted his *Nautilus* by means of simple electrical impulses. It was only once he had taken refuge on Lincoln Island and was weakened by the loss of his crewmen that he imagined uniting himself with it more permanently."

They had arrived in a series of rooms with low, arched ceilings, without corners or ridges, where everything, from the roundness of the arches to the soft curves of the walls and woodwork, seemed to going through a process of liquefaction. Marine lamps capped with green opaline radiated the light of an aurora. On the floor made from the deck of a boat, carpets muffled the sound of their steps.

After crossing an anteroom papered with large nautical charts under which were arranged various measuring instruments, sextants, compasses, and complex armillary spheres, they passed into a gallery with several alcoves distributed symmetrically on the sides, all fitted with purple hangings pulled back by tasseled cords. They saw, in passing, a small bathroom with a marble table and gilt washtub; a narrow box bed, neatly made, under a portrait of a bare-breasted Haitian woman inspired by Girodet; a lady's writing desk inlaid with camphor wood; and a boudoir furnished with a spherical mirror and a satin brocade ottoman.

These rooms, which were clean and tidy, as if they were tributes to the memory of a missing person, led in a row to a long hall whose old ivory ribs gave the unpleasant impression of a chest cavity. The apparent heart of this anatomy was an organ that stood out against the dark wood of the paneling on the left. A Cavaillé-Coll with tin pipes that fanned out above a double keyboard with twenty-two stops. Supported by burr-walnut dolphins, the casing was adorned on both sides with faded gilt cornucopias. At the top of the carved entablature that held the flue pipes, an coat of arms sported a capital N above a phrase in black letters: *Mobilis in mobili*, Captain Nemo's motto. By its wear, an embossed velvet piano stool revealed that it had been much used.

Across from this instrument, behind two Voltaire chairs, a large, faceted, oval bay window showed nothing but bluish darkness.

"I'll wait for you here," said Martyrio, inviting Verity to sit in an armchair, "this is not a sight for young girls."

Cyrus Smith continued toward the chamber that the nautilus occupied. Here, the partition had a potbellied look; a bulky collector had been implanted using rivets, its piping then split before disappearing into the vaulting. Under a switchboard bristling with inert coils, wiring, and dials, they saw a seated man, dressed in a moth-eaten gold lace tunic. His back partially hid an oculus where a purple-veined membrane throbbed. He looked like a surgeon bent over the skull of a trepanned patient, the only difference being that his face and hands, reduced to a tree of nerve fibers and blood vessels, had fused with the living matter that he was examining.

"The poor man," said Lady MacRae, averting her eyes.

"Is he dead?" asked Canterel.

"Yes, clinically speaking, since his heart stopped beating years ago. No, if we are taking into consideration the fact that he reacts to the sound of the organ and alters the nautilus's actions accordingly. Shortly before he took this step, he entrusted me with the series of musical chords that allow us to correspond."

"An anastomosis of the lymphatic system?" asked Sanglard, his lips trembling. "How did he do it?"

"I wouldn't know how to tell you, but Captain Nemo sees through this animal's eyes, uses its beak to feed himself, manipulates its tentacles. He has realized his dream of being no one. He himself is the *Nautilus*."

They walked back to Martyrio and Verity in silence, foreheads glistening with sweat, chests tight from the sudden transfiguration of the space where they were moving.

"Cyrus, please," said the Reverend Mother, "would you stabilize the boat."

Cyrus Smith sat down at the organ and played a triad on the keyboard. The *Nautilus* responded almost immediately with a hiss of air being sucked into some tank above them. Martyrio then pressed a button, releasing a cone of light from a reflector.

Gathering near the porthole, they watched as the black curtain of the abyss opened slightly before them.

Almost at equilibrium, the *Nautilus* descended gently down a wall whose mass they could not guess. It was a Dantesque tangle of more or less floating objects that were dragged along and trapped in the depths by the force of the vortex. Stroke by stroke, as if under the feverish brush of a Hell Brueghel, before their eyes was born a Gehenna of tortured bodies, with details like greenish tumors, scalps, absurd disembowellings, unwound entrails. Everything that had been cast into the sea but had not fallen to the bottom could be found here, but unlike what they had seen on the island's surface, this substratum of debris brought to mind an illegal dumpsite, where they could see, intermingled with big, twisted trees, here the shape of a foam mattress, a tire, a lawn chair, there a child's plaything or a garbage bin. From this dreary stratography—tinged glaucous, the achromic color of absence—a scrap of plastic would sometimes break away and begin a slow ascent toward the surface.

It was on the edge of the slope that they saw it.

The *Nautilus* was finally freeing itself and returning to open water when it skirted the battered wreck of a submarine, its bow hanging, held down by a mass of old nets. Its turret showed its name: *Eurydice*

S644. Embracing it, half enveloping it with its broken wings, a black angel seemed to want to share in its fall.

Ward glued his face to the window.

"The *Black Orpheus*," he murmured, his eyes wet with tears.

"Cyrus, rise to fifteen meters, helm to midships," said Martyrio.

And, as the organ resounded once again, injecting into their souls a hazy promise of hope, she turned out the light.

LXII

O Captain! My Captain!

This last page, Arnaud had read stiffly, his voice cracking with the emotion specific to stories that are coming to an end. Thirty nights to try to bring Dulcie back to the living heart of her first readings, the only medium in which it is possible to rediscover the taste of being born. Thirty nights of magical invocations and prayers, thirty nights for the miracle of an awakening. He has dreamed for her, assembled unknown lands of beings and things that he knew only as poetry, as strict nuclear charge. He has gone so far as to reconstruct for her a wondrous *Nautilus*, swelled by a century of fervent and youthful explorations; so far as to place her inside the ship herself.

"We all died at the age of twenty, without realizing it": for he spoke the truth, the black-eyed bard who, one sunny day, shouted this evidence on the forum. Arnaud has tried everything to disprove this, but the seal of misfortune has not been broken, no miracle has taken place.

For lack of faith? Who more than he could have believed in the possibility of a rebirth, who else could have put so much love and conviction into the daily ritual of her advent?

It is almost impossible, however, to plan a world; we are barely able to dream of its fall, an easy nightmare that resists all of the drugs, all of the narcotics of anguish. In the end, nothing is left, besides the feeling of having been true to oneself, a consistency—the feeling, perhaps, of a fulfilled logic.

Arnaud is testing how much writing involves risking one's life. In the literal sense, for once. Not because of the morbid revocation of the present in which we write, but because of that gaunt shade that constantly reads over our shoulder, and the certainty, tonight, that it will take action. An effect of reality that brings him closer to all those who, while in prison, have learned the date set for their execution.

The moment has come to give up, to put a stop to even the wildest of hopes. He is going to snuff out the flame. It is his thankless role in this comedy. To die here, where he was born, with her, without negligence. They had sworn this to each other in Petrópolis, before the abandoned house of Stefan Zweig.

Together they are going to take the most unexpected of secret passageways, the most frightening, but also the most sure. Everything has been ready for a long time, tidied up, filed away, dusted in anticipation of this voyage.

The feeding tube, the catheter, the nasal tube. Arnaud unplugs Dulcie, drops her moorings one by one. He removes her incontinence pad, washes her body with the care one brings to a funeral toilette.

And now, he thinks, I kill myself, past tense, *I killed myself.*

The little rods of the sleeping pills three shucked blister packs—make such a small pile in the cup, he swallows them in installments, drowned in long swigs of a Barbancourt Five Star saved for the occasion. Haitian rum whose burn has an incurable aftertaste.

His beloved's chest rises and falls weakly. Dulcie is having trouble breathing, it seems. Arnaud lies down naked beside her, so as to feel her skin against his, pulls the sheet over them. Takes her hand. "Goodbye, my love," he says, head turned toward her face, not realizing that he only moved his lips. His leg is shaking in slight tremors, his muscles' equivalent of the force that moves the paw of a sleeping dog in its basket.

Somber organ chords have already started rumbling in his ears, so familiar, so natural to his distress, that when his eyes finally close, he does not wonder to hear rising *Tu se' morta, mia vita, ed io respiro*, Orfeo's heartbreaking lament in Monteverdi's aria.

You are dead, my life, and I still breathe? sings the voice, more and more faintly, as Arnaud's pulse slows, keeps time with the plaint of the music, and after the final measure all that remains in him is the silence of impending disaster, then that dizzy sensation that sleepers share with the dying, of being swallowed by what is suddenly negating and erasing them.

Bear witness, however, to what love means and to the wonders that a word can accomplish. Behold, he perceives this pulsation with his whole body, this stiffening and then this gush that propels him in long jolts beneath the surface of the ocean.

There was no looking glass through which to pass, no March Hare to follow into his home: just his continued dream.

Dulcie has just woken from her sleep.

With a sensory acuity that owes nothing to his organs, Arnaud senses her lips on his neck, the caress of her hand in his hair, a smell of fresh bread, the sweet warmth of her breath.

Through a hundred gazes that are not his eyes, he sees her leaning over his body, sees himself in a cut-away view of the nautilus, a limp god among his manyfold creatures.

On a higher floor, the Reverend Mother has just ushered her guests into a room lined with books, twelve thousand bindings that look like lines of cigar boxes embellished with gold and colors.

"A library!" cries Lady MacRae, her face flushing.

Other exclamations clamor forth. Hands reach forward, pull works out at random, open them ceremoniously.

"What a pleasure," says Holmes, "it must be more than forty years since I've held one of these in my hands. And with their type set on the marble counter of a printing-house! Where did you get them?"

"We make them," Marytrio replies. "All it takes is a press and a few font sets. I'll show you a little later, if you're interested."

Canterel, too, has not been able to keep from consulting one of the books, touching its paper fervently, breathing in its scent like old Burgundy. As the others continue to rhapsodize, he walks along the shelves: the *Grand Robert*, the *Alain Rey*, the *Furetière*, the *Dictionnaire de l'Académie française*, the *Littré*, the *Trévoux*, Samuel Johnson's *Dictionary of the English Language*, the *Godefroy*, the Brothers Grimms' *Deutsches Wörterbuch*, Niccolò Tommaseo's *Dizionario della lingua italiana*, the *Webster*, the *Woordenboek der Nederlandsche Taal*, the *Du Cange*, the *Grand Larousse universel du XIXᵉ siècle*, the *Bailly*, the *Gaffiot*, the *Daremberg et Saglio* . . . The advanced weaponry of language, every parlance and century mixed together, veritable treasures bound solidly, but printed without pomp and all in the same typeface.

"Do you have a literature section?" he asks, concerned.

"No," says Martyrio. "This decision, however, was not easy. To preserve *Don Quixote, Pantagruel,* or some other so called definitive work? Montaigne's *Essays, The Golden Ass, Bouvard and Pécuchet*? If you think about it, every book is the anagram of another. Perhaps even several. Only the dictionary can be an anagram of them all. We copy nothing but dictionaries, in living and extinct languages, in the assurance that they each contain the infinity of all conceivable literature."

"What do you do with it?" asks Sanglard. "Who can really read these dictionaries, remarkable as they may be?"

"We entrust them to the 'International Hawking' and other offshoots that see to it that they are left on subway benches, in refugee camps, hospital waiting rooms. You can't imagine how many times they are consulted."

"Or stolen . . ." says Miss Sherrington, with an incredulous grimace.

"Never, I assure you. It is a fact well known to the police that burglars, alas, do not take tools or books. When these works disappear from the places where we have left them, we rejoice: a library has been planted."

During this interval, Canterel has approached a chessboard whose appearance intrigues him. It is in the form of a box that is deeper than it is wide, wherein the red and black pieces of a classic game are arranged. On its sides, little cranks and sliders enable the adjustment of an internal mechanism.

Marytrio gives a demonstration. As she moves the pawns, she explains that the board includes two booby-trapped squares, assigned at random. When a player places a chessman on one, it is snatched away through a hatch. The square in question then becomes playable again, while a different mousetrap is activated instead. This means that there are only sixty-two squares instead of sixty-four, and there is always the possibility for each of the players to turn the tables up to the last move of the game.

"A game after the image of a dream," she concludes, dropping a red bishop and having it suddenly vanish, "where even a child can beat the grandest master."

"What would you have done with Mardrus," says Canterel, "if he had not left the game so abruptly?"

"I would have put him with the others."

"The others?"

"The other bastards of his kind."

She goes over and opens the two doors of a frosted glass cabinet. Lying on the shelves are some of humanity's most despicable products, criminals who have long been thought to be dead and buried, immobile in their jars, tiny fetuses breathing oxygen from the water through the bracken of their gills. Human tadpoles smiling like fools. They all look so perfectly alike that, without their labels, it would be impossible to identify them. On one of them, the name "Moriarty" gives Canterel a shiver of alarm. As on a notice board at a train station, the letters scroll through his mind at top speed.

"Martyrio!" he sputters once the word is reconstructed.

"Well seen," she says, unmoved. "This is not a secret to anyone close to me; I have the misfortune of being his daughter."

"Son of a rogue!" whispers Sanglard, reacting not to this revelation, but to the piteous sight of the homonculi. "How did you achieve this result?"

Martyrio grabs a stick and replies, all the while tickling her father at the bottom of his jar, nettling him to make him move.

"Two principles: that of neotony, the capacity that axolotls have to preserve their infantile characteristics in their adult stage; and that of transdifferentiation among *Turritopsis nutricula*, jellyfish that have the power to reverse their aging process indefinitely. You saw some of them in our aquariums."

"I don't dare believe . . . You mean to say that the process is reversible? That these 'things' are . . . immortal?"

"As long as I provide them water and food, anyways."

She sprinkles the surface with a pinch of freeze-dried brine shrimp and closes the cupboard.

"Isn't it dangerous?" asks Grimod.

"No more than preserving strains of smallpox or other viruses. Evil must be studied, and closely, for us to be able to confront it effectively: to say your adversary's name is already to exercise a kind of control over him."

A note folded in quarters is brought to her. Martyrio reads it, her face lights up.

"Ah," she says, "I am happy to know she has recovered. Come, I have more to show you."

They follow her into a long hall that is entirely surrounded by water. It is a part of the nautilus's upper curvature, converted into a glass tunnel. Held up by arches, these curved lenses above them form an allegorical sky traversed by shadowy forms, white streaks, dancing bayonets. Schools of fish, barracudas, bonitos, dolphinfish revolve around the submarine like electrons around a nucleus, branch off and come together, skim against it suddenly, exposing bulging foreheads, yellowed teeth, bodies with blank eyes, similar to ours, no doubt, when amazement glues us to the windows of a fish tank. Farther off, in the murk, two manta rays are making their way in a measured flight.

It is not until after this vision that they notice the dozen bustling people in the room, over the seafloor, binding books. Sitting or standing at their workbench, each of the artisans is working on a step of the process. This one is gathering the printed sheets of a large volume into folios, that one is scoring the interior and sewing on the thread, one young woman is cutting a hide, another is gluing it to the boards, a big redhead, cigar in mouth, is already smoothing them. Triskelès is at the board shear. They're grinding, they're decorating, they're putting the books in the nipping press. The room is perfumed with tobacco and strong glue.

Martyrio invites them to sit down in seats arranged in a semicircle before them. The workshop, she stresses, uses only sharkskin and the leather of marine mammals that were beached on the island. It takes sixty hours of steady thoroughness to complete a binding, but for the satisfaction, in return, of having given the book its armor, its passport to longevity.

"We've even started making some shoes, haven't we, Giorgio?"

Triskelès winks in assent.

"This work is vital," she continues, "but it is also a very pleasant distraction. My comrades will take great pleasure in teaching any of you who grow bored along the way."

"How did you find out about the *Nautilus*?" Canterel asks, point blank. "Who are these people? What does all this mean?"

"The voyage will be long," says Martyrio, "we'll have plenty of time to imagine that."

A door opens at the other end of the hall, freezing the movement in the workshop for a moment. Dulcie has just appeared, several handwritten folios in her hands. As she comes forward, haloed with blue light, the *Nautilus* makes a sharp acceleration that knocks her off balance. Her hand on the glass wall, she is heard murmuring "O Captain! My Captain!," and the pacified vessel resumes its slow course. She then walks up to the lectern set up between the tables and steps onto the platform.

She is a black Isis, a priestess of Hecate focused on the exorcism she is preparing to perform. Her turn has come to escort Arnaud, to validate his faith in the soft power of rhapsodes.

"Everything happens," she says, as a preamble, "everything happens as if there were only a single story to tell, a single tale in which certain sections reappear in snatches, complement or negate one another as they surface in the memory. The long, spiraling approach of a dark heart that only shows itself in hints through the recurrence of persistent and mysterious patterns."

She sets her papers on the podium, inhales deeply, then begins to read:

"*Narragonia*, by Arnaud Méneste. 'At this point in the story, the voice stops, immediately replaced by the kind of background music that increases cows' milk production. Monsieur Wang looks at his watch and shakes his head at the punctuality of the performance. Five o'clock on the dot, good work.'"

As the reading continues, Verity turns her face to Martyrio, looking amazed, as if she has recognized the text and is becoming aware of the refolding that is occurring.

Holding a finger to her lips, the Reverend Mother signals to her to keep quiet; she affects a serious expression, but her two little legs are wriggling with happiness between her skirts.

B orn in Algeria, Jean-Marie Blas de Roblès is a truly international writer, having spent significant time in Brazil, France, Taiwan, and Libya. His novel *Where Tigers Are at Home* won the Fnac, Giono, and Médicis Prizes. *Island of Point Nemo* is his ninth novel.

Hannah Chute has an MA in Literary Translation from the University of Rochester. In 2015, she received the Banff Centre Scholarship to work on *Island of Point Nemo*, her first full-length translation.

**OPEN
LETTER**

OPEN LETTER

WWW.OPENLETTERBOOKS.ORG